Also by Marian D. Schwartz

Realities

The Last Season, The Story of a Marriage

The Writers' Conference

Harry Danced Divinely: Collected Giffort Street Stories

War on Giffort Street, a novella

SARA BAREFIELD

MARIAN D. SCHWARTZ

Jefferson Madison
Regional Library
Charlottesville, Virginia

Gristmill Publishing, L.L.C.
Ivy, Virginia

Sara Barefield is a work of fiction. The characters and events portrayed in this book are the product of the author's imagination. Any resemblance to actual persons, living or dead, events, or places is entirely coincidental and not intended by the author.

Sara Barefield

Marian D. Schwartz

Copyright ©2016 by Marian D. Schwartz

All rights reserved.

This book or any portion thereof may not be reproduced or used in any manner whatsoever without the express written permission of the publisher except for the use of brief quotations in a book review.

ISBN 978-0-9886076-7-5

Gristmill Publishing, L.L.C.
P.O. Box 193
Ivy, Virginia 22945-0193

In Memory of Emilie Jacobson

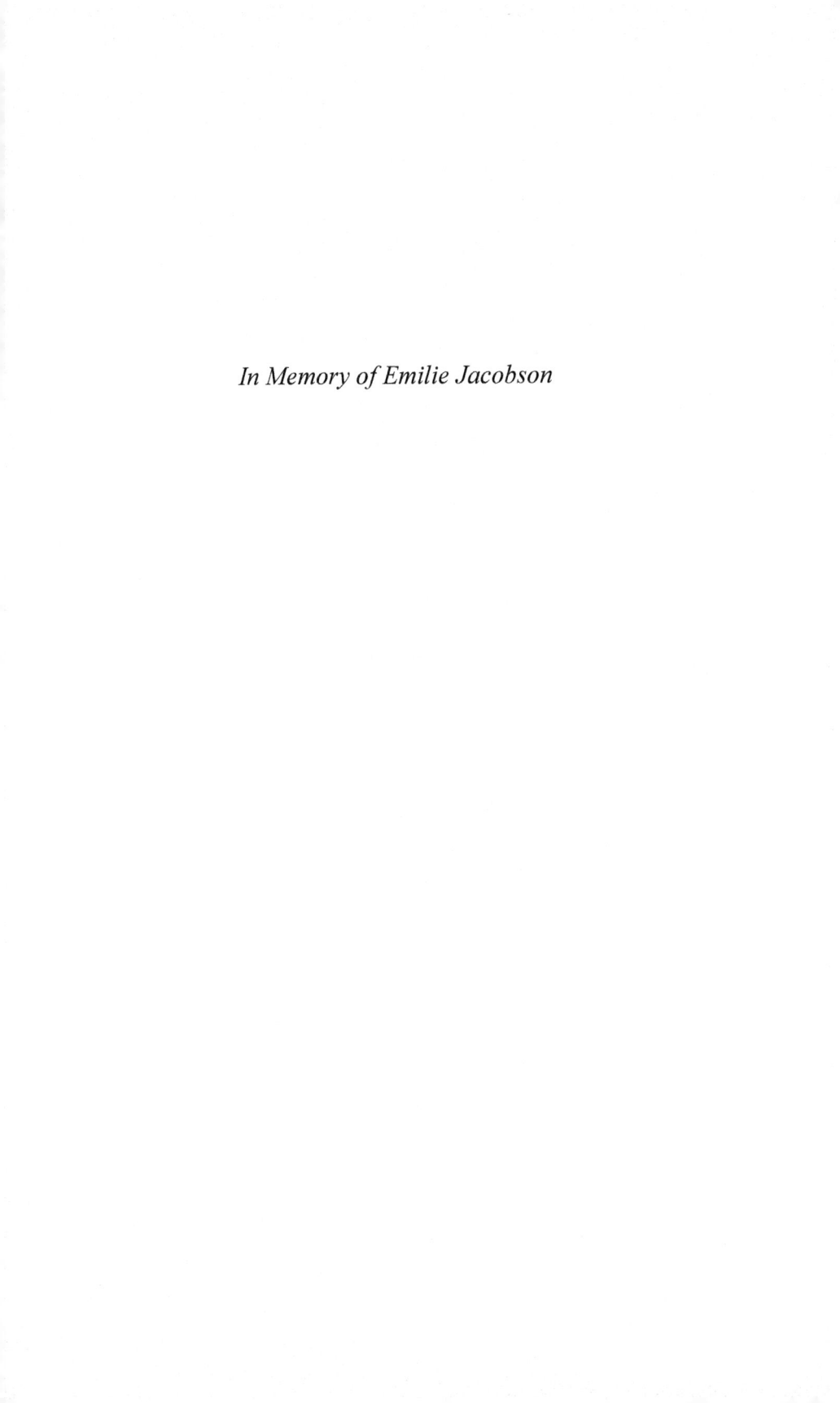

Prologue

He couldn't run anymore. Exhausted, he stopped and leaned forward, resting his hands on his thighs. It was dusk and the mountains were darkly silhouetted against a violet-infused horizon. As his breath returned to normal, he spotted a wide ledge of rock about eighty feet below. It was a steep drop, but there was just enough light to reach it.

He half-walked, half-slid down the mountain, breaking his descent by grabbing hold of trees. The ledge was flat and wider than he expected. He slipped off his backpack and the sleeping bag he hadn't used; he had been in the mountains for three days and he hadn't slept. He couldn't take the risk of another nightmare that would plunge him into the jungle, into monsoon rains, into stifling humidity and the stink of rot, so he forced himself to stay awake, and the incessant voices no one else could hear came back, as unremitting as the tropical rain. He opened his backpack, removed a Glock 22 from its case and held it with his finger lightly on the trigger. Soon the voices stopped.

The gun was the solution, he knew it. The gun could hush the voices, the gun could end the nightmares, the gun could give him peace. But then he thought of Sara, as he did every time he was ready with the Glock in his hand. When he had tried to tell her after he had missed her birthday, she had gotten so upset that he knew she would never be prepared. For her sake, for what they could have had once, he purposely didn't have a formal will drawn to stop him from killing himself. He knew she wouldn't get anything if he didn't have a will—not the cars, not the property, not the bank accounts—and the unfairness of it always stopped him. Sara deserved everything he had; she had been his anchor on this earth. He loved her more than he had imagined he could love anyone.

Tears streamed down his cheeks. The voices were back, louder, more insistent. He tried to concentrate on Sara, on the will, but the voices wouldn't let him think. His grip on the gun tightened.

Animals took off as the shot broke the stillness of the cold night air. Then it was quiet.

AUTUMN, 1991

Forty. Tomorrow I'll be forty. On the Friday before my birthday that thought kept circling in my head as if it were an omen.

It felt like a birthday gift when all of the teachers turned in their attendance sheets on time so I could make copies and complete the official attendance report by four o'clock. I was the school secretary at Creekside Elementary, and the attendance reports were my responsibility. After I sent the report downtown, I was free to leave; most of the teachers were already gone. The principal was at a meeting, so I was spared forcing myself to wish him a pleasant weekend. This was Dr. Bert Sidley's second year at Creekside. Although it was only September, I already knew that this year wouldn't be any easier than the last. Of the four principals I'd worked for, Sidley was the worst; petty and demanding, he was often impossible. As much as I loved the children, last year I had quietly looked for another job without success. At the time I had blamed my failure on the fact that good jobs in Owings, Virginia, were always hard to come by, but deep down I knew that my lack of skills was what stood in my way. I didn't know how to use a computer and had never transcribed dictation from a machine. Like it or not, I was stuck with Sidley until he left for another school, which could take years. A more realistic hope was that the school office would get a computer. There was talk of that happening, but with the recession and budget cuts it could be a while, especially for Creekside, which was the poorest school in Owings and always the last in line.

Instead of going directly home as I usually did on Fridays, I drove to a Winn-Dixie on the other side of town close to where I lived. The trip didn't take long. With a population of less than twenty thousand, Owings doesn't stretch more than a fifteen-minute ride in any direction. By squeezing in my grocery shopping, I could sleep late tomorrow and postpone facing that number: *forty*.

I went through the store quickly, automatically picking up what I needed. While I waited at the deli, I watched a clerk put a tray of fried chicken in the case; it looked so good that I decided to buy some after I ordered my usual cold cuts. Instead of having pizza as we always did on Friday nights, Tully and I would have chicken. I bought potato salad and coleslaw, and got ice cream for dessert. Tully nearly always treated. It felt good to be the one who was giving instead of receiving.

Landscape workers were cutting the grass and clipping shrubs when I pulled into my reserved parking space in the Altavista Gardens apartment complex. Although I wanted to put the ice cream in the freezer, I sat in the car for a moment looking at the contemporary cedar-sided buildings and well-kept grounds, thinking that I had at least accomplished something by the age of forty. Altavista Gardens was a world away from the shotgun house in which I was raised and the shabby apartments I had lived in for years while I first struggled to clear family debts, then struggled again to pay for a decent car and furniture. The rent was more than I could afford but worth any sacrifice. The apartment was new when I moved in; bright and airy, it had large windows in the living room and bedroom that caught the morning light, which was perfect for my plants. My galley kitchen had a dishwasher, a microwave oven, and a stove and refrigerator that no one else had ever used. After living there for two years the place still felt new, and I still felt lucky when I unlocked the door and stepped inside.

I put the groceries away and set the table while I waited for Tully's call. Our routine had been the same for years: if everything was all right, he'd call between five fifteen and five thirty to tell me when he'd be over. Then I'd order a pizza, double cheese and sausage, that he'd pick up on his way to my apartment. After we ate we'd go out for a few beers and then come back to my place. Tully never stayed the night. He always left after I fell asleep, so quiet that I wasn't awakened by the bounce of a bedspring or the sound of footsteps or the closing of a door. He was quieter than a ghost.

At five forty-five I began to worry. Although I hadn't talked to Tully all week, that wasn't unusual. Besides working during the day at Ready's Garage, he had his own business on the side repairing and restoring vintage cars. I knew how absorbed he got while he was working, how he'd even forget to eat, so I didn't expect to hear from him. But he always, always called on Fridays between five fifteen and five thirty unless…

Biting my lip, I dialed Ready's Garage at six o'clock. There was no answer. I hung up and stood in the galley kitchen looking at the beige-laminated cupboards trimmed in oak and the gleaming appliances, the nicest kitchen in the nicest apartment I'd ever had, but the smooth, shining surfaces gave me no comfort. Tully knew tomorrow was my birthday, my fortieth. He couldn't have gone. He couldn't.

I dialed Tully's number and let the phone ring until I couldn't stand listening to it before I called Bob Ready, the owner of Ready's Garage, at home. "I tried to get a hold of you late this afternoon, but no one answered," he said. "I wasn't sure you knew."

"When did he go?"

"He didn't come in this morning, and there's no answer at his place," Bob said. "Sure took us by surprise. It's been a while since he's done this. I thought maybe he was finished with taking off, but I guess not."

"I guess not," I echoed, fighting a lump that was rising in my throat.

"Left us short. People want their cars, they want the work done when they're promised. I had to turn work away. Can't run a business like that," he said.

"He'll be back."

"I know," he said. "But when? Why should I have to put up with this?"

And why should I? I said to myself. And then I answered for both of us. "Because Tully's the best."

"I suppose," he said grudgingly, "But sometimes even with the best it just ain't worth it."

Tears were streaming down my cheeks. I didn't want Bob to know that I was crying; somehow I had to end the conversation quickly. I don't remember what I said, but I was grateful that I didn't start sobbing until the connection was broken.

I went into my bedroom, collapsed on the bed and sobbed until I couldn't catch my breath, until my eyes swelled and my head pounded and my throat felt raw. I kept telling myself that I had to stop, that Tully had taken off like this so many times I should be used to it. And then I cried harder. He knew my birthday was tomorrow, he knew and he left anyway. All the other times I could excuse it because I understood his need to go; the war had done something to him that couldn't be fixed. But tomorrow was my fortieth birthday. The prospect of spending the day alone gave me a feeling of hopelessness that my tears couldn't ease.

I cried for hours. Every time I stopped I'd think of something that would make me start again. Finally I got up, washed my face with cold water, and went into the living room. It was dark, but I didn't turn a light on. I curled up in a corner of the sofa and closed my eyes. It was my fault. I should have broken off with Tully years ago. I could still hear Mama saying, "That boy ain't been right since he got back from the war."

But I didn't listen to her. Besides, Mama had been telling me to break off with Tully before he went to Vietnam. Mama liked Tully well enough, but Tully's family didn't like Mama, or any of the Barefields for that matter, not that Mama cared for the Rutlands; there wasn't a positive thought between the families. But Mama knew that the Rutlands blamed her for the trouble, and she couldn't shift that onto anyone else. She started the problem like she started everything: she spoke first and thought later. Except with Tully, she didn't just speak. She exploded.

It happened the day I met Tully, on the fourth of July when I was seven years old. The whole family—my mama and daddy, my younger brother Ronnie Lee, and Grandpa Loudermilk—had gone to Hazard Park for a picnic and to see the fireworks. The park, named for John Owings Hazard who donated the land, was rapidly filling with families despite the sizzling weather, so it took a while to find an empty table. After we were settled, I went to look for one of the swings that were scattered under the large oaks. The first swings I found were taken, so I kept walking until I came upon a group of boys playing baseball. I saw a wiry blond boy pick up a bat and step up to the plate, but I didn't stay. Someone cried, *"Watch out!"* Not sure if the call was to me, I hesitated and then turned around. The ball hit me on the side of my forehead over my right eye.

I fell backward, stunned. For a minute or so everything was fuzzy and gray. When my vision cleared I saw the blond boy kneeling over me. His eyes were startling, a vivid blue ringed in black. I touched my forehead, which was throbbing, trying not to cry. I didn't want the boy to think I was a crybaby. My hand was covered with blood when I took it away.

The boy walked me back to my family's table, glancing anxiously at my forehead. Before he could finish explaining, Mama exploded, lighting into him like a thousand fireworks going off at once. His parents, who were at a table nearby, came running over. Soon everyone was yelling. They all forgot about me except the boy. He took some paper napkins from the table and walked me to a fountain, where he helped me wipe the blood off my face, but the wound wouldn't stop bleeding. "I think you need stitches," he said. "I had them once. They're not bad. My name's Tully Rutland. I'm really sorry."

"It wasn't your fault."

He smiled, a crooked smile that made me love him right then.

"Tell that to your mama," he said.

We went back to the table. Nothing had changed; our parents were still having words. Grandpa Loudermilk, who had tuned out the whole business to concentrate on his beer, spotted the blood-soaked napkin that I was holding to my forehead. He belched and cleared his throat. "While y'all's arguin', this child's goin' to bleed to death."

Mama took me to the hospital emergency room, where I got nine stitches. "This ain't comin' out of our pocket," Mama said. "Them Rutlands are goin' to pay."

"It wasn't Tully's fault, Mama."

"What do you mean *it wasn't his fault*? He hit the ball, didn't he?"

"I wasn't watchin' out like I should've."

Mama's chin stuck out stubbornly. She had a strong jaw line, high cheekbones, and thick auburn hair that was as unpredictable as she was. When she laughed you could see that she was missing molars, but she was still beautiful. People have told me that I favor her, but I don't see it except for my eyes, which are more hazel than gray, and my cheekbones. I did inherit her height. I'm five feet nine, an inch taller than she was. Her name was Ruby, which fit her perfectly: she was full of fire. "He hit the ball, and they're goin' to pay!" she said.

The Rutlands finally agreed to pay the bill, but at a price. Mrs. Rutland let Mama know that they were paying not because Tully was at fault but to rid themselves of the Barefields. Mama never forgot the insult; nor did Mrs. Rutland, a spare blond woman who was as determined in her way as Mama was in hers. Although Mrs. Rutland was pleasant to me, at times extravagantly so, as if she were performing a chore for Tully's sake, she always managed to let me know just what she thought of the Barefields. And it was less than nothing. Over the years I tried my best to change her opinion—I bought her Christmas presents I couldn't afford, I overlooked her insults, I studied a book on etiquette until I knew the use of every fork that was put on a table, I scrubbed the Southern out of my speech until Tully started teasing me that I sounded like Jane Pauley—but her feelings stayed the same. Nothing would have pleased her more than for Tully to stop seeing me. I was always so intimidated by Mrs. Rutland that I was in my twenties before I realized that her people, the Morrises, weren't much higher on the social scale than the Barefields. The Rutlands were a peg higher. Mr. Rutland was a supervisor in the highway department after years of working his way up. I always liked Mr. Rutland, and I believe he liked me as much as he dared without antagonizing his wife.

Eventually the scar on my forehead faded into a faint line that was barely noticeable, but Tully knew it was there. Every once in a while he would gently run his fingertip along the scar and say, "Guess I knocked you out from the very first."

"You sure did," I'd agree.

I never told him that I loved him from that first day in Hazard Park. Young as we were, we had an understanding that didn't need words. Although we didn't go out on a formal date until Tully, who was two years older than me, got his driver's license when he was sixteen, everyone who knew us knew that I was Tully Rutland's girl. Besides going to college to become a teacher, all I ever wanted was to marry Tully and have a home and children. College was an impossible dream, but not Tully. He was real and he wanted me as much as I wanted him.

Then Tully was drafted. Nearly twenty, he was tall and angular and still blond. When he graduated from high school he got a job as a mechanic at Ray Clark's Ford dealership. The mechanics who worked at Ray Clark's were all considerably older. No one in Owings had ever heard of a boy right out of high school being hired to work for a dealer like Tully was, but no one in Owings had ever seen a gift like Tully's for fixing cars. Before he got his driver's license people were already saying that there was nothing on wheels that Tully Rutland couldn't fix. Ray Clark, a large man who had a broad, ruddy face and a salesman's smile, paid for Tully to get training at a school for mechanics run by the Ford Motor Company.

Tully did so well at the school that Ray Clark couldn't stop bragging. "Tully wasn't only the top in his class," Ray told everyone who'd listen, "he's the best the Ford people ever saw."

Tully made good money at Ray Clark's, but he didn't plan on staying there. He was saving to open his own garage. "I mean to have the biggest, best garage in the county." he said. "It'll take a while before I have enough saved to do it right, but once it's established we can get married and have a good life."

A good life. Before the draft notice came we'd go on Sunday drives and walk through modest new homes that were for sale. When I'd say how nice they were (the houses were palaces compared to mine), Tully told me that they were fine for starters. "After I have my own garage, I'm going to make enough money to buy us a *really* nice house, and you can fill it with as many kids and as much furniture as you want."

I couldn't believe how lucky I was. The future looked as bright as the blue in Tully's eyes.

Ray Clark wanted to fight the draft notice. He said he knew people on the draft board and told Tully that he had other connections as well. It all sounded good, but in the end Tully had to go. "The draft board has to fill a quota," Ray said. "I tried, but I just couldn't fight that damned quota. You can be certain your job will be here for you when you come back."

Ray didn't tell Tully that he didn't try his most important connection, which was with a state senator; he was saving that card for his son, who had just turned eighteen.

I was afraid that Tully would be sent to Vietnam. The television news was full of students demonstrating against the war on college campuses and the sight of body bags being unloaded from airplanes. I had never seen a body bag before. There were so many body bags on the news that a horrible thing happened: I became accustomed to seeing the remains of human beings being taken off planes like ordinary cargo. "Don't worry," Tully said. "The Army isn't stupid. I'm a mechanic. They aren't going to send me off to fight. They're going to have me working on their vehicles."

What he said made absolute sense. I told myself that even if the worst happened and he was sent to Vietnam, he wouldn't be crawling through the jungle; he'd be repairing jeeps and tanks. He'd be safe.

The weekend before he left, Tully took me to Roanoke for dinner and then to a motel. "I want this night to be as special as a honeymoon," he said.

We had made love before, but in his car or at his cousin's cabin. I felt like a bride in the motel on the fresh white sheets. I had no way of knowing that it would be the only time with Tully that I would feel like one.

Tully was sure that the men who ran the Army weren't stupid, but he was wrong. After basic training, he was assigned to an infantry unit. When he protested that he could better serve as a mechanic, he was given orders to ship out a few weeks sooner than he would have gone otherwise as a punishment. Tully had only one night home, which I had to share with the entire Rutland family, before he left.

Tully served in the Army his full two years. Overjoyed that he was back, I tried not to notice how much he smoked and how edgy he was, how he couldn't seem to stay in one place for long, and how quickly he reacted to sudden noises, even the most innocent ones, jumping to his feet at the first whistle of the teakettle like it was an air raid alert. He started working at Ray Clark's again, and he wasn't home more than a week or so before he told me that he was going to look for his own apartment. "I thought you wanted to save all you could for the garage," I said, suddenly fearing that his problem might be deeper than his nervousness.

"I'm still saving, but it won't be as much," he said, lighting another cigarette.

While he was in the Army I had graduated from high school and had started working at a bank. As soon as I had completed my training to be a teller, my mama and daddy told me they wanted half of my paycheck for room and board. I remember looking at them from across the chipped kitchen table astonished, wondering whose idea it was, not that it mattered. I could appreciate their need for the money. My daddy, Vernon Barefield, a powerfully-built man who had a temper to match his size, was a roofer by trade and had been out of work for weeks. I was accustomed to giving in to their demands; they were both so volatile that I always tried to do what they wanted, which was easier and less frightening than to risk doing otherwise. But this demand was so unreasonable that for the first time I refused them what they wanted. "I can't give you that much," I said. "I'll have nothing left for myself, not even to buy lunch, after I make my car payment, and I need the car to get to work."

Reasoning was as foreign to my daddy as French food. He was a brutal man. All his life he reacted with his fists, and this time was no exception. "Pay half or leave!" he said, banging his fist on the table so hard that the dishes rose and skittered off onto the floor.

To their shock, I left. I had always contributed what I could, even in high school when I wanted to save the money I earned for college, but to work all week and not have a penny left to save or spend as I chose just wasn't fair. I was scared to be off on my own, especially with Tully in Vietnam, but it was the only reasonable thing to do. The small basement apartment I found was cold and damp in the winter, but it was pleasant in the summer, and the owner of the house, a kind widower in his seventies who was crippled with arthritis, gave me credit on my rent for the repainting I did and let me use an old sofa and tables that he didn't need.

We were in my apartment when Tully told me he was going to look for his own place. It was a Friday night, the first evening since he'd been back that we had to ourselves, and we had just finished a pizza he'd picked up for dinner. "Maybe you could spend the night here," I said tentatively. It was always Tully who initiated sex.

He rewarded me with the crooked smile I had missed for so long. "Maybe I could," he said, drawing me to him.

While he was gone I had wondered if he was doing it with any of those Vietnamese girls who sold themselves to American soldiers. I knew he'd have the need and that he'd want relief, but it was one more thing to worry about so I put the thought in the back of my mind and let it stay there. When he came that night he shuddered above me as though each spasm was tearing him apart, and all I could do was wrap myself more tightly around him and hang on. I felt almost sure there had been no one else.

I wanted him to stay the night, but he refused. "Please, Tully," I said, thinking that in the morning I'd ask him to move in with me. It would save him the expense of his own apartment and we could get married even sooner.

I started playing with him until he was hard again. "I don't sleep well," he said uneasily after he agreed to stay.

"Maybe you have to get used to being back, the time difference and climate and all."

But Tully's problem wasn't a simple matter of adjustment. During the night he woke me, thrashing and screaming in his sleep. *"Where are they...Where are they...I've got to find them..."*

"Tully?" I said, reaching out to him.

My touch didn't awaken him. He sat straight up in bed, his spine stiff, perspiration and tears dripping off his face, sweat running down his chest and back. *"WHERE ARE THEY?"* he howled. *"I CAN'T FIND THEM..."*

I was terrified. "It's a bad dream," I said, grabbing him by the shoulders. "You've got to wake up. *Wake up, Tully, wake up, PLEASE WAKE UP!*"

He opened his eyes and looked at me as if he had no idea of who I was or where he was. Then it came to him and he covered his face with his hands and wept.

That night was the only time he ever talked about what happened in Vietnam. After he showered and dressed, he sat on the edge of the bed. "I guess you've got to know," he said, his eyes so full of pain that I hurt for him. "Something happened over there...my unit...we were attacked...a surprise...somehow I got separated...a lotta guys got killed...days I was in the jungle, looking,

looking…days…finally I found some guys who brought me in…I never got back with the others…with my unit…they put me in a different unit…"

He couldn't say any more.

I held him, repeating, "It'll take time, it'll just take time," until we both believed it.

A month later Tully disappeared. Ray Clark called at dinnertime asking if I knew where he was. "He didn't come in to work today. We tried his apartment and called his parents. Mrs. Rutland said to call you."

I had no idea of where he might be. "This isn't like him," I said, afraid that Mr. Clark might think Tully wasn't responsible. "Something must have happened. I'm sure he'll be in first thing tomorrow morning."

Tully wasn't in the following morning. The Rutlands called the police. When they searched his apartment, they discovered that his guns and hunting knives were gone; his army clothes were missing, too. But investigators who were called in couldn't find any leads that might help them. Tully had simply vanished.

He was gone for thirty-six days. I had just about given up hope of ever seeing him again when I came home from work on a cool November evening and found him waiting for me. It was dark, and from a distance I didn't recognize him. He was rail thin, thinner than he'd been when he came back from Vietnam, and he had a full, light brown beard. When I saw it was Tully for sure, I ran into his arms crying with joy.

He didn't tell me where he'd been right away. As soon as the door shut behind us we went straight to bed. It wasn't until later when he was sprawled naked on the sheets, smoking, that I asked him. "In the mountains," he said.

Owings sat between the Appalachians and the Blue Ridge. "Which mountains?"

"The Blue Ridge."

"Where in the Blue Ridge?"

He inhaled and let out the smoke in a long stream before he answered. "What difference does it make?"

His reply set me off. I got up, forgetting my modesty. "What difference? I'll tell you what difference! I was worried sick about you! We all were. Your mama looks like she's aged twenty years, and your poor daddy's gotten so quiet he hardly talks at all. We called the police. There was no note, no clue…"

"I'm sorry," he said, interrupting. "Really, Sara, I'm sorry. I couldn't help it. Something made me go. It was like I had to, like I didn't have a choice."

"Couldn't you have called or left a note or told someone instead of just disappearing?"

"I…I wasn't myself."

I looked into his eyes, those vivid blue eyes ringed in black, and for the first time since I'd known him I saw fear. Then I remembered his nightmare and understood what he meant by not being himself: he'd been out of his mind, looking, looking.

Suddenly I felt cold and slipped under the covers. "Maybe you had to get it all out of your system," I said. "That's probably what it was."

"Probably," Tully said.

Our voices had the hollow sound of the unconvinced.

For a while he was fine, but then it happened again. And again. And again. In a period of two years Tully disappeared seven times. He left without telling anyone and was gone anywhere from a week to nearly a month. Ray Clark finally fired him. "I hate to do this, you bein' a veteran and all. You're the best mechanic I've ever had, but you're no good to me if you're not reliable. You need to get yourself some help. Go to a V.A. hospital, see someone. As soon as you're okay, I'll be happy to have you back."

Tully went to a V.A. hospital in northern Virginia and came home bitter and angry. "All's they know how to do is run a lot of tests," he said. "I saw vets from 'Nam. They're treating them like shit."

He started working for another automobile dealer, and then

another as the pattern repeated itself. I kept waiting for the right time to talk about marriage and children and all the dreams we'd had, but the right time never seemed to come. If he was stable for a while, I'd start thinking about saying something, but then he'd disappear again and my hopes would vanish with him. My mama died about a year after he returned from Vietnam, and one of the last things she told me was to find someone else. "You'll never have a life with him," she said one day, as if it were a fact so obvious it barely needed mentioning. But I couldn't believe that. Tully just needed to heal; eventually he would be fine. I knew that he didn't leave by choice, that the demons that propelled him were beyond his control, and when he came back he was always apologetic and embarrassed. He was the best person I'd ever known: kind, loving, smart. There wasn't another man in the world as wonderful as Tully.

Years slipped by until I realized one day with shock that I was approaching thirty and I was no closer to the life I'd hoped for than I was before Tully had left for Vietnam. I happened to see Lureen Davis, who had been my classmate in high school, in the supermarket. Lureen, a short, brassy blonde, was a nonstop talker, and despite having her children with her, she gave me a complete accounting of who was married, who was divorced, and how many children they all had. It was a remarkable feat, an update on the lives of over fifty people in six minutes flat. When she was finished, Lureen took a much-needed breath and said, "So tell me about you."

Tell me about you. My head was swirling with the accounts of how everyone I'd gone to school with had gotten on with their lives. I felt as though my life hadn't gone anywhere, that it had stopped short, frozen in time like an ice cube stuck in a tray.

Lureen's sons, towheads who were four and six, started taking pokes at each other. "I heard a while ago that you were still seein' Tully Rutland," Lureen said, separating the boys by stepping between them. "I also heard that he was wounded or somethin' in Vietnam."

Or somethin'. I had to get away from Lureen. "I see you've got your hands full," I said, tightening my grip on the shopping cart to better make my getaway. "We'll have to get together real soon."

If Tully had been around, I would have talked to him that night, but Tully had gone off the day before. He hadn't disappeared in five months, which was the longest period he'd been stable since he'd returned from Vietnam. He was gone for six days. I was always careful around him the first weeks after he returned because I could feel his fragility. Although outwardly he appeared normal, I knew what he had been through, how shattering it was for him each time he left and what effort it took to pull himself together again. So I waited to talk to him, but I didn't wait long. As soon as I sensed that he was all right, which was about a month after I saw Lureen, I decided to tell him that I wanted to get married. I made the decision on a sunny Friday in April when Owings, usually drab even on sunny days, was flooded with the pinks, reds, whites, and corals of blooming azaleas. "I want us to have a home and babies and all the things we used to talk about," I said that night after we shared a pizza in my apartment, a one-bedroom I had lived in for several years.

He leaped to his feet, tipping his chair over. "I won't bring a child into this world!"

The apartment was small and cheaply built and the walls were thin. In the years since he'd been back he had put on the weight he'd lost, plus a few pounds. He still looked slender, but at six two and one hundred eighty pounds, he wasn't a small man. I felt the floor vibrate when his chair fell. I didn't want the neighbors to hear, I didn't want a scene, but I couldn't believe what he said about not wanting children. "Why?" I said.

"It could be a boy and he could be sent off to war. I'd kill my son before I'd chance that happening!"

I saw the anguish in his face and knew that he meant every word.

We stopped seeing each other. Afterward I thought of that period as the worst in my life, for I saw my situation and it frightened me. I was almost thirty years old and had no family except for my brother, Ronnie Lee, who was as brutal as our daddy, and his wife,

Ardelle, and their three children, whom I cared for. But Ardelle and my two nieces and nephew weren't enough to fill my life. The only men I knew were friends of Tully's, and most of them were married. I had a number of casual acquaintances but only a few really close friends, Eileen Payne and Peggy Carver. Eileen and Peggy had been my friends since high school, but they were both busy working and raising their children, so I rarely saw them except on Monday nights when we went bowling. Without Tully I was truly alone. I felt as if my life had narrowed into a tunnel from which there was no hope of escape.

My thirtieth birthday fell on a weekday. Tully arrived at my door with two boxes, the larger containing a cake, the smaller holding a gold bracelet. He had shaved and showered after work and was wearing a fresh pair of jeans and a blue-and-green plaid shirt. I almost cried with relief when I saw him. We slipped back into our old familiar routine—pizza on Friday nights, dinner out on Saturdays—as if it had never been interrupted. But one thing changed: for a while Tully used condoms even though we had depended on my diaphragm for quite a while. When he stopped using them I knew he trusted me again.

Another ten years gone and now I was alone in the dark on the eve of my fortieth birthday with no tears left to shed.

Early Saturday morning the telephone rang. It was my sister-in-law, Ardelle. "Happy birthday," Ardelle said.

"Thanks."

"Ronnie Lee heard about Tully. How are you doin'?"

"Okay."

Apparently I didn't sound convincing. "Let me take you out to lunch," Ardelle said.

I knew that Ardelle couldn't afford to treat me. Ronnie Lee was a roofer like our daddy, and he had been laid off for over a month. But if I didn't go out with Ardelle, I would spend the entire day and evening alone. Then I had an idea. "It's my birthday, so I'm treating."

"No," Ardelle said, "I asked you."

"I once read about a man who gave gifts to everyone on his birthday because it gave him pleasure. Now I want to take us out on my birthday. You can't deny me that pleasure."

Ardelle laughed. "You sure have a way of turnin' things around."

"I'll meet you at Franny's at a quarter to twelve so we can get a table."

Eileen Payne and Peggy Carver also called to wish me a happy birthday. Both women mentioned their plans to take me out to dinner before we bowled on Monday night. When Peggy asked how I was celebrating, I said, "Quietly." I couldn't trust myself to tell her about Tully, not yet.

It was unusually warm for late September, close to ninety degrees, when I pulled into the restaurant parking lot at twenty minutes to twelve. More than half the spaces were taken. Franny's was the most popular restaurant in town. As I walked toward the red-and-white building, I looked for Tully's black pickup. I knew he was gone, but habit made me look anyway.

It was past noon when Ardelle came into the restaurant. When I spotted her from the booth where I had been waiting, I smiled and waved. Ardelle waved back, and I noticed that she was wearing a long-sleeved blouse. A long-sleeved blouse on such a blistering hot day. I felt my smile fade.

"Sorry I'm late," Ardelle said, sliding into the booth. "I had to drop Darlene off at a friend's house."

Although I tried not to show it, Darlene was my favorite of Ardelle's and Ronnie Lee's three children. She was a spunky, redheaded twelve-year-old who was blossoming into a beauty. "How are the kids?" I said.

"They're fine," Ardelle said. "Growin' like weeds."

I noticed that Ardelle hadn't taken off her sunglasses. Long sleeves and sunglasses. For years I had suspected that Ronnie Lee beat Ardelle like our daddy had beaten our mama, but the few times I'd broached the subject—once when I saw a nasty bruise on

Ardelle's leg and the times Ardelle had a broken arm and a fractured jaw—Ardelle looked frightened and wouldn't talk. I had often wished that I could help Ardelle and felt powerless because I didn't know how. When Ardelle and Ronnie Lee were married, Ardelle was as pretty as she was sweet; with her creamy skin, fluffy blond curls, and tiny figure people thought she looked like a real-life Barbie doll. The years she'd been married to Ronnie Lee had been hard on her. Ardelle's face had gotten puffy, her figure bloated. But by some miracle she had retained her sweetness. I didn't know anyone who had a kinder heart than Ardelle.

A young waitress wearing jeans and a red T-shirt that had FRANNY'S printed across the front in white came to take our order. "The Frannyburger plate," I said. It was a lot of food—an oversize hamburger covered with cheese and bacon, coleslaw, and enough fries for two people—but it was my birthday.

"I'll have the same," said Ardelle.

"How's Ronnie Lee?" I said to be polite. Even though he was my brother, I had no feeling for Ronnie Lee; I neither liked nor loved him. He had a vicious temper and a cruel streak that made me wonder when we were children if he had the same feelings as other people. Once I caught him flicking the eyes out of live frogs with the point of his knife; when I tried to stop him, he grabbed another frog out of the bunch he'd caught and flicked its eye out in my face.

"Bein' laid off is hard on him with the kids goin' back to school. They need so much." Ardelle sighed. "And they want so much. Glenn's been naggin' for them sneakers that cost over a hundred dollars a pair. Ten years old and he says he has to have 'em. Can you imagine? My job at the laundromat don't pay enough to make a dent in it."

It was difficult to feel sympathetic toward my nephew, Glenn, who lately was displaying signs of growing into a replica of his daddy. "Maybe construction will start picking up."

"It usually slows down in the fall. Every year it gets harder—fewer builders, less jobs to bid on. And Ronnie Lee don't know how to do anythin' else."

Ardelle leaned forward. Her sunglasses slipped and I glimpsed her left eye, which was a livid purple and swollen shut. She pushed the glasses back with her finger. "I heard of a way I could work less hours than I do now and make a lot more money."

"How?"

"Cleanin' houses," she said in a voice too low for the people in the next booth to overhear. "I can make fifty dollars for not even five hours work. That's better than ten dollars an hour. And I wouldn't have to pay taxes on it, either. That's two hundred fifty dollars a week, free and clear, more if I work on Saturdays."

The waitress brought our lunches. I reached for the ketchup to put on my French fries. "How can you not pay taxes?"

"No one will know that I'm doin' it except the people I work for, and they're not goin' to talk because they don't want to pay my Social Security."

"But don't they have to?"

"Not if no one knows. My friend Marietta's been cleanin' for over six months. She goes to the same people week after week but to a different house every day. They pay her in cash. Most of them aren't even there while she works. They just let her in and leave the money for her. Marietta says she can get me as many days as I want."

"Do you want to clean other people's houses?" I said, thinking about Ardelle's house, which wasn't dirty but didn't shine, either.

"Not really, but I want the money. There's a lot worse I could do. That's what I told Ronnie Lee. He's dead set against it, says no wife of his is goin' to clean up other people's messes. Of course, it's okay for me to clean up his messes!"

Ardelle put down her fork and reached into her purse, a blue canvas satchel large enough to pack for an overnight trip, for a tissue. "We had an awful fight about it," she said after she blew her nose. "I know he's havin' a hard time, but..."

It took her a few minutes to compose herself. I wanted to help her, but I couldn't think of anything to say except, "I'm sorry."

"You've done nothin' to be sorry for," Ardelle said, sniffling.

"It's your birthday and I'm sittin' here tellin' you my troubles. I'm the one who should be sayin' I'm sorry."

To change the subject, I asked what the girls had been doing. I hadn't seen them in several weeks, and I always enjoyed hearing about their activities. As Ardelle talked, her mood brightened. When we left the restaurant, we were both laughing over something Darlene had said.

Before we started walking to our cars, Ardelle reached into her canvas bag. "It's the after bath lotion you like," she said, handing me an awkwardly wrapped present. "I wish it could've been more."

I knew that the gift meant sacrifice. Ardelle didn't have a spare penny. "It's perfect," I said, giving her a big hug. Ardelle felt warm and comfortable, a sweet, soft cushion.

"I feel bad about Tully. I thought you'd be celebratin' with him, so I didn't plan a party or nothin'."

"Which is good, because no one will know how old I am!"

"You sure don't look forty," Ardelle said. "You don't look a day over twenty-five."

Nor did I feel forty. I felt the same as I did when I was twenty, but the calendar didn't lie. I *was* forty, and as I drove to the library, a stop I made every Saturday, I thought about Tully. At twenty I'd had a heart full of hopes; at forty I had none. My life would go on year after year as it was now. It wasn't a bad life; millions of people had it much worse than I did. But I'd had my dreams, and it had been hard to let them drift away, one after another, like brightly-colored balloons floating beyond my reach: college…marriage…children. It was no one's fault, not mine or Tully's. He couldn't help being the way he was and I couldn't help loving him. Maybe I wouldn't have felt so down if the future had some possibilities, but all it seemed to hold was more of the same.

I decided to buy three lottery tickets instead of my usual two, and on an impulse stopped at the video store as well. My budget didn't permit many movie rentals, but it was my birthday. Selecting the movie was easy: without hesitation I took the last copy of a movie about a handicapped young man that had won an Oscar. I'd heard about the movie on television and knew something about the story. Seeing someone overcome a terrible handicap had to be uplifting, just what I needed to perk up my spirits.

I enjoyed the movie, but I was sorry later that I had rented it. The hero's father reminded me of my own daddy, of his heavy drinking and brutish ways. That night I fell asleep thinking about the roofer's knife that was always tucked into my daddy's belt, the gleam of the curved steel blade that could cut through the thickest shingles as though they were made of paper, the knife that could slice through the rind of a melon or human flesh with equal ease. The knife I was told would quarter me and slice me into small pieces if I didn't do what I was told. He never touched me with the knife because I always, always obeyed. When he died unexpectedly of a stroke, my eyes filled with tears at his funeral. Although I feared more than loved him, he was still my daddy.

On Sunday morning I cleaned my apartment, polishing and vacuuming rooms that probably looked as neat when I started in them as when I finished. While I was wiping the kitchen cupboards, I thought of my mama. She didn't believe in cleaning; it took too much effort, and everything got dirty again anyway. I remembered the film of grease that covered everything in her kitchen, and worked even harder wiping the cupboards and counters. When I was done, I tended to my plants, which were my one indulgence. I couldn't afford many luxuries on my salary of $15,927 a year, but occasionally I'd buy a plant as a treat. Now I had a jungle of them: they were hanging from the ceiling, perched on plant stands, and resting in large pots on the floor. I was pleased when I saw that a spathiphyllum the size of a large shrub had three new flower buds. Then I spotted the fine telltale webs of spider mites on the heart-shaped leaves of an ivy that was spilling out of a white pot. As I carried the plant outside to spray it, it occurred to me that the ivy, like Tully, had a susceptible weakness. But I immediately felt guilty for the thought. The ivy's susceptibility to spider mites was a characteristic of the plant. There was nothing inherently wrong with Tully; he was fine until he was sent to Vietnam.

And it looked like I'd be spending the rest of my life waiting for him to come back.

***

The new week didn't begin well. At five minutes to nine I looked up and saw a child standing in front of my desk. It was Jessica Ann Mawley, a first grader who would have been pretty if she'd been properly cared for. Her hair, which was white-blond when it was clean, hung in dirty clumps down her back, and her jeans and T-shirt were dotted with an assortment of stains, some recent, some old. But it was Jessica Ann's expression, the strained look in her eyes and the odd set of her mouth, as if she were holding it shut with effort, that grabbed my attention. After twenty years as the school secretary, I didn't have to ask what was wrong. "You don't feel well, do you, Jessica Ann?" I said, guessing that she was sick when she was shooed out the door to catch the bus. It was too early in the day for her to come to the office sick unless she was ill when she was sent to school. Jessica Ann was a Mawley. The Mawleys didn't take care of their children any better than they took care of their animals, and their animals were among the sorriest in the county.

Jessica Ann shook her head, then put her hand over her mouth.

I was up in a flash. I grabbed Jessica's free hand and led her to a room off the reception area, ignoring the ringing telephone. "Quick, quick," I said, urging Jessica Ann to move faster.

We made it just in time. Jessica vomited what little she'd had for breakfast. "Better now?" I said, stroking her shoulders. The child's bones felt as fragile as a sparrow's.

She started to cry. "It isn't that bad, is it?" I said, trying to ignore the insistently ringing phone.

"M…My stomach hurts."

No longer able to tune out the phone, I told Jessica Ann to rest on the cot and promised to be back in a few minutes.

The ringing stopped before I reached my desk. When I heard the rumble of Bert Sidley's voice through his closed door, I braced myself for what I knew was coming.

The principal's office wasn't more than twelve feet from my desk. Dr. Sidley opened his glass-partitioned door and emerged head first, like a groundhog coming out of its hole. "That was Mrs. Frazier on the phone," he said, his bulk filling the doorway. "She's picking Hugh up today at two fifteen, in case you're interested."

Hard as I tried, I couldn't brush off his sarcasm. I resisted an impulse to march over to the wall intercom that connected the teachers' rooms to the office to call Hugh's teacher; just talking into the intercom with my back to him would have given me satisfaction. But I knew how full of self-importance he was (much too important to answer the school telephone), and it simply wasn't worth antagonizing him. I jotted Hugh's name and the time he was to leave on a pad. "I have a sick child," I said, unwilling to give him another word.

I found Jessica Ann bent over the toilet, dry heaving. "I don't feel good," she wailed.

I shook my head sympathetically, wondering if the cause was bad food or a virus. I hoped it was bad food, or it would be a nasty day.

It took several calls to locate Mrs. Mawley. The number that was listed in Jessica Ann's file was for the largest dry cleaning store in town; however, Mrs. Mawley didn't work in the store. She worked in the plant, which was in a separate building that had a different telephone number. Some parents made it difficult to contact them at work. They needed their jobs, and when they sent their children to school in the morning, they expected them to remain there for the day, the *entire* day. I more than understood their need for money—children from the poorest families in the county attended Creekside Elementary—but their need didn't absolve them of their responsibilities. Leaving a sick child at school just wasn't right, and that is what I told Mrs. Mawley, who gave me a difficult time. "I'm sorry you'll get behind in your pressing, but Jessica Ann is real sick.

I can't keep her here at school," I said. "She needs to be home with her mama."

But when Mrs. Mawley planted herself in front of the desk an hour and a half later (the school was ten minutes away from the dry cleaning plant), I had second thoughts. Mrs. Mawley's irritation at having been called had colored the woman's plump cheeks a splotched pink that matched the T-shirt stretching across her ample hips. "Well, where's she at?" Mrs. Mawley said, impatiently setting her purse on my desk.

Jessica Ann was curled in a miserable ball on the cot when I went to fetch her. "C'mon, honey, your mama's here."

As I watched them start to leave, I was thinking that one of the worst things that could happen to a child was not having a good mother. Then it happened. Jessica Ann wasn't moving fast enough to suit Mrs. Mawley. I could feel myself wince when I saw the woman turn, grab Jessica Ann's thin wrist, and yank her through the doorway as though she had no more feelings than a bag of straw.

That gesture pulled me back thirty years.

I was ten years old, in Mrs. Hartman's fifth grade class at Creekside Elementary. My ear ached so badly that it was an effort to hold my head up straight. I was hot, then cold, then hot again. The hands on the black-rimmed wall clock in the front of the room seemed to barely move. Ten thirty. Eleven. Eleven fifteen. I couldn't tell Mrs. Hartman I was sick until after the lunch recess. Mama would be angry if she was pulled away from her tables at the restaurant during the lunch hour.

After I took my place in line to leave for the lunchroom, Mrs. Hartman put her hand on my forehead. "Sara Jean, I believe you have a fever. Is it your ear again?"

I didn't want to lie, but I didn't want to catch Mama's wrath if I told the truth. "I'll be okay."

"Come stand by me," she said so kindly that I had all I could do not to cry.

Mrs. Hartman kept her arm around me all the way to the school office. I was conscious of how good she smelled, of soap and chalk dust and a sweet floral perfume. Mrs. Hartman was the best teacher I'd ever had. She was the best person in my small world.

The school secretary, Mrs. Wallace, gave me a sympathetic smile when we came into the office. "Please call Sara Jean's mother," Mrs. Hartman said. "She has a fever."

Instead of going to the teachers' room for lunch, Mrs. Hartman sat with me on a bench against the wall near the door. I hoped she wouldn't notice that a button was missing on my blouse and that the hem of my skirt was torn. "If you're absent for more than a few days, I'll bring you your books and assignments. Then you won't have to work so hard catching up like you did the last time."

Mrs. Hartman at my house! The prospect made me panic. "My brother can bring my books home. Ronnie Lee is in Mrs. Bonner's class."

Before Mrs. Hartman could reply, Mama charged past us into the school office with her arms swinging, her gray eyes the color of storm clouds. Strands of auburn hair that had escaped the bobby pins holding her waitress cap were flying in all directions, and the green uniform she was wearing had a long coffee stain slithering down one side from her hip to her knee. A stranger looking at her would have noticed how young and striking she was, but I was so embarrassed by her stained uniform that I couldn't see anything else. "I've come for Sara Jean," she said, irritation underlining every word.

"Here, Mama," I said, hurrying up to the desk.

"I hope you feel better soon, Sara Jean," Mrs. Wallace said.

"Thank you, ma'am," I said.

Mama didn't have time for pleasantries. She started for the door, expecting me to follow. "Sara Jean should see a doctor about that ear," Mrs. Hartman said, intercepting us. "This is the second time in the past month that it's acted up."

Mama's spine stiffened. "That's her parents' business," she said, yanking the door open. With her other hand she shoved me into the hallway, as if to remove me as quickly as possible from the well-intentioned woman.

The push was unexpected. I lost my balance and fell forward, landing hard on my hands and knees. Any physical hurt I felt was nothing compared with my shame. Mrs. Hartman saw, and so did Mrs. Wallace. I scrambled to my feet and rushed to the heavy doors that led outside so they couldn't see my tears.

Mama didn't apologize. "What a nerve that woman has, tellin' me how to take care of my child!" she said after we got into the car, an old brown Ford that had a portion of the grill missing and a badly dented front fender. She reached into her purse for a Marlboro, lit one and inhaled deeply. It's none 'a her business! I heard she don't even have kids of her own. It's a wonder she's married! The woman's as plain as a potato!"

"She was tryin' to help, Mama. She didn't mean any harm. Mrs. Hartman really cares. She's goin' to send my books and assignments home with Ronnie Lee so I don't fall behind."

"Hrrrumph." Mama cleared her throat derisively and tossed the cigarette out the window. "Hettie's got all my tables. I ain't never goin' to make the payment on this car at this rate. And then I won't go nowhere unless somebody comes to get me. Your daddy won't help. You know that he don't want me to have a car. Even if he did..."

I sat in miserable silence, the smoke from another cigarette assaulting the mucous membranes in my nose and throat. I'd heard Mama's complaints about being stranded without a car so often that I knew the litany by heart. All I could think about was my embarrassment at Mrs. Hartman and Mrs. Wallace seeing Mama in her dirty waitress uniform, and even worse, my shame at them seeing Mama pitch me out the door onto my hands and knees. It felt like the best year I'd had in school had been ruined. Unlike my previous teachers, Mrs. Hartman made me feel as though I could accomplish anything. She was new in town. She hadn't heard about the Barefields yet, that they were shiftless and untrustworthy, lazy and stupid. With her encouragement I had become first in the class in spelling and math, and my name was on the very top of the reading ladder. I was already dreaming of becoming a teacher when I grew up. I wanted to be just like Mrs. Hartman.

Mama drove fast, talking and smoking all the way home. She made a sharp turn into our gravel driveway, which was more dirt than stone, and stopped short in front our house. There was a tunnel of dust behind the car when we got out.

She didn't stay long. After she filled the hot water bottle, she said, "Take a couple aspirin and keep this on your ear. I got to get back. Maybe I can still catch some of the lunch crowd."

The ear got worse and worse until Mama finally took me to the doctor. By then the infection was so bad that I had a slight hearing loss. "It ain't much," Mama said. "Your other ear will pick up anythin' that ear misses, and no one will ever know. It ain't like a deformity or nothin'."

Bert Sidley came up to my desk. Stocky and dark-complexioned, he always looked like he needed a shave. "Here," he said, handing me a piece of paper. "This letter needs to go out today."

His handwriting was almost as impossible as he was, but I was glad to be rescued. Deciphering one of his letters was preferable to reliving a bad memory.

No one else came into the office with Jessica Ann's symptoms, thank goodness. It gets unpleasant fast when there's a school full of children coming down with the stomach virus. I saw what I called my "regulars," the children who came to me every day for their medicines, and two children who needed extra attention: a second grade girl who skinned her knees in the playground, and a sobbing kindergartner who was accidently poked near his eye. Fortunately, nothing happened that I couldn't handle. Creekside Elementary didn't have a nurse. I was grateful to be busy so I wouldn't have time to think about my birthday.

***

Tully was gone for nearly two weeks. He arrived at my apartment on a Wednesday evening looking haggard. He had lost weight, and the skin on his face where he'd shaved was pale and tender-looking. He handed me a black velvet box. "The jeweler told me sapphires are your birth stone," he said. "I got it Labor Day weekend because I knew your special birthday was coming, and I didn't want to get you a last-minute gift."

The box held a sapphire-and-diamond ring.

I had always tried to overlook any inconveniences his disappearances caused, but it was hard to do this time. "It's beautiful," I said, gazing at the ring, "but I would have rather had you here on my birthday than a present."

My hurt was too open to hide. "I'm sorry, Sara, so sorry...I tried to hang on...I almost made it...but I couldn't..."

"Not for one day, just one more day?" I cried, unable to hold back what seemed like unending tears of disappointment that came every time I thought of that awful Friday night.

"Maybe I shouldn't have come back. Maybe I should have done it this time."

"Done what?"

His eyes clouded. "Ended it," he said, his voice so low I could barely hear him. "I can't stand being this way. It's like I don't have control of my own life. More than anything I wanted to be here for your birthday. I knew how important it was to you, how much it meant...

"One night up there I put a gun to my head. It wasn't the first time I've done it, but I guess I wasn't ready before. That night I was ready. All that kept me from pulling the trigger was the ring, wanting to give it to you. Oh, God," he said, breaking down. "We had so many plans, so many dreams..."

We held each other and wept.

An urgent need grew out of our tears. We went into my bedroom and made love until we were breathless, until we lay panting and exhausted. I didn't want to let go of him. "Please, Tully, promise me that you'll stop thinking about doing away with yourself. Please..."

He rolled off me and mumbled what I wanted to hear, the words almost unintelligible, like they were caught in his throat.

I knew that making him promise wasn't fair, but I couldn't stop myself any more than he could stop himself from going off into the mountains. With sudden clarity I realized that whatever it was that he lost in the jungles of Vietnam would claim him. Then I would be alone, left with an empty life and memories. It was an effort of will for me not to cry out my pain.

Before he left, Tully put the sapphire ring on the third finger of my left hand. The diamonds surrounding the deep blue stone sparkled like stars. "It's so beautiful," I said. "It's really too much, too nice a gift."

He kissed me gently. "Sara, nothing I could ever give you would be enough."

Somehow I managed to hold back my tears until he was gone.

Later, as I was falling asleep, I realized that I hadn't been wearing my diaphragm. I didn't think I had anything to worry about. At the age of forty I was too old to get pregnant.

***

The stripes on the pregnancy test I bought confirmed what I suspected: I was pregnant. My period was three weeks late; for days I had been able to think of little else. After so many years of denying my dreams, they were alive again: a baby, a family. Instead of settling into the dullness of middle age, at forty I was starting a whole new life! My happiness would have been complete if I could have shared the news with Tully.

I didn't know how Tully would react. I hadn't forgotten his refusal to bring a child into the world, or his threat to kill it if it was a son. But that was years ago. Tully was mellower now, and he certainly enjoyed his brother Jimmy's boys. According to Carol Ann, Jimmy's ex-wife, Tully spent more time with the boys than Jimmy did. "While Jimmy's screwing around with his women, Tully is taking the boys fishing and teaching them how to work on cars," Carol Ann said.

And there was the worry of Tully's confession that he had put a gun to his head when he was up in the mountains. I believed that he had been ready to pull the trigger and that he could be ready again. Since he'd been back, there had been times when I had felt him drifting away from me, his mind in a place I couldn't reach. Maybe my pregnancy would give him the reason to live that he needed. But what if it didn't? What if he did pull the trigger?

After a sleepless night during which I imagined everything from Tully's insisting that I have an abortion, to our wedding (a simple ceremony), to the birth of the baby (a perfect little girl), to Tully's disappearance (his death was too horrible to imagine), I made a decision: I would wait until I was a full three months pregnant before I told him. Then we couldn't argue about an abortion because it would be too late for me to have one. My decision made me uncomfortable. I had never deceived Tully before, but I couldn't see an alternative. And if the absolute worst happened, if Tully didn't want the baby, I would raise it myself. Separating from him would just about kill me, but except for Tully, I wanted this baby more than I had ever wanted anything in my life.

On my Saturday visit to the library I skimmed books on pregnancy; with relief I read that most women have their first appointment with the doctor between their twelfth and sixteenth weeks. My gynecologist, Dr. Healy, brought his cars to Tully to work on, and he never failed to ask how Tully was doing when I came in for my checkups. I knew doctors were supposed to keep confidences, but I didn't want to take the risk. I also read about the importance of having a healthy diet. Afterward, when I went grocery shopping, I put more fruits and vegetables than usual in my cart, and added a box of unsalted crackers that the books recommended for nausea.

It was impossible to suppress my happiness. Just thinking about the baby made me want to laugh out loud with joy. Some of the teachers at Creekside Elementary noticed. "Sara, do you have a wonderful secret that you're not telling?" said Gail Wood, an energetic, sweet-faced woman who had been at Creekside as long as me. "Your eyes shine like you won the lottery."

"Don't I wish," I said, thinking that my baby was better than any lottery.

With the exception of odors bothering me and being more tired than usual at the end of the day, I felt remarkably well. Nausea was rarely a problem; however, at Thanksgiving dinner at Tully's parents' house I could hardly swallow a bite. Later I wondered if it was the house itself that triggered the nausea, the air overwarm and heavy with cooking smells. Or was it the fussy lampshades and the sentimental ceramic figurines perched everywhere that made my eyes blur? Or was it the realization that Mrs. Rutland, with her forced pleasantries and partiality to anything that had little hearts stamped on it, would be my baby's grandmother? "Why, Sara, you've hardly eaten a thing," said Mrs. Rutland when the meal was nearly over.

"There's so much," I said. "Everything is delicious."

"I always like to make some new recipes with the old standbys," said Mrs. Rutland, who took pride in her cooking and had prepared enough for double our number. "I forgot that you aren't accustomed to such a full table."

Usually Mrs. Rutland was careful to save her barbs for when we were alone. Her meaning was unmistakable: *Your people, the Barefields, were too poor to set a decent table.* I looked around. Tully's father and brother Jimmy were busying themselves with what was left on their plates. I felt the gentle pressure of Tully's hand on my thigh under the table; our eyes met, his apologetic and cautioning. He was right. A confrontation with his mother would accomplish nothing except spoil the meal for everyone else.

Fighting anger as well as nausea, I sat quietly until Tully finished his pumpkin pie. Then, explaining that I wasn't feeling well, I asked Tully to take me home. It didn't bother me a bit that Mrs. Rutland was left with the job of clearing the table and doing the dishes herself.

Hiding my nausea was difficult, but there was nothing I could do to conceal my frequent trips to the rest room from Bert Sidley. Though I tried to stay at my desk when the principal was around, the pressure of my uterus on my bladder didn't always make that possible. On the second Friday in December, Sidley was leaning against my desk when I returned from the teachers' lounge. "You're supposed to be at this desk," he said. "What if a child was here waiting instead of me?"

"I was only gone for a few minutes."

"The past week or so you seem to be gone more than you're here."

I knew his nastiness would continue until he saw that I was close to tears; only then would he be satisfied. It had become his pattern. Not this time, I decided, having a sudden inspiration. Over the years I had accumulated weeks and weeks of sick days that I would probably never use. "I don't feel well," I said. "I'm going home."

Sidley's heavy jaw dropped, the meanness in his face conquered by surprise. "It's only ten fifteen."

"Are you telling me that I have to stay when I don't feel well?"

"What about the phone, the children?" he said, backing away from the desk. "It's Friday. There are the attendance sheets…"

That's your problem, I wanted to say. Instead, I suggested that he get the help of a teacher's aide. Walking calmly out of the building to my car took self-control. I wanted to laugh, to dance, to shout to the world that I had finally stood up to Bert Sidley. And to think: it happened because of my pregnancy!

It was impossible to conceal the changes in my body from Tully. My nipples were darker, my breasts fuller. I started turning the lights off when we made love. When we were undressing in my bedroom a week before Christmas, Tully came up behind me and cupped my breasts in his hands. It was semi-dark; the only light was from a single lamp in the living room. "You seem a lot bigger," he said, nibbling at my neck.

I felt his organ stiffening against my backside. "I might have gained a few pounds."

"I like where you gained 'em."

I stepped away and lay down on the bed so my breasts would lose some of their fullness as they spread to my sides. He eased his body next to mine. Tully had gifted hands for more than just cars; it felt like my whole body was humming when he entered me. Never had I been so happy.

I was two and a half months pregnant. More than anything I wanted to tell him, but if I told him then and he took the news badly, the holidays might be spoiled. I had already decided to wait at least until New Year's Eve. This year I wanted to make New Year's Eve special, the best we ever had.

We were expected at Bob Ready's New Year's Eve party. I didn't want to go to the party, which ended every year with everyone drunk. It seemed to me that the people got drunk deliberately, as if it were expected of them because it was New Year's Eve. Even Tully, who always prided himself on being able to hold his liquor, got so loaded last year that I had to drive him home. The next day he had a brutal hangover, the worst in his life, he said. It would probably happen again if we went.

Hard as I tried, I couldn't think of a way to avoid the Readys' party until the day before New Year's Eve. Then it came to me, a solution so simple that it immediately felt right: I'd have my own party, just Tully and me. We would have a late supper. I'd buy a couple of steaks and champagne, and I'd put music Tully liked on the CD player he gave me for Christmas, romantic music that would set the mood for the evening. It could be the perfect time to tell him about the baby.

Rather than talk to him about my plans on the phone, I decided to catch Tully after work. I arrived at Ready's Garage a few minutes before five, parked in the gravel lot behind the concrete-block building, and went directly to the first of six bays, where I found Tully lowering the hood on a gray Oldsmobile. His face broke into a grin when he saw me. "What brings you here?" Then his smile faded. "The Buick again?"

For the past couple of months I had been having trouble with my car, a 1984 Buick Century. "It's running fine," I said, noticing that he had a streak of grease on his forehead. "Are you finished for the day?"

He took a pen out of the front pocket of his blue coveralls and reached for a clipboard that was suspended from a hook on the wall. "I just have to write this up and turn it in. It won't take but a minute. Want to go to Franny's for a quick bite? Later I have to work on that '67 Mustang I told you about. I promised I'd have it done by tomorrow."

"I can go on ahead and get us a table."

Tully turned and looked across the garage to a glass-enclosed office. "Maybe you should stop and say hello to Bob. It'll take me a couple of minutes to wash up and change anyway."

I nodded. If Bob saw me, he would be offended if I left without speaking to him. It would be rude not to take a minute with the other mechanics I knew as well. My mind was so occupied with New Year's Eve that I wasn't thinking properly about anything else.

We drove to Franny's separately. Tully got there first and was waiting outside when I arrived. He was wearing the black leather bomber jacket I had gotten him for Christmas. I preferred the jacket in brown, but Tully always liked black best. "Guess you didn't time the lights right," he said when I walked up to him.

The sly smile on his face made me laugh. As usual, he was anticipating a remark from me about his speeding. "I know," I said, "you weren't speeding at all. You just have those lights on your own private timer. They all turn green when they see your truck coming."

"You got it!" he said, holding the door.

I waited until after the waitress brought our Frannyburger plates to talk about New Year's Eve. He had given me a bottle of my favorite perfume and one hundred dollars besides the CD player for Christmas. "I spent some of my Christmas money today," I said, salting the fries. "I got a new black bra and panties. I also bought champagne."

He held the giant hamburger in midair, his blue eyes gleaming. "Sounds like a party."

His gaze was so suggestive that I felt my cheeks color. "I thought I'd make us a late supper tomorrow night, maybe eight thirty or so, to celebrate New Year's Eve—steak, baked potato, champagne.

"Mmm," he said approvingly. Then he frowned. "What about the Readys' party?"

"We can go late," I said. "Or if we decide not to go, we can call and say one of us isn't feeling well. They always have such a crowd, we won't be missed."

"Good idea." He leaned forward. "Are you going to be wearing the new stuff you bought?"

"Sure."

He shook his head. "It's a damn shame I have to work on that Mustang tonight!"

The next morning I was out early. Before going to the supermarket, I decided to shop for a tablecloth instead of using the old vinyl place mats. I wanted candles, too. This evening would be truly special.

Hours later I looked at the table with satisfaction. Most of my Christmas money was gone, but it was worth it. The blue tablecloth I found on sale at K-Mart matched the blue flowers on my dishes. The white candles and lucite candlestick holders were also on sale, but I had to pay full price for the champagne glasses. I had never set a table like this before. As nice as it looked, it seemed as though something was missing. Flowers, I realized, recalling pictures in magazines. I placed an African violet that had clusters of white flowers edged in pink between the candles. It was perfect. Now I could relax in a hot bath.

While I was soaking in the tub, I thought about all I had done. I knew that my effort wasn't necessary. Tully wouldn't care about a tablecloth or candles or fancy glasses for the champagne. As long as his steak was rare and there was plenty of butter for his baked potato, he'd be satisfied. But I cared. I wanted tonight to be like evenings I had read about in novels and had seen on television, where couples celebrated special occasions with romantic dinners in a halo of candlelight. Tully and I had loved each other nearly our entire lives. If we had gotten married as we had once planned, we would have celebrated twenty anniversaries. Now we were going to have a baby. Tonight could be the beginning of the life we never had.

As I sank lower in the tub, uneasiness began to overtake my happy thoughts. Maybe tonight wouldn't be the right time to tell him. Maybe he'd feel that all I had done—the fancy table and the steak and champagne—was a trick to soften him for the news about the baby. Maybe it would be better to wait until Friday. After waiting so long, just a few more days wouldn't make a difference.

I dressed with special care, deciding on a pair of black slacks that still fit passably and a polyester blouse in a rich shade of red that looked like silk. I put on jewelry Tully had given me over the years, a gold necklace and gold hoop earrings, a gold watch and the sapphire-and-diamond ring. My effort was rewarded. "You look terrific," he said when I opened the door to greet him. He leaned over to kiss me. "Mmm, I smell that Christmas perfume."

He was carrying a six-pack of beer in one hand and a bottle of wine in the other. I noticed that he'd gotten a haircut. He was wearing gray slacks and a blue-and-gray sweater his mother had given him for Christmas. The sweater accentuated the intense color of his eyes. I remember thinking how lucky I was that he loved me. "You don't look bad yourself," I said.

"I'll put these in the refrigerator," he said, heading for the kitchen. He stopped when he saw the table. "Hey, this is something! No beer. It's definitely wine tonight."

"There's champagne for later."

"I think I'd better call Bob now. We're not going to make it to the party."

"What will you say?"

"I'll tell him you're not feeling well."

"What if he wants you to come?"

Tully grinned. "He'll have to drag me out of here!"

While I made the salads, Tully put the potatoes in the microwave and broiled the steaks. After so many years it was a division of labor done without discussion. We both knew that if I cooked the steaks, there was a risk that they'd either be too rare or too well done. Before we sat down to eat I lit the candles and turned off the lights. Tully poured the wine, then lifted his glass. "Happy New Year, honey," he said.

"Happy New Year," I said, loving him more than I had ever thought possible.

I tried not to notice that he was drinking more wine than usual, that he was smoking more, that there was a quickness in his movements, a kind of nervous energy that wouldn't let him relax.

After dinner we cleared the table together. Tully put another disc in the CD player while I loaded the dishes into the dishwasher. Then we drifted into the bedroom, Tully saying, "I haven't forgotten about that black bra and those black panties."

I was conscious of him watching me undress in the semi-darkness. When I stepped up to him in the lacy black bra and black panties, I hoped he wouldn't notice the slight swell of flesh in my stomach. He took me in his arms. "You're beautiful, Sara, really beautiful."

As if articulating my thoughts, Elvis' voice crooned *"Love me tender..."* from the CD player. Listening to the words, I felt as though all of my dreams had been fulfilled.

WINTER, 1992

Two days later Tully was gone. My telephone rang at nine o'clock on Friday morning, just as I was finishing a second cup of coffee. I had been mentally rehearsing how I would tell him about the baby that evening. The moment I heard Bob Ready's voice, I knew. "I'm calling on the chance that Tully might be at your place," he said.

"No," I managed to say, the coffee rising in my throat.

"Didn't think so," said Bob. "But I thought I'd give it a try anyway. He's gone again. I wonder how long it will be this time."

I couldn't answer. I put the receiver down and ran to the bathroom, where I vomited until I dry heaved. Afterward, weak and shaking, I went to bed and lay under the covers with my eyes closed, wishing for night and darkness, wishing I could sleep so I could escape the fear that was coiling itself around me like a snake. If only I had told him, I kept thinking, if only I had told him.

The weekend was a nightmare of worry, and Tully's absence was all I could think about when I returned to work on Monday. My pulse raced each time the telephone rang. Despite my being busy the day seemed endless, and I knew the night would be worse. Tuesday was the same. Then, on Tuesday evening, the waiting was over. I heard three sharp raps on my door followed by Tully's brother's voice. "Sara, it's Jimmy…"

He didn't have to say another word. I was crying when I opened the door.

There was a definite family resemblance between Jimmy and Tully, but Jimmy wasn't as blond and his eyes were a paler blue. His face, less angular than Tully's, crumpled when he saw me; however, he quickly regained his composure, perhaps sensing that my need for comfort was greater than his. He held me while I cried uncontrollably, patting me like a child. "Hunters found him this morning," he said when my sobbing eased.

"Wh…When did he…?"

"On Sunday, they think. We don't have the report yet."

Tully dead for days, alone. "Oh God," I cried.

"The funeral's going to be on Saturday at eleven o'clock," Jimmy said, exhaustion creeping into his voice.

"Where?"

"At Buckley's."

Buckley's. The name made me clench my teeth. "Your mama and daddy," I said. "How are they? When should I go see them?"

Jimmy hesitated. "It might be best if you waited a while. Daddy's quiet like always. But Mama…" He shook his head. "It's like she's lost her mind with grief. Sara, I don't know how to tell you this, it hurts me to say it. She's…She's kind of blaming you for what's happened."

I gasped. "Blaming me?"

"She keeps going on and on about Tully not getting married and having a family, that he's gone and there's nothing left of him on this earth."

"Tully didn't want to get married. He didn't want…" I couldn't say it.

"I know that, but you can't tell Mama. She has it fixed in her mind that he'd be alive if he'd had a wife and kids. And once Mama's mind gets set on something, you can't change it," Jimmy said wearily. "Ever since me and Carol Ann got divorced, Mama's been after me to get custody of the boys. It must be a thousand times that I've told her I can't take care of the boys like Carol Ann, and a judge wouldn't take them away from their mother even if I could. But

Mama won't accept a word of it. As far as she's concerned, if it's got the name *Rutland* on it, it's hers. And that includes the boys."

I crossed my hands over my stomach. "Then I'll just go to the funeral."

"I'm sorry for this, Sara, really I am." Jimmy bent down and kissed me gently on the cheek. "Tully loved you more than anything in this world. I know he did, and I know it would hurt him to see how Mama's acting. All's I can say is that grief is making her behave like this. I hope you understand."

"Oh, I understand."

He would have been surprised to know how much I understood. From the moment he told me about his mama's carrying on, I could almost hear Mrs. Rutland wailing about the Barefields being trash, wailing about how Tully wasted his life with Sara Barefield instead of marrying a girl from a decent family, as if that alone would have saved him.

Hard as I had tried, over the years it had been impossible to change Mrs. Rutland's opinion of me, and now it didn't matter. Tully was gone. Again, my hands crept over my stomach. *As far as she's concerned, if it's got the name* Rutland *on it, it's hers,* Jimmy said. If it was the last thing I did, I'd make sure that Mrs. Rutland would never know about the baby.

I couldn't sleep. When I wasn't crying, I was torturing myself over whether Tully would still be alive if I had told him about the baby. The hellish combination of guilt and grief didn't allow me a moment of peace.

And when I finally did fall asleep sometime before dawn on Friday, I dreamed of what I had struggled to forget. I dreamed of death and Buckley's funeral parlor. *After the doctor took my mama's breast off, she wouldn't go anywhere. I begged her to come out, even if it was just for a short drive, but she refused. Then one day she came to my apartment. I was so happy to have her come for a visit that I didn't notice later that my Visa card was missing. Mama had taken the card off my dresser. A bill for over eight hundred dollars* for clothes and jewelry charged to my account came after I had seen Mama wearing a new blouse and slacks that looked expensive. I was working at the bank then, barely earning enough to survive on, and when I confronted Mama with the bill, nearly hysterical, she said, "I wanted to have me some nice things before I die."

No amount of pleading could get her to return anything she'd bought. "What I got, I'm keepin'. You can think of it as a gift."

"I can't afford to give you gifts, Mama. I can hardly afford to live."

"You can pay it off on time," Mama said. "You've got lots of that. Mine's almost gone."

So I started paying the Visa bill, a few dollars a month, and hadn't made more than four or five payments when she died. There was no money for a funeral or a burial plot. My daddy didn't have enough for a pine box. Ronnie Lee had dropped out of high school, and he didn't have any money, either. Mama had died at home; her body was in the bedroom, getting stiff, and her husband was in the kitchen, getting drunk. "What are you goin' to do, Daddy?" I said, sobbing part out of grief and part out of fear of what might happen next.

"Can't do nothin'," he said.

"You've got to do somethin'. Mama has to be fixed up. She has to be buried. You can't keep her in the bedroom."

"Ain't nothin' I can do with no money."

"We might could bury her out back," said Ronnie Lee, who'd had more than a few beers himself.

I glared at my brother, furious. "That's your mama you're talkin' about!"

Ronnie Lee shrugged.

"I guess I'll have to call the county," I said, not knowing what else to do.

"NO!" Daddy exploded. "We don't take nothin' from nobody. We never have and we never will!"

I had to sign for the funeral and the plot so Mama could be buried *proper. I knew that Buckley's funeral parlor was overcharging me, but I had to use Buckley's because it was the only place that would extend me credit. It took me years and years to pay them. No one knew, not even Tully. I had been too ashamed for anyone to know that my daddy couldn't afford to bury my mama. Tully didn't know about the Visa bill, either. But when my daddy died and I had to pay for his funeral and burial plot, Tully did know about it. He was with me when I asked Ronnie Lee to pay his fair share of the expenses. Ronnie Lee refused, claiming he had all he could do to take care of his wife and kids. Tully tried to reason with him, and Ronnie Lee got nasty. After that Tully would have nothing to do with him. Tully's disgust with Ronnie Lee was so deep that I never got over my shame.*

Tuuullllly. I cried out his name in my sleep and wept for him when I was awake. Finally Ardelle, who was spending every moment she could spare with me, said, "Sara, you have to try to think of Tully at peace after so many years of being troubled, and be glad for him even though it's so hard for you."

I knew she was right: Tully was at peace. But would I ever have a moment's rest from the guilt of not having told him about the baby? I ached to share my secret with Ardelle, but nothing could pry a word out of me until after the funeral, until there was no risk that it might get back to the Rutlands.

Ardelle had brought supper and was dressed to go to the funeral parlor. "I didn't expect you'd still be in your bathrobe," she said. "We should be at Buckley's before seven."

"I'm not going."

Ardelle's china-blue eyes widened. "You have to go! People will be expectin' you there."

"Mrs. Rutland's blaming me for Tully's death. She thinks that if he'd gotten married—not to me, to someone else—and had a family, it wouldn't have happened."

"Who told you that?"

"Jimmy," I said. "And when he called this afternoon, he told me that nothing's changed."

"It's grief that's makin' her say that. She'll come around," Ardelle said.

It would have been hurtful to reveal how Mrs. Rutland felt about the Barefields. Ardelle had carried the name long enough to know what it felt like to be labeled *trash* and treated accordingly. "Mrs. Rutland's mind is set," I said. "I'll just go to the funeral."

Ardelle thought I was wrong. "Tomorrow mornin' there'll be a place for you in the front row with the family," she said. "You'll see."

The following morning Ardelle insisted upon picking me up at nine fifteen so we would be at the funeral parlor an hour before the service. "Since you weren't there last night, you have to be there early so your friends can pay their respects."

Although I would have preferred to go later, I didn't argue.

I was bent with exhaustion when we entered Buckley's, but when I walked into the familiar green chapel and saw the first row—the family row—packed from end to end with Rutlands—my spine straightened. I would never let Mrs. Rutland hurt me again, I vowed, looking at the woman's bony backside. After the funeral I would never see her again.

"I don't believe it!" Ardelle sputtered, staring at the end-to-end Rutlands.

Fearing that Ardelle might confront them, I put a restraining hand on her arm. "Forget about them. We're here for Tully. Let's sit in one of these back rows. If you don't mind, I'd like to be on the aisle in case I get to feeling sick."

Jimmy came to apologize after we were settled in the next-to-last row. He looked uncomfortable in a new dark gray suit. "Sara, I wish it wasn't like this. I'd sit the boys with Carol Ann so you'd be up front where you belong, but Mama's barely hanging on."

"I'm fine here," I said, looking straight up at him. Since I had entered the chapel, I had been unable to bring myself to look at the casket.

"You were too nice about it," Ardelle said after he left.

Before I could reply, Eddie McCauley entered the chapel and came up to me to offer his condolences, his long face somber. Eddie had worked with Tully at Bob Ready's Garage. Benny Thomas came after Eddie, then George Powell and Harold Mills, Dave Jenkins and Billy Goodloe, Donnie Tribby and Henry Blankenship. And they kept coming, one after another, blocking the aisle at the back of the chapel, offering me their sympathy. Men who had worked with Tully as far back as when he first started at Ray Clark's Ford dealership stopped to tell me how highly they regarded him and how much they felt for me in my loss. Their words, simple and heartfelt, moved me deeply. I was grateful and thanked each one. After the service Ardelle told me that Mrs. Rutland had kept glancing toward the back of the chapel at the mourners who had clotted around me instead of flowing up the aisle to her.

People said later that every mechanic in Owings was at Buckley's that morning to pay last respects to Tully. The chapel was filled when the sallow-complexioned minister from Mrs. Rutland's church began the service. Tully hadn't been to church since he'd come back from Vietnam; he'd never met the minister, yet the minister was talking about Tully with an intimacy that belonged to old friends. I knew the information had been supplied by the Rutlands. I didn't hold it against the minister. He was doing his job, like thousands of clergymen do every day, pretending to know the strangers they're eulogizing, but I couldn't bear to listen. His words were bought and paid for. They had nothing to do with Tully.

My head felt as if it was going to burst with memories: Tully as a skinny, tow-headed boy of ten in Hazard Park, wiping blood off my forehead; Tully in his Ford coveralls after he finished his training at the school for mechanics; Tully lean in his Army uniform before he was sent to Vietnam; Tully bearded and haggard the first time he came back after disappearing into the mountains; Tully putting the sapphire-and-diamond ring on my finger the night we made our baby; Tully wearing the bomber jacket I had gotten him for Christmas; Tully raising his champagne glass to wish me a happy New Year.

Silently, with tears streaming down my cheeks, I gave Tully his eulogy.

***

Tully was the center of my world. He was my lover and my oldest and best friend. His death made a gaping hole in my life that left me dizzy, weak, and frightened. After the funeral I had no desire to do anything except stay in my bedroom with the shades drawn, huddled under the covers with my grief; however, circumstances didn't give me that option. The shock of Mrs. Rutland's treatment of me made it clear that I would have to leave Owings. I knew without question that the woman would make every day of my life miserable once the baby was born. Even if the baby didn't have the name Rutland, the infant would be all that remained of Tully on this earth, and Mrs. Rutland would lay claim to it, attaching herself and interfering in any way that she could.

Mrs. Rutland wasn't the only reason for me to leave Owings. I was positive that Bert Sidley would force me to quit my job at Creekside Elementary when my pregnancy became obvious; he wouldn't want an unwed pregnant woman working in the school office. To be fair, I didn't think it was right, either. Even though it seemed that everyone was having babies without husbands—teenagers, movie stars, career women—I didn't feel that an unwed pregnant woman was a proper example to set before children. Nor did I want to be a subject for gossip, which is what would happen when my pregnancy became known.

The prospect of moving was frightening, but the problem of money was overwhelming. Before Tully's death, I hadn't given a thought to money. No one was kinder or more generous than Tully. Even if he didn't want to get married, I was certain he would have helped me and the baby. I had nine hundred fifty dollars in the bank, which was all that was left of my savings after paying for Christmas presents. If I worked weekends at a part-time job, I still couldn't save enough to tide me over once my job at Creekside Elementary was gone; the rent and utilities for my apartment ran over five hundred dollars a month. If I moved away from Owings, I might find a job where I could work until I was ready to deliver. But that would probably mean a low-paying job, and I would have to get it before my pregnancy showed. All of my reasoning pointed to one conclusion: unless I won the lottery, when the baby was born I would have to go on welfare.

Welfare. The very thought of it affected me physically. Even my parents at their most desperate had never applied for public assistance. As poor as they were, to them welfare was a dirty word, and people who were on it were beneath contempt. When I was a child and my daddy wasn't working, which was often, Ronnie Lee and I were given peanut butter, crackers, and water for supper. Sometimes there wasn't any peanut butter. It was entirely possible that I had lived poorer than people on welfare and just didn't know it. Some of the children at Creekside Elementary whose families were on welfare came to school better dressed than I was at their age, and people on welfare didn't live in places any worse than the falling-apart house I grew up in. But those things weren't as important to my parents as being able to hold their heads up. They had their self-respect. They weren't charity cases.

There was a bitter taste in my mouth and a leaden feeling in my stomach. I wanted everything for this baby that I hadn't had as a child: a nice home, enough to eat, decent clothes, the opportunity to go to college. And now, after years of struggle, I was about to sink even lower than where I started. To the absolute bottom.

I didn't go to work on the Monday after the funeral, but it wasn't time taken off to grieve. I knew that if I started crying, I might not be able to stop, and I couldn't risk that. Tears wouldn't help me with the decisions I had to make. I still had the miracle of the baby, the precious gift of life, which was worth more than any amount of money. And welfare wouldn't be forever. I had been able to rise out of poverty once and I could do it again. I was determined to be strong for both of us; our survival depended on it.

I needed information, fast. I called the Department of Social Services and asked to speak to a caseworker. My call was transferred, and a recorded message stated that the caseworker was presently unavailable. I didn't leave my name and telephone number; I decided to try again later. Next I called obstetricians' offices and might as well have been talking to answering machines. The doctors' receptionists would not divulge fees for delivering babies over the telephone. "You mean I have to make an appointment and ask the doctor how much he charges?" I said in frustration to the receptionist at the third office I called. "What if I can't afford his fee? Wouldn't it be better to find out in advance rather than waste his time and mine?" The receptionist still wouldn't give me a straight answer, but she did reveal that fees were based on the allowable amounts insurance companies paid for obstetrical care, which ranged from fifteen hundred to twenty-one hundred dollars for a normal vaginal delivery. "Check with your insurance company," she said.

I called my insurance company, but not to find out their allowance for obstetrical care. I wanted to know how much it would cost to keep my health insurance after I left Creekside Elementary School. The figure was so high I didn't bother to write it down. Health insurance would be as far out of my reach as a diamond necklace.

Finally, after four tries, I was able to speak to a caseworker at the Department of Social Services. Pretending that I was calling for someone else, "a friend who was pregnant," I asked how much the "friend's" monthly allotment would be if she applied for welfare. "Does your friend have any other children?" the caseworker asked.

"No," I said.

"Then she wouldn't get anything," he said. "AFDC is Aid to Families with Dependent Children. Single women without dependents don't qualify."

"But she's going to lose her job. She has very little money, not enough to pay an obstetrician for medical care."

"How many months pregnant is she?"

"A little over three months."

"All she can get before the birth of the baby is Medicaid and food stamps. She could also be eligible for WIC. Prenatal care is important. She should apply for Medicaid soon."

"How much money will she get when the baby is born?"

"Two hundred ninety-three dollars a month."

"Oh," I said, too shocked to ask more questions.

No one could live on two hundred ninety-three dollars a month. I realized that I should have asked more about food stamps. I should have asked if other help was available. I had more questions, although asking them wouldn't have changed anything. Somehow I would manage, I always had. But I had managed with Tully's help. My television set, my VCR, my cherry bedroom set, all the repairs on the cars I had owned over the years, were gifts from him. Thinking that it was impossible, I struggled for self-control. I still had other calls to make.

At eleven thirty I called Ardelle at work. "Can you get away for lunch?"

"I'm alone here," Ardelle said.

"Then I'll bring lunch," I said.

Located across the street from the oldest apartment complex in Owings, the laundromat where Ardelle worked was in an area of town that looked seedier to me each time I came by. The laundromat seemed seedier as well, the windows on the washers cloudy with soap scum, the beige floor tiles curling from age and water damage. Ardelle, wearing jeans and an extra-large T-shirt that nearly reached her knees, was wrestling with a huge peach-colored comforter when I walked in. "I'll help you with that," I said, setting the McDonald's bag on a washer.

Together we folded the comforter and managed to fit it into a clear plastic bag. "Thanks," Ardelle said, taking the oversize package. "I just have a few loads to check on and then we can sit."

While I was waiting for Ardelle, I wandered over to an area where a small group of women were watching a television set that was suspended from the ceiling. The women were gazing at the screen in rapt attention, several nodding in agreement as an attractive middle-aged actress berated her soap-opera husband for his infidelity. "You tell 'im, honey," said a woman who had a receding chin and sad pouches under her eyes. "You tell 'im!"

"Uh-huh," chorused the others, as though she were speaking for all of them.

Ardelle motioned to me to follow her. We went behind a counter at the back of the laundromat into the office, a narrow windowless room that was furnished with a desk, an old filing cabinet, and a battered wood table and three mismatched chairs. "This is a treat," Ardelle said, removing Big Macs and fries from the bag I brought. "I'm starved!"

The food had no appeal to me. I picked at the fries, leaving my hamburger untouched, until Ardelle said, "You've got to try to eat, Sara. A bird couldn't survive on what little you've had this past week."

"I know. It's important for..." I had held the secret for so long that now I was having trouble saying it. "I have...I want to tell you something, but I can't unless you promise that you'll never tell anyone, not a soul, not even Ronnie Lee. I want you to swear on my life that you won't say a word."

Ardelle was extremely superstitious; she squirmed uncomfortably. "That isn't necessary. You can trust me."

"Swear," I insisted.

"I swear I won't say anything."

"I'm pregnant."

Ardelle's eyes bugged. "You're what?"

"I'll be three-and-a-half months pregnant on Wednesday. No one knows."

"Oh my God," Ardelle said, putting down her hamburger.

"Tully didn't know. He didn't want children. He once told me that he'd kill his son rather than risk having him sent off to war, and I knew that he meant it. I could see it in his face. I had planned to tell him the Friday after New Year's, but it was too late. He was gone. I keep thinking that if I'd told him sooner…"

Ardelle reached across the table and took my hand. "What if you'd told him and then he'd done it?"

"I hadn't thought of that."

"You can't blame yourself. Tully was troubled for a long time. People are sayin' that if it wasn't for you he wouldn't have lasted as long as he did."

The mention of people talking about Tully and me stopped my tears. It made me feel exposed. I had always been protective of Tully, unwilling to discuss his problem or answer people's prying questions. "I wish people would mind their own business."

"That'll never happen, so you better get used to it, especially now," Ardelle said, her face full of concern. "How are you going to manage? Will you be able to keep your job?"

"I've decided to move away from Owings."

"Move away?" Ardelle said, her eyebrows rising in shock "Why?"

"I don't want the Rutlands to know about the baby, especially Mrs. Rutland."

"I know how bad she treated you at the funeral, but it'll pass."

"No," I said. "It was always there and it always will be."

"Where will you go?"

"I'm not sure yet except that it'll be on the other side of the Blue Ridge. I want to put the mountains between me and the Rutlands. I'm thinking of either Stalling or Charlottesville. I should be able to find some sort of job until the baby is born."

"And then?"

I swallowed hard. "I guess I'll have to go on welfare for a while."

"Oh, Sara, welfare is so awful. How will you survive?" Ardelle's eyes welled with tears.

"On food stamps, I guess. Other people manage. If they can, I can, too."

Again, Ardelle reached for my hand. "Sara, you don't have to do this. Ronnie Lee says Tully left a big estate—the cars he restored, that property with the house and garages. Ronnie Lee says that all together it's worth more than a quarter of a million dollars."

Nothing had changed. Ronnie Lee was still counting other people's money. "Tully didn't have a will. He had a dislike for lawyers from the time he bought his property and the lawyer he hired messed up on getting proper title. It cost him a couple thousand dollars to get it straightened out. Since he left no will, everything will go to the Rutlands."

"But don't you see, the baby is a Rutland. By law Tully's child must be entitled to a portion of his property. I just heard about a couple who'd been separated for years, and she got a share of what he had when he died suddenly because they were still legally married."

"If I made a claim, the Rutlands would know about the baby. There's no way that's ever going to happen."

"I can't believe you'd go on welfare rather than let them know about their grandchild!"

"Yes," I said.

"In my opinion you're foolish to deny yourself a claim to his estate. You stuck by Tully for years, for your whole life really. A lot of wives don't do as much. But for you to deny the baby's claim is just plain wrong. That inheritance could give your baby a chance in life. Because you dislike Mrs. Rutland is no reason to deprive your baby."

I didn't want to tell her about the insults I'd had to endure over the years, the slights and barbed remarks, although they weren't the whole reason I was determined to keep knowledge of the baby from the Rutlands. I would fight with every bit of strength I possessed to prevent my child from looking at me through Mrs. Rutland's eyes. "I can't explain it to you, but it's more than dislike that's making me do this."

"Choosing welfare over an inheritance?" Ardelle shook her head "You're as pig-headed as your brother, and even he wouldn't do that."

I remembered how my mama had always accused me of having too much pride and Ronnie Lee of not having any. "Probably not," I said, opening my purse. "Before I came here I got these forms to open a savings account at First Trust. There's a check made out to you for two hundred dollars. I want you to open the account in your name so the money can't be traced to me. If I can, I'll add to it before I move. It'll be my emergency money. I hope you don't mind."

Ardelle took the papers and the check. "When do you plan to go?"

"I'll give notice on my apartment at the end of the month, so I'll be moving at the end of February."

"The kids will miss you. We'll all miss you." Ardelle started to cry.

"I haven't gone yet." I got up to give Ardelle a hug. "Thank you for doing this for me. You're the only one in the world I can trust."

After I left the laundromat I thought about Ardelle's reaction to my plan to leave Owings, forfeiting any claim to Tully's estate. For days I had been so lost in a fog of grief that I hadn't given a moment's consideration to what he had left behind. It was a shock to hear Ardelle say that his estate was worth more than a quarter of a million dollars. As I drove home, I began to realize what Tully had accumulated.

A few years after he'd gotten out of the Army, Tully had painstakingly restored a 1955 Corvette. Recently a man from Newport News had offered forty-seven thousand dollars for the car. "I'd never sell the Corvette at any price," Tully had said at the time. To my surprise, I had felt relieved. The white Corvette was special to me, too; I had enjoyed going for drives in it as much as he did. He had also owned two T-Birds that he had restored, a 1957 and a 1960. A fellow from Richmond had offered him thirty-three thousand dollars for the 1957 T-Bird less than a month before he died. Tully didn't consider the offer for even a second; the 1957 T-Bird was as special to him as the Corvette, not for sale at any price. There was also the land that he owned, six acres located a few miles beyond what had been the outskirts of town when he bought the property.

The land had been cheap at the time, the house on it a three-room shack. Tully had insulated the house, put on a new roof and new siding, and had made the inside livable. Then, with the help of his brother Jimmy, who owned a small construction company, he had built a long, low building divided into five garages. Three of the garages were for Tully's cars; he worked on cars people brought to him in the remaining two. Tully had always had more work offered to him than he could possibly take. Over the years he had become selective, and I was proud of his glowing reputation. Although he had often mentioned what he had charged for work he had completed, I hadn't paid much attention. Most of the money went into the bank. I had no idea as to the size of the accounts. Tully had spent relatively little on himself; his one luxury, which was really a necessity, was his insistence on the best tools he could buy. I knew the tools were valuable, as was the land. Owings had spread, moving out to Tully's property. He had had a number of offers for his land, several well over one hundred thousand dollars, but he hadn't been interested in selling. Content where he was, he had reasoned that it would cost a good portion of what he would be paid to duplicate what he had.

For once Ronnie Lee was right: the cars, the property, the bank accounts, the tools, even the black pickup truck that was new last year, all added up to a lot of money. The pain was almost unbearable when I thought of Tully's possessions, things that he cared about, being sold to strangers.

"*For you to deny the baby's claim is just plain wrong. That inheritance could give your baby a chance in life,*" Ardelle said. Maybe she was right. The money would mean that I wouldn't have to go on welfare, that the baby and I could live decently. But at what price? Again, I thought of my child looking at me through Mrs. Rutland's contemptuous eyes. If I stayed and made a claim, it was inevitable. The woman's mind had been fixed for over thirty years and it would stay fixed until she died; no amount of effort had been able to change it.

My chin set with determination and my eyes glittering with tears, I made my decision: the Rutlands could have everything that Tully owned. I had the baby, which was all I wanted.

***

On the last Monday in January I told the manager of Altavista Gardens that I would be moving at the end of February. "You have my security deposit of four hundred fifty dollars," I said. "When can I get it back?"

The manager was an older woman whose hair was dyed the color of black shoe polish. "It takes at least thirty days."

"I'd appreciate the money sooner. I'm moving out of town."

"That's the owner's policy. I'm sorry, but there's nothing I can do."

I had been counting on that money to help with my moving expenses. After I left the rental office, I tried to remember if I had given deposits to the telephone and electric companies. Every penny mattered now. I called Virginia Power when I got back to my apartment and was told that my deposit had been refunded. "Since you're moving, you might want a letter of credit," the fellow said.

"What's that?"

"It's a letter stating that you have a good record for paying your bills on time. Most power companies will accept a letter of credit instead of a deposit when you start new service with them."

Yes, I did want the letter. And immediately after I hung up, I called requesting letters of credit from the telephone company and the county water authority. Afterward I thought about all the years I had struggled to pay my bills on time, occasionally wondering if the effort was worth it. Now I felt rewarded.

Giving notice that I was moving wasn't as upsetting as I had expected it to be. Although Tully and I hadn't lived together, the hours I had spent in the apartment since his funeral, particularly the weekends, had been excruciatingly lonely. It was in the apartment that I felt his death most: never again would he call on Friday afternoons between five fifteen and five thirty; never again would we share a pizza or make love; never again would he arrive on Saturday nights to take me out to dinner; never again would we go out for a drive in one of his cars. On Saturdays I stayed out as long as I could. I went to bargain movie matinees. I shopped at end-of-season sales for clothes that would hide my pregnancy and bought two cotton tunic sweaters, a long oversize blouse, and two pairs of knit stirrup pants. I didn't plan on wearing the clothes until it was necessary, but shopping kept me out of the apartment. It made me think about something besides Tully.

Although it wouldn't have been questioned if I had taken more time off, I went back to work the day after I told Ardelle about my pregnancy. I had hoped that keeping busy would ease my grief, but the teachers were so solicitous that I often found myself choking back tears. I would have almost preferred their indifference to their concern. If they had ignored my loss it would have hurt; however, their kind words of sympathy were reminders that constantly reopened the wound of my grief. The same thing happened when I resumed bowling with Eileen and Peggy. One Monday night, unable to see the pins through a blur of tears, I threw the ball blindly and made two strikes in a row.

Determined to put the Blue Ridge Mountains between me and the Rutlands, I decided to move to Stalling, Virginia. Charlottesville had a high cost of living and would be too expensive. With a population of about thirty-five thousand, Stalling was larger than Owings but small enough so that I'd feel comfortable. Stalling had a community college and a university; a major credit card company had its headquarters there, as did a chain of restaurants. I didn't want to leave Virginia; staying in the state where I was born somehow made the move seem less upsetting. From my research, Stalling seemed as good a place as any.

On the first Saturday in February, I left my apartment before seven in the morning and was in Stalling by ten o'clock. Even in winter the ride was beautiful. Gentle, rolling hills became deeper and more dramatic as I approached the Blue Ridge Mountains. As I drove through them, their stark, rugged beauty rising all around me, I thought of Tully wandering lost in these vast mountains. It was three weeks to the day since he was buried. Would my tears ever end? I wondered, brushing them away.

Soon after I passed a sign saying **WELCOME TO STALLING, pop. 34,974**, I saw a Shoney's restaurant and decided to stop. I bought the local newspaper, *The Stalling Record*, from a machine before I went inside. The only booth available was in the smoking section, which I decided to accept rather than wait. When a waitress came to take my order, I was absorbed in the classified section of the paper. She looked surprised when I asked for tea and toast. Nearly everyone had the breakfast buffet on Saturdays.

I didn't take more than a few bites of the toast. I went over and over the columns of apartments for rent, circling possibilities with a black ballpoint pen. There weren't many circles. Too upset to eat, I kept thinking about the figure the caseworker I had spoken with at the Department of Social Services had given me, two hundred ninety-three dollars a month. I didn't see a single two-bedroom apartment for less than four hundred dollars, or a one-bedroom for under three hundred twenty-five, and those didn't include utilities. Realizing that I had better call about the few apartments I had circled as soon as possible, I folded the newspaper and left the waitress a tip. I bought a street map of Stalling at the cashier's stand when I paid my bill.

There was a pay telephone in the vestibule of the restaurant, but the constant flow of people entering and leaving would give me no privacy, so I decided to find another phone. After driving about a half mile, I spotted a public telephone at a corner gas station and pulled in.

It was sunny, but there was a steady cold wind that numbed my fingers as I called the numbers I had circled in the paper. By the time I had finished making the calls, my fingers felt like sticks of ice. I had an icy feeling in the pit of my stomach as well, a chill of uncertainty close to fear. Two of the four apartments I inquired about were still available; the other two had already been rented.

Following directions I had been given, I drove past the edges of subdivisions and a commercial area before entering the city. I passed through a section that had a mixture of light industry and automobile repair places, then stayed on a street that ran parallel to railroad tracks until I made a right onto Lilydale Street.

The apartment was in the basement of a decrepit-looking house. As I followed a toothless old woman down a sagging staircase, I started to gag from odors of raw sewage and ancient mildew. "The sewer problem's supposed to be fixed today," the woman said. She was difficult to understand because of her missing teeth.

The apartment was a horror, a long, dank room that had paint curling off the ceiling and walls. At the far end, in an alcove, there was a chipped sink that had a torn skirt around it, a small stove with the oven door hanging askew, and an ancient refrigerator. I guessed that a closed door near the sink opened into a bathroom, which I definitely didn't want to see. The stench was overwhelming. "I...I have to go," I managed to say between gags. "Thank you."

I rushed up the stairs and ran to my car, taking in gulps of fresh air. As I drove away, I wondered how anyone would pay two hundred eighty dollars a month to live in that hellish place.

The other apartment was across the railroad tracks in an even older part of town where the lots and houses were smaller and closer together. Mature trees lined streets named Lemon, Peach, Grape, Plum, and Cherry. When I pulled up in front of 410 Cherry Street, the address I had been given, a large black man was easing his bulk out of a shiny new white Lincoln. His skin was a deep chestnut color, his face full; his features ran into each other like pudding. He was wearing an expensive brown wool coat, and there was a massive gold ring on the third finger of his right hand. I had guessed that Mr. Daniels was black when I had spoken to him on the telephone about the apartment so I wasn't surprised, but I hadn't expected someone this prosperous. The shiny white Lincoln, the expensive coat, and the gold ring should have served as a warning, but they didn't. I was still shaken over the unspeakable condition of the first apartment I saw.

His heavy brows rose slightly as I approached him. "You the lady I talked to about the apartment?" he said.

"Yes," I said, suddenly realizing that with my car and the short red wool coat and navy slacks I was wearing I must have appeared prosperous to him.

He pursed his lips, openly studying me. "I'm goin' to be direct, right to the point," he said finally. "Why are you interested in this apartment?"

"The rent," I said. "It's as low as I could find."

"Where do you live now?"

"In Owings."

"Why are you movin' to Stalling?"

I stepped back. "Do you always ask so many questions?"

"I have to protect myself, my property. This ain't a neighborhood someone like you would pick, if you understand what I mean." He glanced pointedly at two black women walking on the other side of the street, and then toward the corner where a group of tough-looking adolescent boys had gathered.

I followed his gaze and nodded. The group of adolescents made my pulse skip with fear.

"What do you do for a livin' in Owings?"

"I'm a school secretary."

"How long you have that job?"

"Twenty years," I said, the tone of my voice registering my resentment at his digging.

Again, he pursed his lips thoughtfully. "I have another apartment that'll be available the first of March. It's a little better than this one. I can give it to you for the same rent, two ninety a month."

"When can I see it?"

"We can drive over there now and see if the tenants are in," he said. "Follow my car."

The apartment was on Lemon Street. Daniels barely managed to squeeze his Lincoln into the driveway of a green-frame house. There were two cars ahead of his, a beat-up blue Nova and an ancient black Ford missing a rear bumper. He waited in his car while I parked at the curb.

I followed him into a small dark vestibule, where he rang the doorbell and then knocked impatiently on one of two doors. There were footsteps on the stairs, the slapping sound of backless slippers. "Who is it?" a female voice called.

"Mr. Daniels," he said. "I have a party here to see the apartment."

"Someone's sleepin'."

"Wake 'em up!" he said in a tone that demanded obedience.

A few minutes lapsed before the door was unlocked. The narrow staircase was so dirty that the wood steps were black from imbedded grime. Daniels went up first, stepping directly into a room that had double windows facing the street. A man and a woman were sitting on a torn sofa that was set against a splotched wall. The man, whose skin was a deep brown, had his arms folded in front of him so his head could rest on his knees. Daniels nodded at the woman, then said to me, "I call this apartment a studio. It has a good amount of space."

Besides the sofa, there were two worn chairs near the front windows; a bed and dresser were on the other side of a half-wall that partially divided the room. The kitchen, which consisted of a sink with a counter on either side that had cupboard space below, a battered refrigerator, and a chipped stove, was on the wall opposite the front windows, no partition marking it off. Torn linoleum so old that it was impossible to tell its original color covered the floor. Every wall was marked with splotches and cracks in the plaster. A section of the ceiling over the kitchen sink was missing, the area around it marked with brown water stains.

I forced myself to go into the bathroom. There was no lid on the toilet; the bowl and seat were badly stained, as was the tub, stains I guessed were so deeply imbedded that they wouldn't respond to bleach and cleanser. Water was dripping steadily from a corroded faucet into the sink. The floor was badly warped, all ridges and ruts, as though it had been repeatedly flooded. And the room smelled, a nasty sour smell that I was afraid no amount of scrubbing would ever remove. I swallowed hard.

"Well," Daniels said expectantly when we were outside.

I didn't know what to do. I thought of the last place I had seen and of the two apartments that had been taken when I called. "This place is nicer than the one on Cherry Street," Daniels said. "And I want you to know that I knocked ten dollars off the rent. The people in there now are payin' three hundred a month. You can go back up and ask them. They'll tell you."

"N...No," I said, "that isn't necessary."

"Then you want it?"

No, I don't, I don't, I felt like screaming. But I couldn't. I had to either take the apartment or risk not finding anything better and ending up in a place as bad as that hellish basement room I had just seen, and I had to decide now. In Owings I knew where to look for cheap housing; in Stalling I was lost. And I had so little to spend that I couldn't expect much. "How big a deposit do you want?" I said.

"A month's rent and a two-hundred-ninety-dollar security deposit. How will you pay?"

"By check."

"Make it out to Grover Daniels."

During the week I had transferred six hundred dollars from my savings to my checking account. After I handed him the check, I realized that I had acted too quickly. "The walls," I said, "they need repainting, and the linoleum on the floor is coming up."

Grover Daniels was immense, but he was quick. The check was already deep in his pants pocket. "For that rent there ain't any improvements. You gettin' a bargain as it is, and you remember that. Also remember: I expect the rent the first of the month, no excuses."

I didn't like the belligerent tone of his voice, but it was too late. Rather than respond, I got into my car and drove away. I tried not to think about Grover Daniels and Lemon Street on the way back to

Owings. Instead, I kept telling myself that I could overcome anything. But when I walked into my apartment in Altavista Gardens and saw the fresh white walls and nubby gray carpeting that ran unbroken from the living room to the bedroom, I sank down on the sofa and wept.

Exhausted, I went to bed soon after I ate supper. As I was falling asleep I felt a sensation in my abdomen, a light but definite stirring, like the fluttering of butterfly wings. I lay perfectly still, hoping that I wasn't mistaken, that I hadn't been dreaming. Again, I felt a definite stirring, the quickening of life. For the first time in weeks the weight of grief I'd been carrying eased. I gently placed my hand on the small swell in my belly. "Everything will be all right," I whispered. "It will be all right."

***

The money I gave to Ardelle and Grover Daniels cut my savings account down to one hundred seventy dollars, and I still had to pay for moving. Professional movers I called were too expensive. Then I thought of Lester, the school custodian, who occasionally did outside work with his son, Monroe. I hoped they would be willing to help me.

Lester Johnson had been at Creekside Elementary since the day it had opened thirty-three years ago, the only black in the building until the school was required by law to desegregate. He knew and remembered every child who went to Creekside, and he recognized me when I returned to work there as the school secretary. "You and I were both here when the doors opened," he'd said, welcoming me with a broad smile. "We got a long history."

Glad to see a familiar face, I had agreed, but my smile wasn't as warm as his had been. There was a reason for my attitude, not that an explanation excuses it. Prejudice is learned, and my mama and daddy taught it to me early. They believed that by virtue of their white skin they were superior to blacks, that this was their privilege and their birthright. And they needed to believe it. They were

Barefields, the lowest of the low, the whites all other whites looked down upon. The cruelest jokes I heard when I was growing up were about Barefields: some were the usual redneck jokes, like Barefield boys looking forward to family reunions so they could pick up girls; but some were truly ugly, like asking why Barefields always hit their children in the head when they punished them (their heads were the one place they couldn't get hurt). My parents' need didn't excuse them—or me—and I am grateful that I have learned better.

Although I wasn't conscious of it happening, over the years my attitude toward Lester changed. As time passed I came to respect him for his quiet dignity and the care with which he performed his duties. If he noticed the change in my attitude, he never acknowledged it. Our relationship was pleasant, an alliance forged by daily contact and an unspoken awareness that we were on the lowest rungs of the Creekside Elementary staff.

I asked Lester on the Monday after I went to Stalling. I found him in a third grade classroom, guiding a heavy buffing machine over the floor. "Do you have a minute?" I said.

Lester stooped to turn off the machine, then straightened to face me. We were the same height. "I need...I want..." I didn't know how to begin.

"Is somethin' wrong?"

Like the teachers at Creekside Elementary, Lester had been especially kind since Tully's death. The expression of honest concern on his face made me relax. "I'm moving to Stalling," I said, "and I'd like to hire you and Monroe to help me move."

"Movin'?" he said with surprise. "I didn't know."

"No one knows yet. I'm not giving notice until next week, and I'd be grateful if you didn't tell anyone."

"Sure," he said. "What date you goin' to move?"

"Everything has to be out of my apartment on February twenty-ninth, and I'm not sure I can move into the place in Stalling until March first."

"February twenty-nine—what day of the week is that?"

"It's a Saturday."

"How much stuff you got?"

Lester listened, nodding as though he were memorizing each item, while I described my belongings. "All that'll take a good-size rental truck," he said when I was finished. "Do you want to rent the truck or do you want me an' Monroe to rent it?"

"You and Monroe."

"A Saturday is no problem," Lester said. "But you think you'll be movin' into the new place on Sunday?"

"I'm sorry, but I have to," I said, knowing that he kept Sundays for church. "I hope you can manage it."

"I'll talk to Monroe," he said.

All week I thought about what I would say when I quit. Since I knew I wasn't coming back, I was tempted to tell Sidley exactly what I thought of him. In the end, however, I decided to keep it simple; I didn't want to risk putting myself in a bad light by attacking him. At seven thirty on Monday morning I sat at my desk and typed a simple letter stating that I was giving two weeks' notice. The letter began, *I regret having to resign my position as school secretary, but I feel it would be best at this time.*

After I checked the letter for errors, I signed it, made three copies, and put the original on the principal's desk.

Bert Sidley gave me a perfunctory nod when he arrived at a few minutes before eight. He went into his office and then almost immediately summoned me. "What's the meaning of this?" he demanded, waving the letter.

"Just what it says: my last day will be February twenty-eighth."

"You can't leave before the end of the year! You have a contract!"

"No, I don't," I said, thinking that, as usual, he didn't know what he was talking about; only he and the teachers had contracts. "I didn't put it in the letter, but I'll be happy to train the person who will be replacing me. I'll add that in my letter to Dr. Howell."

Sidley's manner changed at the mention of the superintendent's name. "It really isn't necessary for you to write to Dr. Howell," he said with a let's-be-friends smile that was as phony as any I've ever seen.

"Dr. Howell has known me since I started working here twenty years ago. I wouldn't think of leaving without giving him the courtesy of a personal letter."

Perspiration had formed on his upper lip. He looked so uncomfortable that I would have felt sorry for him if I hadn't detested him.

I had intended my letter to Dr. Howell to be more like a thank you note, but Sidley's reaction made me reconsider. I was aware that a number of the teachers had complained about him; there was no reason why I couldn't at least let the superintendent know that the atmosphere in the school had deteriorated badly. But the letter I finally sent didn't give a hint of any trouble. Although I felt guilty, as if I were betraying the children by my silence, I wanted to leave as smoothly as possible without calling any more attention to myself than I already was by leaving before the end of the school year.

News of my resignation spread quickly through the school. "I hear the secret's out," Lester said when he came into the office after dismissal.

"Is it ever!" I said, tired from fielding questions all day. Whoever Sidley told had spread the news to everyone. "I didn't think it could travel that fast!"

"Big news in this small school? It moves like lightnin'," he said with a chuckle. "I talked to Monroe. We can help you move. With the cost of the truck rental, it should run 'bout three hundred fifty dollars."

"Thanks, Lester," I said, relieved that the five-hundred-dollar paycheck I expected the following week would cover what I would owe him. "I really appreciate it."

***

Nothing could have prepared me for my last day at Creekside Elementary. Dressed in one of my new tunic sweaters and a pair of stirrup pants, I arrived in the morning without any expectations, and as the day progressed I was at first surprised, then amazed, then astounded. As the teachers came into the office in the morning to get their room keys, they each made an effort to speak to me, either to talk about it being my last day or to thank me for favors I had done for them. Gail Wood asked me to meet her in the teachers' lounge at noon. "We both started working here the same year," she said. "I want us old timers to have lunch together on your last day."

I almost forgot about the lunch in my excitement over Dr. Howell's visit. The superintendent came into the office at eleven thirty with a long white box that held a dozen red roses nestled in a cloud of baby's breath. A stout man whose hair and moustache were nearly white, he shook his head, saying, "I can't imagine this school without you, Sara. Everyone downtown feels that way, especially Mabel, who swears that there is nothing neater or more dependable on this entire earth than your attendance reports. She's been talking about those reports all week."

Sidley hurried out of his office to greet Dr. Howell, but the superintendent brushed him off with barely concealed impatience. "Sara, I am aware of your recent loss, for which I am truly sorry. Should you ever decide that you want to come back, there will always be a place for you in this school system," Dr. Howell said. "Everyone downtown wishes you the very best."

Dr. Howell, who has a tendency towards speechmaking, would have continued if the telephone hadn't started to ring. The new secretary had gone for an early lunch. "Excuse me," I said, taking the call.

After I hung up I thanked him, feeling flustered and embarrassed. As happy as I was, I was afraid that the gratitude I expressed was inadequate for the wonderful tribute I'd been given.

I was thinking about the roses as I walked to the teachers' lounge at noon. Although I ate my lunch in the lounge every day, I had never felt really comfortable there. The teachers were polite and friendly, but I wasn't one of them, an equal member in their circle of friendship. So when I entered the lounge and the teachers gave me a standing ovation, it was so unexpected that I stood in a daze, blinking like an owl that had been suddenly thrust into the sunlight. The teachers had arranged for the cafeteria to prepare a special lunch: turkey salad made with wild rice and water chestnuts, fresh rolls, and chocolate cake for dessert. Instead of the usual two tables placed parallel to each other, a third table had been brought in to make a horseshoe. I was led by Gail Wood to the place of honor at the center table. "I had no idea," I said. "How...How can I ever thank you?"

Gail squeezed my hand. "You can enjoy yourself."

Unlike the cafeteria's usual bland fare, the salad and rolls were delicious, but I hardly touched them. Instead, too excited to eat, I chatted with the teachers seated near me. Before the chocolate cake was cut, Gloria Snyder, a first grade teacher who was so tiny she seemed tailored in size for the children she taught, stood up and hit her spoon against a glass to interrupt the hum of conversation. "I don't know why I was chosen to give you our gift," she said, walking up to me with a large rectangular box wrapped in silver paper, "unless it was because this box is almost as big as I am so y'all can have a good laugh. Whatever the reason, I'm delighted to give this to you."

"Thank you," I managed to say, overwhelmed.

The box contained a small suitcase covered in a heavy gray-and-mauve fabric that looked like tapestry. They had all written brief messages wishing me well on a large card.

The suitcase was just the right size to take to the hospital when I had the baby. It was almost like a sign. I truly believed that nothing could happen that would make me feel better about the years I had spent at Creekside Elementary than I did at that moment.

I was wrong. About an hour before dismissal, a woman I hadn't seen in four or five years came into the office. Thin and sharp-featured, she was wearing a white uniform on which a pink AIDE pin was fastened, and white stockings and shoes. "I don't know if you remember me," she said, "but you'll remember my boy, Kenny Lang. He had asthma real bad."

"Oh, yes," I said, recalling Kenny and the frightening attacks he had, gasping and wheezing as though he might die for lack of a decent breath. "I remember Kenny. How is he?"

"He's doin' all right," Mrs. Lang said. "I heard you was leavin', so I decided to stop by on my way to work and thank you for what you done for Kenny. It was always you that helped him when he had an attack, not the teachers."

"It's hard for the teachers because they're responsible for so many children."

"Kenny told me the teachers always sent him to you at the first sign of any trouble," said Mrs. Lang. "His daddy and me believe that he wouldn't have made it through Creekside with the rest of his class if it wasn't for you, and I wanted you to know how we feel. I should've done this long ago."

By dismissal time more than a half dozen parents came in to thank me for past kindnesses to their children. The new secretary, a slim young woman who had reddish-blond hair and masses of freckles, watched and listened. "I'll never be able to take your place," she said, her shoulders sagging after the last parent left.

"Sure you will," I said, feeling giddy from the attention I had received. All those parents coming to see me, the special effort they made: it was hard to believe. And the nice things they said, so many compliments. I had always tried my best, but no one had ever seemed to notice; some days I'd felt that I wasn't accomplishing anything, that what I did wasn't important because I wasn't a teacher. How good it was to know that my efforts had meant something after all!

At a few minutes before four, Sidley emerged from his office. His manner was subdued, almost embarrassed, as though he was aware that his eventual departure from the school wouldn't get the response that mine had. "Goodbye and good luck," he said in a tone so flat it sounded like he was reading from the telephone book.

Out of habit, I wished him a pleasant weekend as I had done every Friday to all the principals I had worked for for twenty years. Then I picked up the box that contained the suitcase and a bag that held a few personal things, and took them to my car. Sidley was nowhere to be seen when I returned. "Thank you for all the time you took with me this week. I hope I don't mess up," the new secretary said.

The young woman looked so anxious that I hugged her. "You'll be fine," I said.

There was nothing left to do but take the roses and go home. I removed the flowers from a vase I had put them in and gently placed them inside the florist's box, leaving the box uncovered so the baby's breath wouldn't be crushed. Cradling the flowers in my arm, I walked out of the office and stood in the center hall, looking up and down the corridors for the last time. The halls were so crowded with memories that they became an indistinct blur. More than half my life had been spent in this building. Now the thought that I would never see these halls again filled me with an almost overwhelming sense of loss. Creekside Elementary had been my refuge as a child and my place of opportunity as an adult; it was part of the fabric of my life, and tearing myself away hurt more than I had expected.

On my way home I decided to give the roses to Ardelle, who had invited me for supper. Maybe the flowers would give her some needed cheering up. After working for less than a month, Ronnie Lee had been laid off again. I wasn't expected there until six thirty, so I had time to enjoy the flowers while I did some last-minute packing.

Ardelle and Ronnie Lee lived in a double-wide trailer on an acre of land outside of town. They owned the trailer (at least a portion of it) and rented the land. When I arrived at six thirty, Ronnie Lee looked like he'd been drinking all afternoon. His eyes were glassy and mean, his speech slurred. I shuddered at the sight of him. As he had gotten older, he had become a mirror image of our daddy, Vernon Barefield. The hard lines between his eyes, his gestures, the swagger when he walked, even the roofer's knife hooked menacingly into his belt were the same. "I unnerstand you quit your job. Tully must've left you a bundle. For a guy who had more 'n a few screws loose, he sure made him some money," Ronnie Lee said, the drink in his voice as unmistakable as the envy.

Too angry to speak, I went into the kitchen to give the roses to Ardelle. Every year Ronnie Lee got worse. I detested him more than ever. As hard as it was to leave Owings, he was one person I wouldn't miss.

If it weren't for Ronnie Lee and ten-year-old Glenn, I would have enjoyed every minute of my visit. No one made better fried chicken and apple cobbler than Ardelle, and the girls, Darlene and Lisa, were fun to be with, especially Darlene. I loved Darlene's quick sense of humor and bubbly laugh, and I could see the intelligence in my niece's clear gray eyes. I also saw how Ronnie Lee looked at Darlene, how his eyes followed her when she walked in or out of a room. Nearly thirteen, she was tall for her age and already had full breasts and a nicely-shaped behind. Her face was maturing, too, showing the promise of high cheekbones and fine features. But she was still a child. Seeing Ronnie Lee's eyes fixed on Darlene made my stomach do nervous flip-flops. I hoped Ardelle would watch Ronnie Lee, that she would always be there to pay attention.

After dinner I caught Glenn going through my purse, which I had left on one of the girls' beds. He had my wallet in his hand, and when he tried to put it back, I grabbed his arm and held it firmly. "I was...I was lookin' for your keys," he said, trying to wrest his arm free.

"Next you're going to tell me that you have your driver's license," I said, tightening my grip.

Glenn had Ardelle's blond coloring, but his features were like Ronnie Lee's. "Let go of me," he said, his face hard and mean.

With my free hand I ruffled through the bills in my wallet. "Twenty dollars is missing. Either you give it to me now or I'll strip your clothes off you until I find it."

He glared at me with pure hatred while he reached into his jeans pocket for the money. "Since you need it so bad, take it," he said, throwing the bill on the floor.

"Pick it up," I said, keeping my voice low. Ardelle had enough troubles without hearing this.

I almost wished I hadn't caught him. As much as I needed the money, it was a shame to leave with such a bad memory of my nephew.

Ardelle walked to the car with me. The night air was cold, the sky flooded with stars. "I should have my security deposit back from Altavista Gardens by the end of March. Be watching for a check from me the first week in April," I said. "I'll send it to you at the laundromat."

"Oh, Sara," Ardelle said with a sob. "With things like they are here, I don't know when I can get to Stalling to see you. I'm goin' to miss you somethin' terrible."

"I'll miss you, too," I said, trying not to cry. With Tully gone, Ardelle and the children were the only family I had. Although it was no more than a three-hour drive away, suddenly Stalling seemed so far; Owings was the only home I'd ever known. Despite my efforts, tears welled in my eyes.

Ardelle and I clung to each other and wept.

***

Saturday morning Eileen Payne and Peggy Carver met me for breakfast at Franny's. "I really wish you wouldn't move," said Eileen, looking sadly at me over a mug of steaming coffee. Although it was only seven thirty, Eileen's lashes were thickly coated with mascara and her eyelids were shaded with gray-blue eye shadow that perfectly matched her eyes.

"Won't you reconsider?" said Peggy, whose round face was still puffy with sleep.

"It's too late. Lester and Monroe are coming early this afternoon to load my stuff on a truck."

Eileen put down her coffee mug. "I know how hard it's been since Tully died, but movin' away isn't going to make it easier. Your home is here, your life is here. And we're here!"

"That's right!" Peggy said. "Unless there's some deep, dark secret you're not tellin' us."

I hesitated. Neither Eileen nor Peggy could keep a confidence. If

I told them, Mrs. Rutland would know about the baby before it was born. "What secret could I possibly have?" I said, hating to deceive my friends after so many years.

Before we parted we promised to keep in touch. Despite my enthusiasm, I knew I wouldn't be able to afford to call them and that they wouldn't write. Realizing it might be years before I had contact with them again, a lump rose in my throat as I walked to my car. Eileen and Peggy were once-in-a-lifetime friends. Their friendship had been a refuge during the difficult years I was growing up in my parents' house. I had stood up for their weddings and had rocked their babies. They had watched over me, protective and concerned, each time Tully had disappeared. Tears came then, tears so hard and fast that I don't know how I managed to drive back to my apartment.

Later, shivering in a light rain, I stood on the sidewalk watching Lester and Monroe load the last boxes into the rental truck. It was chilly and I was concerned about my plants, which were packed in long cardboard cartons that filled the entire back of my car, both seat and floor. "I don't know about this plant," Lester said doubtfully, bracing himself before he picked up the huge spathiphyllum. The plant was wrapped in an old sheet and tied with twine to protect the leaves from breaking. "It might not fit. Them boxes is piled near to the top."

"Maybe you can shift a few," I said. "Please try."

Finally, after some maneuvering, they managed to wedge the spathiphyllum between columns of boxes. While Lester locked the truck, I gave Monroe a piece of paper on which my new address was written. "I have an extra map of Stalling if you'd like it," I said.

Monroe was considerably larger than his father, at least six feet tall, and muscular from years of loading heavy sacks of feed and fertilizers onto farmers' pickup trucks. "No, thanks," he said. "My wife's from Stalling. I know it pretty well." He glanced at the address, then looked again as if he weren't sure he'd seen it correctly. "Lemon Street? Is this right?"

"Yes."

"That's…" Monroe rubbed his chin thoughtfully. "It's not a good neighborhood," he said in measured words. "People from Stalling, they call that area the Fruit Belt."

"Oh," I said.

"Well, just so you know to be careful."

"Thanks," I said.

I didn't go into the apartment after they drove away. There was no point in teasing myself with what I was leaving. And I wouldn't dwell on what Monroe said about the Fruit Belt. It was temporary, not forever. Tonight I would find an inexpensive motel, and tomorrow I would start a new life.

My hands drifted over my abdomen. No, I thought, correcting myself. Tomorrow *we'll* start a new life.

SPRING, 1992

The first thing I saw when I woke was a long crack creeping across a yellowed ceiling. For a moment I didn't know where I was. But when I focused on a splotched wall the realization came to me and I squeezed my eyes shut. I didn't want to see walls that were covered with ugly stains, linoleum worn paper-thin where it wasn't torn, the gaping hole in the ceiling over the kitchen sink, the bathroom I had scrubbed until my body ached. With all the scrubbing I had done, even with the new toilet seat I'd bought, the apartment still didn't feel clean; some dirt was embedded too deep to ever get out. At least I didn't see a lot of bugs. I hoped the spray I had used and the traps I had set out would take care of any problems.

The worst part of my move from Owings to Stalling wasn't the scrubbing. It wasn't seeing all the dead and damaged house plants in the back of my car that had been caught by an unexpected overnight drop in temperature to below freezing. It wasn't discovering that only one burner on the stove worked, that the fruit and vegetable crispers in the refrigerator were missing, that there were no screens for the windows. What was hardest was watching Lester and Monroe drive off in the rental truck after they carted the last of my belongings upstairs.

Lester and Monroe had arrived at about four in the afternoon; when I spotted the truck, I hurried downstairs to meet them. Monroe insisted that I go back inside, and I soon understood why. Teenage boys and tough-looking older fellows had started collecting across the street, almost as if they'd been summoned by a bell, when Lester and Monroe began unloading the truck. Frightened, I asked Monroe why the men were congregating. "They want to see what you got," he said angrily. "They no better than vermin! I'll use blankets to cover what I can, like the TV and VCR. No sense lettin' them see what they could steal."

Before they left to drive back to Owings, Monroe cautioned me to be careful. Lester, whose face was creased with exhaustion, shook his head sadly. "I hate to leave you in this place," he said.

"I'll watch out," I said, sounding braver than I felt.

I stood at the window until the truck disappeared down Lemon Street, feeling utterly alone. Lester and Monroe were my last contact with Owings. With home. And they were gone.

These were dangerous thoughts, I decided, forcing myself out of bed. I had unpacking to do, and there were some plants that might be saved with extra care. Activity always helped keep my thoughts away from paths I didn't want them to take.

But the very first thing I had to do was to go to the Department of Social Services and apply for Medicaid. I was already into my sixth month of pregnancy, and the movements of the baby, which were easy to recognize now, were daily reminders that I still hadn't seen a doctor. I had learned from reading that pregnancies in older women carried greater risks. I was concerned that the trauma of Tully's death may have affected the baby, and worried that the depression I was feeling with the move to Stalling might also be harmful. More than anything I needed a doctor to tell me that my baby was fine.

While I was getting dressed I decided to apply for food stamps as well. All I had left after my moving expenses was one hundred twenty-seven dollars. I hoped I didn't look too prosperous in my stirrup pants and tunic sweater; the waists on my skirts and slacks had all become too tight. Reluctantly I took off the sapphire-and-diamond ring Tully had given me and put it a plastic bag with my other gold jewelry. While I was looking for a hiding place, I remembered a novel I had read in which a woman hid her jewelry in a hollowed-out cake that was stored in a freezer. I tied the bag shut and put it in the freezer compartment of the refrigerator. Later I'd buy a cake to hollow out like the woman did in the book.

Although it was sunny and pleasant when I stepped outside, I didn't pay attention to the weather. I had all I could do not to cry out when I saw my car: the hubcaps were gone, all four stolen! I circled the car looking for clues and found nothing. The morning before when I went to my car at the motel, the first thing I saw was the long cardboard boxes like coffins, holding dead plants. Today it was my hubcaps. I couldn't blame what had happened to the plants on anyone but myself; if I had taken them into the motel room for the night, they would have been fine. Maybe there was a lesson in the hubcaps: I had better not leave anything of value in the car while I lived on Lemon Street.

I probably overreacted to the stolen hubcaps. I had been so proud of the Buick. It was the first decent car I had ever owned, the first new car. I had chosen a Buick over Tully's objections; he had wanted me to buy a Toyota, which he said would last longer with fewer problems. But I had wanted a Buick for reasons that had nothing to do with what was under the hood. When I was growing up, the families who lived in nice houses that were in respectable neighborhoods owned Buicks. In the end, though, Tully was right. Over the years the Buick had needed more than its share of repairs.

There was considerably more traffic on Lemon Street than there had been over the weekend. Soon the reason became clear: Lemon Street emptied into Main Street a few blocks before City Hall. Because it was nestled in the foothills of the Blue Ridge Mountains, Stalling was hilly, and its streets often took unexpected dips and turns. I drove past the Plummet County Courthouse, an imposing building that had a perfectly-kept front lawn anchored in the center by a statue of Robert E. Lee. The Plummet County Municipal Building, in the same red brick and nearly as impressive, stood opposite the courthouse. A block past the county buildings Main

Street twisted, dipping down to Stalling City Hall, a three-story brown-brick building so plain that I would have missed it if I hadn't glimpsed the black letters over the double front doors. There were two paved parking areas behind the building, one below the other, set into the side of the hill. I found a space in the lower lot and climbed a steep flight of stairs, then a short flight, to reach the building.

The Stalling Department of Social Services was on the lowest level of City Hall. The door opened into a narrow tweed-carpeted reception area where nine black vinyl chairs that had metal arms and legs were lined up against the longest wall; three additional chairs took up the space along a side wall. Although it was just a few minutes past nine, all but one of the chairs were filled. I went to a counter opposite the long row of chairs. At least two feet deep, the black counter jutted out like a barrier between the reception area and a huge office beyond in which there were close to a dozen desks, filing cabinets, and a copy machine. Half of the desks were occupied by women who were either talking on the telephone, typing, or sorting through papers; one young woman, a hard-looking blond, was studying her eye makeup in a red plastic mirror; another woman was chewing on her thumbnail while she stared dreamily out the window. I waited for two women who were standing behind the counter to finish talking. The women were aware of me; occasionally they glanced beyond the counter, but they continued talking as if I didn't exist.

Five minutes passed. The women kept their voices too low for me to hear their conversation, but I caught snatches about paint and choosing colors. A thin black woman who was filling out a form at the end of the counter didn't look at me; nor did the people in the chairs. No one seemed to be looking at anyone else. It was as if the people in the reception area were bound by an unspoken pact to give each other as much privacy as they could under the circumstances; or maybe it was simply that they were all as embarrassed as I was at being there and were trying to be as inconspicuous as possible.

Whatever the case, it had the feeling of a dream, everything suspended.

Ten minutes passed. The women continued talking as if I was of no more significance than a speck of dust that had settled on the counter. I couldn't believe their rudeness! In my twenty years as a school secretary I had never let anyone, adult or child, stand at my desk for more than a moment or two without receiving attention. From the corner of my eye I saw that the thin black woman had finished filling out the form. But the woman was silent. She stood motionless, her hands clasped together, waiting for someone to see that she was done.

Fifteen minutes passed, each second making me more anxious. A red-headed toddler who had been sleeping fitfully on his mother's lap woke and started whining that he wanted to go. His mother, a pale girl dressed in jeans and a sweatshirt who looked no more than fifteen or sixteen, told him to hush, which made him whine louder. I began to wonder if I would have been treated differently if I had worn my best clothes and jewelry. Probably not, I decided, feeling as though each minute I waited was taking something from me more precious than time.

Nearly twenty minutes passed before the two women behind the counter finally stopped talking. The older of the pair, a middle-aged woman who had deep scowl lines between her eyes and a small, pinched mouth, stepped up to the counter. "Yes?" she said, peering at me through smoke-tinted glasses.

The woman's voice seemed unnaturally loud. "I...I want to apply for Medicaid and food stamps," I said, conscious of all the people sitting in the chairs behind me.

"Do you have children?"

"I'm pregnant."

The woman reached under the counter for the applications. "Fill this out first," she said, showing me a folded form that said **Base Document**. "Then fill these out. Return them to me when you're done." She gave me the forms, a clipboard and ballpoint pen, then turned her attention to the thin black woman.

The Base Document, which had **Commonwealth of Virginia, Department of Social Services** printed in the upper left-hand corner of the first page, asked what assistance I was applying for, my marital status, and where I lived. I had to list any savings, checking and retirement accounts, all real property I owned, members of my household, and my living expenses, including rent, utilities, water and trash collection, as well as any income. The form asked whether I was now or had ever received medical assistance, financial assistance, or food stamps. In a space provided to list any needs or problems, I wrote: *I am forty years old, in my sixth month of pregnancy, and I haven't seen a doctor. I have no income.*

I hesitated over a question about whether I expected to receive money from any source. A final paycheck of two hundred fifty-one dollars for my last week of work at Creekside Elementary would be coming, as would the return of my four-hundred-fifty-dollar rental deposit from Altavista Gardens. I realized that the paycheck could easily be traced, so I listed it in the space provided. But I didn't mention the four hundred fifty dollars; nor did I answer truthfully about transferring money within the past three months. The two hundred dollars I had deposited in Ardelle's name, plus the additional money from the rental deposit that I planned to send, was all I would have for the baby. With no relatives or friends to help me, I had to save as much as I could. I hated being dishonest, but I didn't see an alternative. I skimmed over a sentence about the statements I had made being true and correct to the best of my knowledge and, with my pulse skipping, signed the Base Document. I felt terrible. All my life I had tried to be a better person, to be truthful, to be honest, to be responsible, to be someone Tully would be proud of. I felt as if I had wiped away all my efforts with that one signature.

The Medicaid application asked if I owned any items worth over five hundred dollars such as silver, fine china, antiques, or expensive jewelry except for one engagement ring and wedding band per person. Without hesitation, I checked the box next to **NO**. I considered the sapphire-and-diamond ring that Tully had given me an engagement ring. As for my other jewelry, I doubted that it met the requirements.

A separate paper entitled **Know Your Rights When Applying for Food Stamps** came with the food stamp application. It stated that if my resources and income were very low (one hundred dollars in resources and one hundred fifty in income), I might be eligible for expedited services. This meant that I was entitled to receive Food Stamps within five days following the date my application was filed at the social services department. I had no income; however, I did have one hundred twenty-seven dollars in my purse. Again, I didn't want to lie, but I was concerned that I might need the money to buy something to wear for a job interview. While I had waited for the women behind the counter to stop talking, I had started fighting fear that was threatening to become hysteria. Moving away from Owings seemed like the right decision when I had made it. Now it felt disastrous. How would I pay my rent? My utilities? How would I be able to live?

I hesitated when I wrote twenty-seven dollars in the space next to *Cash on Hand*. When I signed the application, I avoided looking at a statement stating that I might be subject to criminal prosecution for knowingly providing false information. I already felt like a criminal.

The woman behind the counter took the clipboard and quickly went through the applications. "You'll have to wait until a food stamp worker can see you," she said. "It's first come, first served. As a pregnant indigent, you'll get a form from Medicaid in the mail."

I caught my breath. To be called *indigent* in front of a roomful of people was worse than anything I had anticipated. Even my parents at their poorest didn't have to endure that. I took the last vacant chair, wanting to disappear.

Hours passed. People's names were called; they left and others took their places. Most of the chairs remained filled, occupied by people sitting quietly except for those who had children with them.

For the lucky ones, their babies slept or their toddlers played contentedly with toys they'd brought from home. The others, struggling with tears or tantrums, coped as best they could. I sat as though nothing was going on around me. Since I had entered this room I had been ignored, I had signed documents on which I had lied, and I had been stripped of my dignity. Devastated beyond tears, I sat with these thoughts buzzing in my head like flies trapped in a jar, unaware that the skin behind my lower lip was bleeding where I had bitten through it. When my name was called at twelve forty-five, I stood up as dazed as if I'd been awakened from a trance.

A large, round-faced woman wearing a denim skirt and a blue-and-white striped blouse was standing behind the counter holding my Base Document and food stamp application. Although she looked no more than forty-five or fifty, her short curly hair was completely white. "I'm Frieda Stowe," she said. "I'm going to review your application. Then I'll come back for you. It shouldn't take long."

It was about one o'clock when Frieda Stowe returned. After we left the main reception area, I spotted a drinking fountain in the corridor. I had had nothing to eat or drink since seven in the morning. "Would you mind if I stop at that fountain?" I asked.

"Not at all," she said.

The water was cold and I drank eagerly, chasing the parched taste from my mouth. "Thanks," I said when I was finished.

We walked through a series of narrow corridors that twisted and turned like a rat maze, passing signs jutting out from the walls that said HOUSING, MEDICAID, EMPLOYMENT SERVICES, DAY CARE. We made so many rights and lefts that I lost sense of where I was. "I don't think I could find my way back alone," I said.

"No one can. I've worked here for two years and I still get lost when I go into one of the departments I'm not familiar with. Each department has its own set of hallways."

"It's certainly confusing."

"Yes," she said. "People often take a wrong turn and end up

where they had no intention of going. Some think it was deliberately designed this way."

Frieda Stowe's office was a cubbyhole no bigger than eight by ten into which a metal desk, three chairs, and a filing cabinet were squeezed. "I see that you live on Lemon Street," she said after we were settled. "How did you happen to pick that particular area?"

"It was the cheapest rent I could find. I just moved here from Owings."

She picked up the food stamp application. "You state here that you quit your job with the Owings Board of Education within the last sixty days, and the reason you give is your pregnancy."

"I was the secretary in an elementary school, and I'm not married. I felt that I had to leave before I started showing."

"According to food stamp regulations, if you quit your job within sixty days of applying, you're not eligible for food stamps for ninety days from the day you quit."

Even though it was in English, it took me a moment to sort out what she said. When I finally understood, I couldn't believe it. "I'm pregnant! I couldn't have continued working at Creekside Elementary!"

"Pregnancy isn't considered good cause. If, however, you quit to re-locate…"

I didn't wait for her to finish. "I did," I said, leaning forward earnestly. "I really had to move. I couldn't stay in Owings."

She wrote something on a pad, then looked up. "You've indicated that the only cash you have on hand is twenty-seven dollars. That's barely gas money. How long have you been living in Stalling?"

"I moved here yesterday."

"Yesterday?" she said, her eyes wide. "What are you going to do? How are you going to live?"

Hearing her voice my thoughts made my anxiety worse. "I'm going to have to find a job right quick," I said, my proper speech gone with the strain I was under.

"The employment picture isn't good in Stalling. Even minimum wage jobs have been drying up in this recession."

"I'll find something."

"Do you have family, anyone who can help you?" she said, her pen moving rapidly across the pad.

"I have no one," I said, looking directly at her so she could see the truth in my eyes.

Maybe I imagined it, but for a moment she looked sympathetic. "Your rent is two hundred ninety dollars a month. Does that include utilities?"

"No."

"To receive expedited food stamps, your rent and utilities have to be more than your expected gross income for the month."

"All I'm expecting is a check for two hundred fifty-one dollars and some change for my last week of work."

"The two hundred fifty-one is your net income. I need the *gross* figure, the amount before taxes."

"I used to get paid every two weeks. The gross was six hundred sixty-three dollars."

She reached for a calculator and put in some numbers. "Your gross for that last paycheck is more than three hundred thirty dollars, which puts you over your shelter expense of two hundred ninety dollars."

"But my utilities aren't included in my shelter expense because I don't know what they'll be. My electricity and water bills will add up to over forty dollars."

"If I follow the rules and use the figures you've just given me, I'll have to put your application at the bottom of the pile, which is now so high that I won't get to it until the end of the month. I can, however, expedite your case with a reasonable declaration, but to do that I need monthly estimates of your electric and water bills based on past use. You should be able to get the information from the utility companies or your landlord. Call to give me the figures as soon as possible so I can start working on your application," she said, writing her name and telephone number on a scrap of paper.

"Thank you," I said, starting to rise.

She held up her hands in a gesture to wait. "I'm afraid we're not done. Your stamps for this month will be given to you based on your declaration, in other words, on what you've told me. For you to continue to receive food stamps, we must have written verification," she said, withdrawing papers from a file drawer in her desk. "Your landlord has to fill out this residency statement, and your former employer will have to complete the verification of termination statement. In addition, you'll have to provide the information that I'm marking on this checklist."

The verification of termination statement had **CITY OF STALLING, DEPARTMENT OF SOCIAL SERVICES** printed in bold letters at the top. There was a place to fill in my name. Below it read: *The individual named above has authorized us to obtain the following information, which is needed to evaluate his/her eligibility to receive public assistance. Thank you for your cooperation.*

I was so upset I could hardly talk. "I...I can't send this. I don't want the people back in Owings to know that I'm applying for assistance. It...It's humiliating."

"Can you get a letter giving the date and reason for your termination, and the dates and gross amounts of your last paychecks?"

"I think so," I said with relief.

Ms. Stowe took a booklet from a stack on her desk. **VIRGINIA SOCIAL SERVICES BENEFIT PROGRAMS** was printed on the cover. "Read this through when you get a chance. You're eligible for WIC."

"What's that?"

"A supplemental food program for pregnant woman, infants, and children. Participating in WIC won't affect your food stamps."

She picked up my food stamp application. "I'm going to go over some rules that are very important. If any of the rules are broken, you could be fined or sent to prison and prevented from participation in the program."

After clearing her throat, she told me that the food stamps I would be receiving couldn't be sold or given to anyone, that they couldn't be altered, that they couldn't be used to buy alcoholic drinks or tobacco or non-food items. Further, I couldn't obtain or use food stamps belonging to someone else.

She paused. "Do you have any questions?"

I shook my head.

Then she continued, reading aloud from a statement warning me that the information I had given in my application was subject to verification by federal, state, or local officials to determine if it was true. If any of the information was found to be false, I could be denied food stamps and could be subject to criminal prosecution.

My mind was fixed on the one hundred dollars I hadn't declared. I felt like I was one step away from jail.

Ms. Stowe picked up the Base Document and turned to the back page. "You've already signed this Base Document, which means you certify that the statements you've made are true. As a food stamp applicant, you've agreed to notify the Department of Social Services within ten days of any changes that occur in your situation. Your signature indicates that you understand, under penalty of perjury, that if you've given false information, withheld information, or failed to report changes promptly, or on purpose, you may be breaking the law and could be prosecuted."

I felt her eyes on me, studying, searching. I nodded woodenly, unable to speak. To my relief, she seemed satisfied.

I didn't talk until we had gone back through the winding corridors and were close to the reception area. "Is there a public telephone here?" I asked. "I want to call about the electric and water bills for my apartment. I also need the number of the telephone company so I can arrange for service."

"There are two telephones off the main lobby on the first floor. Unfortunately, the telephone books are missing. The covers were attached to the wall with chains, but people managed to rip them off anyway."

"That's terrible," I said, hoping she wasn't putting me in the same category as the people who stole the telephone books.

"I'll see if I can't get a book for you to use at the reception counter. If you call me with the figures before noon tomorrow, I'll try to have your stamps ready on Wednesday."

"Thank you," I said, wondering if I could ask how much I would be getting in stamps. I had practically no food in my apartment and would have to buy groceries today. Despite telling myself that it was a perfectly reasonable question, I began hesitantly, afraid I'd be penalized for asking. "Do you have any idea..."

"Of how much you'll be getting? It should be about one hundred dollars."

One hundred dollars. From the moment I had entered the reception area in what seemed like a lifetime ago, I'd felt as if I had descended into hell. And it was all for one hundred dollars.

Rather than use one of the public telephones, which weren't in booths, I decided to drive directly to the utility company offices. It was two thirty, but I didn't take time to eat. Arranging for telephone service and getting an average monthly electric bill were more important. Fortunately, I had the letter of credit for the telephone in my purse.

My business with the telephone company was accomplished easily, but I had to speak with two different clerks and a supervisor before I was able to get the average monthly electric bill for my apartment. The first clerk, a woman who was wearing a black-and-white polka dot dress and too much perfume, told me that the information wasn't readily available. When I questioned this by asking if the power company used computers for their billing and accounting, the woman left me standing while she summoned another clerk, who wanted to know the reason for the request. Despite my weariness and a grinding headache, I suddenly sensed that they wouldn't be giving me any difficulty if I wanted the information about an apartment in a nice neighborhood. When I expressed this thought aloud, the second clerk scurried away and returned with a supervisor, a wiry-haired fellow who had a mustache that looked like a rusty Brillo pad. "What is the problem here?" he said.

His manner was polite, but I didn't miss the condescension in his voice; carrying the name *Barefield*, I had fought that tone all my life. My chin shot up like a reflex. With my shoulders squared, I repeated what I said to the clerk. He got me the information in what seemed like seconds: the average monthly electric bill for the apartment was fifty-four dollars.

My chin still high, I left the offices of the Blue Ridge Power Company without uttering a word.

It was after four o'clock. The power company was on Lee Avenue, a heavily trafficked street that led to the suburbs. Lemon Street was in the opposite direction. I started the car and headed out Lee Avenue. I had to live in the Fruit Belt, but I didn't have to shop there.

Soon I was passing landmarks that were starting to become familiar. When I spotted a high red sign in the distance that said WESTMARK PLAZA, I switched into the right-hand lane. Yesterday I had been in the Westmark Plaza, where I had bought a new toilet seat and bug spray at a store called Magnolia's, and had gotten milk, juice, cereal, and a carton of Pepsi at Kroger's. As I pulled into the shopping center I recalled seeing an extremely pregnant cashier working at Magnolia's, which I decided to keep in mind if I had trouble finding a job elsewhere.

Inside Kroger's, the price of everything I looked at loomed larger than the item: ninety-nine cents a head for lettuce, ninety-seven cents a pound for apples, fifty-nine cents a pound for bananas. Navel oranges were fifty cents apiece; grapefruit were priced at three for a dollar nineteen. The books I'd read on pregnancy had all stressed the importance of eating fresh fruits and vegetables. But my car needed gas, and I didn't want to spend any of the one hundred dollars I hadn't declared, which was the only money I'd have until my last paycheck came. I thought of the food stamps I'd be getting, approximately twenty-five dollars a week, and decided to start living on that budget now. Adding as I shopped, I put a head of lettuce, three apples, three grapefruit, four bananas, and a bag of carrots in my cart. Grapes, which I would have enjoyed, were on sale for a dollar thirty-nine, but I had already spent well over four dollars and I still didn't have anything to eat for supper.

Even if my apartment was equipped with a microwave oven, I could no longer afford the frozen prepared dinners I used to buy, so I headed for the meat department. The ground beef was nearly white with fat; the ground chuck looked better, but it was a dollar seventy-nine a pound. I steered my cart toward people who were clustered further down the aisle. Immediately I saw what was attracting them: whole chickens were on sale for forty-nine cents a pound. I don't care much for dark meat, but a whole chicken could be stretched for four meals. The refrigerated case was well picked over; I took the largest bird I could find for a dollar seventy-six.

There was still a starch to buy, a vegetable, salad dressing, and eggs. Now everything I put in the cart became a major decision. I would have liked to cut up the chicken and cook it with Shake 'n Bake, but the prepared mix cost more than the chicken. Frozen peas were on sale, as were frozen French fries. I put a can of hearty beef soup in the cart to heat up for supper, and a package of chocolate chip cookies that I could stretch over the week for desserts. Although I suspected that it wasn't particularly healthy, I couldn't find anything cheaper to have for lunches than peanut-butter-and-jelly sandwiches, which made me think of the peanut-butter-and-cracker suppers of my childhood. This was only temporary, I told myself as I took the items off the shelves. Before I started toward the checkout lines I remembered the cake I needed to hide my jewelry in. The store bakery didn't have a cake for under two ninety-nine. Mentally recalculating what I'd already spent, I crisscrossed the store to the bread section, where I found a packaged angel food cake on special for two dollars. Then I went to wait in line with other late afternoon shoppers. I watched intently as the clerk ran my groceries over the scanner. The total, including tax, came to nineteen dollars and seventy-six cents. That left me seven dollars for gas and a newspaper, maybe more than one paper, so I could look for a job.

When I pulled into the driveway on Lemon Street, I realized that I hadn't called the police to report my stolen hubcaps. I'd call tomorrow. Now all I wanted was to go upstairs and have a bowl of warm soup. This had been one of the longest, most difficult days of my life. Exhausted, I was glad that it was over.

But the day wasn't over. When the doorbell rang as I was finishing my supper, I thought it was a mistake, someone ringing my bell instead of the bell for the apartment downstairs. But then the bell rang again, this time accompanied by insistent knocking. Remembering Monroe's warning to be careful, I took a knife from a drawer that I had scrubbed and lined with paper. "Who's there?" I called out from the top of the stairs, my heart pounding.

"It's Joletta Hall. I live downstairs. We need to talk about the cars in the driveway."

I loosened my grip on the knife, yet I still wasn't sure. What if it was a trick? I wished the door had a chain like the one in my last apartment. "I'll be right there," I said, starting down the stairs.

I opened the door a crack and saw an attractive woman who had striking, wide-set eyes and skin a rich caramel color. "I have to leave at seven o'clock on weekday mornings, and your car is blockin' mine," she said.

"I'll get my keys," I said.

After I came back I introduced myself and followed her outside. "I noticed that you scrubbed the stairs," she said. "This is the first time I can remember that the staircase smelled clean."

"How long have you lived here?"

"Fifteen years. When we moved in, we thought it would be temporary. The neighborhood was different then. We were savin' to buy a house. We had almost all we needed for a down payment when my husband was killed. I had to use the house money for his funeral."

The evening air was pleasant, but after we switched the cars we immediately went back into the house. It was dark, and although she didn't say anything, I sensed she felt as vulnerable as I did. "Weekdays I'm usually home by five," Joletta said, locking the front door. "If you come in later, just knock. Sometimes movin' the cars gets to be a hassle, but I have a long drive every mornin' and I don't want to be late."

"Where do you work?"

"Over in the valley at the processin' plant."

"What processing plant?"

Joletta looked at me with surprise. "I thought everybody in Stalling knew Golden Farms chicken. Where do you work?"

"I just moved here from Owings. I don't have a job yet."

"Unless you have a strong back and a stronger stomach, you don't want to work at Golden Farms. What did you do in Owings?"

"I was a school secretary," I said, wanting to change the subject. "Before I forget, I'd like to ask if you heard any unusual noise last night. My hubcaps were stolen."

Joletta shook her head. "They're quick and quiet around here."

"I'll call the police tomorrow."

"You'll…call…the po-lice?" Joletta said, laughing so hard she barely managed to get the words out. "You'll…call…the po-lice?"

"What's so funny?" I said, offended.

Joletta couldn't stop laughing; tears were streaming down her cheeks. Finally, gasping for breath, she said, "The po-lice don't care what's stolen down here. They call this area *'the Market'* 'cause of all the drug dealin' that goes on."

"I thought this neighborhood was called the Fruit Belt."

"It was, in better days," she said, the laughter gone from her face. "Now it's the Market. Drugs rule these streets, and not a day goes by that I don't worry over that. I've had to raise my daughter here. It seems like I spend my life worryin'. Next year she'll be graduatin' from high school. I want her to go to college. Then maybe I'll be able to relax some."

We said good night and I went upstairs to bed. Sleep should have come easily after all I had been through, but it didn't. My mind kept flipping back to the two women behind the counter in the reception room at the Department of Social Services who had deliberately ignored me for twenty minutes while they were talking. In my other life, the one I had before Tully died, I wouldn't have waited more than a minute or so before saying a polite "excuse me." Such a simple thing, two words, but I couldn't say them because I was afraid of irritating women who had been hired to help me. I thought of all the papers I signed, of feeling like a criminal because I didn't declare one hundred dollars I needed to live on until my paycheck came. I thought about my interview with Frieda Stowe, of worrying over every word I uttered as if she were God deciding my fate. My decision to move to Stalling and give up a claim to Tully's estate seemed foolish. I should have listened to Ardelle. But then I thought about Mrs. Rutland. I remembered the party she had for her twenty-fifth wedding anniversary. It was after my mama died. I was struggling with debt from Mama's Visa bills and funeral expenses, but I bought a new dress anyway because I wanted to look my best for the party. Then, the night before the party, Tully said he couldn't bring me. "I guess I misunderstood," he said. "Mama told me the party is just for family and a few of their close friends."

He knew I'd bought a new dress. I didn't tell him that I'd had it altered so I couldn't return it.

The party was on a Saturday night. Tully was at my door early Sunday morning. I could see from the way his jaw muscles were working that he was upset. "I have something to tell you," he said.

For the first time in all the years I'd known him he was having trouble looking me in the eye. "Jimmy brought a date to the anniversary party last night."

"A date?" I said, trying to take the news calmly.

"Carol Ann Pickett. When I asked, Mama said she didn't know Jimmy was bringing her."

We both knew that wasn't the truth. Jimmy wouldn't have dared bring a date without Mrs. Rutland's permission. Carol Ann was the mayor's niece.

Despite my effort not to let Tully know how hurt I was, I started to cry. Tully put his arms around me. "I'm sorry, Sara. If it's any consolation, I left the party early. I would have come here, but I was too angry. It never should have happened."

But it did happen. And it continued to happen. Mrs. Rutland never missed an opportunity to shut me out, to let me know that I wasn't an acceptable choice for her son. Even after Tully died, she was still making her feelings known. If I made a claim against the estate, she'd make those same feelings known to Tully's baby.

That thought settled my doubts. I finally fell asleep, convinced I had made the right decision.

***

I went over and over the want ads hoping that I had missed something. There were openings for mechanics and medical personnel, for waitresses and cooks, and for experienced salespeople. Even if I were qualified, I sensed that most of the sales jobs were based on commission. The two jobs that were advertised for secretaries wanted dictation and computer skills that I didn't have. Reading the ads made me realize how narrow my possibilities for employment were. Most of my clothes no longer fit, and maternity clothes, which I had priced on the long Saturdays I had wandered through stores after Tully's death, were expensive. The wardrobe I would need to work in an office or a bank—if those places would even consider hiring a pregnant woman—was way beyond my reach.

The only job prospects I found were for a motel desk clerk that required evenings and weekends, a companion for an elderly woman, and an operator for a professional answering service. There was also a housecleaning job for one day a week that made me think of Ardelle; the description didn't mention pay, and the job required references.

My telephone service wasn't scheduled to be connected until the afternoon, so I drove to Lee Avenue early in the morning to make my calls. From the beginning I'd been apprehensive about living on Lemon Street, and after my conversation with Joletta, my nervousness became fear. If there were public telephones in the Fruit Belt—the Market, Joletta called it—I wasn't going to look for them. The extra gasoline to drive to Lee Avenue was an expense I couldn't afford, but I wasn't about to set myself up to be robbed, or worse. Once I got my telephone and found a job I'd plan my trips carefully.

After I called Frieda Stowe to tell her my estimated monthly telephone and electric bills, I called about the motel job. The man I spoke with told me the job paid minimum wage, and he couldn't guarantee me more than thirty hours a week. "It'll be easy for someone with your experience," he said after he asked me about my previous job. "Mainly it's just checking people in and out and keeping the coffee pot going. Why don't you come by, and we can talk."

"I'm sorry," I said. "I need more hours and more money."

"Maybe we could work something out."

"I'll have to get back to you," I said, thinking that if I found a day job I might be able to work at the motel nights.

As I suspected, the pay for an elderly woman's companion was less than minimum wage. "It is a hundred fifty dollars for a forty-hour week," said the elderly woman's daughter (who sounded ancient herself). "It includes your lunches. And some snacks, too," she added brightly.

I thanked her and hung up, wondering how the woman expected to get someone competent to work for snacks instead of cash.

Although I had tried it first, the number for the telephone answering service had been busy. I tried again, and a woman who had a soft, lilting drawl answered. She asked me if I had any switchboard experience.

"No," I said, "but I was a school secretary for twenty years. I handled all incoming calls."

"What school?"

"Creekside Elementary in Owings. I just moved here."

"You have a pleasant voice. Would you be available for an interview this mornin'?"

"I can come over right now," I said, hoping that the clothes I was wearing, a loose-fitting jumper and blouse, would be appropriate.

After the woman gave me directions, I asked about the pay. "It's four fifty an hour."

My shoulders sagged. Just pennies above minimum wage.

The directions I was given took me to an older, well-kept section of town. I found the building, which had three stores with offices above, and went in through the door to the offices. As I climbed a long flight of stairs, I noticed a strong odor of stale cigarette smoke. When I reached the top, there was no doubt where the odor came from. The first door on the right, which was ajar, opened into the answering service's office—a single large room where four women, each of whom had to weigh over two hundred pounds, were sitting at switchboard stations answering calls and smoking. In their pink, mint green, yellow, and lavender sweat suits, the women looked like enormous Easter eggs. The stations were littered with empty cups, filled ashtrays, and piles of empty candy wrappers and potato chip bags. My eyes stung from the smoke, my throat burned. I didn't think I could last an hour in this room. Rather than take up the woman's time (the supervisor was wearing the lavender sweat suit), I politely explained that I was bothered by cigarette smoke and left.

I walked to a drugstore at the corner, bought a newspaper, and went back to my car to read the want ads. A few more jobs were listed, but none were possibilities. Common sense told me to be patient until Sunday, when the largest number of jobs were advertised, but Sunday seemed like a year away. Again, I felt panic stirring deep in the pit of my stomach, as I did when I was at the Department of Social Services. I couldn't wait until Sunday. I started the car and drove directly to Magnolia's in the Westmark Plaza.

A black woman behind the service desk in Magnolia's gave me an application for employment. It was a simple form that I quickly filled in until I got to the last page, where the names of three people with whom I had worked who were not relatives were required for references. Hesitating, I wrote the name *Mabel Baxter* with the address and telephone number of the Owings school system; in the other spaces I put the names of two women who worked under Mabel's supervision, doubting that they'd be called.

I could feel seeds of panic sprouting. I couldn't drive back to Lemon Street without the prospect of a job. "I'd like to speak to the manager," I said to the woman behind the service desk after people ahead of me were helped with exchanges.

"The manager don't talk to people until he reads the application. I'll make sure he gets it," she said, holding out her hand for the form. A name tag pinned to her green-and-white apron-style top, which all Magnolia's female employees seemed to wear, said *Delilah*.

I wouldn't give her the application. "I understand, but there's something I have to explain."

"Welllll," Delilah said reluctantly, "I'll page him. You can wait at jewelry. I have to keep the service desk clear."

The jewelry section was on the opposite aisle. I stood with my back to a glass display case filled with Timex watches, trying to calm my nervousness, amazed that I had pushed so hard. Desperation gave me nerve I hadn't had before. Nearly five minutes passed before a chunky man wearing a green knit shirt and khaki pants arrived at the service desk. Delilah briefly spoke to him, pointing in my direction. He nodded, then ambled across the aisle. It seemed like he was deliberately taking his time, that making me wait pleased him. I guessed he was somewhere in his thirties; his face was full, his receding hair a straight, lifeless brown. His eyeglass frames, which were made of gray plastic, reminded me of the type old men wore. The name tag attached to his shirt said *Linwood Cagle, Manager*. "I understand there's a problem with your application," he said.

"My telephone won't be connected until this afternoon," I said, handing him the form. "I just moved to Stalling. I'm really anxious for a job, and I didn't want you to call and find that the number wasn't working."

"According to what you've written here, you worked for your last employer for twenty years," he said, scanning the application.

"Yes. You can check with my references."

He stepped back and looked me up and down, squinting suspiciously. "Why are you applying here?"

"I need a job right away."

"So you'll work here until you can find a better job?"

"No," I said, which wasn't quite true.

"Why should I believe you?" he said in a belligerent whine. "People do it all the time. We hire 'em, we train 'em, and then they leave."

"How much do you pay?"

"Uh…well…it's four fifty an hour."

"Can you promise me a full work week—forty hours?"

"Right now the most I can give you is thirty-five. But that's a guarantee if you'll work evenings and weekends."

"Then I'm hired?"

"I want to call your references first. You can check back with me this afternoon at four," he said.

"Thank you," I said, as if the job were already mine.

I had to break into the one hundred dollars that I'd promised myself I wouldn't touch to call Mabel Baxter from a pay phone. "It isn't the same without you," Mabel said. "I know I'll never see the likes of one of your attendance reports again."

"I hope that means you'll give me a good reference. I've moved to Stalling and I've applied for a job."

"It would be my pleasure. Have you applied at a school?"

I winced with embarrassment, glad that Mabel couldn't see me. "No," I said, "at a Magnolia's. It'll only be temporary, something to tide me over until I find the right place."

"Well, it is near the end of the school year."

"I hate to put you to the trouble, but I need a letter, something on official stationery giving the date and reason I left, and the dates and gross amounts of my last paychecks. Since I'm not living in Owings anymore, I might have to prove how much I earned and that I wasn't fired."

"I'll see to it this afternoon," Mabel said.

Mabel's eagerness to help made me feel guilty; although I hadn't actually lied, I had misrepresented. For years I had prided myself on being different from my parents and brother, who lied as effortlessly as they breathed. But ever since I'd gone to the Department of Social Services, it seemed like I was being pushed into telling one lie after another. In each instance the truth would have hurt me but a lie wouldn't.

My telephone was installed early in the afternoon, and promptly at four o'clock I called Magnolia's and asked to speak to the manager. "Come in tomorrow morning so I can go over some things with you and give you the employee handbook," Linwood Cagle said.

"Can I start work tomorrow?"

"I like people to read the handbook first so they know what's expected of them."

"I can read it during my lunch break."

"I suppose Mrs. Early could start training you," he said.

I put the receiver down with relief. Maybe I'd find a better job in the Sunday paper and work at Magnolia's on weekends or evenings. Meanwhile, it gave me some security.

The next telephone call I made was to Grover Daniels. Rather than begin with a list of complaints, I told him that I'd scrubbed the apartment from top to bottom and replaced the toilet seat before I mentioned that only one burner on the stove worked and that the vegetable crispers in the refrigerator were missing. When he didn't respond, I asked if he was still there. He made a sound like a grunt. "I have a form I need you to fill out," I said, flustered by his response.

"What kind of form?" he said loudly.

"A residency statement."

"You got a child living with you?"

I moved the receiver away from my ear. "No."

"Then why do you need a residency statement?"

"For food stamps," I said, hating him for making me say it.

"Do you have a job?"

"I start work tomorrow."

"I expect the rent on the first of the month, cash or money order. I usually collect there late in the day. If you won't be home, call me to make other arrangements."

"What about the residency statement?"

He gave me an address and told me to mail it. Then, before I had a chance to ask about the stove and vegetable crispers, he hung up.

Almost from the moment I had given Grover Daniels the deposit on the apartment, I had felt as though I had made a terrible mistake. Now I was sure. I took a deep breath and forced myself to think of something else. Supper. I had to make supper.

I took the chicken I had bought yesterday out of the refrigerator and put it on the narrow counter next to the sink. The bird was still in the plastic bag, pale and watery, a sad-looking thing. Small as it was, it took up most of the meager workspace. I pictured my kitchen in Altavista Gardens, the generous counter tops without gouges and scratches, the sleek beige cupboards, the new appliances. I thought of New Year's Eve, of Tully cooking steaks while I made salads, and my eyes filled with tears. Missing him hurt more than I had imagined anything could.

Sobbing, I tried to concentrate on cutting up the chicken, which was cold and rubbery and kept slipping out of my hands.

***

At least I didn't have to worry about clothes for my job at Magnolia's. From what I had seen yesterday, slacks, stirrup pants, even jeans were acceptable. Still, I wore the nicer of my two tunic sweaters, wanting to look well on my first day.

The manager, Linwood Cagle, walked with me to the far end of the store, where we went through a door marked **EMPLOYEES ONLY** and climbed a flight of stairs to the offices and employees' rooms. A bank of metal lockers lined one side of the hallway. Cagle selected a key from a large ring that hung from a chain hooked to his belt and unlocked the door to a storage room. "What size apron do you think you take?" he said, fixing his eyes on my breasts.

"Large," I said, turning away.

Linwood Cagle wasn't quick at getting messages. "They run pretty big," he said with a smirk.

"Large," I repeated coldly.

The tone of my voice told him that he'd badly overstepped. He awkwardly handed me the green-and-white apron. "I'll get your name pin and the handbook from my office."

"And my time card?" I said. "I saw the clock in the hall. Shouldn't I punch in?"

"Uh...yes," he said, as though he'd forgotten. "I won't be long. Feel free to look in the employees' rooms."

I waited until he was gone before I put on the apron. As I expected, it was too large, but it would conceal my pregnancy for a while.

After I peeked into a small employees' room for smokers, I went into a large room that had tables and chairs where employees could eat, a small television set bolted to the wall in a cage-type device, and soft drink and snack machines. The room was as stark as a jail cell, dull grays and blacks, all hard surfaces including the chairs. It wasn't a room a person could get comfortable in, I thought, beginning to get an idea of what it was going to be like working for Magnolia's.

When Linwood returned, he showed me how to punch in and assigned me a locker opposite the employees' restrooms. "Don't give anyone the combination," he cautioned after I put my purse, the handbook, and my bag lunch inside the locker.

We went back downstairs, Linwood talking nonstop. "On days that you work nine to five, you get a ten-minute break in the morning and a ten-minute break in the afternoon. Your lunch will be from one to two, not always right on the hour. We try to stagger employees' times to keep the floor covered. Your supervisor will let you know when it's okay to take your lunch break. There are always two supervisors on the floor—they're really assistant managers—one for the hard lines like cosmetics and one for the soft lines, which are clothes and linens. There's also the office manager, Mrs. Petty. I forgot to introduce you to her when we were upstairs. You should see her to give her the payroll information she needs. Finally, there's Mrs. Early. She's the customer service manager. You're going to spend the next few days with Mrs. Early learning the register. Then you'll get your regular schedule. How flexible can you be?"

"I want as many hours as I can get," I said.

He introduced me to employees we passed as we walked toward the cash registers. His introductions were so brief, a mere calling out of names, that all I remembered was a jumble of faces. What made the biggest impression me was that most of them were black.

I knew immediately by the way he introduced her that the short, middle-aged black woman wearing a string of keys around her neck was important. "Sara, this is Mrs. Early. For the next couple-three days she'll be teaching you how to run a register. No one knows more about registers than Mrs. Early."

Mrs. Early was all business. She explained the scanner to me, the keys, the importance of paying attention to the monitor, wasting neither words nor motion. "You must always concentrate," she said. "Most mistakes are the result of a lack of concentration. You can't be thinking about anything but the transaction."

As pleasant as Mrs. Early was, I felt like I'd slid to the very bottom of the job ladder. "What happens if I make a mistake?" I said, remembering the two years I had worked as a teller. Every penny had to be accounted for at the bank.

"For a shortage or overage under five dollars, you're reprimanded and told to be more careful. If you have three overages or shortages in excess of five dollars in a ninety-day period, you're fired. If you have a large shortage—fifty dollars or more—you're fired immediately.

"Mistakes can happen, but these new registers do everything for you, even remind you to close your cash drawer."

After I had practiced on the register for about an hour, Mrs. Early said, "You're doing very well. Have you worked on a register before?"

"No," I said. "But I did work in a bank once."

A light above one of the registers started flashing. "That light's for me," said Mrs. Early. "Probably an override. I hope it isn't going to be one of those days. Why don't you take your break now? You have ten minutes. When you come back, you can watch for a while."

We had been working at the register nearest the front door; the entrance to the employees' rooms was diagonally opposite at the rear of the store. Walking as fast as I dared, it took me close to two minutes to reach the stairs. I needed to use the bathroom and I wanted to call Frieda Stowe to see if my food stamps were ready. I raced up the stairs, wondering if I could do it all in under six minutes.

A black girl who looked eighteen at most was using the phone. I signaled that I wanted to make a call, then hurried to the restroom. The girl was still on the phone when I came out, laughing, and from the sound of the conversation, flirting. I went to my locker and took a quarter and the scrap of paper Frieda Stowe had given me from my purse. I glanced at my watch: less than three minutes left.

The name tag pinned to the girl's green-and-white apron said *Nikki*. I stood what I thought was a polite distance away, an expectant look on my face. "Gotta go now," Nikki said to whoever she was talking to. "I'll catch you later."

The receiver went down harder than necessary. "You didn't have to get in my face!" Nikki said nastily.

Before I could respond, Nikki was jogging down the hall to the stairs, her break apparently over.

There wasn't a direct line to Frieda Stowe's office. My call had to be transferred by a receptionist, which ate precious seconds. After four rings, I heard the click of a machine turning on. *"This is Frieda Stowe. I am not available to take your call. At the sound of the beep, please leave..."*

Disappointed, I decided to try again at the beginning of my lunch break. The hour I was allowed was the only time I'd have to get my stamps.

I went back downstairs through the store to the registers, passing the paint department, hardware, linens, housewares, toiletries, cosmetics, cards and gift wrap, and ladies' sportswear. There was no time to look at the merchandise. I made it to the front of the store in just under ten minutes.

Frieda Stowe was in her office when I called again at one. "Your stamps are ready," she said.

Traffic was heavy; the drive to city hall took close to twenty minutes. Hungry, I ate an apple from my bag lunch while I drove. As I rushed into the building, I thought about the form I had signed promising to give Social Services notification within ten days of getting a job. If I told Frieda Stowe about my job at Magnolia's today, it might change the amount I would get in food stamps. But not telling would be dishonest. Maybe it wouldn't be dishonest. The form did say ten days.

Walking into the Department of Social Services reception area triggered a rush of the emotions I had experienced the first time: embarrassment, shame, feelings of unworthiness, as if my presence there was an admission that I was somehow inferior, a failure. I averted my eyes so I wouldn't look at the people waiting in the chairs that were lined against the wall and went directly to the counter, where I stood far enough behind an overweight blond girl and a slender black boy to give them privacy. The girl, wearing a pink jacket and jeans that were straining at the seams, was talking to the clerk while the boy held a baby against his chest like it was a trophy. The clerk slipped papers into a clipboard that she handed to the girl, then nodded at me to come forward. "Ms. Stowe told me that my food stamps are ready," I said, remembering the clerk from my last visit. She had been sitting at her desk staring out the window while I had stood waiting to be helped.

"I believe Ms. Stowe is with a client. What's your name?"

"Sara Barefield."

She picked up the phone to call Frieda Stowe. "There's a Sara Barefield here for her stamps," she said, her high-pitched voice carrying throughout the room.

I shut my eyes, wishing I was invisible. "She says she'll be done shortly," the clerk said.

What did shortly mean? I wondered, glad that a chair near the door was available. Almost thirty minutes of my lunch hour was gone. I had to allow at least twenty minutes to get back to the store, and time on top of that to park the car, go to my locker, put on my apron, and report to Mrs. Early. A rumble of hunger came from my stomach. The rest of my lunch, a peanut-butter-and-jelly sandwich and two cookies, was in the car. I had brought nothing to drink. I started thinking that it had been stupid to come here, but I needed those stamps so I wouldn't use up what was left of my reserve money. I was working all day tomorrow. Probably Friday, too. If I didn't get the stamps today, there would be no point in coming back until I had time to wait. I would be forced to use the reserve money.

Just as I was deciding to leave, the clerk called my name. I hurried to the counter. "Ms. Stowe will meet you in the hall," she said.

I stepped into the corridor and saw Frieda Stowe approaching with a heavy-set, middle-aged man who looked so miserable that I felt sorry for him. He probably lost his job, I guessed, staying at a distance until they parted.

"Here is one hundred seven dollars in food stamps," Ms. Stowe said, handing me what looked like oversized books of tickets and a green card. "You'll need the green card for identification, so always keep it with you. Stores are supposed to check to see that the numbers on the stamps match the numbers on the green ID."

"Thank you," I said, so grateful that I decided to tell her about my job. I had to tell within the next ten days anyway, and I didn't want Ms. Stowe to think less of me for waiting to disclose it. "I got a job."

"Really?" she said, looking surprised. "Where?"

"At Magnolia's. I'm getting four fifty an hour. It isn't much, but it'll help until I can get something better."

"According to the rules, I should re-figure your stamps, but they've already been issued and I have six people waiting. The amount of extra stamps you might be getting is negligible anyway," she said, more to herself than to me.

"When can I expect to hear from Medicaid?"

"I have no idea," she said with irritation. "My department is food stamps."

Stunned at her response, I mumbled goodbye and left. When I was in the car, I examined one of the food stamp booklets. The booklet, which was worth seven dollars, had a cream-and-lavender cover; inside there was a five-dollar cream-and-purple stamp and two one-dollar cream-and-brown stamps. The stamps looked like play money that belonged to a child's game.

I got back to the store without a second to spare and again went back and forth past the paint department, hardware, linens, housewares, toiletries, cosmetics, cards and gift wrap, and ladies' sportswear. I spent most of the afternoon with Mrs. Early observing clerks working at the registers. For a while I watched Nikki, the girl who had been rude to me earlier. "She's so fast," I said to Mrs. Early, admiring how quickly Nikki handled customers' purchases. The girl ran items over the scanner and put them in plastic bags in what seemed like one continuous motion.

"She's fast all right," Mrs. Early said. "But being careful and accurate is more important. When you're too fast, items can miss the scanner or get damaged when they're put in bags. If the customer has coupons, you'll probably lose time looking back at the tape because you won't remember if the item was purchased. And if you're too fast, it's likely that your register will be off. Nikki's been warned: if her register is off again, she'll have to leave. It seems like she hasn't taken the warning to heart."

I used my one break in the afternoon to eat my sandwich. Unaccustomed to standing for hours at a time, by the end of the day my feet hurt, my back ached, and my head throbbed with all I had to remember about the register and the differences in processing Visa, MasterCard, Discovery, and American Express cards. Bone weary, all I wanted was to eat a light supper, soak in the tub, and go to bed.

The blue Nova was in the driveway when I got home. I knocked on Joletta Hall's door, hoping we could switch cars. A teenage girl peeped through the door before opening it. The girl had Joletta's striking wide-set eyes, but her face was longer and thinner, a perfect oval; her features were finely chiseled and her skin was a light honey color. As tired as I was, I was astonished by the girl's beauty. She was exquisite. "I'm Sara Barefield. I'd like to switch cars now if I can," I said.

"Be a minute," the girl said.

Joletta came out dangling her keys from her index finger. "Is she your daughter?" I said.

"Yes, that's Symone."

"She's beautiful."

"Thank you," Joletta said, getting into the Nova. She sounded as weary as I felt. "But let me tell you, beauty ain't always easy."

***

Though I would have liked to put my aching feet up for a while, I didn't linger in the employees' room after I finished my lunch. There were several groups eating at other tables, but I had eaten alone. The only white person in the room, I felt as conspicuous as a piece of lint on a dark dress. I was particularly conscious of Nikki, the girl who had been rude to me yesterday. Nikki was sitting at one of the other tables, laughing and joking as if she was at a party. Less than an hour earlier, while I was observing the cashiers, I saw Nikki double-up two pairs of stockings and run them through the scanner as one pair. Nikki's movements were fast—the merchandise run across the scanner and dumped into a waiting plastic bag in one continuous motion—almost too fast for anyone to see. But I did see. I also saw that Nikki and the customer, a girl Nikki's age, knew each other. The customer tilted her head in my direction; Nikki turned and looked at me with a defiant smirk. I responded with a hard, steady gaze that told Nikki I wouldn't be intimidated. I didn't want trouble and sensed that Nikki would give it to me if I showed any sign of weakness.

It was payday at Magnolia's. Wondering when I could expect my first check, I left the employees' room and went to the office, where an immense woman was sitting behind a metal desk. A black-and-white nameplate on the desk said GLADYS PETTY. "I'm Sara Barefield. I started working here yesterday."

Mrs. Petty gave me forms to complete for tax information. "When will I get my first paycheck?" I asked when I was finished.

"Two weeks from today. Payday is every two weeks on Thursdays."

"Do you have any idea of how much my check will be? Mr. Cagle said he'd give me thirty-five hours a week."

Despite cushions of fat, Mrs. Petty's fingers moved rapidly over the keys of her calculator. "Your check should be $253.80."

"For two weeks?"

"Here, I'll give you the breakdown," Mrs. Petty said. She tore the paper from the machine and wrote beside each figure before handing me the tape:

  $18.10 State of Virginia Tax
  19.00 Federal Tax
  4.57 Medicare
  <u>19.53</u> Social Security
  $61.20

  $315.00 Gross
  <u>61.20</u> Deductions
  $253.80 Net

I stared at the tape with disbelief. For two weeks of work at Magnolia's I would be taking home what I made in a week working at Creekside Elementary. "The deduction for Social Security is almost twenty dollars," I said finally. "Is this right?"

"Social Security takes the same percentage out of everyone's salary no matter how much you earn," said Mrs. Petty. "You're being taxed at the same rate as a bank president, but a bank president doesn't feel it. The people with the low-paying jobs are the ones it hurts."

I thanked her and headed downstairs. I would have to think about my finances later. Mrs. Early was waiting to supervise me while I checked out customers.

There was only one difficult transaction all afternoon. A woman of about twenty who was holding a baby and had a toddler in her cart gave me a check for $40.53 to pay for her purchases. The register rejected the check after I punched in the woman's Social Security number as I had been instructed. "I'm sorry," I said, returning the check to the woman with a slip of paper that gave a brief explanation of the rejection and telephone numbers to call.

"There's a mistake," the woman said, furiously pushing strands of oily brown hair off her face. "I'm a good customer. You can trust that check is good. You must've punched them numbers in wrong."

Conscious of Mrs. Early watching, I tried again, carefully punching in each number. The check was again rejected "I'm sorry," I said. "Maybe you'd…"

The woman didn't give me a chance to finish. "I ain't shoppin' in this store again!" She yanked the toddler out of the cart and stalked out of the store, both children crying.

Upset by what had happened, it was difficult for me to concentrate on the next customer's order. I was so intent on not making a mistake that I didn't notice Mrs. Early put the chain across the aisle to close it. When the customer left, Mrs. Early came up to me. "You did fine with that rejected check," she said. "With some people I can smooth things over, but not with that young woman. She's pulled the same thing in here before, and each time I hope she'll make good her threat and really never come back. But she will. You did exactly what you were supposed to do: you gave her the

SCAN slip, you were polite, and you didn't let her bully you into taking her check."

"I felt sorry for her," I said. "Having her check refused had to be embarrassing."

"Don't you start feeling sorry for people. She knew her check wasn't good. I stayed back and watched her pick your aisle because you're new."

"I didn't realize..."

"You will," Mrs. Early said confidently. "You catch on fast."

Late in the afternoon I was given my hours for the next week. I was scheduled to work from five to eleven on Tuesday and Wednesday nights, Friday and Saturday from nine to five, and Sunday from ten until seven. Linwood Cagle had kept his promise. And he reminded me of that as I was leaving. "You got your thirty-five hours," he said.

I didn't like the eager expression on his face, as if he were expecting praise or payment of some kind for a gift he had given. "That was the deal," I said, walking away.

Since the food I had bought early in the week was nearly gone, I decided to go grocery shopping before driving back to Lemon Street. Tomorrow I might be too tired after my first full day of cashing out customers. There was no way I would shop at the Kroger's in the plaza and risk having the people I worked with at Magnolia's see me using food stamps, so I drove to a Food Lion several miles farther out Lee Avenue, never considering that the people I wanted to avoid were very likely using food stamps themselves. So it came as a shock to glimpse a woman I had seen stocking toiletries on shelves in Magnolia's several people ahead of me in line at Food Lion pay the checkout clerk with food stamps. Quickly, I looked away, and my eyes happened to meet those of the young man standing behind me. With his well-cut sandy-brown hair and the designer logo on his shirt, he looked like a rich college boy. "This line sure isn't moving fast," he said in a commiserating tone, one fellow sufferer to another.

Swallowing hard, I managed a weak smile. More than anything I didn't want that boy with his blow-dried hair and designer shirt to see me paying with food stamps. I could move to another line, but no matter which line I was in someone would see me.

When my turn finally came, the overhead lights seemed brighter, shining down on me like spotlights. Instead of watching the monitor as I always did while the checkout clerk weighed and scanned the groceries, my eyes were fixed on the floor. I didn't look up when I handed the clerk my books of stamps; shame wouldn't allow me to make eye contact or to count the change I was given. Conscious of the college boy, conscious of all the people around me, I rushed out of the store feeling the cool air on my flushed skin as if I had been publicly humiliated, though no one had made a comment or had even seemed to notice. They didn't have to. I knew. I had paid for my food with stamps; my poverty was out front for strangers to see.

This was only temporary, I told myself as I put the groceries in the car. But the thought gave me no comfort as I drove home to Lemon Street.

After I ate supper, I tried to figure out a budget based on what I would be earning at Magnolia's. No matter how I juggled the figures, I would be left with no more than twenty dollars a week after I deducted what I needed for my rent, utilities, and the gas for my car. My food stamps would surely be cut because I was working, and the payment for my car insurance was due next month. It was impossible. There was no way I could live.

Sleep gave me no escape from my worries. That night my mama was in my dreams—vivid, loud, puffing on Marlboros in the clothes she'd bought with my credit card. *"You've really gone and done it! Pregnant with no husband! Livin' with niggers! Payin' for your food with stamps, a charity case!"*

The litany went on and on. "Please stop, Mama, please. This is only temporary."

"Temporary my foot! Once you hit bottom you're trapped! Me an' your daddy had all we could do to keep one step away. But we managed, because we knew if we didn't we'd never get out."

"I'm not you and daddy. I'll do it!"

"You always had them fancy ideas, your head in books all the time. Now you're goin' to get a good dose of the real world!"

I struggled until I was able to force myself awake. Anything, even sleeplessness after a hard day, was better than listening to my mama.

***

Although there was double the number of jobs listed in the Sunday newspaper, there wasn't one to which I could apply: either they wanted experience I didn't have or they required a wardrobe I couldn't afford. Even if I wasn't pregnant, most of the ads were for minimum wage jobs that were no better than what I had.

Monday was my first full day off since I had started working at Magnolia's. After I cleaned the apartment and threw out the plants I hadn't been able to save, I decided to go to the library and then to a park. The day looked inviting, sunny and warm, and it had been weeks since I'd had the pleasure of escaping in a book. Before I left, I checked the mail and found my Medicaid card. To my surprise I was able to get an appointment at the hospital clinic on Wednesday morning.

The library nearest to Lemon Street was so small and beaten-looking with its peeling paint and boarded broken windows that I drove to one on the other side of town. Checking my map, I discovered that the parks were on the other side of town as well. It seemed that everything desirable was on the other side of town. From what I could see the Fruit Belt was an island of misery standing all by itself with little to offer the people who lived there. When I returned to my apartment, I felt trapped.

Late that afternoon I knocked on Joletta's door. "I got my work schedule," I said, "and it might be a problem. On Tuesdays and Wednesdays I have to work until eleven at night. What do you want to do about the cars?"

"I have to be up before six in the mornin'. I can't be movin' cars at midnight."

"Maybe I could park on the lawn," I said.

"That would work as long as you move to the driveway in the mornin'. You don't want your car on the lawn durin' the day."

"Why not? There's hardly any grass there."

"You don't want to do anythin' that Grover Daniels could give you trouble for," she said. "Where are you workin'?"

"Magnolia's, but I'm..."

I started to say that I was looking for something better, but Joletta's eyes had shifted, focusing past me. I turned and saw Symone. "*Where you been?*" Joletta demanded.

"Just...uh...hangin' out," Symone said.

An angry vein rose on the side of Joletta's neck. Feeling like an intruder, I started back upstairs. "You been with Darrell Lawson, haven't you!" I heard Joletta say. "You been with him, I know it! That Darrell's nothin' but trouble! Can't you see it? He'll ruin your life like he's ruined all those other girls. How many has he gotten pregnant? Five? Six? A dozen? You think I don't know what goes on? Everybody know about Darrell Lawson. His mama died of drugs and now he's killin' other people with them! They say his mama didn't even know who his daddy was!"

I turned on the television so I wouldn't hear them through the thin walls. I had enough to think about as it was.

On Wednesday morning, I arrived at the OB/GYN clinic at Cornelius Dearth Memorial Hospital at nine o'clock, as I'd been instructed. Dearth Memorial was a teaching hospital affiliated with the university. Located in an older part of Stalling, it was a factory-like complex of brick and stone buildings that covered several city blocks. To get to the clinic I had to walk through three connected buildings, following a map given to me by a receptionist at the main desk. I didn't know what to expect. I had never been to a clinic before.

The first half hour or so I was kept busy filling out forms. But after I was finished it didn't take long for me to become aware that certain women in the large common waiting room were called soon after giving their names at the reception area while others, like me, remained in the pink and blue upholstered chairs, their names uncalled. Puzzled, then annoyed, I finally went up to the receptionist and asked why those other women had been called and I hadn't. "They're private patients," the receptionist said.

Private? At first I didn't understand. Then, with the realization that *private* meant *paying*, I could feel my face color. "Oh," I managed to say through a haze of embarrassment.

The magazines in the waiting room were dated and dog-eared, a *Time* over a year old, a *McCall's* missing a cover, a *National Geographic* that was falling apart. There were also stacks of complimentary magazines full of ads selling everything imaginable for babies. The infants pictured in the ads looked so winning—bright-eyed and smiling, possessing perfectly formed limbs and the proper number of fingers and toes—that I became even more anxious for my name to be called. All the questions I'd wanted to ask a doctor for weeks were going through my head, all the fears and worries that had been weighing on my heart. It wasn't surprising, then, that my blood pressure was a full forty points above my normal reading when a nurse took it at eleven thirty-five.

The nurse, a brunette in her thirties whose figure was as sleek as a teenager's, remarked about my small weight gain. "Isn't six pounds enough?" I asked, concerned. "Will it hurt the baby?"

"The baby will take what it needs from you, so you must have a healthy diet. I'll give you a booklet on nutrition."

After she finished drawing my blood, she gave me the material on nutrition and a pamphlet about natural childbirth. "Have you thought about natural childbirth?" she said.

"No," I said.

"It's much healthier for the baby. The pamphlet explains. Whatever you decide, you should definitely go to the childbirth classes. You'll learn relaxation and breathing techniques that will make your labor easier.

"There is, however, a decision you will have to make today. You have a choice between seeing a nurse practitioner or a doctor when you come here for your checkups. If you choose the nurse practitioner, you'll see the same nurse every time, which is an advantage because she'll be familiar with you and your progress. If you decide to see a doctor, you'll be seen by whoever is available at the time of your visit, usually a resident."

I stopped listening after hearing that I'd have a choice between a nurse or a doctor. There was no way I'd settle for a nurse, not after having to wait all morning because I wasn't a private patient! "I want a doctor," I said firmly.

Again I had to wait, this time perched on an examining table, a flimsy drape across my lap, my bare backside getting chilly. When the doctor finally came in, I nearly gasped. Of medium height and build, his face was so boyish, full and pink-cheeked, that he looked no more than eighteen. "Hi, I'm Dr. Prentice," he said without looking at me, his attention completely taken by the papers in my folder. "Please place your feet in the stirrups, lay back and slide your bottom forward."

Aided by the nurse, I did as I was instructed. Thinking that it would be better not to distract him, I decided to wait until he was finished examining me before I started asking questions. But immediately after he was through with his uncomfortable probing, he slipped off his gloves and said, "Rather than giving the date of your last period, you put down October eighth as the date of conception. Are you positive about that?"

"Yes," I said, relieved that he was finally paying attention to me above my waist.

"Pregnancy in a woman your age is considered high risk," he said after the nurse left.

"Did you find something wrong?" I said with alarm.

"No," he said, hesitating as if he weren't sure. "But my examination, by its very nature, is limited. What you need is a procedure called amniocentesis. You'll be given a local anesthetic and a hollow needle will be inserted through your abdominal wall into your uterus to withdraw a small amount of fluid. This fluid will be able to tell us if the baby is normal."

Normal, the magic word. More than anything I wanted the baby to be normal, to be healthy. But what if the baby moved unexpectedly and was hurt by the needle? "I don't know…"

"The procedure is absolutely safe," he said.

There was something in the intensity of his brown eyes that made me uneasy. I recalled reading in the library that amniocentesis was usually performed sometime around the third or fourth month of pregnancy. I was far past that, already in my sixth month. "No, I don't think I want that done."

"It's the best test that we have. I don't want to frighten you, but the incidence of problems like Down's syndrome—mental retardation—goes up with the mother's age."

"Oh, my God." The words escaped my lips. I'd been worrying about whether the baby had all of its parts and that they were in working order; I hadn't considered that the baby's mind could be defective.

"You also have the option of ultrasound, though it won't tell us as much."

I had had an ultrasound of my breast several years before for a suspicious lump that was judged harmless. "I'll have that," I said, "the ultrasound."

"It's your choice," he said with a shrug. He leaned over the desk and quickly filled out the Medicaid form I needed to verify my pregnancy, and an order sheet for the ultrasound test. Then, wordlessly, he handed me the papers and left. He didn't even bother saying goodbye.

Stunned by his abrupt departure, I stayed on the examining table for a moment or two, the questions I'd wanted to ask for weeks still unanswered. Instead of reassurance, all I'd gotten was a new set of worries. At least I knew the baby's probable birth date, I thought as I scanned the Medicaid form. Next to *Probable Date of Delivery* he'd written June 28.

Before I left the hospital I was directed to the pharmacy, where I was charged only three dollars for a month's supply of vitamin pills. My gratitude for the reasonable price didn't last long; there was a three-dollar charge for parking in the hospital-owned ramp.

When I returned to the hospital the following day for the ultrasound test, I was both hopeful and nervous. Sure that I would be able to see the baby on the small screen I remembered from my previous test, I would know if anything was obviously wrong. But the screen was set at an angle away from my line of vision, and the technician, a young woman in her early twenties who had the scrubbed, plastic look of a cheerleader, conducted the test in silence. "Please," I said, "can I see the baby?"

"Sorry, I can't let you do that," she said with a flat Midwestern accent, her eyes fixed on the screen as she continued to move the probe over my gel-slick abdomen.

"Just a glance?" I said.

"Sorry."

"Then can you tell me if everything is all right?"

"I'm not allowed to say. You'll have to ask your doctor."

Frustrated to the point of tears, I wondered how anyone, especially another female, could be so unfeeling that she wouldn't let me have even a peek at my baby...unless there was something terribly wrong. "My next appointment isn't for another four weeks."

"You could call him. The report will be ready on Monday," the technician said, her left hand adjusting dials. "Now please take a deep breath and hold."

The remainder of the test was conducted as it had begun, in silence. The technician asked me to wait after I got dressed in case it was necessary to take more pictures. Ten minutes later she appeared in the waiting room. "You can go now," she said with a bright plastic smile, as though our session had been a great success.

From the hospital I drove directly to the library, thinking that perhaps it wasn't too late, maybe I could still have amniocentesis. It had to be luck that led me to the information I needed. In the first book I opened I learned that not only was I four weeks beyond the ideal time to perform the procedure, but amniocentesis had a three percent fetus death rate.

I caught my breath. If I had trusted Dr. Prentice, I could have lost the baby.

***

Money. I couldn't stop worrying about money. I had only fifty-five dollars left from the one hundred that I hadn't wanted to touch. Every dollar I had been forced to spend made me feel more insecure: money for gasoline, money for the laundromat, money for parking in the hospital ramp, money for non-food items like toilet paper and soap that my food stamps wouldn't pay for. The booklet on nutrition the nurse had given me suggested that a pregnant woman eat a minimum of six servings of fruit and vegetables a day. I couldn't afford more than half that amount on food stamps, even with eating peanut butter for lunch every day. And I needed maternity clothes. My stomach had really blossomed, and all I could wear was a loose-fitting jumper and the few things I'd bought before I left Owings, which wouldn't fit by the end of the month. Years ago when I left my parents' house, my ignorance of the world made the poverty I faced a challenge. Now I knew it for what it was: more than a threat, it was a monster waiting to consume me and the baby if I let my guard down for a minute.

On Friday afternoon there was still over forty minutes of my lunch hour left, enough time to open a bank account. My final paycheck from the Owings school system was tucked in my wallet. Though I would have liked to send the $251 check to Ardelle to deposit in the account I had opened for the baby, it wasn't possible. I needed to have some money set aside as a cushion. I wouldn't get my first paycheck from Magnolia's until next Thursday; a portion of the $253.80 paycheck would have to go toward next month's rent.

The bank was on the opposite end of the plaza from Magnolia's. I walked briskly, feeling the tension in my body from working at a cash register all morning loosen with each step. I passed clothing shops, a kitchenware store, a fabric store, barely glancing in the windows until I came to a florist. A graceful rattan flower cart in the window that was brimming with African violets and begonias, ivy spilling over its sides, caught my attention. I stopped to look at the charming cart and noticed a small sign that said PART TIME HELP WANTED taped to a bottom corner of the window. I decided to go in.

"Is anyone here?" I said, seeing no one inside.

"I'll be right there," a female voice called.

A woman who I guessed was in her mid-to-late forties emerged from the back of the shop carrying a delicate arrangement of pale pink roses and white carnations. She was wearing jeans and a loose-fitting blue smock that had large, deep pockets; reading glasses dangled from a chain around her neck. Her bright coloring—reddish-blond hair, a dusting of freckles, and clear blue eyes—rescued her face from plainness. "How can I help you?" she said with a smile so warm that I immediately liked her.

"Your sign in the window," I said. "Are you looking for help?"

"I sure am," she said, putting the arrangement in a refrigerated display case that was against the wall. "I need someone on Fridays to answer the phone and help with customers."

"I'm already working on Fridays, but if I could get my schedule changed, I'd be interested. How much are you paying?"

"Four twenty-five an hour," she said. "I wish it was more, but I can't afford it yet. I've only been open for a few months. Where are you working now?"

"At Magnolia's," I said. "Before that I was an elementary school secretary for twenty years."

"Do you know anything about plants and flowers?"

"Mostly plants. I do pretty well with them. I noticed your sign because I stopped to admire the African violets and begonias in that wonderful flower cart."

"What's your name?"

"Sara Barefield."

"Well, Sara, I'm going to be honest with you. I've had the sign up for two weeks and you're my first good prospect. If you want the job, it's yours." She extended her hand. "I'm Bev Garland."

I hesitated. "I think I should tell you: I'm pregnant."

"When are you due?"

"At the end of June."

"Let's give it a try and hope I'm still in business at the end of June!"

"I'll have to see if I can get my schedule switched. I work until five."

"Can you stop by afterward to let me know? I'll wait for you."

"Sure," I said, thinking that if I hurried, there was still enough time to go to the bank.

I couldn't open a checking account. The monthly service charge and the cost of the checks, even for an economy account, was more than I could afford. "What are the charges for a savings account?" I said.

"Nothing, as long as you maintain a minimum balance of two hundred dollars," said the assistant manager, a middle-aged woman whose eyebrows were carefully drawn with brown pencil. "If your balance goes under two hundred, there's a service charge of three dollars a month."

I filled out the card I had been given and endorsed the check, realizing that I would have to buy money orders to pay my rent and utilities. Money orders, which to me were like flags signaling poverty. Only the poorest of the poor didn't have a checking account.

On my way back to Magnolia's, I thought about the job at the flower shop. Even though it paid only minimum wage, I would be surrounded by plants, and Bev Garland seemed nice. Besides, it was the only prospect for employment I had or was likely to have in my condition. I decided to talk to Mrs. Early rather than Linwood Cagle about changing my schedule. He might give me a hard time, and Mrs. Early seemed to run the store anyway.

Mrs. Early wasn't at all happy about the request. "Fridays are one of our busiest days," she said. "I need you on a register."

"I can't live on what I'm making here," I said, resenting having to give an explanation. "I need this other job."

"What if you can't be switched?"

Mrs. Early's expression was stern, not at all like the sweet-talking woman who soothed disgruntled customers. This was a side of her I hadn't seen. I knew she was pushing me, so I had to push back. "Then I'll have to look for another job. I shouldn't have trouble finding one with the good training you gave me on the register."

"That won't be necessary," she said, her voice full of honey again. "I think we can work something out."

"I need to know today."

"I'll get back to you before five."

But it was Linwood who got back to me as I was heading upstairs on my afternoon break. "I moved you to Thursdays, nine to five. If you need to switch in the future, see me instead of Mrs. Early. I'm in charge of scheduling."

Wednesday nights I worked until eleven o'clock; the switch to Thursday meant that I would barely get enough sleep before I had to be at work again. I wondered if I dare ask if I could switch nights from Wednesday to Monday. Before I had a chance, he said, "How's about going for a couple of beers after work tonight?"

"Uh...Oh," I said, struggling for a tactful excuse. "Thanks, but I can't. I have an appointment. And thanks for switching me to Thursdays," I added, wanting to steer the conversation in a different direction.

"Yeah, sure," he said sullenly.

There were customers in Garland's Floristry when I returned after work. "I can take the job," I said when the last one, a gray-haired man who bought a dozen roses, left.

Bev Garland beamed. "That's great! You've already helped me, you know."

"How?"

"By staying open while I waited for you, I picked up more

business. I should have realized that men would be good last-minute customers late on Fridays. I sold two dozen roses after five o'clock. Can you believe it? Either those guys were in the doghouse or they just remembered a birthday or an anniversary. Whatever the reason, from now on I'm going to stay open until six on Fridays!"

Her enthusiasm made me smile. "What time do you want me here next Friday?"

"Come at eight thirty so I can show you around and explain a few things. There really isn't much for you to learn. Mostly you'll be answering the phone and waiting on customers so I can be free to work in the back. After next week you can work from nine to five thirty."

I wanted to ask when I would get paid but decided that it would make the wrong impression; however, there was nothing I could do about the negative impression my address made. When I wrote it on a piece of paper, along with my telephone and Social Security numbers, I saw Bev's mouth pucker with surprise. But no comment was made, which reinforced my feeling that I was going to like this job.

Working Saturday and Sunday would have made the weekend pass quickly if I hadn't been so anxious for the results of the ultrasound test. Although I was exhausted from standing at a register both days, I slept poorly at night, battling worry and bad dreams. Then on Monday, after waiting endlessly on hold, my anxiety was swept away in seconds. "The results of your ultrasound test are positive," a doctor said. "The baby seems fine."

"Thank you, thank you," I said, so elated that I didn't realize until after I hung up that I hadn't caught the physician's name; nor had I asked if he knew the baby's sex. Somehow it seemed unnatural to know.

The baby is fine, the baby is fine. I couldn't stop saying it to myself: *The baby is fine.* Never had I felt such joyous relief!

I wanted to share the news, but I didn't have a single friend in Stalling. Ardelle, I thought, realizing with a pang how much I missed her. Despite the cost, I decided to call the laundromat. Ardelle always worked on Mondays.

Ardelle was delighted. "I'm so happy for you, Sara," she said, her voice bubbling in a way that made me picture her smile. "How have you been doin'?"

I told her about my job at Magnolia's and the new one I was starting at the flower shop. Then I asked how everyone was in Owings. "The girls are fine. Darlene made the honor roll again, and she's the captain of the girls' softball team. But Glenn's a real handful. He's gettin' some mouth on him."

Like Ronnie Lee, I thought. Out of politeness I asked about my brother. "He still ain't workin', but he has a chance for a job in April. It's been rough."

I imagined Ronnie Lee drinking away the idle hours, and shuddered.

"I know this call's expensive, but I have to tell you what's happenin' with Mrs. Rutland. She goes to Tully's house every mornin' and sits there all day like she expects him to come walkin' through the door. She's been doin' this since the funeral, but they were able to keep it quiet for a while. And that ain't all. She won't allow any of Tully's stuff to be sold: not the cars, not the tools, not the property, nothin'. People have been makin' inquiries, especially about the cars. Mrs. Rutland wants everything to stay like it is, like a museum.

"You know how I thought you should stay and make a claim on Tully's estate for the baby? Now I think maybe you did the right thing by leavin'. That estate is goin' to be tied up for as long as Mrs. Rutland lives, and her people live long. Her mama was close to a hundred when she died, her daddy was in his nineties. Mrs. Rutland is sixty-three. Jimmy's been tellin' people that he'll be an old man before he sees a cent of what Tully left, if he ever does."

"Mrs. Rutland has always held on to things," I said, feeling the scars I bore as proof. "She was never one for letting go."

Saying goodbye was as hard as it had been in Owings, perhaps harder. I wept when I put the receiver down. Losing the comforting warmth of Ardelle's voice made me feel the depth of my loneliness. I could almost understand Mrs. Rutland's compulsion to sit in Tully's house. Sometimes I caught myself thinking that he really wasn't dead, that he would come and rescue me from Lemon Street and food stamps and Magnolia's.

But that wasn't going to happen. Tully was dead and it was up to me to rescue myself and our baby. What Ardelle told me confirmed that I had done the right thing by moving. "We'll make it," I said, patting my belly with one hand while I wiped my tears away with the other.

***

Coming home at eleven thirty at night was the most difficult part of the passing weeks. Even with the car doors locked and the windows closed, my pulse started racing as I approached the Fruit Belt. At that hour there was little traffic; occasionally my car was the only one on the street. My knuckles were white with tension as I gripped the steering wheel when I had to stop for a traffic light; getting safely from the car to the house put me in a state close to panic. Every sound, every shadow was a threat. Taking only a few dollars and my driver's license in my purse didn't ease my fears: I could as easily be attacked for a lack of money as for the possession of it. And what Joletta had told me was always in my mind: I was living in a neighborhood ruled by drugs. I was living in the Market.

I wanted something I could use to protect myself. A gun was too expensive, and I knew too little about Mace to trust it. Then I thought of a roofer's knife, of the curved steel blade that could slice through the thickest shingles as if they were made of butter. The knife I bought looked so much like my daddy's that for a moment it seemed as menacing as it was in my childhood, but my pulse still raced when I drove down Lemon Street late at night praying that all the traffic lights would be green. Still, the knife was a comfort to have in my hand as I hurried from my car to the safety of the house.

Although coming home was a trial, I much preferred working

nights at Magnolia's. On Tuesday and Wednesday evenings another woman, Lolita Huggins, and I straightened stock and put out new merchandise in the lingerie and ladies' departments. "Lolita?" I said when we were introduced.

"That's right," said Lolita, a heavyset woman in her thirties whose skin was a chestnut brown. "My mama heard the name Lolita around the time I was born and she liked it. When I got to high school, I found out that Lolita was the name of a book and a movie. Since I wasn't goin' to change my name, I decided not to look at either one in case I didn't like what they were about."

Lolita offered this information with a good-natured smile. She worked only nights, explaining, "My husband works days on construction. He minds the kids while I'm here. We're strict with them; kids can turn fast if they're not watched. I didn't give birth so one of mine would take the wrong path."

I felt as if I was on probation with Lolita until I proved myself to be a steady worker. Once Lolita was sure of me, we often worked side-by-side, chatting while we put out new merchandise. One night my eyes began burning and tearing while I removed blouses from the plastic in which they were wrapped. "It's chemicals," Lolita said. "A lot of this stuff is treated, 'specially the permanent press. I've opened some plastic bags and nearly passed out from the fumes."

"I'm pregnant," I said.

Lolita beamed. "I knew it!"

I thought my Magnolia's apron still concealed my condition. "How did you know?"

"You got the look and you're gettin' the walk. After four kids, I'm an expert."

"Maybe the chemicals could hurt the baby."

"I was workin' here when I was pregnant with my last one and he's fine," Lolita said. "First thing when I go on my break, I wash my hands. And I always wash whatever I buy before anyone in my family wears it."

One night I asked Lolita about Mrs. Early. "From what I've seen, she runs the store," I said. "Linwood Cagle is next to worthless."

"You got it!"

"Then why isn't Mrs. Early the manager?"

She didn't answer right away. Instead, she looked at me as if she were making a decision. "Magnolia's has only white managers," she said finally. "Mrs. Early can never be a manager at a Magnolia's because she's black. When the manager position opened up and they brought Cagle in here, she saw how worthless he was and she gave him notice that she was leavin'. Someone who saw it told me that he was sobbin' and pleadin' like a child when he was beggin' her to stay. She agreed on the condition that she was raised to management. Somehow he was able to get her promoted to save his own sorry ass. She was runnin' the store; without her, he would've sunk for sure."

"Thank you for telling me," I said, not knowing what else to say.

"The big chains like K-Mart let blacks in management, probably because they're all over the country. Magnolia's is just a small, Southern chain. Nobody pays attention to them so they get away with a lot."

"Like not having enough merchandise for the specials they advertise."

"And substitutin' cheaper stuff on the first day of a sale." She shook her head. "People ain't stupid. They're startin' to catch on. This store has been losin' business; it used to be a lot busier."

Lolita had an obsession for finding misplaced items. "Lookit this," she said on the first night I worked, holding up a pair of navy slacks. "A size sixteen in with the size eights! Sometimes people is just careless. But sometimes they do it to hide the item until the end of the week when they can afford to buy it so they can save the two dollar layaway charge."

One evening I found a glob of chewed gum stuck to a pair of bikini underpants. Lolita wasn't surprised. "I don't put nothin' past people. They're gettin' worse and worse. If the world is in anywhere near the mess that's made in this store, then we're sure in a whole lot of trouble!"

Since I had been working at Magnolia's, I had seen more than enough to agree.

Fridays were the high point of my weeks. From my first day working in the flower shop I felt at ease waiting on customers and answering the phone. In the morning, Bev Garland was always in the back workroom designing arrangements for delivery later in the day. But during lulls in the afternoons, we often talked. I had never met anyone who was as open about her life as Bev. "All the settlement money from my divorce is in this shop," Bev said one afternoon. "If it's a success, it'll be the only good thing to come out of that marriage besides the boys."

Bev has two sons, both in college. "My ex-husband cheated on me for years, but I waited until the youngest went away to school before filing for a divorce. I didn't want him home in case it was messy. But it wasn't, which made me think I should have done it years before. So much time wasted!" She sighed. "The funny thing is that the boys knew it all the time. They were waiting for it to happen."

Bev chuckled bitterly. "You know, with all the cheating my ex-husband did, he didn't learn much. He was lousy in bed from the day I married him until the day I filed for the divorce twenty-three years later."

I found myself telling Bev things that I never thought I would tell anyone. I told Bev how I met Tully and what happened when he came back from Vietnam. For the first time I talked about his death; the words came freely, spilling out as if they'd been waiting for release. Bev reached for my hand. "I'm so sorry," she said with such sincerity that I choked back tears.

My first paycheck from my Friday job was for $31.40. "I had to take out $2.11 for Social Security and $.49 for Medicare," Bev explained. "The state and federal taxes weren't deducted because the amounts were negligible, so you should put a little money aside to pay your taxes at the end of the year."

The check didn't quite cover the cost of a maternity outfit. The maternity clothes at Magnolia's didn't look like they'd last through a half-dozen washings, so I went to K-Mart and bought a top and slacks for $16.99 each. I found three more tops and another pair of slacks that I put on layaway rather than use my Visa card, which was paid up. The Visa card was my insurance, the only easily accessible credit I had in case of an emergency, and I wanted to keep the balance at zero. The layaway terms were three dollars down and a minimum payment of twenty percent of the total every two weeks for ten weeks. Since I needed the clothes as soon as possible, I planned to cover what I owed with my next two paychecks from the flower shop. As I filled out the layaway form, it occurred to me that I had lived most of my life on the layaway plan, struggling to get things by paying for them a little bit at a time until they were mine.

After so many months of hiding my condition, wearing the new maternity clothes made me feel as though I finally had permission to enjoy my pregnancy. When I came into the flower shop wearing my new top and slacks, Bev said, "How nice you look. You're just glowing."

Bev wasn't the only one who noticed. Leroy Bunting, the owner of Bunting's Delivery Service, stopped short when he came into the shop to pick up plants and flowers for delivery. A tall, lean black man who walked with a bounce in his step, he always called out his motto, *Bunting delivers*, when he came in. "Bunting de…" he started to say automatically Then he smiled. "I got to remember to look before I talk."

"You mean there are some things that Bunting doesn't deliver?" I said, remembering how he'd boasted the previous week that he'd deliver anything.

"Bunting delivers *most* things," he said, laughing.

Before I left the shop that day Bev offered me an African violet. I hesitated, not sure that I should accept. The previous Friday I had mentioned that all of my violets had died when I moved; I didn't want charity. "Take it," Bev said. "It's my way of saying thank you for the great job you're doing with the plants."

I wasn't the only one living at 936 Lemon Street who received a gift that afternoon. As I was unlocking the front door, I overheard Joletta say, "Everybody talks about how Darrell Lawson gives heavy gold necklaces to the girls he gets pregnant. *So I'm askin' you again, are you pregnant?"*

"No!"

"You better not be!" Joletta said. "Give that necklace back and stay away from him! If you don't, you'll end up bein' like all the other girls in gold chains livin' in the Grady Street project with babies!"

I hurried upstairs with the African violet, remembering what Joletta said about beauty not always being easy.

***

The weather turned unseasonably warm the last day in March. There were no screens on the windows, and by late afternoon my apartment was suffocating. Nauseated from the heat, I met Joletta in the driveway when she came home from work and asked if she had a key to unlock the basement door. "There are no screens on my windows," I said.

"There aren't any screens. The frames rotted and Daniels wouldn't replace 'em."

"What did the other tenants do? It's stifling up there."

"They bought those adjustable screens, you know, the kind you insert in the window," she said. "I see you're expectin'. When is the baby due?"

"The end of June."

Maybe it was my imagination, but Joletta seemed to react to my pregnancy as an unwelcome surprise.

I had barely enough time to get to work. During my break I looked in Magnolia's hardware department, but they didn't carry the screens. In a way, I was almost glad. Tomorrow I would call Grover Daniels and demand screens because the living conditions were unhealthy. Confident that I could handle the situation, I told Lolita about it while we were unpacking bras. "Who's your landlord?" she asked.

"Grover Daniels. If he doesn't get me screens, I'm going to file a complaint against him."

"That Daniels, he's the worst! Last year they did a series on TV about slumlords in Stalling. They said his properties are worth over two million dollars and that he's been cited for more housing violations than any other property owner in town, black or white. My mother-in-law once rented from him. He gave her nothin' but grief! There are hundreds of complaints against Grover Daniels, and he weasels out of every one of 'em."

"Not this one," I said determinedly.

Early the following morning I called Daniels. "I need screens. Yesterday it was eighty-nine degrees in this apartment."

"You don't need screens to open the windows. The windows work fine."

"This isn't a barn. I'm not keeping windows open without screens."

"Then keep 'em closed."

"The heat is making me sick. I'm pregnant."

"Oh," he said. There was a long pause. "The rent will be adjusted when the baby comes."

"What do you mean *adjusted*?"

"The rate you're gettin' is for one person, not two. And don't forget, you got ten dollars knocked off besides."

"There were two people living here, so I should be paying less. What about the screens?"

"Open the windows or keep 'em closed, your choice."

"I'll report you to the Board of Health."

"You do that and you'll be lookin' at an eviction notice!"

"You can't evict me for reporting you!"

"No," he said. "But I can evict you for ruinin' the front lawn by parkin' your car on it at night."

"You're not serious," I said, stunned. "There was no lawn, just a couple blades of grass and weeds!"

"I got a picture of this house with a lawn that I'll be happy to take to court," he said, his voice full with satisfaction.

Later at work, I told Lolita what had happened, but talking about it didn't give me any relief; my anger wouldn't rest. I was as furious with myself as I was with Grover Daniels. If I hadn't rented the apartment so hastily I wouldn't be in this position. I felt as if I had placed myself in his trap.

Sleep that night was impossible. The air in the apartment simmered, and when I wasn't chewing over my confrontation with Daniels, I was worrying about how I could manage to live on my new food stamp allotment of forty-two dollars a month. I had called Frieda Stowe after receiving the stamps in the mail and was told that Ms. Stowe was now a supervisor; my new case worker was Daphne Slovene, who was attending a meeting all day. Also in the mail was a new Medicaid card, valid for the month of April, and a bill for $288 for my car insurance that had been forwarded from Owings. I had spent most of the afternoon calling agencies in Stalling to find less expensive insurance. In order to get payments that I could afford, I had to settle for the lowest possible coverage, less than half of what I had before, at a premium of $33.92 a month, which came to $407.04 a year. "This low coverage and the monthly payments is the least economical way to go," the agent said.

"Don't you think I realize that? I'd take the better coverage with fewer payments if I could afford it," I said, stifling the urge to tell him that being poor didn't mean I was stupid.

Still wide awake at dawn, I rose wearily and tried to work out a budget. One of my paychecks from the flower shop could cover most of the car insurance payment, but that would leave only $94 from my Friday job to spread over four weeks for food and other necessities. I expected my telephone bill to be close to fifty dollars to cover the cost of hook-up charges; my electric would be another fifty, if not more, and I still had to make another payment to get the maternity clothes I needed out of layaway. Gasoline for the car was running fifteen dollars a week, and I needed more than one $253 paycheck from Magnolia's to cover the rent.

I stared at the figures. Not even a magician could make this work. On an impulse I added up the deductions that had been taken out of my pay from Magnolia's and the flower shop for Social Security and Medicare. The total was so high—$34.50 every two weeks, $69 a month—that I reworked the figures, thinking that I had made an error. There was no mistake. Nearly seventy dollars a month was being deducted from my pay to take care of old people, and I couldn't afford to buy food for myself!

There had to be a mistake in calculating the amount of food stamps I had been given. "No, there's no mistake," said Daphne Slovene, whose voice sounded young when I called social services during my lunch break at Magnolia's. "The forty-two dollars you received in stamps is correct."

"But it's not enough," I said. "I can't manage on that amount."

"Your application says you're pregnant. Have you applied to WIC?"

"No," I said. Applying for food stamps and Medicaid was the most degrading experience I had ever had; I wasn't about to subject myself to something like that again.

But the two adjustable screens I bought at a hardware store after work came to fifteen dollars, and the groceries I purchased afterward at Food Lion consumed over half of my food stamp allotment for the month. Bitterly, I realized that WIC was no longer an option; I had to apply if I wanted to survive.

With a feeling of defeat I called WIC the following morning during my break. "Are you on Medicaid?" the receptionist asked.

"Yes."

"Then you qualify. We have three clinics a week: Monday, Wednesday, and Friday."

I made an appointment for Monday morning. "Be sure to bring your Medicaid card," the receptionist said.

The WIC clinic was in a squat brick building that had **PLUMMET COUNTY HEALTH DEPARTMENT** in bold block letters above the front door. At a few minutes before nine, I entered a spacious reception area that had bright posters hanging on cheerful yellow walls. Two playpens were tucked into corners of the room, and toys that had overflowed from a large wooden toy box were piled nearby. After I filled out several forms, I was ushered into a small room by a young black woman who took my height and weight and pricked my finger to get a few drops of blood that would tell if I was anemic. "You can go back to the waiting room and the nutritionist will call you," she said.

The waiting room was filling with women in various stages of pregnancy; some looked shockingly young. After a short wait my name was called. I followed a woman of about fifty whose dark hair was streaked with gray into a simply furnished office "I'm Mrs. Chalmers," she said after we were seated. "This may seem strange, but could you please tell me what you ate yesterday for breakfast, lunch, and dinner?"

I hesitated. I felt like saying, *It's none of your business.*

"Really, I'm not asking to pry. I'm here to help you."

"For breakfast I had corn flakes and a banana," I began reluctantly. "For lunch, a peanut-butter-and-jelly sandwich, an apple, and cookies. I had spaghetti for dinner."

"What was on the spaghetti?"

"Tomato sauce."

"Any meat?"

"No."

"Do you recall having any juice?"

I shook my head.

"You need a minimum of six servings of fruits and vegetables a day," Mrs. Chalmers said. "Even if I count the tomato sauce as a serving, you had only half the minimum amount."

"Will that hurt the baby?"

"It won't help, and it could certainly contribute to your discomfort, particularly in regard to constipation."

I could feel the skin on my face color. "Fruits and vegetables are expensive."

"Try to buy whatever is on sale, and what is in season. Look for generic and store brands in canned goods, which are always cheaper.

Today I'll give you vouchers that you can use to get juice. A serving of juice can be substituted for a serving of fruit."

Mrs. Chalmers discussed protein with me, which my diet was also lacking in sufficient amounts. "I'm going to give you two months' worth of checks today that will help you get the protein you need. You're allowed three checks a month. You can't use a portion of a check: the check has to be turned in when you use it. Most grocery stores in Stalling accept WIC checks. You must buy the cheapest brands, and any cereal you chose must have no sugar. Your corn flakes are acceptable, but you'd be better off nutritionally with a whole grain cereal."

I waited until I was in the car before examining the checks. The first was for two gallons of milk, one dozen eggs, two forty-six-ounce cans of single strength fruit juice or two twelve-ounce cans of concentrated frozen juice, and thirty-six ounces of WIC-approved cereal. The second check was for one gallon of milk, two pounds of WIC-approved cheese, eighteen ounces of peanut butter or one pound of dried beans, and two forty-six-ounce cans of fruit juice. The last monthly check was for one gallon of milk, two pounds of cheese, and two cans of juice.

Food stamps and now WIC checks. I would feel like shriveling up at the grocery check- out counter for sure. But I had no choice, I needed the help. At least at WIC I had been treated kindly.

A check from Altavista Gardens for $450, the refund of my security deposit for my apartment in Owings, was in the mailbox when I got home. Although I would have liked to send the full amount to Ardelle to deposit in the savings account for the baby, I decided to send $350 and to deposit the remaining one hundred dollars in the new account I had opened in Stalling so that I would have the security of one month's rent in the bank. *I wish I could send more,* I wrote in the letter that I enclosed with the money order, *but money is tight here. Although it isn't much, it's a good feeling to know that there's a little something set aside for the baby. I hope things are better at home since I talked to you. Give my love to everyone. Please write if you can.*

I addressed the envelope to the laundromat, trying not to think about how much I missed Ardelle and the girls. I told myself that it was ridiculous, but I had an awful feeling that I wouldn't see them again.

***

I had never met anyone as persistent as the nurse in the hospital clinic. On my April visit the nurse had asked if I had signed up for the childbirth classes, and now on this May visit she was asking again. "A new class is starting next week on Tuesday night at seven o'clock. You can sign up today."

"I can't," I said. "I work on Tuesday nights."

"There will be another class starting the following week on Thursday night, May twenty-first."

"I can't."

"There's no charge for these classes, and taking them will make your labor so much easier," she said. "Maybe you can get your schedule switched."

"Maybe," I said, unwilling to admit that I didn't have anyone to ask to be my coach.

The nurse left the examining room with her mouth fixed in a line of frustration. I'm sure she thought I was being either impossibly stubborn or truly ignorant.

As I expected, the doctor who came in was one I hadn't seen before. He had a long thin face and a pleasant smile. "My name is Dr. Bennett," he said. "How are you feeling?"

He was the first of the three young doctors who had come to examine me at the clinic to ask that simple question. "Fine," I said, instantly warming to him. "My back seems to be aching more, though."

"That's normal," he said, scanning the nurse's notes. "The weight of the baby puts a strain on your back. Try not to be on your feet for long periods of time."

It was hard not to laugh as I imagined how Linwood Cagle and

Mrs. Early would react if I followed his advice at Magnolia's; however, I was concerned when Dr. Bennett told me to make an appointment to come back in two weeks. "Two weeks?" I said anxiously.

"There's nothing to worry about," he said. "You're coming into the home stretch."

"And I have the stretch marks to prove it!" I said, smiling with relief.

It did seem closer now. The baby had begun moving at regular times during the day, almost as if it were on a schedule, and it seemed to respond to music, particularly the Elvis Presley discs I played. I had begun thinking of it as *her*, a little girl, and had decided on calling her Audrey, which was Mrs. Hartman's name, the teacher whom I had adored. Audrey Barefield. At least in Stalling the name Barefield wasn't an ugly joke. My daughter wouldn't be marked with two names as I had been—Sara Jean—the second name sticking to me like a label marked *TRASH* until I had it removed legally.

I was thinking about the baby when I returned to the apartment. My baby wasn't going to come home to these ugly walls, I decided. Sometimes dented cans of paint were reduced at Magnolia's. I would check it out tonight.

At work Lolita had so much news that I almost forgot about the paint. "You must know Nikki Goins, the girl who works days on checkout," Lolita said.

"Yes, she's fast," I said, thinking that Nikki still seemed to go out of her way to be rude to me.

"Not fast enough for the new cameras."

"What new cameras?"

"On Sunday night, after everyone was out of the store, cameras were put in to watch the registers; they're hidden in the ceilin'. Everythin' that happens at the registers is filmed. I hear there's a monitor like a television in the manager's office. Nikki was caught on Monday. She was runnin' two items over the scanner as one— socks, underwear, lipsticks, you name it! She thought she could get away with it because it was Mrs. Early's day off. Her line was packed with her friends. They had this scheme goin': they'd get two items, keep one, and bring the other one back later for a cash refund. Then they split what they got with Nikki."

"What's going to happen to her?" I said, deciding that it might be best not to mention that I had seen Nikki doubling up items.

"The po-lice came and arrested her. They got her cold, everythin' on film. And she ain't the only one who's in trouble. The big management was here. They chewed Cagle out for not seein' what Nikki was doin' right under his nose! He's been switched to nights. The talk is he's on probation."

I groaned. "I'm in for it."

Lolita's eyes widened. "What you got to do with Nikki?"

"Not Nikki," I said. "Cagle. He's been giving me grief since the day my pregnancy started showing, hassling me over anything he can find to pick on. He acts like I deliberately got into this condition to annoy him. Last Thursday my register was off thirty-six cents. He wouldn't stop chewing me out until I handed him a couple of quarters I had in my pocket. 'This will cover it,' I said. I told him he could keep the change. We were short two people working registers all week so I knew he wouldn't fire me."

"Shhhhh," Lolita warned. "Here he comes."

Paler than usual in his green Magnolia's shirt and rumpled khaki pants, Linwood Cagle came up to us looking like he was suffering from a bad case of heartburn. "Sara, get over to housewares. You're going to work there tonight," he said.

"I need her here," Lolita said. "There's a new shipment of shorts and blouses to put out, and the bras are a mess."

"She's going to housewares," he snapped.

I followed him, deliberately staying several steps behind. When we had gone past housewares to the aisles that held cleaning supplies and I saw a dolly loaded with cartons, I knew I was in trouble. "I want you to redo these two end caps," he said, "the bleach in one and the detergent in the other." He reached for a carton that held four one-gallon containers of bleach. Despite his effort to handle the box easily, the weight of it forced him to let it down with a *thunk* on the floor.

"How much does that box weigh?" I asked.

Ignoring my question, he removed a utility knife from his back pocket. "You put closed cartons on the bottom. Cut the others like this before stacking them," he said, making diagonal cuts on two sides and a straight, low cut several inches above the bottom of the box. "Be careful that you don't cut through the bottles."

"She ain't cuttin' through nothin," said a voice behind us.

We turned and saw Lolita, who was looking at Cagle with disgust, as if he were a cockroach sitting on a cupcake. "Go back to your department," he said.

"Not without Sara."

"Either you go back there now or you're fired!" he said, the skin on his neck turning a spotty red.

Lolita remained where she was standing, solid as a tree. "I bet this store could get closed down for forcin' a pregnant woman to tote them heavy boxes like you're orderin' her to do. For sure you'll be in trouble. And what if movin' them boxes causes her to lose the baby? Then you'll have a big-time lawsuit. Instead of firin' me, you can thank me for savin' your sorry ass!" she said. "C'mon, Sara, we got shorts and blouses to put out."

"Thank you, Lolita," I said as we walked back to our department. "I owe you one."

"You don't owe me nothin'," Lolita said "I just did what any friend would do."

I couldn't say anything. Suddenly I felt deeply ashamed.

***

I found the letter in my mailbox when I came home from work on the twenty-first of May. The postmark on the envelope was from Baltimore, Maryland.

May 19, 1992

Dear Sara,

I don't know how to start this letter. I guess I should begin by telling you that I had to spend the money that was in the savings account for the baby. I know how you were counting on it and I feel terrible, I'm really sorry. But I had no choice.

This next thing I'm going to tell you is so hard that I can't even think about it without crying. Ronnie Lee raped Darlene. Two weeks ago Friday I had to work late at the laundromat. When I got home no one was there but Darlene. She was in her room on her bed crying in this awful way, a tearing sound like nothing I ever heard. She wouldn't talk and I couldn't quiet her. I was close to my wit's end, ready to call the rescue squad, when she told me.

I didn't cry then. That night was probably the only time I didn't cry because it seems like I've been crying ever since.

I changed the sheets on her bed while she took a shower. After I gave her one of my tranquilizers and got her to bed, I took the rifle out of the back of my bedroom closet, loaded it, and went into the living room to sit and wait.

Glenn was staying over at a friend's house. Lisa was working at Gino's Pizza and wouldn't be home until midnight.

Ronnie Lee came home drunk at about ten. When he saw the gun he thought I was fooling, so I fired a shot that missed his head by inches to show him I meant business. Now I'm sorry I didn't take better aim. He sobered up right quick. I told him that he didn't deserve to live for what he done to Darlene and that I was going to shoot him in the heart because he broke his daughter's heart and my heart. I told him that he was the worst bastard that ever lived. He *just stood there crying while I was yelling and pointing the gun, crying and begging like a big old baby. He was a disgusting sight, such a stupid slobbering mess, that I decided he wasn't worth the jail time I'd get for killing him. As much as I wanted to pull that trigger, Darlene needed me, so I told him to leave and never come back.*

But I knew he would come back. Maybe not that night, but he'd be back. I wouldn't have a moment's peace knowing that he was anywhere near Darlene and Lisa. That's when I realized that the only way I could be sure of keeping the girls safe was to leave town.

I called my mama and told her what had happened and what I was going to do. She came right over and gave me all the money she had in the house—twenty-three dollars. I had only a few dollars in my purse. Mama said I didn't even have enough to get across the state. Then I remembered the bank account with the five hundred fifty dollars in it.

Lisa and Mama helped me pack. In the morning I picked up Glenn, went to the bank and took out the money, and left Owings. I drove for four days, one eye on the road and the other eye on Darlene sitting next to me in the front seat, putting as big a distance as I could between us and Ronnie Lee. When we got to where we are now, the Salvation Army put us in contact with a shelter for battered women, and the shelter took us in. I never told you this out of respect for Ronnie Lee being your brother, and also because I was so ashamed and scared, but over the years he beat me real bad.

The shelter has saved us. Volunteer tutors are helping the children keep up with their schooling, and counselors are helping them and me with our other problems. Next week I'm starting a course to become a beautician. I always did like doing hair.

When you left Owings I missed you something terrible.

Now I miss you and Mama and my sisters. I feel like I've lost all of my best friends. I feel like I've lost almost everyone I love.

But the hardest thing is seeing what's happened to Darlene. Even though you tried to hide it, I know you was always partial to her. I never faulted you for it. Darlene was the quickest of my three children and the most fun to be with, and she was growing up to be as beautiful as your mama was in the pictures I saw of her when she was young. That girl is gone now. Ronnie Lee killed something in her that she'll never get back. Darlene is going to be thirteen next week and she has the eyes of an old woman—the light in them is gone.

I can't stop blaming myself. If I had left Ronnie Lee years ago, this never would have happened. The counselor here at the shelter keeps telling me that I have to look forward and not back. It ain't easy.

Tomorrow is Mother's Day. I'll be aching to hug my mama, but I'll try to look happy for the sake of the children.

You won't get this letter from the city where we're living. Even though I've told the people at the shelter that Ronnie Lee doesn't know where you are, they're taking care of the mailing so our whereabouts can't be traced. They say it's best not to take any chances.

Sara, not a day goes by that I don't think of you and the baby. You were as close to me as my sisters. I pray that someday we'll see each other again, and that you'll forgive me.

Love always,
Ardelle

I sat holding the letter, tears streaming down my cheeks. Darlene. Ardelle. And there were other thoughts, darker, a memory so long repressed that it came back with a sickening shock: my daddy coming into my bedroom, filling the darkness with the stench of liquor, then my mama coming in and pulling him away as he was about to touch me, the cracking sound Mama's jaw made when he hit her, the guilt Mama made me carry for the missing teeth.

The two small screens I had bought weren't enough to catch a breeze. But even if it hadn't been uncomfortably warm in the apartment, I doubt that I could have slept anyway. There was too much to think about, too much to worry about, too much to grieve over.

The hard night I spent must have shown on my face. "Did the baby give you a difficult night?" Bev said when I came into the shop Friday morning.

As burdened as I was, I looked at her, this clean decent woman, and I couldn't say a word about Ardelle's letter and my own dark memories. "The heat," I said. "My apartment really heats up."

"Don't you have air conditioning? It can get brutal here in the summer."

"Air conditioning on Lemon Street? I'm lucky that I have windows." I tried to laugh, but it sounded forced.

"I have an old air conditioner in my basement that still works. Do you want it?"

"I'd love it, but I'm afraid I can't afford it."

"Oh, I don't want to sell it to you! It's just a loan for as long as you want it. My boys are both home now. When would a convenient time be for them to bring it over?"

"I don't work on Monday."

"Then Monday it is," she said. "I have some good news. I got two weddings this week, one of them really big—a bridal party of twelve, a guest list of three hundred, flowers for the church and the country club."

"That's wonderful!" I said, truly happy for her.

"It's a relief! I used to do a lot of weddings, operating out of my house, and I had built up a nice word-of-mouth business. It was on the basis of that business that I opened this shop. Then I stopped getting weddings. People must have been afraid that my prices were no longer competitive. But now they are calling again, thank goodness!"

I tended all the plants in the shop that day as I usually did. The store was much busier than it had been when I first started working there, but I also managed to clean the display shelves and dust the ceramic containers though it wasn't expected of me. "It looks terrific," Bev said when she came out of the work room and saw me wiping the last shelf, "but you're doing too much."

"No," I said, wishing I could do more to repay her for her kindness. "It's hardly anything at all."

Bev's sons arrived at the apartment with the air conditioner early Monday evening. I was glad that I had painted the walls. Even though the blue was a darker shade than I would have chosen if I had been able to afford an undamaged can, the paint covered most of the ugly splotches. Andy, the taller of the two young men, was fair like Bev. I guessed that Tom, who had brown hair and eyes, looked like Bev's ex-husband.

They installed the unit in one of the living room windows. "Thanks," I said when they were finished. "I want you to treat yourselves." I started to hand Tom a twenty-dollar bill.

"No, thank you, ma'am," Andy said, putting his arm out before Tom could accept the money. "We're under strict orders not to take anything or there will be hell to pay."

"Are you sure?"

"Positive," Andy said, giving me a grin that reminded me of Bev.

The air conditioning unit was large, and it cooled the apartment right away. That night I slept better than I had in weeks.

***

I had always assumed that if I was attacked on Lemon Street it would happen at night, darkness giving the attacker the advantages of cover and surprise. So when I came home from work on the Saturday of Memorial Day weekend and pulled into the driveway, I didn't notice anything other than that Joletta's car wasn't there. It was five thirty in the afternoon, sunny and hot. The air conditioner in my car wasn't working, and I was thinking gratefully of the air conditioner Bev had loaned me. All I wanted to do was turn on the unit and sit with my aching feet up.

He came out from behind a scraggly bush next to the house, a skinny youth of about seventeen wearing baggy jeans and a filthy T-shirt that hung on his bony shoulders. His face was glistening with sweat and the brown skin on his arms looked ashy. I smelled him before I saw him, a strong sour smell that made me turn as I was pulling the door handle of the car to make sure it was locked. "Gimme yo purse," he said, coming toward me, a knife with a long blade in his left hand, his right hand outstretched.

I had planned to go shopping on Monday for some things for the baby at Memorial Day sales and had seventy-five dollars, money I had withdrawn from the bank, in a zippered compartment in my purse; a money order to pay my rent was also in the compartment. The roofer's knife was in another compartment, more like an open pocket, the blade pointing down. "C'mon, c'mon," he said, moving closer as I backed away, his bloodshot eyes glancing nervously toward the street.

It would be impossible to replace the money. "This is my only summer purse, my only one," I said, as desperate as he was. I clutched my purse, a leather-trimmed straw bag. "I'll give you my wallet…everything in it…my money and my Visa card…you can have it all…"

Still inching back, I opened my purse and thrust my hand inside, grabbing the wood handle of the roofer's knife. "Here," I said.

My arm shot towards him, the curved blade of the knife catching the skin of his outstretched hand between his thumb and index finger. The boy's body jerked as the blade slit open his palm like a ripe piece of fruit. Blood gushed from the wound as I started to run to the safety of the house. Somehow I managed to get the door unlocked, my heart pounding so hard I could feel a rush of blood in my ears.

After I locked myself inside the apartment, I collapsed in a chair panting, my heart still beating wildly. There was a sudden, sharp pain in my abdomen. No, no, it's too early, I thought, noticing that my maternity top and slacks were spattered with blood. I felt the baby move and forced myself to take deep breaths. I had to be calm, I had to think clearly. The police. If I called the police and told them what had happened, they probably wouldn't look for the boy. Joletta said the police didn't care what happened in the Fruit Belt. But they'd have to file a report, and they'd talk about it because I was white and very pregnant. It was the kind of story newspaper and television reporters would be interested in: PREGNANT WOMAN DEFENDS HERSELF AGAINST THIEF. *The Owings Gazette* was partial to that type of story, and it would surely be in *The Gazette* because it happened in Virginia. The Rutlands would see it, and people would talk about it to Ronnie Lee.

But if I didn't report it to the police, what would happen then? I hurt the boy badly. And I didn't have the roofer's knife. I dropped it when I ran to the house. The boy was alone and he looked sick, like he was strung out on drugs. He'd have to get his hand sewn up. No matter where he went to get it fixed, even to a hospital, he wouldn't tell how it happened because I had acted in self-defense when he tried to rob me. But would he come back to get me for what I had done to him? Did he have friends who would avenge him? He looked desperate, and he was nervous and filthy. He looked like a boy who needed help and wasn't getting any from anyone, family or friends. The police wouldn't protect me if I told them because I lived in the Fruit Belt. That settled it: since the police wouldn't do anything for me anyway, I wouldn't call them. No one would know except me and the boy, and he wouldn't tell.

It was still light out when I went back outside. There was no traffic; Lemon Street looked deserted, as it did earlier. I found the roofer's knife on the ground near the front of my car and slipped a plastic bag over my hand before I picked it up, afraid to come in contact with the boy's blood. Rather than wash the knife, I decided to throw it out and buy a new one. As much as I hated to spend the money, the few dollars it would cost wasn't worth the risk of getting AIDS. I noticed blood splattered on the car. Tomorrow I would go to a cheap car wash that was near Magnolia's before I went to work.

As I climbed the stairs to my apartment, I happened to glance down at the roofer's knife and a thought occurred to me that made me smile: all my life I had struggled to be respectable, to be better than the name I carried, and a knife like my daddy's had rescued me.

I got out of my clothes and took a long bath, trying to relax. The fright didn't go away easily. I kept feeling the precariousness of my life, of the baby's life. If that boy had gotten my money, I couldn't have replaced it. But what had happened wasn't just about money. The scare could have cost me the baby. I was lucky. We were lucky. I had to keep that luck.

SUMMER, 1992

"Mah discount," the woman said with a deep Southern accent after I rang a total on her purchases." You didn't give me mah senior citizen discount." She was well dressed, in her late sixties. Her blond hair was professionally done, and her manicured nails were polished a true red, one of which was pointing at the monitor that read $14.96. "That total isn't correct."

I tried not to stare at the diamond in the woman's ring, which was the size of a large pea. I also noticed the embossed duck on her handbag. Purses with that duck on them were locked in a special glass case in the Belk store in Owings. Although I couldn't recall the brand name, I definitely remembered the prices: there wasn't one purse in that glass display case for less than two hundred dollars. "Today is Thursday," I said, thinking of the disproportionate chunk of money that was taken out of my paycheck for Social Security. "Senior citizen discounts are on Wednesdays."

"Ah you sure?" the woman said, her mouth twitching with irritation.

Instead of responding with a "Yes, ma'am" as I usually did, I lost what little patience I had left. I was tired of senior citizens pushing for discounts on days they weren't entitled to them, tired of belligerent teenagers arguing over prices, tired of customers commenting on my pregnancy. And I was tired of my back aching, of having indigestion, and of what seemed like a constant need to empty my bladder. "It was Thursday when I got up this morning, and I don't believe that's changed," I said.

The woman took her time removing money from her wallet. Finally she slapped a twenty-dollar bill on the counter to show her displeasure, a display I easily ignored. After working at Magnolia's for nearly four months, there was a lot I had learned to ignore.

I took care of another customer, a fellow who bought spackling paste and sandpaper, and barely glanced at the next one, a buxom woman wearing a denim blouse that was embroidered with metallic gold thread, before running her purchases—four mugs, a roll of gift wrap, and a bag of potato chips—over the scanner. "That'll be $20.94," I said, feeling that I needed to take a break again.

After the woman paid, I gave her a receipt and started wrapping the mugs in tissue paper. "This charge is wrong. It says $1.09 on this bag of potato chips, and I was charged $1.39!" the woman said, studying the register tape. Her r's sounded like awe's.

A Yankee. I had encountered enough Yankees working at Magnolia's to know that they generally weren't shy about showing their displeasure. I took the bag of potato chips and the register slip from the woman. "I'm sorry," I said, picking up a form to get the price changed in the computer. "You can get a refund at the service desk."

"Why do I have to take it to the service desk? Why can't you refund the money?"

"I'm not allowed," I said. "The register's already closed."

"Then open it!" the woman said, her voice carrying throughout the front of the store. "I shouldn't have to stand in line to get my money back when I was overcharged!"

"I wish I could, but it's against store rules."

The woman bristled. "That's ridiculous!"

Mrs. Early glided up to us. "Is there a problem here?" she said in a tone that could calm a tornado.

"I was overcharged, and she's telling me that she can't refund my money, that I have to go to the service desk!"

"That's correct," Mrs. Early said. "I'll take care of it for you right now. You can pick up your refund on your way out of the store. We're sorry it happened."

"Well," the woman said, somewhat mollified.

After my next customer, I signaled to Mrs. Early that I needed to take a break. It was after four o'clock, but I didn't think I could last until five.

I walked past cards and gift wrap, and was at cosmetics when I had a sudden pain that felt like a menstrual cramp, only much stronger. I gasped, steadying myself against a display rack. Delilah, the woman who usually worked at the service desk, was returning from a late break and hurried up to me. "You all right?" she said.

The past few weeks I'd had some minor pains, but this one was different. "I think my labor has started. Please tell Mrs. Early. I'm going to get my things and leave."

Besides my purse, there was nothing to remove from my locker other than an old pair of sneakers that I wore when my feet were especially swollen. I punched out for the last time, glad that I had made it to payday. Luckily, during my lunch hour I had gone to the bank and then to the post office to get a money order to pay my rent. It was as if someone were watching over me.

Mrs. Early was waiting at the bottom of the stairs. "Delilah told me that your labor has started. Will you be able to make it home on your own? I can drive you."

"Thanks, I'll manage," I said. "And thanks for being so understanding about my extra bathroom breaks."

Mrs. Early put her arm around me and walked me to the door. "I know you'll have a beautiful baby," she said, giving my shoulder a squeeze. "You're one of the best cashiers we've ever had. I knew you would be from your first day. I hope you'll be back."

"Not for a while," I said, hoping that day would never come.

Again, I was lucky. My next pain came while I was waiting at a traffic light on Lemon Street. I gripped the steering wheel and looked at the Blue Ridge Mountains in the distance. Tully, I thought. Tully was watching over me and the baby.

Joletta was already home. I explained that my labor had started, and we moved the cars. "How far apart are your pains?" Joletta said.

"Twenty minutes."

"I'll be here, so just holler if you need anythin'."

The suitcase the teachers at Creekside Elementary had given me had been packed for weeks. I took it out of the closet and set it by the door, ready to go. Then I called Bev at the flower shop to tell her that I wouldn't be in tomorrow. "Are you walking?" Bev said.

"Walking?"

"Yes, walking," Bev said. "My niece had a baby last month. She took one of those childbirth classes and was told that walking speeds up labor, so she walked. She had the baby in no time at all, maybe five or six hours from start to finish, and she's a tiny thing."

"I'll start walking now."

"How will you be getting to the hospital?"

"I'm going to take a cab."

"No, no," Bev said. "I'll take you. I'd come sit with you, but I have to get tomorrow's orders done tonight so I can start working on the arrangements for a wedding on Saturday. I'll be here at the shop until nine, at least. If I don't hear from you, I'll call you then."

After I hung up, I started walking. I walked back and forth, back and forth, around and around the small apartment, pausing only when I had a pain, then gripping whatever was close—the kitchen counter top, the bedpost, the railing on the white crib I bought for the baby—to help me through it. Not once did I consider resting. Each pain was harder than the last. I didn't want this labor to linger.

At about eight fifteen I felt tremendous pressure and got to the bathroom just as my water broke. A few minutes later there was rapping on my door. "It's Joletta. Are you all right?"

It took a few moments to get to the door. I must have looked a sight. "My water broke."

"I knew it had to be somethin' when the floor stopped creakin'. That was some walk you took! You want me to take you to the hospital?"

I thought of Bev's offer, but Bev was loaded with work. "If it isn't too much trouble," I said gratefully.

My pains were five minutes apart when we approached the reception desk at the hospital, Joletta carrying my suitcase. "Do you want me to stay?" she said.

"Thanks, you've done more than enough. I'll be all right."

But I wasn't all right after I had been examined by a resident and left alone in a labor room. As the contractions became harder, I tensed and started holding my breath as they circled my body in a girdle of pain. "*Breathe!*" ordered a nurse who had come in to check on me.

"I can't," I said through clenched teeth.

She was a dark-haired woman of about forty who had deep-set brown eyes and a determined chin. The name tag pinned to her uniform said Angela Blakey. "Were you able to attend the childbirth classes?" she said.

"No," I groaned. Those damned classes seemed to be all that the nurses had on their minds.

"I'm going to teach you how to breathe. It's easy to learn, and it will help you get through the pain. You have to work with the contractions—not fight them—or your labor will be harder and last longer. We'll practice now so you'll be ready for the next one. First, you'll take a deep cleansing breath: in through the nose, out through the mouth..."

Except for a few minutes she took to check on the only other woman in labor, Angela Blakey stayed with me for better than two hours, coaching my breathing, rubbing the tension out of my back and shoulders, wiping the perspiration off my face. "You're doing a great job," she kept saying, urging me on. "You're almost there."

When the pains were coming so hard and close together that I barely had enough time between them to say "I can't do this anymore, I can't do this anymore," she left to get the resident.

Angela Blakey stayed with me until my son Adam was born. I will be grateful to her forever.

***

"Look at how he's latched on!" marveled a nurse who came in the room to see if I was having any problems nursing. "He's got the whole areola in his mouth."

Just like his daddy, I thought, smiling as I gazed down at him. I hadn't planned on nursing, but Angela Blakey had encouraged me. "Your milk is so much better for him than anything you can buy," she said. "And nursing helps the uterus contract."

I could feel the contractions, a pleasant sensation, as the baby sucked, which compensated for my aching bottom. I wondered if nursing would help my stomach, which was soft and spongy, the skin hanging in pleats like a sagging fan. My waist was gone, too. But the baby was worth it, even if I did have the shape of a wood post. He wasn't marked by any of the trials I had gone through while I carried him. He weighed seven pounds and he was perfect. Though his eyes were the deep blue-gray that all babies had, I could already see a black ring around the pupils, like Tully's.

A different nurse came to take the baby. Exhausted, I would have liked to sleep, but an elderly couple who were talking nonstop were visiting the woman in the next bed. They had arrived with flowers to add to the collection already massed on the woman's small dresser. I tried not to look at my dresser, which was bare.

A petite woman wearing a pink volunteers' smock came into the room pushing a cart. She approached me first. "Would you care for some juice?" she said. "I also have a morning paper, if you'd like one."

"The paper, please," I said.

Unable to afford the few dollars a week for a subscription, it had been months since I had read a newspaper. I savored each page, scanning articles that I normally would have passed over, until I started reading the *Life Styles* section. Then, despite my sore bottom, I sat straight up in bed, reading the headline again: **Welfare Mother Gets Nursing Degree**.

Below a picture of the full, beaming face of a middle-aged woman wearing a nurse's uniform, there was an article about Yolanda Washington, a single parent with five children who had been able to go back to school to become a nurse with the help of the Stalling Women's Center. The Women's Center had a program called Reach Up that offered financial aid and support groups to single mothers, disadvantaged women, and displaced homemakers. The purpose of the program was to help these women get the education and training that would enable them to become self-sufficient. *There is no charge to speak to the Center's trained counselors*, the article said. A telephone number was given to call for an appointment.

I put down the newspaper, my mind racing. College had always seemed unattainable, so far beyond my reach that I hadn't allowed myself to think about it. I had wanted to be a teacher since I was ten years old. I still wanted to be a teacher. If Yolanda Washington could go to college, I could, too!

Then another thought came to me: to find this article about the Reach Up program after not reading a newspaper for months had to be more than just a coincidence. And to find it today, on the first day of our son's life. *Tully*. It was Tully's gift to us. He had watched over us during my labor and delivery, and he was watching over us now.

A lean brown arm reached in, knocking on the door to the room. "Bunting delivers," a familiar voice called. "Is it okay if I come in?"

"Leroy?" I said. "It sure is!"

Leroy Bunting entered carrying a spectacular basket of flowers that made the arrangements on the other side of the room look meager in comparison. "Oh, it's beautiful!" I said, touched that Bev had taken the time to make the arrangement with all the other work she had.

"Bev really outdid herself on this one," Leroy said. "It's the nicest I've seen. Where do you want it?"

"On this tray table by my bed so I can enjoy it up close for a while," I said, suddenly aware that the nonstop chatter from the other side of the room had stopped. I knew what they all were thinking and didn't care. I also knew that I must have looked dreadful, and that didn't bother me, either. Leroy had taken time from his busy day to bring me the flowers instead of leaving them for an aide to deliver, and I was so pleased that I wouldn't let anything bother me.

"I stopped at the nursery and peaked in. You got yourself a fine boy," he said. "How are you feelin'?"

"Like I put in a good night's work!"

He smiled. "That must be why they call it labor."

"Do you have any children?" I said, realizing that I knew nothing about his personal life.

"Not that I know of, which is a good thing since I'm not married."

Although he didn't stay long, I enjoyed his visit. Leroy Bunting's personality was like his walk, easy and upbeat. My next visitor, however, was as sour as spoiled milk.

While I was dozing early in the afternoon, a stout woman of about sixty came into the room carrying a clipboard. Gray curls sat stiffly on the woman's head; an extra chin drooped down her neck like a turkey wattle. The name printed on the tag pinned to her broad bosom was Fidelia Swinton. Instead of letting me rest, she marched directly to my bed. "I need you to answer some questions for your baby's birth certificate," she said.

Yawning, I forced myself awake.

The questions were easy to answer until they wanted information about the baby's father. "Father's name and place of birth," she said, her pen poised over the clipboard.

I didn't know how to respond. It was unlikely that I would ever have contact with the Rutlands again, but sometimes life took strange turns. If Tully's name were on the birth certificate, it would be a matter of public record. "Leave that blank," I said, deciding that it would be best to keep it simple since the baby would be called Barefield. I would tell him about his daddy when he was old enough to understand.

Fidelia Swinton's dark eyes glinted like pieces of glass. "This is an application for a legal document. The father's name has to be filled in."

"And if it isn't?"

"It's saying publicly that you don't know who the father is. Your baby is branded for life!"

Stung by the insult, I stared at her: she looked so smug that her neck had disappeared. Smug and self-satisfied, like the people in Owings who had made me a target for their meanness because my name was Barefield. That no-neck woman wasn't going to insult my son on the first day of his life! "Give me that application," I said, furious.

Before Fidelia Swinton could protest, I leaned over and snatched the clipboard and pen. Within seconds, the blank spaces were filled in. "Now get out of here," I said, thrusting the material at her, "and don't come back!"

She left as fast as her thick legs could carry her, which was a shame. I would have liked to see her expression when she read: **FATHER:** *Santa Claus*; **PLACE OF BIRTH:** *North Pole*.

Shortly afterward an older nurse came in whom I hadn't seen before. "I wanted to meet the patient who let Fido Swinton have it. I've been waiting for years for someone to send her running!"

"Fido?" I said.

"That's what we call her. She's as mean and persistent as a pit bull. She picks on single mothers. You're going to become a legend around here."

I don't know about becoming a legend, but sending Fido Swinton running could have been the reason that a nurse who came into the room after dinner to take my temperature and blood pressure warned me that I would probably be discharged early the next morning. "But I just had the baby last night," I said. "I haven't even been here twenty-four hours."

"I know," the nurse said kindly. "If it were up to me, you'd be able to stay at least one more day, but I don't make the rules. I thought you'd want to know tonight so you wouldn't be surprised in the morning."

"I appreciate it," I said, feeling so tired and sore that I wondered how I could manage alone.

Bev Garland called after the nurse left. "I really missed you today. Friday just wasn't the same. How are you doing?"

"All right, but not ready to go home tomorrow morning."

"What?"

"A nurse told me that they're discharging me in the morning."

"But you just had the baby!"

"That's what I told the nurse, but it didn't seem to matter," I said. "Thank you for the flowers. They're beautiful. Everyone who comes in comments on them. They've attracted a lot of attention. People want to know where they came from."

"That's wonderful! I need all that good word-of-mouth advertising!" Bev said. "Before I forget, I want to mention that I put your paycheck for last week in the mail. You should get it Monday or Tuesday."

Again, I thanked her. The paycheck meant more than ever now.

In the morning, after I had been examined by a resident and declared fit to be discharged, I showered and dressed. "Will someone be picking you up?" asked a nurse whose bifocals were perched at the end of her nose.

"No, I'll have to call a cab," I said, feeling shapeless in the maternity top and slacks I had worn to the hospital. I had been unable to button the clothes I'd packed in my suitcase.

"I'll call while you finish packing."

The nurse returned holding the baby; an aide was with her, pushing a wheelchair. "I'd rather walk," I said.

The nurse smiled sympathetically. "I'm sure you would, but it's hospital rules."

The cab driver was a grizzled-looking man wearing a dirty gray cap. "Where to?" he asked after Adam and I were settled in the back seat.

"Nine thirty-six Lemon Street."

He turned and fixed watery blue eyes on me. "Say that again?"

I repeated the Lemon Street address.

The cab jerked forward. Perhaps it was the sudden motion, or maybe it was the charged atmosphere that woke the baby. Despite doing everything I knew to soothe him, Adam cried all the way to Lemon Street.

"That'll be ten dollars and ten cent," the driver said after he pulled into the driveway. "And in the future, don't call Confederate Cab. We don't service this part of town."

I could see that he had no intention of helping me. His thoughts were so obvious, the same as what my daddy's or my brother's would have been—*a white woman livin' with niggers, probably a nigger baby*—that I wanted to slap him. Luckily, I had the exact amount of the fare in my wallet. Ignoring his outstretched hand, I dropped the money on the floor of the cab. Then, cradling the baby, I managed to get out with the suitcase and the flowers.

Late in the afternoon Joletta brought me supper, pork chops and greens. "I was surprised when I heard the baby cryin'. You were hardly in the hospital any time at all."

"Thank you," I said, taking the plate. "It smells so good. I really don't feel like cooking."

"You need to rest," she said, handing me a gift-wrapped box. "This is for the baby."

The box held a duff-colored, floppy-eared stuffed dog. "It's Adam's first toy! Thank you. Would you like to see him?"

Adam was sleeping on his back in the white crib. "I'd forgotten how tiny new babies are, so fragile," she said, her voice barely above a whisper. "They're fragile when they grow up, too. It's just a different kind of fragile."

"Symone?"

"This mornin' when she was in the shower I went into her room to put some laundry away and saw a pair of diamond stud earrings on her dresser. When I asked, she told me that she got them from a fellow who's been chasin' her. He gave her a gold chain, too."

"Those are expensive gifts."

"They're nothin' for him. He makes thousands every day. He's the boss of the Market—born on the street, runs the street. He's not givin' her gold and diamonds because he wants to hold her hand. He picks out the prettiest girls and then dazzles them with his money. He'll do to her what he's done to all the other ones: get her pregnant and then dump her. But she can't see it. I don't know what to do. I can't keep her locked up in her room."

"Maybe the police will catch him."

"Darrell Lawson?" she said with a bitter laugh. "They'll never touch him! The street is what he knows, it's where he got his education. His mama was an addict and an alcoholic; he's got no family and no sense of shame. He's survived on his own since he was a kid, left school at the age of eleven or twelve. By then he was already dealin' drugs big time."

"How old is he now?"

"About twenty, I think. Symone's seventeen, a baby in what she knows compared to him. I keep tellin' her how important school is, how she needs to get an education. Even at Golden Farms chicken they don't hire anyone who doesn't have a high school diploma. I wear boots all day and wade through chicken shit and I wouldn't have the job if I didn't have my diploma! She needs to go to college to have a future, but she can't see it. All she can see is the dazzle of gold and diamonds.

"Oh, how I wish her daddy was still here," Joletta said with a great sigh. "It's hard bein' alone."

"Yes," I said, feeling Tully's loss more than ever.

***

Although I had been told by the doctor who examined me before I was discharged from the hospital that I shouldn't drive for two weeks, I called the Stalling Department of Social Services early Monday morning to ask about applying for welfare. "I just had a baby," I said, "and I have no means of support."

"The first appointment I can give you is on Thursday morning at ten thirty," said a woman who sounded as if she had a summer cold.

"Bring the baby's birth certificate, documents verifying any bank accounts, and your most recent pay check stubs. Get here a half hour early so you can fill out the forms."

"I don't have the baby's birth certificate yet. He was born at midnight on Thursday."

"Then you'll have to bring a proof of birth statement from the hospital."

I decided to go to the hospital to get the proof on Wednesday so as not to risk being late for my appointment. The first of July was on Wednesday; I would be getting my food stamps, which I needed badly. There was nothing left to eat in the apartment but cheese, macaroni, and a half-box of cereal. I had intended to go grocery shopping Friday after getting my check from Bev, but I didn't make it to the flower shop. Even though I knew that the baby could come at any time, I desperately needed the money that each day of work would bring. My food stamps for the month of June were gone, my WIC checks, too. I had only fifteen dollars in my wallet and my car needed gas; the tank was nearly empty. I also needed diapers for the baby. The only money I could expect now was the paycheck Bev sent and my final paycheck from Magnolia's, which would be under $130. The money in the savings account I had opened was gone, spent on things for the baby. The cheapest crib, mattress, and bedding I had found had come to over two hundred dollars; a car seat, which was required by law in Virginia, cost forty-five dollars. Then there were receiving blankets and undershirts, bottles, nightgowns, and diapers to buy. Money flew out of my hands. A carriage was too expensive, so I bought a baby carrier I could strap on for forty dollars. I agonized over every purchase except one: on an impulse I spent twenty-two dollars for a mobile of brightly-colored butterflies that I could attach to the crib. It was the purchase that pleased me most. The baby would wake to focus on butterflies instead of the cracked, stained ceiling.

The past four weeks I had stinted on food and gas, and now it had caught up with me. The meal Joletta had brought was the only decent one I'd had since I had come home from the hospital. Hungry enough to eat the cake in which I'd hidden my jewelry, I decided to call the WIC clinic. Maybe they could see me on Wednesday so I could get my set of checks for the month of July. "You can come in next Monday morning at nine," the receptionist said.

"I'd like to come sooner," I said.

"I'm sorry, but we're jammed up this week because we're closed on Friday for the Fourth."

The Fourth of July. I had completely forgotten about the holiday, which had always been special to Tully and me. It was the anniversary of the day we met, and we celebrated every year, usually with a picnic. Thinking of Tully and the Fourth made my eyes fill with tears. If the telephone hadn't started to ring, I would have wept.

It was Lolita. "How you been doin', girl?"

"I had a baby boy Thursday night."

"Ha!" Lolita said, sounding as if she'd won a prize. "I *knew* it was a boy! I knew it!"

"Did you really? Why didn't you tell me?"

"'Cause you were wantin' a girl. What did you name him?"

"Adam. I decided to keep it short and simple. His initials are the first two letters of the alphabet."

Lolita asked me if I needed anything. I didn't want to take advantage of her generous nature, but I sorely needed help. "Diapers for the baby, if it isn't too much trouble."

"It ain't no trouble," Lolita said. "Do you need anythin' else, any groceries?"

Mentally adding while I was speaking, I said, "A half-gallon of milk, a loaf of bread, a can of frozen orange juice, and a couple of bananas."

Lolita arrived early in the afternoon with the diapers and the groceries, which came, to my great relief, to under fifteen dollars. She also brought a gift, a set of bibs for the baby, and a plate of cold fried chicken. "I made extra chicken yesterday," she said.

I had just finished nursing Adam, and he was yawning

contentedly. I yawned, too. "Is he up a lot at night?" Lolita said.

"Every two hours, but it seems like every two minutes."

"How long do you let him go between feedin's durin' the day?"

"Between four and five hours. The doctor said he'd make his own schedule."

"Uh, uh." Lolita shook her head. "He's gettin' his days and nights mixed up."

"What should I do?"

"Don't let him sleep more 'n three and a half hours at a time durin' the day. Wake him up and wait 'til he's good and hungry before you feed him."

Lolita noticed the basket of flowers on the coffee table in front of the sofa. The flowers still looked fresh. "They're from Bev, the owner of Garland's Floristry where I worked on Fridays."

"Now that's nice," she said. "Not like Magnolia's, where they can't even squeeze out a card."

We both laughed, then talked for a while about babies and Magnolia's. Before Lolita left, I thanked her again for all she had done. "Let me know if there's anythin' else you need," she said.

I needed nursing bras. I needed to get to a laundromat because the baby's clothes, which I had hand washed and hung over the tub, weren't drying well. But Lolita had already done more than enough. Her visit was a godsend.

***

The upper parking lot behind Stalling City Hall was full when I pulled in at ten o'clock on Thursday morning, so I had to park in the lower lot. It was sunny, the temperature already a humid eighty-five degrees. Perspiring as I climbed the steep flight of stairs to reach the upper level, a diaper bag draped over one shoulder and my purse draped over the other, the baby in a carrier that was strapped to me, I could feel the bleeding start again. Yesterday, after going to the bank to cash the check from Bev and then grocery shopping with my new allotment of food stamps, I had bled what seemed like an alarming amount. I didn't want it to happen again, especially not now when I had this appointment.

Again, I was given a Base Document to fill in. I was also given a form titled **Supplement C, Aid to Dependent Children (ADC)**. In the space provided in the Base Document to list any needs or problems, I wrote: *My son Adam was born a week ago today. I can no longer work. I have no savings and no income other than a final paycheck that I expect next week for $126.90.*

I immediately regretted what I had written. Even though every word was true, putting my situation on paper made me look as needy and pathetic as a street beggar.

On the ADC form, I left the space blank for the name of the father.

The waiting room was full, and two toddlers squabbling over a toy started to cry. Adam stirred in the baby carrier. The toddlers' mothers weren't having success distracting them. I shifted in my chair, hoping that Adam wouldn't wake up. I had fed him at nine and had brought a bottle, but when I had tried to give him a bottle yesterday to prepare him for today, he had fussed, wanting my breast. I hoped he wouldn't wake up. I hoped I wouldn't be kept waiting long. I hoped I would stop bleeding.

Adam didn't awaken, but the intake worker didn't call my name until almost eleven o'clock. A wisp of a man, barely five feet tall and one hundred pounds at most, he had an oversize mustache that looked like it had never been groomed: scraggly brown hairs hung over his upper lip and floated down below his chin. "I'm sorry I'm running late," he said as I rose from my seat, towering over him. "My name is Mr. Ryle. Please come with me."

I felt as if I were being led into the bowels of the building. We made a right turn, then a left, then a right again. More turns, more confusing corridors. Finally we entered a small office furnished with a beige metal desk, black filing cabinets, and two straight-back wood chairs. A nameplate on the desk said ALEXANDER RYLE. Eyeing the baby as if he were a bomb that could explode at any time, Mr. Ryle gestured for me to be seated. Then he leaned against the desk and said, "We'll begin by going through your Base Document."

He carefully reviewed my responses to each question. When he came to the bottom of the first page and read aloud what I had written, I was embarrassed and fixed my eyes on the floor. "Is there anything you want to add?" he asked.

I shook my head, again wishing that I hadn't humiliated myself by putting my situation in writing. And I continued to shake my head as he went on, asking, "Do you own any stocks or bonds?...Machinery, tools, or other equipment?...Have any bank accounts?...Trust funds?...IRA or Keogh plans?...Real property?...Medical insurance?...A cemetery plot, burial plot, or prearranged funeral?...Your car is a 1984 Buick Century that you own free and clear?"

"Yes," I said.

He reached for a book that was on a shelf above his desk and looked something up. "You're under the $1500 limit."

Finally, I raised my eyes. "What does that mean?"

"You're entitled to a $1500 exemption on a vehicle you own. If your car was worth more than $1500, anything over the $1500 would have to go toward your resource limit."

"Resource limit?"

"To qualify for ADC, you can't have more than $1000 in personal resources—bank accounts, property, insurance policies, and so on."

He said this as if it were good news. I was dismayed. The car, my one major investment, had cost $10,800 six years ago. Now it seemed to be worth next to nothing.

After he went over the amounts I had given for my household expenses, he told me to re-read the closing statements. When I was done, he put an X where I had to initial that I understood. He signed as witness.

Mr. Ryle sat at his desk and scanned the ADC form. "You didn't complete this section for the absent parent," he said.

"I can't."

"You realize that you just initialed a statement that stated: *I understand, under penalty of perjury, that if I withhold information I may be breaking the law and could be prosecuted for perjury, larceny, and/or welfare fraud."*

I nodded that I understood.

He picked up a stack of pamphlets, each a different color, and started reviewing what was in them. I sat quietly while he talked about the ADC program, appeals and fair hearings, child support services, food stamps, and WIC. But when he came to a rose-colored pamphlet entitled ESP-JOBS and started talking about education and job skills training, I took the baby out of the carrier and leaned forward. *"When you become an ESP-JOBS participant, you can get day care, transportation, and help with family problems,"* he said, reading from the pamphlet.

"In last Friday's newspaper I read about a woman on welfare who became a nurse," I said.

"Yolanda Washington," Mr. Ryle said, smiling. "She was one of my clients."

Thinking how lucky I was that I was seeing him, I said, "I want to go to college like Yolanda Washington did."

"To become a nurse?"

"No," I said. "A teacher."

He looked at me sharply. "What is your background?"

"My background?"

"What did you do before your baby was born? How did you support yourself?"

"I worked at Magnolia's. Before that I was a secretary in an elementary school."

"What school?"

"Creekside Elementary in Owings."

He leaned back in his chair. "Well then, you have job skills."

"Not really," I said. "I don't know how to use a computer or take dictation from a machine. You need those skills today to get a decent job."

He glanced at his watch and frowned. "That can easily be

remedied," he said.

He hurried through the remainder of the pamphlet, which stressed commitment to an employment goal, then asked me to sign indicating that my rights and responsibilities had been fully explained.

But I didn't feel that my rights and responsibilities had been adequately explained. I wanted to know more about going to college, more about any financial help I could expect; however, I didn't want to antagonize him. It was obvious that he wanted to move on, so reluctantly, I signed.

We went through the remaining pamphlets—an assignment of rights to medical support form and a declaration of citizenship. After I signed the two forms, he gave me the pamphlets to keep, cleared his throat, and picked up yet another paper. *"If you knowingly make a false statement, withhold information..."* he began.

Again, the threat of prosecution for fraud. "Do you understand what I just read?" he asked.

I nodded, wondering from the grave tone of his voice what was coming next. I didn't have to wonder long. He picked up a form that detailed changes in my circumstances which required immediate reporting. *"I understand that if I give false information, withhold information, or fail to report changes to the Department of Social Services, I can be charged with a criminal offense. I am aware that such an offense is punishable by a jail sentence, fine, or both,"* he read aloud, each word burning in my brain. Then he paused. "Any questions?"

"No," I said.

I signed the statement where he indicated, and he put his signature and the date below mine before setting the statement aside.

"Now, Ms. Barefield," he said, his eyes seeking mine. Like his mustache, his eyes were a flat brown. "On the ADC form you didn't complete the section for the absent responsible parent. I have this Notice of Cooperation and Exception. Its purpose is to advise you concerning your cooperation in establishing the paternity of your child. Your cooperation is required by state and federal law for you to be eligible for ADC."

"I can't tell you who the father is."

He handed me the notice, his expression stern. "You'd better read this carefully."

The notice stated that cooperation included naming the parent of the child, giving help to obtain money and property, and, if necessary, appearing at the Department of Social Services, Division of Child Support Enforcement office, or in court to sign papers or give information. I read about *good cause*, which might excuse me from cooperating if I believed that my cooperation would not be in the best interest of my child. But to claim good cause I had to supply evidence within twenty days that cooperation would result in physical or emotional harm to the child or to me; or that the child was conceived as a result of incest or rape; or that legal proceedings for the adoption of the child were presently pending; or that I was currently being assisted by a social agency to resolve the issue of whether to keep my child or give him up for adoption.

It was impossible. My circumstances didn't fit into any of the acceptable definitions of good cause. "What will happen if I can't tell you who the father is?"

"Then all you'll get is support for the baby, which is one hundred sixty-three dollars a month."

I gasped. No one could live on that.

He pulled on the wispy strands of his mustache, waiting for me to say something, but I couldn't. He looked at his watch with irritation. "I must also inform you that the DSCE—the Division of Child Support Enforcement—will take you through the court system if you refuse to reveal the father. A judge can hold you in contempt and put you in jail."

The sharpness of Mr. Ryle's voice made Adam stir. I rocked him on my arm, the motion automatic while my mind raced. If I were put in jail, Adam would be placed in a foster home where he could be hurt or abused. I would die before I would let that happen. I thought of Mrs. Rutland, rooted in Tully's house like she was welded to the floor. Nothing, not even the Commonwealth of Virginia, could force that woman to sell any of Tully's things until she was ready. But if Mrs. Rutland knew about Adam, she would probably start her own legal proceedings to take him, claiming that she could provide a better home, security, a family.

"I can't reveal the father," I said, nearly overwhelmed by my impossible situation. "I have no money and no one I can turn to for help. No one. All my life I worked and paid taxes that helped other people. I worked two jobs, over forty hours a week, until the day my baby was born. Now I need help. I don't intend to be on welfare forever. I'll get off it as soon as I can. Coming here has been the most humiliating, degrading experience of my life. Can't you help me?"

Maybe I imagined it, but for a moment his expression seemed to soften. "I'm required by the Commonwealth of Virginia to establish your baby's paternity. The Commonwealth believes, and rightly so," he said slowly, as if he were choosing his words, "that parents must be held responsible for their offspring. The only time an exception is made is in rare instances when the mother doesn't know who the father is."

The mother doesn't know. I couldn't say that I was raped because I couldn't provide evidence. Maybe I could make up a story. Maybe I could say that I was drunk...

I shifted in my chair so he couldn't see my face. "I...I met a man in a bar. I...I had too much to drink. I went with him to his motel room. We...we had sex. In the morning he was gone."

"What is the man's name?"

"His name is..." My free hand went to my face, covering my eyes. "His name is Willie. Or maybe it's Wayne. I was so drunk."

"You're saying that you don't know the name of the man who fathered your child?"

Though I had never belonged to a church and I wasn't even sure I believed in God, I had been comforted since Tully's death thinking that he was in heaven. Praying that Tully would forgive me, I nodded, too filled with shame to speak.

Mr. Ryle asked me the name of the bar, the name of the motel. I named a seedy motel and a bar that Tully and I never frequented. I told Mr. Ryle that I had been depressed since my fortieth birthday. With all the lies I had told, I needed to say something that was true. I watched him write everything down. I couldn't prove my story, but they couldn't disprove it, either.

We went through three additional forms pertaining to the baby's paternity. I responded to the questions Mr. Ryle asked and signed the papers without looking at him. The air in the room had gotten close. I wiped perspiration off my forehead; it was difficult to breathe. "We're almost finished," he said, coming to yet another form. "I need verification of the baby's birth, a birth certificate or a letter from the hospital. Also, I have to see your Social Security card, if you have it with you."

I gave him the card and the proof of birth statement I'd gotten from the hospital. I also gave him my cancelled savings account book and my last three pay stubs.

Adam started to whimper. "This is a residency statement that must be completed by your landlord," he said, eyeing the baby nervously as he handed me the form. Then he handed me another form to sign that gave the Department of Social Services permission to obtain information on my account from the bank. I also had to sign a release allowing the Department of Social Services to get information on my earnings from Magnolia's. "You'll have to sign a verification of termination release for that flower shop where you worked, too," he said, rummaging through the papers on his desk to find another release.

It was one thing for the office staff at Magnolia's to know that I was applying for welfare, and quite another for the Department of Social Services to send the form to Bev. "I only worked at the flower shop one day a week for minimum wage. It would really embarrass me to have you contact the owner."

"Sorry, the rules are the rules."

Adam's whimpers became wails. I shifted him to my shoulder. There was no comforting him. And there was no comfort for me, either, as I signed the release that would go to Bev.

"This last form is a No Income Statement," he said. "It has to be filled in and signed by someone who has known you for more than a year."

There was no point in trying to give Adam the bottle I had brought if this was the last form. Returning him to my arm, I took the paper and read it quickly. "This asks about my work history and how I pay my bills. I don't have anyone who can answer these questions. I've only lived in Stalling since March, and I haven't made close friends here who know my private business."

"Then it will have to be someone from where you used to live."

"There is no one in Owings."

"How long did you live there?" he asked, raising his voice to be heard above the baby's wails.

"All my life until I moved here, but I didn't discuss my personal finances with anyone. I always felt that how I paid my bills was no one's business but mine," I said, doubting that he discussed how he paid his bills with anyone.

"It has to be completed," he said, the tone of his voice leaving no room for argument.

"I'll send it to the woman in the rental office where I had my apartment in Owings," I said with a sigh of resignation. "She knows I always paid on the first of the month."

On our way back to the reception area, I asked how much money I could expect. "If your case is approved, you'll get $245 a month. And you'll have to come back in six months for a re-evaluation of your situation. You'll get a notice in the mail with the date and time of the re-evaluation appointment. Failure to keep the appointment will mean termination of your benefits."

I wasn't concerned about six months from now. The figure he gave had to be a mistake. "In Owings, welfare pays $296 a month."

"This is Stalling, not Owings."

"But my rent is going up to $300 a month! How will I be able to live?"

"You'll have to make an appointment with housing," Alexander Ryle said, practically running in his eagerness to escape us. Adam was still squalling. I felt like wailing, too.

***

"Your son weighs seven pounds five ounces," said the nurse at the WIC clinic on Monday morning. "How much did he weigh at birth?"

"Seven pounds," I said. "Since Friday I've had problems nursing him. I think my milk has pretty well dried up. He's on a bottle now, though he doesn't like it much."

"The switch probably explains his small weight gain. He's a smart little fella. He knows your milk is better for him than what he's getting in a bottle," the nurse said, lifting Adam off the scale so she could measure him. Close to me in age, she had alert green eyes and a friendly manner.

"I'm sure it is, but I can't do it anymore."

She returned the baby to me. "We have volunteers that work with first-time mothers who are having problems nursing. I'd like you to talk to one of them."

"It won't help."

"Did the problem start because of sore nipples?"

"No."

"There must be something we can do," she said kindly.

"I only wish," I said. I missed nursing Adam. I missed the closeness, the indescribable feeling of my body nurturing his. He wasn't even two weeks old, and I already felt as though I'd failed him. I started drying up after my visit to the Department of Social Services. I was sure that worry was the cause. Even if I combined the check I expected from Magnolia's with the money I would get from welfare, I still wouldn't have enough to pay my rent and utilities. I didn't know what to do or where to turn.

"Do you have a pediatrician?" the nurse said.

"No," I said.

"Adam should be seen on a regular basis. We'll be checking on him as well. Be sure to bring him back here in six months."

I was given WIC checks for myself that covered a period of six weeks. Since I wasn't nursing, they were the last WIC checks I would receive. For Adam there was a voucher for thirty-one cans of baby formula concentrate, which he would continue to receive until he was eleven months old.

When I got home, I called over half of the pediatricians listed in the telephone book. None of them accepted Medicaid patients. Rather than try the remaining pediatricians, I called WIC. "We're not permitted to recommend anyone," said the receptionist. "A lot of people go to the clinic at Dearth Memorial."

I decided to try a few more pediatricians. Again, none of them took Medicaid patients. I had to resign myself to the thought of another clinic at Dearth Memorial. Suddenly it seemed as if all of my choices were gone, that my circumstances were making choices for me whether I liked them or not.

That night, as in every night since my appointment at the Department of Social Services, my mama was in my dreams, hounding me like a bill collector who wouldn't go away. *"So you don't know the name of your baby's father! What a whoppin' lie that is!"* Mama said. *"And you always actin' so superior, like you was better than the rest of us. Miss Better-than-the-Barefields! Miss High 'n' Mighty! What a story you told! Them lies came out of your mouth one after another fast as bullets from a gun. And now you can't even pay your rent or choose your baby's doctor! Some high 'n' mighty you are!"*

***

I was able to get an appointment with Fletcher Hargrave, the Assistant Director of Housing, a week after my interview with Alexander Ryle. It was a scorching ninety-four degrees outside on the Wednesday afternoon we were scheduled to meet; without air conditioning it felt twenty degrees hotter in the car. I glanced at Adam sleeping in the car seat and saw tiny beads of perspiration beneath the fine blond down on his scalp. I hoped he wouldn't get a heat rash.

City Hall was mercifully cool. Mr. Hargrave, a large, rumpled man, led us through a maze of corridors to the offices of the Department of Housing. His office was nearly a duplicate of Alexander Ryle's. After we were seated, he said, "How can I help you?"

I briefly explained that I had applied for welfare and could no longer afford to live in my apartment. "I don't plan on being on welfare any longer than I have to, but right now I have no choice. I'll be getting $245 a month. I need a place to live that I can afford."

Mr. Hargrave shook his head. Pouches sagged beneath his mustard-brown eyes. "I'm sorry, I wish I could help you, but right now there's nothing I can do. There will be an advertisement in the newspaper, probably in January, when the Section 8 waiting list opens up."

"Section 8?" I said.

"About twenty years ago Congress passed a law called Section 8, HOUSING AND URBAN DEVELOPMENT, commonly known as HUD. It's federally-subsidized housing for people who qualify under the HUD guidelines. You qualify, but unfortunately, I can't give you an application. Since we can't get housing for people in a reasonable length of time, we open the waiting list to new names only once a year for thirty days. Look for the ad in the newspaper."

"I can't afford the newspaper. My rent is $300 a month and I don't have the money! Where am I going to live?" I said, my voice rising in desperation.

"Perhaps you can live with some relatives for a while, or stay with a friend."

I leaned toward him, nestling Adam against my shoulder. "I don't have anyone I can stay with! I'm all alone. My baby is two weeks old. Are you telling me that we'll have to live on the street?"

"You could try the Salvation Army. If they have room, they'll let you stay for a while. They've been letting people stay for up to six weeks..." His voice trailed off.

"The Salvation Army?" I said, as if it weren't a sane option. "Isn't there anything else, some housing besides that Section 8 you talked about?"

"Grady Gardens, which is city-owned housing," he said. "It's full."

"Can I get on the waiting list or do I have to wait until January for that housing, too?"

His jaw dropped, as if he were surprised. "Uh...you can get on the list."

"How long do names stay on the list?"

"It depends," he said. "Sometimes it can be months. Names move faster on that one than on the other list, which can take four years."

Somehow I had to make this man understand. "I don't have four years! I don't even have four weeks! My rent will be due August first, and I don't have the money to pay it! I *must* have someplace to live!"

"I'm sorry, there's nothing I can do," he said wearily. Placing his hands on the desk, he pushed himself up, rising to tell me that our meeting was over.

I didn't budge. I couldn't let him shuffle me out the door. "When I came in here, you asked how you could help me: I need a place to live! Isn't that your job, helping people like me who are desperate?"

Mr. Hargrave's face went from pink to red to purple. "You can tell me all day that you need a place. *I have nothing to give you.* I'm not an uncaring, unfeeling person, but I can't do the impossible! Federally-subsidized housing has been cut seventy-five percent since 1982. Each year it gets worse: there is greater need and fewer available units. It's gone from bad to worse to insuperable. There are four hundred fifty-eight families on the Section 8 waiting list; three hundred sixty-nine of those waiting are priorities, like you. Last winter people came to see me who were living in their cars on days when the temperature was forecast to drop to fifteen degrees overnight, and all I could do was send them to the Salvation Army.

"Do you think I enjoy telling you and all the others like you that the cupboard is bare? I've come to hate my job, but I have a family to support so I'm lucky to have it. I don't know how you got into your predicament, it's none of my business, but as an adult you are responsible for at least some of the choices you made that led you to the situation you're in."

He was right: some of the choices I made did lead me to my predicament. Too stricken to speak, I followed him through the maze of corridors to the reception area, fighting back what felt like a wall of tears.

By the time I reached the bottom of the long flight of stairs to the lower parking lot, I was in a place beyond tears. The blazing sun, the burning metal door handle, the intense heat inside the car barely seemed to register. I kept thinking that this was all a bad dream, that until a few weeks ago I was a hard-working, tax-paying citizen, that Adam and I couldn't end up living on the street, not us, not here in America. Certainly the system I had contributed to all my life would come to my rescue.

So I waited. On the last Monday in July, I called the Department of Social Services and asked to speak to Mr. Ryle. The past week I had gone to my mailbox every day expecting the ADC check, and every day I had been disappointed. Again today the check wasn't there, and Grover Daniels would be coming to collect the rent at the end of the week. I had to give him something.

My call was connected after a brief wait. "Alexander Ryle," he said.

"This is Sara Barefield. I was in your office on July second to apply for welfare. I'm sorry to bother you, but my rent is due this Saturday, and I haven't received the check for $245."

"It generally takes forty-five days to determine eligibility."

"Forty-five days! That won't be until next month! I went to the

Department of Housing like you suggested but they couldn't help me. What will I do? I have a baby and no place to go!"

"Did you give the landlord a security deposit?"

"Yes, two hundred ninety dollars."

"Maybe he'll accept that for your rent."

"Maybe," I said doubting it. I wondered how hard I could push. "Is there a chance my eligibility could be determined sooner?"

"We need to have all of your documentation in," he said. "At the earliest, it won't be until the first week in August. But then you can expect a check for the full $245. Your food stamps will also be increased."

I managed to thank him and say good-by before I wept.

The first week in August. I couldn't pay Grover Daniels and I was down to my last eight dollars. Needing the air conditioner to fight the brutal July heat, the only bill I had paid was my electric bill, which was seventy-eight dollars. Unable to pay the telephone and car insurance bills, I had used the remainder of my one hundred twenty-six dollar paycheck from Magnolia's to pay for diapers for the baby, the laundromat, and a few dollars' worth of gas for the car. There was no money for food. I had lost all the weight I had gained during my pregnancy, and then some. I had stopped watching the evening news; reports of millions of dollars wasted by the Pentagon, millions wasted by government agencies, huge subsidies to rich corporations filled me with hopeless anger. I felt helpless, isolated, alone. Days went by when the only human contact I had was with the baby. At times when I was particularly tired and tense, feeling overwhelmed by my situation and my inability to find a way out, Adam was impossibly fussy. Nothing would soothe him, not feeding or changing or patting or crooning or cuddling or even Elvis singing *Love Me Tender*. It was as if his emotions had become entangled with mine. At those times I felt as if we were both falling to pieces.

***

I always went downstairs to give Grover Daniels the rent when he rang the bell on the first of the month. It wasn't surprising, then, that he looked suspicious when I asked him to come upstairs on Saturday. "The rent is three hundred dollars now," he said, peering with curiosity at Adam, who was sleeping peacefully in the white crib.

Daniels seemed immense, more bloated than usual. I stepped between him and the crib. "I want you to use my security deposit for this month's rent. I'll send you a money order at the end of the week for the additional ten dollars."

"No," he said, giving his full attention to me now. "I want the rent."

"Look at how I've improved this apartment," I said, gesturing with my arm. "I cleaned it up, I painted the walls. I haven't damaged anything."

"The money," he said. "Do you have it?"

"Not today, but we could work it out if you'll use the security deposit."

"I already told you: No."

I didn't know what to say. Then the expression on his face changed; he was looking at me differently. I was wearing white shorts and a blue knit top. Conscious of his gaze traveling up my legs to my crotch, to my breasts, I started backing away from him. "But maybe we could work something out for part of what you owe, if you do me right," he said, reaching down to unzip his fly. He pulled out his member, already getting hard.

The roofer's knife was in my purse. I was always prepared for an attacker when I left the apartment, the knife either in my hand or in an accessible pocket, but I hadn't expected this. "Get out of here," I said, moving toward the purse on my dresser. "Get out now!"

Still facing him, I grabbed the purse. "Get out before you get hurt!" I said, my hand closing around the handle of the knife.

Maybe he thought from the tone of my voice that the weapon in my hand was a gun. He didn't wait to see. Cursing, he left with surprising swiftness.

Adam, who had been whimpering, started to wail. I couldn't attend to him until I stopped shaking.

Three days later the mailman rang the bell and asked me to sign for a certified letter. I waited until I was upstairs before I opened the envelope. Inside there was a Pay or Quit Notice, requiring the payment of rent within five days of receiving the notice. Failure to pay within the five-day period meant forfeiture of my right to possession of the apartment.

I called Fletcher Hargrave at the Department of Housing and left a message on his voice mail. He didn't call me back. I called Alexander Ryle. He was off for a week on vacation. Deciding that my only alternative was to sell my jewelry, I took the hollowed-out cake from the freezer and removed the sapphire-and-diamond ring, the gold necklace, the gold bracelets and earrings. It had been so long since I had seen or worn these things that had once given me so much pleasure that for a moment it seemed as if they had belonged to someone else, but as I fingered each piece, I remembered when Tully had given it to me and I wept.

There was only one pawnshop listed in the Stalling telephone book. I drove there the following morning, wanting to go before the heat became too oppressive. The sign over the store said LEDBETTER'S, Guns & Gold Bought & Sold. Inside, everything seemed to be covered with a film of gray dust, including the bespectacled old man behind a long display case filled with a jumble of items ranging from Swiss army knives to a silver-backed hairbrush. I showed him my jewelry, which he briefly examined under a jeweler's loupe. "I can give you two hundred seventy-five dollars for the lot of it," he said.

"It's worth more than that, much more. The ring alone cost over a thousand dollars."

"That's retail," he said. "Two seventy-five. Take it or not."

Grover Daniels wouldn't accept less than three hundred dollars. I had no money. Adam was almost out of diapers and there was nothing to eat in the apartment besides a nearly empty box of corn flakes and the cake in which I'd hidden the jewelry. But I would rather starve than let this old thief have everything for two hundred seventy-five dollars. Maybe I could sell him one piece, just get enough to tide me over. Reluctantly, I held up the necklace. "How much will you give me for this?"

He took the necklace from me and put it on a scale. "I can give you fifty for it."

I knew Tully had paid at least six times that amount, but I had to eat, Adam had to be changed. "Okay," I said, swallowing hard.

My ADC check came in the mail a week after my trip to the pawnshop. I also received $203 worth of food stamps and new Medicaid cards for myself and the baby. But that same week, on Friday, a sheriff's deputy rang the doorbell and handed me a summons for unlawful detainer. The summons stated that Sara Barefield should be removed from possession of the upper apartment at 936 Lemon Street due to the nonpayment of rent; there was also a $500 claim for damage to the front lawn, which made me furious. There hadn't been a lawn to damage: it had been, and still was, a patch of mud and weeds. The summons commanded me to appear before the Stalling General District Court on August twenty-seventh at two o'clock.

Adam was two months old on the day we went to court. He had become marvelously responsive, a playful baby whose big smiles came easily; he rewarded me with coos and gurgles when I talked to him. And I talked to him all the time. I told him about his daddy, about my plan to go to college, about the wonderful future we would have (though on days when I was especially down it was difficult to believe). I sang him nursery rhymes and the alphabet song, and played patty-cake with him endlessly. He delighted me beyond anything I could have possibly imagined. Adam was, without a doubt, the most wonderful baby in the world. But on the day we went to court I was so preoccupied with worry and what I would tell the judge that I barely responded to his smiles while I bathed and dressed him. Although he was a picture in a new blue romper that complimented the color of his eyes, poor Adam became tearful, expressing his reaction to my lack of response by the only means available to him.

Wanting to give the appearance of respectability, I worried over how to dress, but in the end I had to wear a simple cotton skirt and blouse. I had lost so much weight that this particular skirt, a black-and-white print with a partially elasticized waist, was the only one that fit me. And as I had for weeks, I put my hair in a French braid; there had been no money for a haircut since I'd left Owings. But when I entered the courtroom and saw the people gathered there, my worries over my appearance vanished. Apparently Thursday afternoons in Stalling General District Court were reserved for landlord-tenant cases; with the exception of the landlords and a handful of lawyers wearing dark suits, most of the people sitting on the oak benches were dressed in work clothes. There was an air of anxious weariness about them, as if they were preparing themselves for bad news.

The wood-paneled courtroom was wider than it was long. From the seat I had taken toward the back so I could feed Adam, I could hear without difficulty. While I gave him his bottle, I listened to the cases called before mine. An astonishingly obese woman whose pendulous stomach was straining the seams of her pink shift tried to justify her nonpayment of rent because the landlord hadn't fixed a broken toilet for two days. The landlord, a bald man in his sixties dressed in a sport shirt, navy blazer, and khakis, was represented by a middle-aged attorney who smoothly questioned the woman about the dates and nature of other complaints she had made. When the lawyer finished arguing his case, the judge decided in favor of the landlord, concluding that the woman deliberately caused the damage to avoid the payment of rent. The landlord was awarded a judgment; the woman was evicted.

I listened to three more cases, my nervousness growing. In only one of the cases did the tenant win; he brought cancelled checks and pictures to bolster his case. I hadn't brought any evidence. It would be my word against Daniel's. At least he didn't seem to have a lawyer with him. He was sitting alone, on the aisle several rows in front of me. Adam had almost dozed off when my case was called.

I gathered up the baby, the diaper bag, and my purse and followed Grover Daniels, as big as a walrus in a grayish-brown suit, as he lumbered up to the front of the courtroom ahead of me. The judge was a robust-looking man of about fifty whose deep tan suggested weekends spent on the golf course. The nameplate to his left said SAMUEL WAYLAND. "Sara Barefield?" Judge Wayland said after he scanned copies of the summons and affidavit.

"Yes."

"Mr. Daniels alleges that you owe three hundred dollars for rent for the month of August and five hundred dollars for damage to the front lawn at 936 Lemon Street. Is that correct?"

"There was no lawn," I said. "It was mud and weeds from the day I moved in."

Daniels stepped forward, his hand extended. "Your honor, I have pictures here of how the lawn looked before and how it looks now, and a picture of her car parked on it that caused the damage."

"Since there is a dispute over the lawn, we'll set that for trial," the judge said, gesturing for Daniels to step back. "Now, Ms. Barefield, you still haven't responded as to whether you owe three hundred dollars rent for the month of August."

Stunned, I didn't know what to say. Too late I remembered Daniel's claim that he had a picture of the house with a lawn. The picture must have been taken years ago, but I had no proof, nothing to offer to refute it. Though I had planned to tell the judge that Daniels had exposed himself, I realized that I couldn't; again, I had no proof. It was my word against his. "Your honor," I said, patting Adam, who had started to fuss, "I owe the rent, but Mr. Daniels has refused to fix anything. There are no screens for the windows. Water pours in through a hole in the ceiling when it rains. Only one burner on the stove works."

The furrows in Judge Wayland's tanned forehead deepened. "How long have these conditions existed?"

"Since I moved into the apartment in March."

"Since March?" The judge shook his head. "There are laws to

protect tenants, but laws are worthless unless they are used. You should have filed your claims months ago. You could have paid your rent in court until the situation was corrected."

"I didn't know," I said. "And I couldn't afford a lawyer."

"You could have gotten help from Legal Aid. As it stands now, since you've acknowledged that you owe the rent, Mr. Daniels is entitled to the eviction unless you can pay what you owe at this time."

My throat constricted. "I can't," I said, barely making myself heard. As if responding to my emotional state, Adam started to cry.

Daniels stepped forward. "Your honor, I'd like her out within seventy-two hours. There's only a few days left to the month to find another tenant."

"I don't have another place to live," I said, conscious of the people in the courtroom, all witnesses to my situation. Adam cried harder while I struggled to retain my composure.

"I'm going to enter a judgment for three hundred dollars for the rent. You have ten days to move, an allowance due to your circumstances," he said. "I'm setting a court date for the five hundred dollar claim for damage to the lawn for September thirtieth at two o'clock."

I rushed blindly out of the courtroom thinking that this couldn't be happening to me.

Early the next morning I called Fletcher Hargrave at the Department of Housing. I'd had only an hour or so of sleep, a nightmare in which I'd dreamed that Grover Daniels had all of my belongings moved out of the apartment onto the sidewalk, where the crowd that had gathered the day I moved in had returned. I'd watched helpless, unable to stop them, as they carted away my mattress and box springs, my dresser and bed, my sofa, tables and chairs, the television, VCR and CD player, my dishes, my pots and pans and ironing board, Adam's crib and the butterfly mobile. Then I remembered a documentary I had seen on television of people living on the streets in India, where they were huddled in doorways and sleeping on the sidewalk. Fear took root in me as tenacious as a cancer.

"Nothing has changed," Fletcher Hargrave said. "There are no openings."

"Not even in the city-owned housing?"

"No even on Grady Street," he said.

"What will I do? Where will I live? I have a two-month old baby!" I said, nearly hysterical. "I can't sleep on the street!"

"I'm sorry, all I can suggest is that you stay temporarily with friends or relatives or try the Salvation Army."

The facilities at the Salvation Army were filled to capacity. "We try not to turn anyone in need away," said the woman I spoke with on the phone. "You're welcome to come in and talk about your situation. In a pinch we've sometimes slept six in a room instead of four."

"Six?"

"Usually we have two mothers and two infants or children per bedroom," she explained. "But we can fit six in a room, or even seven, temporarily."

"Oh," I said, shuddering as I tried to imagine what it would be like to sleep in a room with four strangers.

"I can see you at ten thirty this morning."

"I...uh...thank you...I'll have to call you back."

I still had one last option. I had gotten the idea during the night when, feeling helpless and lost, I was aching for Tully. For no particular reason I remembered Ray Clark and his assurances that he had connections that could keep Tully from being drafted. And I bitterly recalled how Ray Clark's son, Ray Junior, got out of the draft a year after Tully was sent to Vietnam. At the time people in Owings talked about the favor that had been done for Ray by a state senator, which must have been the connection Ray had boasted about to Tully. I thought of the hundreds of people whose names were on the waiting lists for housing. Some of them, I was sure, moved up faster on the lists than others. My mama always said that there were two kinds of people in the world, those that had connections and those that didn't. And I knew someone who had connections.

I hadn't seen or spoken to Bev Garland since I had signed the verification of termination release when I had applied for welfare. Although Bev was my employer, I had thought of her as my friend; however, that changed when I knew Bev would receive the notice from the Department of Social Services. I was too embarrassed by my situation to contact her. Now, faced with either living at the Salvation Army or on the street, I had no alternative. During lulls on Fridays when we had chatted, Bev had mentioned that her brother Warren and the mayor of Stalling were close friends.

I drove to the Westmark Plaza late in the afternoon hoping Bev wouldn't notice how haggard I looked; the make-up I put on didn't hide the blue shadows under my eyes and the unnatural paleness of my skin. Sure that Bev had hired someone to replace me, I waited until a few minutes before closing time before entering the shop. To my surprise, Bev was alone. "Sara!" she said with her sparkling smile. "It's good to see you! I've been meaning to call, really. Please forgive me. I can't seem to catch up. I still haven't found a replacement who can come close to you. But enough about me. Let's see your son."

I lifted Adam out of the carrier, concerned about how he'd react to a stranger. When Bev took him in her arms and started talking to him in a bright, happy voice, he rewarded her with wide smiles and coos. She was charmed. "What a delight he is! And those eyes, those unusual eyes! I've never seen anything like them. He's gorgeous."

"His eyes are like his daddy's."

"What a shame it is that his daddy isn't here to enjoy him."

I forced back unwanted tears, thinking that the worst thing I could do was to feel sorry for myself. If I fell now, I would never be able to pick myself up.

Bev noticed. "Oh, Sara, I'm sorry. I shouldn't have said that."

"There's no reason why you shouldn't have. I think about how sad it is every day, but thinking about it isn't going to bring Tully back. I guess I'm more sensitive than usual. I have a problem and...and...you're the only one I know who might be able to help."

"Me?"

I took a deep breath and told her about my problems with Grover Daniels and what had happened in court. "After Tully died I knew that having Adam wouldn't be easy. I knew that I'd have to depend on public assistance for a while. And knowing that, I can't even begin to tell you how I felt, how applying for welfare just about killed me. But I never thought—never—that I might end up living on the street."

"What do you mean *living on the street*?" she said, her expression sharp.

"Grover Daniels has the security deposit I gave him, which I know he'll never return. And I don't have the money for another one. Even if I did have money for a security deposit, I can't afford the rent anywhere but in subsidized housing, and that's full. Fletcher Hargrave, the head of the Department of Housing, told me that there were no openings anywhere. I can't even get on the waiting list until January. I have to be out of where I'm living in nine days, and I have nowhere to go. I hate to ask, but you mentioned that your brother and the mayor are friends. Sometimes openings do come up. What I was hoping..."

I didn't have to finish. "I'll call Warren tonight, Bev said.

"Thank you," I said. "Thank you."

Bev called me Saturday morning. "Warren says the mayor has been on vacation, but he should be back next week; they have a date to play golf on Wednesday. I told him about your deadline. Warren promised he'd do his best."

I don't know how I got through those days waiting for Bev's call. I took care of Adam, I played with him. I read. I packed. I watched television. I tried not to go insane with worry. Finally, early on the following Friday morning, Bev phoned. "I have news for you," she said. "Can you come to the shop?"

The store was empty when we arrived. Bev came out of the back room when she heard the bell. "I have to get an arrangement done before Leroy comes," she said. "Keep me company while I finish and we can talk."

Bev was adding greens to a stately flower arrangement, which contained white gladiolus and lilies. "The only place that I could get for you is a two-bedroom unit in the Grady Street project."

"Oh, thank you!" I said, nearly overcome with relief. "I can't thank you enough!"

Bev snipped the stem of a fern. "Sara, do you know anything about Grady Street?"

"Grady Gardens? It's city-owned housing, isn't it?"

"Yes," she said, placing the fern in the arrangement so that it curved artfully over the side of the container. Then she turned and looked me in the eye. "Mostly blacks live there. It's a tough place."

"It's better than the street," I said.

"You could stay with me until something better comes along. I have a big house, and it's empty after the boys go back to college."

I was astonished and moved by her generosity. "That is so kind, but I couldn't. You've already done more than enough."

The bell rang in the front of the store. "Bunting delivers," a familiar voice called out.

"Leroy!" I said. "I was going to call him to ask if he'd help me move."

"Give it a try. He might have the time since it's Labor Day weekend. And if he has trouble finding a helper, you can call Andy. He won't be leaving for school until Wednesday."

Leroy Bunting seemed as pleased to see me as I was to see him. A customer came into the shop before I had a chance to ask, so I followed him outside, waiting until he put the last of the flowers into the truck. "I'd like to hire you to help me move this weekend."

Squinting, he raised his hand to shield his eyes from the sun. "I don't know. I'd have to remove all the special shelving."

"Didn't you once tell me that Bunting delivers everything but babies?"

"I guess I did," he said with a chuckle. "Where are you movin' to?"

It was difficult for me to say. "Grady Gardens."

Leroy Bunting wasn't able to conceal his surprise. "Grady Gardens?" He shook his head and gave me a sad smile. "How would Sunday afternoon be?"

"Fine," I said. "Do you have a CD player?"

"No, but I've been meanin' to get me one."

"I have a new one that was expensive. Will you accept it as payment?"

"Hey," he said, "that's too much."

"It isn't, not for your help and the use of your truck."

"Well..."

"Then it's settled," I said firmly.

It had to be settled. I didn't have the money to pay him.

When I went back into the shop, Bev told me that I would have to go to the Grady Gardens rental office as soon as possible. "There is paperwork that will have to be done today because of the holiday weekend. The mayor's secretary has notified the office that you're taking the unit."

I thanked her again after she gave me directions to Grady Street. I felt as though I could never thank her enough.

Even with Bev's directions, I nearly drove past Grady Gardens. Tucked between the Fruit Belt, railroad tracks, and a rise of land that formed a berm between the project and its neighbors, Grady Gardens was so isolated that only its residents and their visitors would give it a second look. From the moment I approached the entrance, where men drinking from bottles in brown paper bags were sprawled on the grass between two cinder-block pillars, I sensed that Grady Gardens was located in this particular spot to segregate the people who lived there from the rest of the community. (Months later I learned that what I had sensed about the placement of Grady Gardens was correct. In the late 1950s, a section of the city that had ramshackle housing which had become an eyesore was torn down; the land was rezoned for commercial use, and the people whose homes were destroyed were shunted into Grady Gardens to keep them out of sight.)

To my relief, the two-story painted cinder-block buildings looked well-tended. The narrow strips of lawn in front of the buildings were cut and the shrubs were trimmed. There was a sign in front of the rental office, which occupied a unit in one of the smaller buildings near the entrance. A black woman whose desk was opposite the door was expecting me. "You Sara Barefield?" she said. Attracted by anything that glittered, Adam stared at her ears, which were studded with three pairs of gold earrings.

I signed a lease for sixty-two dollars a month that included heat and an allowance for electricity. Fortunately, I had put money in my wallet before I went to see Bev. The woman gave me a receipt for my first month's rent. "Here's your keys," she said. "You can move in any time."

Adam needed his bottle and nap, and I needed to finish packing, but before I left Grady Gardens I drove to see where we would live. We had been given an end unit in an eight-unit concrete-block building that was four blocks from the entrance. The building was painted a pale green. Like the rest of the complex, it looked well-kept; there was no reason to think the inside wouldn't be up to the same standard. A group of black girls were playing double Dutch in the side street. At the corner men were playing dice on the sidewalk. I turned the car around and headed out, wondering if I could ever think of this place as home.

***

On Saturday morning before I drove to Grady Gardens to clean the unit I'd rented, I knocked on Joletta's door to tell her that I was moving. "Oh, I'm sorry to hear that," she said. She was wearing shorts and a loose cotton shirt; a red-and-gold scarf was tied turban-style over her hair. "Where are you movin'?"

"Grady Street."

Joletta's expression became as solemn as if she'd been told of a death. "You've been a good neighbor. No one since I've lived here has had the upstairs so nice."

"You were right about Grover Daniels when you told me that I shouldn't do anything he could give me trouble for. He's suing me, claiming that I ruined the front lawn."

"Uh, uh. That man is as mean and greedy as they come! How much does he want?"

"Five hundred dollars."

"Five hundred dollars for nothin'! There was no grass there, hasn't been in years."

"Would he give you trouble if you said that in court?"

"Would he ever!" Joletta said. "I'm sorry, I'd help you if I could, but…"

"I understand," I said. "Is Symone home? I want to ask her if she can babysit Adam this afternoon. I'll keep him in the car seat while I clean this morning, but I'd like him to nap in his crib later."

"She's workin' this afternoon; she starts at eleven. But I can watch him, I'll be home. I'm plannin' to do my shoppin' this mornin' before the heat gets too bad."

"If you'll let me treat us to pizza for supper," I said, knowing that she wouldn't accept money for the favor.

"You got a deal!" she said.

Later, after I saw the task ahead of me, I was glad that I had asked her.

The well-tended exterior of my unit in Grady Gardens gave no clue as to what the inside would be like. What I would have to clean up. It was indescribably filthy, a shock.

The front door opened directly into the living room; the kitchen, which had metal cupboards, was behind it. Upstairs there were two bedrooms and a bathroom. The concrete-block walls, painted beige, looked like prison walls. All of the floors were covered with beige vinyl tile.

I had lived in worse places, but never one this filthy. As dirty as the Lemon Street apartment had been, it was immaculate compared to this. I spent the entire morning cleaning the bathroom, gagging constantly. I vomited twice. When I went back to Lemon Street at noon, I took a shower, then bathed and fed Adam before I left him with Joletta. On my way back to Grady Street I bought more disinfectant and cleansers. I worked in the kitchen scrubbing all afternoon and still wasn't finished when I finally left after five. The metal racks in the refrigerator were so encrusted that I had to use a steel brush to get them clean.

"You look like you're about done in," Joletta said when we sat down to eat the pizza I'd picked up.

"It's been a tough day," I said. "Is Symone home? There's plenty of pizza here."

"She's workin' 'til seven. I told her this mornin' that you're movin'. She's plannin' to come up to see you when she gets home. I'll tell her to make it quick because you're beat."

"It's all right. I've always enjoyed seeing her when she's come up to visit Adam. She's as sweet as she is lovely."

"Thank you," Joletta said. "Sometimes I wish she was still a baby like Adam. When they're little, you can remove them from trouble, just pick them up and put them someplace else. When they're seventeen, all you can do is make rules, then worry and pray that they don't break them."

I insisted that Joletta take the leftover pizza. Symone came up to say goodbye as I was getting ready to give Adam his bottle. She asked if she could feed him. After I got her settled in the rocking chair with the baby, she said, "Mama says you're movin' to Grady Street."

"Yes."

"Is it really bad there?"

"It isn't good. I like it here better, but I have no choice."

"Are you…Are you ever sorry that you had Adam?"

I sensed that I had to be careful. I didn't want to say anything that could hurt her. "No, I'm not sorry. But I thought things would be different. Adam's daddy died when I was three months pregnant. He didn't know that I was expecting. If he had known, he would have made sure that we were taken care of, that we wouldn't have had to move into a place like Grady Gardens."

"Why didn't you tell him?"

Her eyes were so wide, so trusting. "I wanted to surprise him. I was forty years old: it was a surprise. He died before I had a chance."

Later, as I was falling asleep, I wondered if I should have said more, if I should have told her that Tully would have married me, even though it wasn't quite true.

The move into Grady Gardens wasn't too different from the move to Lemon Street. Children gathered to watch Leroy and Andy unload the truck; adults watched, too, but more discreetly from behind their curtains. The air was so thick with heat and humidity that the T-shirts Leroy and Andy were wearing were soaked with sweat. After they carried the furniture in, Andy, who was familiar with it, worked on installing the air conditioner in the living room window while I helped Leroy bring in cartons. There was one little boy with skin the color of cinnamon whose eyes followed Leroy with each trip he made. The youngster's expression was serious, as if he were carefully judging something. Leroy asked him his name.

"Tyrone," the boy said.

"Well, Tyrone, you look like you got somethin' on your mind. What are you thinkin'?"

"You work hard."

"Yes, I do."

"I ain't goin' to be like you when I grow up. I'm goin' to be like my daddy. He don't have to do nothin'."

Leroy set the carton he was holding on the sidewalk and squatted to talk to the boy eye-to-eye. As always, his manner was easy, but his face was dead serious. "If your daddy don't work, then where does he get his money?"

"He get it from my mama and from the mamas of his other kids."

"Tyrone, I'm goin' to tell you somethin' and I want you to believe me: if you study in school and work hard like me when you grow up, you'll have more money than your daddy will ever have."

Tyrone looked at him skeptically. "How much you got?"

"More than you can count."

"I be in the first grade," Tyrone said, puffing up his chest. "I can count high."

"Not high enough," said Leroy with a grim laugh.

When they were finished moving everything in, I tried to give Leroy the box that contained the CD player, but he wouldn't take it. "No, you keep it."

"But we had a deal," I said.

"It's too much."

"Then give it to Andy. He can take it with him to college," I said, thrusting it into his hands. "And thank him again for me."

After the truck pulled away, I checked both doors—the one in front that opened into the living room and the back door that opened into the kitchen—to make sure they were locked. Then I decided to go to bed. I didn't have the strength to even think about all there was to do. There hadn't been time to sweep dirt that looked like dried coffee grounds off the window sills and floors; nor had there been time to wash what looked like soot off the corners of the rooms where the ceilings met the painted concrete-block walls. Moving had put Adam off his schedule. He could be up at any time, so I had to sleep while I could.

I don't know what woke me first, Adam's cries or the sensation of something crawling on my face, on my arm, on my hand. I groped for the lamp in the darkness and switched it on. Then I screamed.

Roaches. There were hundreds and hundreds of them, roaches the size of my thumbnail scurrying in response to the light. The walls were alive with roaches; they dropped from the ceiling like rain. Roaches crawling on my dresser, on the lamp, on the shade, on the fresh sheets and pillowcases, on the slippers at the side of my bed, in my hair, on my nightgown, up my leg. Brushing them off, I ran into Adam's room. The light sent the roaches into a frenzy. They scattered everywhere, crawling on top of each other, moving in waves. Roaches on the crib, on the sheet. Hysterical, I picked a roach off the corner of Adam's mouth, a roach out of his ear. There was a roach in his diaper when I changed him.

Downstairs it was more of the same: roaches running for cover, scurrying from the light. In the kitchen roaches were crawling on the countertops I'd scrubbed, in the sink, on the beige vinyl floor. There were roaches in the metal cupboards; they were crawling on the dishes, on the silverware; there was a roach inside one of Adam's clean, empty bottles. Suddenly I realized that the dirt like dried coffee grounds that I had seen everywhere was roach excrement.

By some miracle there were no roaches in the refrigerator. Quickly, I grabbed a bottle and shut the door. I wanted to run from this horrible place, but where could I go in the middle of the night? I thought of sitting in my car. But the car was parked on the street, and I was more afraid of the street than I was of the roaches. My only alternatives were two hells.

I went into the living room and pulled the rocking chair into the center of the room. And that is where I stayed the rest of the night, rocking, thinking, Adam sleeping nestled against my shoulder, his warm breath on my neck. Unwelcome thoughts crowded into my head. I recalled a television show I'd seen on which childless middle-class couples made public pleas to pregnant women to give up their babies for adoption. I thought of Ardelle and the children in some strange city where I could never hope to find them. I thought of Mrs. Rutland, rooted in Tully's house. And I thought of Tully, of how he would feel if he could see me and his baby in this roach-infested place.

Adam was all I had in this world, my only family. From the beginning I knew that having him would be hard, but I believed that any problems I encountered would be temporary. I never thought I'd end up in a hell like this.

***

Although I knew what was coming, I was no better prepared for my second night on Grady Street than I had been for the first. By the time I arrived at the rental office early Tuesday morning, I was exhausted and hysterical. "The unit you rented to me is infested with roaches!" I told the black woman whose ears were studded with three pairs of gold earrings.

"I'll schedule you for the exterminator."

"I need him to come today. I can't go through another night of roaches crawling all over my baby and me!"

"I'll look at the schedule." The woman shuffled through some papers until she found the one she wanted. "It looks like Thursday's the earliest."

"*THURSDAY!*" I shrieked. "I've been up for two nights! The place isn't fit to live in! It should be condemned!"

The woman shrugged. "There's nothin' I can do."

"Well, there's something I can do!" I said, so angry I was shaking. "If my place isn't exterminated by noon today, I'm going to call the newspaper so they can send a photographer over tonight! I guarantee the pictures will make the front page! There are so many roaches you can't see the walls!"

My threat wasn't tested. An hour later while I was upstairs changing Adam's diaper I heard the front door open. "Who's there?" I called, my heart pounding.

"Exterminator," a deep male voice called back.

I put Adam in his crib and hurried downstairs. A wiry man whose rough brown skin looked like it had been pitted by the chemicals he used was glancing around the living room. "How did you get in here?" I said.

He held up a ring of keys. "Empty the cabinets and cover your food. If you got any goldfish, cover the bowls. I'll be back in a couple hours."

"It's really bad in here," I said, disturbed by the fact that he'd let himself in. I wondered how many other people had keys to my door.

"Yeah, I can see that by the eggs," he said, looking up at the corners of the ceiling at what I'd thought was soot.

There weren't as many roaches that night, but I still couldn't sleep. I was up constantly, checking on Adam and surveying my own sheets for insects. And when I was finally able to doze, I was jarred awake by banging on the front door.

I put on a robe and went downstairs, wondering who it could be at six forty-five in the morning. "Who's there?"

"Verona Finch. I live next door."

I opened the door a crack. A large woman was standing on the walk with her hands on her hips, her anger so visible that the freckles scattered across her nose stood out boldly against her light brown skin. "Are you outta your mind! Do you know what you done! You sent your filthy roaches into my place!"

"They aren't *my* roaches," I said, opening the door wider. "They were here when I moved in."

"Well, I don't want 'em! I got a business to run!"

"Business? What business?"

"That's none 'a your business! Don't you be callin' the exterminator again!"

"I'm not going to live with roaches! I'll keep calling the exterminator until they're gone!"

"All you be doin' is sendin' 'em to my place!"

"No, that's not all I'll be doing," I said. "I'll be keeping my place clean. If you keep your place clean, too, maybe we'll be rid of them."

"*Rid of roaches on Grady Street?*" Verona Finch said, staring at me. "You just plain crazy!

FALL, 1992

For as long as I could remember, the one constant good thing in my life besides Tully was books. From the day I learned how to read I was able to escape my parents' battles, my brother's meanness, the stigma of being poor and being a Barefield. When I read, I heard the authors' voices in their books and heard my own voice responding, my private voice, the voice I used to think with, the one I used to speak to myself. Reading took me to worlds that were better than the one I lived in, and introduced me to people and places I wouldn't have known otherwise. Reading was my education, my solace, my means of escape.

There have been only two times in my life when I couldn't read: the first weeks after Tully died and the first weeks I spent on Grady Street.

Those first weeks in Grady Gardens I felt as if I were moving through a fog. I went outside only to go to my car, which I parked on the side street next to my unit, and when I went to check my mailbox, one of a group of eight metal boxes stacked on a post near the curb at the corner. I avoided contact with the people who lived around me, even though I was almost always given a courteous nod or a pleasant comment on the weather when I encountered another Grady Street resident. I was so disconnected those first weeks that I didn't wonder, even once, if the situation were reversed, if the project were filled with white folks, with people like the Barefields and the Rutlands, and I were one of less than a handful of blacks who moved in, if my presence would have been met with the same tolerance.

On my better days, if the weather was especially nice, I escaped Grady Street by driving across town to a park. It was in the park on a brilliant September morning that I witnessed something so special that for a long time afterward I thought of it as a break in the clouds, a shining moment in what seemed like unending bleakness. Adam and I were on a blanket spread under the shade of a large oak. Adam was on his back, awake and gurgling happily. Suddenly his gaze locked on his hand. I watched as his eyes followed the movement of his fingers, his fist opening and closing, at first tentative, then deliberate, his eyes widening with the realization that this object of enormous fascination was indeed attached to him and that he had the ability to control it. Briefly, all of my trials—food stamps, welfare, Grady Street—were forgotten. For a while one magical morning there was nothing other than the joy of witnessing my son discovering his hand.

On days when I found roach eggs on the dishes in the cupboard (I finally started storing the dishes, glasses, and pots I used in the refrigerator, the one place that was roach-free) or opened the kitchen door and spotted a rat in the tiny fenced yard behind my unit, I escaped by watching television. Hour after hour I saw talk shows on which ordinary people made extraordinary confessions: women revealed that they had been molested as children by their fathers, their brothers, their uncles, their grandfathers; married men confessed to having had affairs with younger women, with older women, with men dressed as women; men and women talked about group sex, about no sex, about failures and fetishes and one-night stands. There were men who lived as women, women who lived as men, and those who couldn't decide how they wanted to live. I saw people who had every kind of phobia, people who were racists, people who were compulsive gamblers, compulsive liars, compulsive thieves. On one particular day I saw a show that featured teenagers who were arrested for having had sex on a department store bed, a rapist who had insisted that he hadn't raped a woman because she'd asked him to wear a condom, feuding neighbors who had destroyed each others' property, a mother who had blackmailed her daughter with a video of her having sex, and people who cared only about having their own orgasm first. I felt like I was watching a long, continuous strip show, an unending procession of people exposing what they should have kept hidden for the entertainment of strangers. After a while their names, faces, and problems became indistinct, a blur of pain and humiliation to which I could respond.

If it weren't for my tooth, I might have lingered in front of the television set indefinitely. The tooth, an upper molar, had been sensitive to cold since Adam was born. I hadn't seen a dentist in over a year and decided to ignore the sensitivity in the hope that it would go away. But by the third week in September I couldn't eat or drink anything cold without experiencing pain. Assuming that I would have to go to Dearth Memorial for dental care as I did for medical care for myself and Adam, I called the hospital and was told that they didn't have a dental clinic; however, there was a dental clinic at the university. But when I called the university clinic, I was told that the only care they provided to Medicaid patients over the age of eighteen was extractions and temporary fillings. "There's only one dentist to see over twenty patients in two hours," a woman said hurriedly. "If you've got pain, bleeding, or swelling, you can come to the emergency walk-in clinic for an extraction."

"But what if the tooth doesn't need to be extracted?" I said. "What if it just needs to be filled?"

"We don't provide preventative care—no fillings, crowns, or bridges—for Medicaid patients," the woman said. "Sorry, I have to go. There are people waiting. If the tooth is really bad, come in and we'll pull it."

I hung up, my tongue curling protectively around the tooth, a gesture I had seen my mama do countless times. Except in Mama's mouth the space was empty; the tooth had been pulled. To Mama, each missing tooth was an announcement of her poverty. "Teeth are a dead giveaway," she often said bitterly. "A smile tells quicker 'n anythin' who has money and who don't."

A good portion of her teeth were gone when she died in her late thirties.

None of my teeth were missing; nor were any edged with decay. The lesson of Mama's anger and unhappiness wasn't lost. The first money I was able to save, cash earned babysitting when I was in my early teens, was used to pay a dentist. And over the years money for the dentist always came before anything else, before a new dress or a new plant or a nice cut of meat at the supermarket. I was never going to be like Mama, self-conscious to the point of shame when I smiled in front of strangers. No clinic dentist was going to pull my tooth!

By the last Thursday in September, I had no choice: I had to see a dentist. But after paying my most pressing bills, all I had was fourteen dollars, which would have to stretch another full week until my ADC check came. Determined to save my tooth, I decided to go to a private dentist and work out payments afterward. My rent was so much less than it had been on Lemon Street that I could certainly manage to pay something.

Reasoning that I would probably be refused if I called for an emergency appointment because I wasn't a regular patient, I decided to go directly to a dentist's office. A dentist wouldn't interrupt his schedule for me, but he might agree to see me late in the day if he had time. I left Grady Street shortly after three in the afternoon and drove to a modern brick building on Lee Avenue near Magnolia's, where I tried several dentists without success. Discouraged, I remembered a dentist's office a few blocks away from Dearth Memorial Hospital. It had caught my attention because the small gray clapboard structure looked like a cottage nestled between two large Victorian homes.

It was four fifteen when I pulled into a driveway that led to a parking lot behind the office of Dr. Carl Shields. I took Adam, who was sleeping in his car seat, and went into the building through the only entrance, which faced the street. There was one person in the waiting room, an elderly woman whose cane was propped against a chair. A prim-looking woman wearing an office smock the color of mint toothpaste was behind a gray counter that served as the reception desk. "Can I help you?" she said, eying Adam as if she expected him to awaken and disturb the gray silence.

"I'm new in Stalling, and I need to see a dentist: I can't eat or drink anything cold without experiencing pain. I was hoping, if the dentist has time, that he could see me after his last patient."

"I don't know. It's already so late in the day…" the woman said, her tone leaving a trail of doubt.

"Could you ask him?"

"He's with a patient now."

"When he's finished?" I said. "Please, I'd really appreciate it."

Before she could reply, I turned and went to the waiting area, where I sat in a chair opposite the elderly woman. "What a lovely baby!" the woman said in a loud whisper. "I wish I could sleep like that. I can hardly sleep at all anymore."

"Oh," I said sympathetically, reaching for a magazine.

"My husband can't sleep, either. But he sleeps during the day; he takes little naps. All those naps add up. Yes, they do!" the woman said, slipping into what sounded like a familiar argument.

I couldn't open the magazine without appearing rude until the woman stopped talking, but she didn't stop. She talked about her arthritis, her digestion, her daughter's worthless husband. One subject seemed to suggest another. Nearly a half hour passed. Then an elderly gentleman wearing a blue knit shirt and brown checked pants emerged from the back, the right side of his mouth sliding toward his chin. "There he is," said the woman, rising heavily.

The receptionist waited until the couple left, then disappeared down a hall that led to the back offices. "Dr. Shields will see you," she said when she returned, her frown registering her disagreement with the decision.

After I filled out a patient information card, I picked up Adam in his car seat, thankful that he was still sleeping. Usually he was up late in the afternoon; it was his fussy time. But I hadn't let him nap long in the morning and I had fed him before we left, so with luck he'd be out for a while longer.

There were three rooms at the end of the hall. Dr. Carl Shields was standing in the doorway to the room on the right. Slightly taller than me, he was wearing a lab coat the same shade of toothpaste green as the receptionist's smock. He had a long, rather narrow face that seemed somewhat mismatched with his chunky frame. Although I guessed that he was in his late forties or early fifties, his shoulders were stooped, perhaps the result of years of bending over patients. "I understand you're having a problem," he said, looking at Adam with interest.

He stepped aside and gestured for me to enter the office. "You can put the baby in that corner," he said, tilting his head toward the only suitable spot in the small room.

After I was settled in the chair, he put on glasses, latex gloves, and a mask. "Which tooth is giving you the trouble?"

"It's sensitive to cold," I said, pointing to the tooth.

"Mmm, the bicuspid." He adjusted the light, picked up his instruments, and peered inside. "The tooth is cracked."

"Cracked? Does that mean I'll lose it?"

"Oh, no! I can stabilize the tooth with a pin and then do a bonded filling. It will look better than it does now with that old silver filling you have."

While he waited for the shot of Novocaine he gave me to take effect, he asked me about Adam. "He's three months old," I said.

"He's very fair."

"His daddy was fair."

"Was?"

"He died last January."

The dentist's brown eyes softened; he shook his head sympathetically. "Then he never saw his son. That's hard. My wife died of cancer last December. We didn't have any children. She was the office manager; she kept the books and did all the billing."

"I'm sorry," I said.

The whine of the drill woke Adam. Immediately interested in the new sounds and sights, he watched intently until he became absorbed in his feet, his most recent discovery. I was also absorbed, thinking about how I would approach the subject of payment. All these months I had resisted using my Visa card so I would have credit in case of an emergency. If Dr. Shields accepted Visa, my problem was solved. If he didn't, I would offer to make payments. But if he wouldn't take payments...

Worried, I tried to think of something else. My birthday was on Sunday. I remembered my fortieth birthday last year, Tully's disappearance, and my lunch with Ardelle. Looking up as the dentist fitted a metal ring around my tooth, I spotted a cobweb in the corner of the room near the ceiling. The cobweb reminded me of what Ardelle had talked about during that birthday lunch, which gave me another idea, one more possibility.

The work on my tooth was finished within an hour. Dr. Shields removed the bib from my neck and handed me a mirror to see my tooth. As he had promised, it looked better than before, really perfect. "I...I'd like to talk to you about the bill. How much will it be?"

"One hundred ten dollars, eight for the pin and one hundred two for the filling."

"Do you accept Visa?"

"No."

"I can't pay all at once, but I can manage ten dollars a month, maybe fifteen."

He grimaced as if he'd bitten into something disagreeable. "That would involve too much bookkeeping. Can't you borrow the money?"

"No," I said, "I can't. But I could work to pay it off. I noticed that cobweb in the corner near the window. I could clean in exchange for the filling."

Dr. Shields thought for a moment. "You'd have to clean the

offices twice to take care of the bill," he said. "And you'd have to use your own equipment—vacuum, bucket, rags, and so on."

"When do you want me to come?"

"I'd have to be here, so it would have to be Saturday afternoon, if you're free."

"I'll be here at one," I said.

***

Carl Shields pulled into the office parking lot on Saturday as I was getting out of my car. I was dressed for cleaning in a pair of old jeans and a T-shirt. He parked his car, a tan Mercedes, next to mine. I was conscious of his eyes on me as I leaned through the back door of the Buick to fetch Adam in his car seat. "Do you need help?" he said.

"You could take the bucket, if you wouldn't mind."

The bucket was filled with cleansers, a roll of paper towels, and disposable rags; there was also a new pair of rubber gloves. I had worn through several pairs of rubber gloves cleaning my unit in Grady Gardens. I bought the new pair because I didn't want to come in contact with strangers' germs, particularly not in a place where syringes were used and people bled.

"I'll be working in my office. It's the door on the left in the back," he said after we were inside.

I put Adam in the office on the right where my tooth had been filled. Again, I had kept him up most of the morning and hoped he would sleep all afternoon. Then I went back to my car to get the vacuum and a broom.

I was able to work steadily for close to three hours before Adam started fussing. There were sticky spots on the imitation leather chairs in the waiting room, fingerprints everywhere, smudges on the walls, pyramids of dust in awkward corners. It seemed to me that the place hadn't been properly cleaned in a long time, and that is what I told Carl (he asked me to call him by his first name) while I worked in his small office. "Then the cleaning service wasn't doing a good job," he said.

I didn't think to ask how long it had been since he had last had the cleaning service.

He followed me when I went to check on Adam. I peeled off the rubber gloves before I picked up the baby. Carl watched while I changed Adam and ran a bottle under hot water to warm it. "How much more do you have to do?" he asked.

"Just this room."

"You've done a nice job. Let me know when you're finished."

Adam took his bottle greedily, and by four thirty I was set to leave. Carl offered to carry the vacuum and the bucket; he watched while I loaded the car. "Then I'll see you next week at one?"

"Yes," I said, fastening the car seat.

"How is your tooth?"

"Fine, thanks."

He seemed to want to talk, but I was anxious to get back to Grady Street while it was still light; and although I wasn't dirty, I wanted to strip off my clothes and take a shower. "See you next week," I said, pulling away.

The next day, Sunday, was dismal. I wished that it weren't overcast and rainy so I could drive to the park and play with Adam in the sunshine, and forget for a while that it was my forty-first birthday. I thought of my fortieth birthday, of the unending tears I had shed over Tully's disappearance. Now he was gone forever, and missing him had become an ache that never went away.

As the day wore on, it felt like the cinder-block walls were closing in. The apartment I'd had in Altavista Gardens with its immaculate white walls and new appliances and carpeting seemed as remote as a dream. Owings seemed as remote as a dream, too. I hadn't kept in touch with anyone there; I couldn't bear the thought of my friends knowing my circumstances. No one in Stalling knew it was my birthday. I hadn't received a note or a call or a card. Ardelle had always remembered my birthday. I wondered where Ardelle and the girls were, and how they were doing.

Early in the evening there was a break in the rain. From Adam's bedroom window I could see a steady stream of people walking on a well-worn path behind the units down a slope to a low, rectangular piece of land set between the slope and a berm, which I learned later was called *The Bottom*. Though I didn't know the name of the piece of land at that time, I had no doubts as to its attraction: drugs were bought and sold there. From Adam's window I had seen people of all ages, males and females, getting high. I had seen boys dealing who were no more than ten or eleven years old. I had seen angry shoving and pushing and the flash of knives. I had seen women gesturing wildly, some getting on their knees like beggars, while teenage dealers looked at them with stony contempt and walked away. For a while I had kept the window shade down, thinking that I could block it out. But blocking out *The Bottom* didn't make it go away. I knew what was going on beyond that window. More than anything, I wanted to be out of Grady Gardens before Adam was old enough to look out and ask questions.

***

The month ended as badly as it had begun. On September thirtieth I returned to court and watched, angry and frustrated, as Grover Daniels stepped up to the bench and handed Judge Wayland his pictures. "You can see, Judge," Daniels said smugly, "in that first picture the lawn is perfect. The next picture shows her car parked on it. And that last picture shows the place now, nothin' but a mess of mud and weeds."

The judge, still deeply tanned, studied the photographs. "When was this picture of the lawn taken?"

"Before she moved in," Daniels said.

Judge Wayland looked at Daniels skeptically. "How long before? A month? A year?"

"I can't say for sure."

"How long have you owned the property?"

"Lemme see..." Daniels studied the ceiling. "About...uh... fifteen years," he said, his voice less confident now.

"Then this picture could have been taken when you bought the house fifteen years ago?"

I could see perspiration forming on Daniels' broad forehead. "No," he said.

"But you can't prove the date," the judge said, turning his attention to me. "Do you have any evidence to present?"

"No," I said. "I didn't think to take a picture. There was no lawn when I moved in. It was the same as it is now, dirt and weeds."

"Do you have any witnesses who can verify that, another tenant or neighbors?"

"I asked the other tenant, but she's still living there so it's hard. She doesn't want any trouble."

The judge handed me the picture that showed the house with a lawn. I looked at the photograph, trying to stay calm. "This picture shows two lights by the front door, but the house has only one outside light; the other one is gone. And there are hardly any of the shrubs that are in this picture. If you drove by, you'd see."

Judge Wayland nodded. "Well, Mr. Daniels?"

Daniels' forehead was coated with sweat. "Vandals," he said. "The light was broke right before she moved in."

"And the shrubs?"

"They got a blight. The winter was hard."

The judge coughed to clear his throat. "Mr. Daniels has shown by a preponderance of the evidence that the damage occurred during Ms. Barefield's stay. He has testified and produced pictures of the property before and after her tenancy. Since Ms. Barefield has no witnesses, no pictures, and no additional evidence, I am compelled to find for Mr. Daniels."

I had all I could do not to scream, *DANIELS WAS LYING!*

My security deposit of $290 was deducted from Daniels' $500 claim of damages. He was awarded a judgment of $210, plus an additional judgment for $300 for the loss of his September rent. Grover Daniels now had a total of $810 in judgments against me.

Gone in an instant was a lifetime of working to have a good credit record.

***

It was easier to clean the dentist's office the second time. "You've done a great job," Carl Shields said when I was finished. "I've marked your bill paid."

I had been conscious of him all afternoon. He had frequently come into the areas in which I was working as if he were looking for something, and each time he had stayed to chat for a few minutes. Dressed in a yellow knit shirt and khakis, he was more attractive than he was in his green clinic coat. He talked about the weather, about repainting the waiting room, about how hard it was to keep up an office and a house when he'd been used to his wife taking charge of these things. His manner was friendly, his tone confiding. I had used some of the money from my welfare check to get a haircut, my first in nearly a year, and I looked better than I had in a long time. His attention was flattering, so I was unprepared when, after he helped me load the car, he said, "I have something to ask. I hope you won't take it the wrong way. I know the only reason you cleaned my office was to take care of your bill. You probably don't do this work normally, but if you'd be willing, I'd like to hire you to clean my house."

A cleaning woman. He thought of me as a cleaning woman. I felt my cheeks burn. How foolish I'd been!

"I'm sorry," he said quickly. "I guess I shouldn't have asked, but I could really use the help."

Despite my hurt feelings, I couldn't afford pride, not when I thought about the clothes Adam needed for the winter; he was growing fast, and baby things were expensive. I wanted a stroller, which would make taking him places easier. But I had signed those papers at the welfare office. Any money I made would be deducted from my check.

"I can give you cash so the money can't be traced," he said, as if he were reading my thoughts.

What he was offering was exactly what Ardelle had talked about.

"When would you want me to come?"

"One o'clock next Saturday is fine. I'm playing golf in the morning." He took a pad and pen out of his shirt pocket. "I live at 1092 Dogwood Lane," he said, writing rapidly. "Do you know where it is?"

"No."

"I'll draw you a map. You shouldn't have any trouble. And I have a vacuum, so you don't have to bring yours."

His map was as precise as his dental work. The following Saturday I found his house easily. It was in an established subdivision off Lee Avenue, a two-story red brick colonial that had white trim and dark green shutters. Fifteen minutes early (I had allowed extra time in case I got lost), I decided to park in the driveway. It had rained most of the morning, and gathering dark clouds looked threatening again.

Carl came to the door smiling broadly. He was dressed in rumpled khakis and a green sweater. "I couldn't play golf because of the weather, so I got a head start straightening up. I'll show you around after you get the baby settled."

The motion of the car had put Adam to sleep. I followed Carl upstairs to a bedroom that had twin beds covered with white ruffled bedspreads that were starting to yellow. "Would you mind if I take one of the bedspreads off and put the car seat on the bed?" I asked, hoping he wouldn't suspect that what I really wanted was a clean spot on which to set the car seat.

"I'll do it."

He whisked off the bedspread, releasing a cloud of dust. I stepped back, shielding Adam's face with my hand.

Carl took me on a tour of the house. There were four bedrooms and two bathrooms upstairs, the master bedroom and bath unusually spacious. I wasn't paying as much attention to what was in the rooms as I was looking at the dust that coated everything, and the fine cobwebs in the corners, and the mildew I could see growing on the grout and tiles through the glass shower door. "I guess the shower doesn't look too good," he said with an embarrassed laugh.

Downstairs, it was more of the same. The rooms he used—the kitchen, family room, laundry room, and half-bath—needed cleaning; the living room and dining room were studies in dust. Though this house and its contents were far nicer, it reminded me of Mrs. Rutland's. There was a fussiness about it, an overabundance of clutter: collections of decorative silver teaspoons displayed in wall racks, a herd of ceramic and glass elephants on an end table, groups of silver and brass picture frames on an unused baby grand piano, hand-painted porcelain birds, boxes of all sizes made of inlaid wood. Too much to dust, I thought, trying to imagine the woman who had bought all these things: a woman who had spent hours and hours of her life shopping, hours and hours of fussing and arranging. Although I liked the colors in the house, the blues and reds and creamy whites, it didn't feel comfortable.

"Where do you want me to start?" I said.

He shook his head, as though the size of the task was beyond him. "Anywhere."

"Would you prefer a light cleaning or a thorough one?"

This time he didn't hesitate. "Thorough," he said.

Four hours later I had cleaned most of the downstairs with the exception of the living room. I had expected the kitchen to be a disaster, but it wasn't as bad as I had feared. The counter tops were relatively clean, although the sponge he must have used to wipe them with was so dirty and sour smelling that I wondered why he didn't buy a new one. Sponges were cheap. Living in a house this grand, he could afford buckets full of sponges. The microwave oven and the kitchen floor needed the heaviest scrubbing; the built-in oven looked like it had never been used.

I had brought Adam downstairs after his nap. He was in the family room in his car seat, which was on the rug facing the television. Carl was sitting nearby on a blue leather lounge chair, his feet resting on a matching ottoman. "Your son seems to like commercials," he said. "They really grab his attention."

"Commercials are louder, and they have music and bright colors."

Carl smiled. "He's certainly a happy baby."

"He has a good disposition, like his daddy."

"I hope you're not offended if I ask what his daddy did for a living."

I looked at the built-in bookcases, the expensive furniture and the Oriental rug, and felt myself becoming defensive. I didn't want Tully judged by this stoop-shouldered man. I didn't want to say that he was a mechanic. Tully wasn't *just* a mechanic. He was gifted, he was special. "He rebuilt and restored old cars."

"Old cars!" he said enthusiastically. "I've always wanted an old T-Bird."

"Tully owned two T-Birds, a 1957 and a 1960."

I regretted the words as soon as they were out of my mouth. Carl was looking at me skeptically, as if he were wondering what I was doing cleaning his house if the father of my child had owned two such valuable cars. I stooped to pick up Adam. "I'm ready to leave."

He glanced at his watch, then reached into his pants pocket and took out folded bills held by a money clip. "Four hours," he said, handing me two twenties. "This should do it."

I hesitated before accepting the money. I had worked longer and harder here than I had in his office, and he was paying me what amounted to five dollars less.

He noticed my reluctance. "I hope you think that's fair. It's ten dollars an hour."

I wasn't sure it was fair, but I vaguely remembered Ardelle talking about fifty dollars for five hours' work. Maybe he was right. Ten dollars an hour was more than double what I was paid at Magnolia's. "It's fine," I said.

"I hope you'll come back next week. It'll take a few more Saturdays to get this place in shape."

"Would you mind if I started earlier?"

"My golf game is usually over by eleven thirty. I can be back here at noon. I'll stop on my way and pick up something for lunch. Will you join me?"

He seemed so pleased at the prospect that I didn't feel I could refuse. "Sure," I said.

He held the door for me and walked me to the car. "It was nice having you and the baby here today. Sometimes the house feels so big and empty. It's much too large for one person. I thought it was too large for me and my wife when we bought it, but Marge—that was my wife's name—always wanted a big red brick colonial. She said it was her dream house."

I smiled sympathetically and got into the car, wanting to get back to Grady Street before dark.

***

Carl had lunch on the table when I arrived on the following Saturday. He had bought chicken sandwiches and French fries at Burger King. Even with the two cans of Coke and two glasses he'd put out, the food looked lost on the large oak table. "I guess I should have thought of something for dessert," he said. "There isn't much in the house. I keep forgetting to go grocery shopping."

He might have forgotten to buy food, but he didn't forget to buy beer. He offered me a cold bottle, already open on the kitchen counter, when I was finished cleaning. "Thanks," I said, "but I'd like to get home before it gets dark."

"Ten minutes won't make a difference."

"Maybe another time."

"I'll take that as a promise for next week," he said.

"If you don't mind, I'd like to skip next Saturday. It's Halloween, and I want to be home in the afternoon in case children come to the door."

"Won't they go away if no one answers?"

"I haven't lived there very long. I don't know what to expect."

He put his arm around me protectively. "Would you like to stay here overnight? I can borrow a crib from one of the neighbors. You can come next Saturday at noon like you did today and park your car in the garage. Then you won't have anything to worry about."

"I have been worried about my car," I said.

"Then it's settled!" he said so enthusiastically that it wasn't until after I was in the car that I realized I hadn't agreed.

All week I wondered about his offer, if his invitation was motivated by kindness or something else. I was aware of how he looked at me and of his efforts to be friendly, which made me sure he had more on his mind than getting his house clean. But once before I had made that assumption and I had been wrong. Also, if I hadn't brought up the subject of Halloween, he wouldn't have made the offer. Carl didn't particularly appeal to me, not in the way I cared for Tully, but he was nice. It felt good when he put his arm around me. For a moment I didn't feel so alone.

I decided to pack for an overnight stay but to give myself an option by keeping the suitcase in the trunk. If he didn't see the suitcase, it would be less awkward if I wanted to leave at the end of the day.

Carl was outside raking leaves when I arrived. He put down the rake and gestured for me to pull into the open garage. Adam smiled when he came up to the car. "Hey, fella," Carl said, clearly pleased. "I'll take Adam. He can sit with us while we have lunch. I ordered a pizza. It should be here soon."

The pizza had anchovies on it. "I hope you like anchovies. Marge hated them, but they're my favorite."

I had never imagined that pizza could taste so awful. "Then you can have mine as well."

"Are you sure?"

"Positive," I said, trying not to think of the mushroom-and-sausage pizzas Tully and I had shared.

"What are you planning on doing today?"

"I'll finish the upstairs, then vacuum and dust down here. If there's time, I'll wash the kitchen floor."

I worked five hours instead of four. When I was done every surface was dusted, the rugs were vacuumed, the bathrooms sparkled, the brick vinyl floor in the kitchen shone. "This house never looked so good. Sara, I truly thank you," he said.

I decided that I would stay. "Would you mind watching Adam while I shower?" I said.

"What if he cries?"

"He's usually happy unless something is bothering him. If he cries, pick him up and he'll probably stop. I won't be long."

In less than a half hour I was back downstairs dressed in navy slacks and a burgundy sweater. I had put on a touch of makeup—blush, lipstick, and mascara. "You look *really* nice," he said.

"I don't always wear cleaning clothes."

"Let's relax with a few beers. Later, I'll light the grill and put on the steaks. I got potatoes and the fixings for salad in the refrigerator."

Steak, potato, salad. The pizza for lunch. Images of Tully flashed through my mind. But he wasn't Tully.

"Is something wrong? Did I say something to upset you?"

"No…Nothing," I said, blinking back tears. "I must have an eyelash in my eye."

"I'm great at getting those out. Manual dexterity, you know."

"I'm fine now."

But he insisted on checking. He put his hand under my chin and told me to look up. "Mmm," he said. Then he kissed me. "I've wanted to do that for a long time."

I was unsure of how I felt, unsure of what to say. "I…I'd better feed Adam before I have that beer."

Our dinner was interrupted by the frequent ringing of the doorbell. Carl was handing out sugarless gum. "Some of the kids are probably disappointed, but it wouldn't look right for a dentist to give candy," he said.

I caught glimpses of the trick-or-treaters and was charmed by their exuberance and the inventiveness of their costumes—a teapot, a bullfighter, a carrot. These children seemed to have more self-assurance than the children at Creekside Elementary. It had to be the homes they came from, the security. Oh, how I wanted that security for Adam.

"I enjoyed dinner," he said while we cleared the table, "but I wish it had been quieter. It seemed like there were more kids than ever this year. They came later, too. I can't believe it's already past ten."

"Time for Adam's last bottle."

"I'll take care of the dishes," he said.

Adam was in the smallest bedroom. Carl came upstairs as I was putting him back in the crib. "He seems to be looking for something," he observed.

"Butterflies," I said. "He has a mobile of butterflies fluttering over his crib."

"It must be nice to wake up and see butterflies, though if I had my choice, I'd want to see you."

I took a deep breath. I knew what was coming and I didn't know what I should do.

Perhaps it was the way he kissed me, tentatively at first, as if he were afraid he might be rejected, that made me respond. It had been so long since I'd been held. We seemed to drift into his bedroom naturally. Then we were undressed and in bed and he was marveling at my breasts, making love to them, I began to feel, rather than to me. He entered me wearing a lubricated condom. After what seemed like no more than a half-dozen thrusts, he came. "It's always a little awkward at first," he said, rolling off me. "The next time it'll be better."

Earlier I had made up one of the twin beds in the bedroom across the hall. As soon as I sensed that he was asleep, I eased his arm off me and crept out of the room.

I couldn't sleep. Never had I imagined that so intimate an act could have left me feeling so empty. Yet at the same time, his attention was flattering. He made me feel attractive. He made me feel desirable. He made me feel good about myself.

Carl greeted me with a kiss when I came into the kitchen in the morning. His breath smelled like mint toothpaste. "I hope my snoring didn't chase you away last night."

"I was restless. I didn't want to disturb you."

He had made coffee, and there were sweet rolls on the kitchen counter. We ate leisurely, reading the paper and playing with Adam. Later, while I showered, I thought about how pleasant the morning had been, how pleasant it was staying in this lovely house, and how Adam was responding so happily to Carl's attention. Maybe he was right, that it was always awkward the first time. The only man I'd ever known was Tully, the one true love of my life. I couldn't expect another love like that. Carl seemed to really care for me. I had to do what Ardelle said, I had to look forward and not back.

It was approaching noon when someone rang the doorbell. I was starting down the circular staircase carrying Adam. I had finished loading the car and we were dressed to leave. "Did you check your windows?" I heard a woman ask.

"No," Carl said.

"Someone soaped ours. I'm just furious! Charles and I handed out treats all night, a fortune in candy."

"I'd better look," Carl said.

I decided to wait at the top of the stairs until the woman left. Making myself known could cause embarrassment. I heard the click of the woman's heels as they crossed the marble foyer floor. "They did soap the windows!" Carl said. "It's going to be a job to clean."

"I want to know who has been cleaning this house. Everything in here sparkles!" the woman said.

"I hired a cleaning woman," Carl said.

"Is she expensive?"

"I don't know the going rate. I've been paying her ten dollars an hour."

"I've been paying more—fifty dollars for four hours—and my house doesn't look anywhere near as good as this. Where did you find her?"

"She's a patient of mine. She cleaned my office, too."

"Do you know if she has any free days?"

"I'll ask her if she's interested. She could probably use the money. She's white, but she lives in the Grady…"

I couldn't listen anymore. My eyes stung, my throat burned. I went into the nearest bedroom and waited until the woman left, then rushed down the stairs, pausing briefly in front of Carl Shields before hurrying into the garage. "You can find yourself a new cleaning woman!" I said.

I don't know how I managed to drive home. I was angry, I was devastated, I felt like a fool. And if I weren't feeling badly enough, when I pulled into Grady Gardens I realized that he hadn't paid me the fifty dollars I was owed for Saturday's cleaning.

***

A week after my experience with Carl Shields, Bev called me on Sunday morning. "I hope you didn't think I'd forgotten about you," she said. "I've had a wedding every weekend but one since mid-September. Today I'm going to relax and make a big pot of soup. Can you and Adam come for supper?"

"We'd love to!" I said.

The invitation pulled me out of what was beginning to feel like permanent gloom. Crushed by the conversation I'd overheard between Carl and his neighbor, I'd had a miserable week. Over and over I'd told myself how stupid I'd been not to realize how I appeared to him, a white woman with a Grady Street address. Trash. He thought of me as trash. And the proof, not that I needed it, was that he hadn't made an attempt to contact me to apologize; nor had he bothered to send the money he owed me, which I was sure I would never see.

Since the day was mild, Bev wanted us to come early enough to spend some time in her garden. Her house was three blocks from Carl's. It was also a red brick colonial, but smaller and less impressive from the street. Inside, however, the house had a tasteful charm that his house lacked. "Do you think Adam will come to me?" Bev said, greeting us with outstretched arms.

Responding to her smile and warm coaxing, Adam went easily from my arms to hers.

Although only a few late asters and chrysanthemums were in

bloom, I was enchanted by Bev's garden. The beds moved in graceful curves around the yard, and each area had its own appeal—whimsical statues, a small pond that had fish swimming beneath lily pads, an old iron bench, carefully placed trees and shrubs. A gold November sun glinted off stone paths that wove between the plants. "If I had a garden like this, I'd never want to leave it," I said.

"Gardens are seductive. I can't count the number of times I've escaped here."

We spread a blanket on the grass where Adam slept fitfully while we sat on wood lawn chairs and talked. For the first time in months I had someone with whom I could share my thoughts, and I had done a lot of thinking since my devastating experience with Carl Shields. "I hate being where I am," I confessed when Bev asked me how I was doing. "I feel like I'm sinking in deeper with each day that passes. I want to go to school—there's a program at the Women's Center that will help me—but I don't feel right about putting Adam in daycare. He's so young. And this time with him is so special; he's doing something new almost every day."

"And you don't want to miss a moment of it," Bev said. "I don't blame you. My niece didn't want to go back to work, but she had no choice. Like most young couples today, she and her husband need both of their incomes. They've adjusted and their baby is fine."

My skin prickled with embarrassment. "I must look terrible to you—like a freeloader— staying home with Adam while your niece goes to work."

"Oh, no," Bev said. "Your situation is completely different. My niece and her husband have a big new house to pay for."

"Owning a house—not a big house, just a small house for me and Adam—is one of my dreams, too. But it will never happen if I don't go back to school soon. I'll be too old."

"You're far from too old."

"Not if I want to become a teacher. It takes five years of college to get certification."

"You want to be a teacher?" Bev said with surprise.

"That's all I ever wanted to be besides a wife and mother. I just never had the opportunity."

"How will you manage it now? Where will you get the money?"

I told her about Yolanda Washington and the Reach Up program. I had read the newspaper article so many times that I knew it by heart. "I really admire you," Bev said. "I don't think I'd have the courage to do what you're doing."

"It isn't courage," I said. "It's a chance to make a decent life for us. I'd be a fool not to try."

"Go for it!" Bev said.

Adam woke from his nap fussing. "I think he might be teething. He's been biting on everything he can get in his mouth," I said.

Bev took the baby and peered in his mouth. "I can see where his gum is swollen. I used to rub a little whiskey on the boys' gums when they were teething. It's an old-fashioned remedy that the pediatrician told me about."

I picked up the blanket and followed her inside. There was a built-in bar in an alcove off the family room. Adam's face puckered at first, but then he opened his mouth wider as Bev rubbed his lower gum. "Andy liked scotch, too," she said, smiling.

We ate in the kitchen, a large cheerful room that had floral wallpaper and a white tile floor. The soup, thick with beef and vegetables, was delicious. "Is there anything you don't do well?" I said.

Bev laughed. "Don't be too impressed. I've been gardening and making soup for years. What I wish I had is more of your gumption."

"What do you mean? You started your own business. That takes plenty of gumption."

"I suppose. But my life has become *all* business, which isn't good. I need a social life, too. I haven't been on a date since my divorce, not that I know anyone who would ask me out."

"Maybe your friends could introduce you to someone."

"Some of my friends are in the same position I'm in. Actually, I do know an unattached fellow—a dentist. He lives just a few blocks from here on Dogwood Lane. His wife and I were once in the same garden club; she died about a year ago." Bev winked mischievously. "I suppose I could make an appointment with him to get my teeth cleaned."

Carl Shields, it had to be Carl Shields. I didn't know what to say. I gave her a weak smile.

It was dark when we were ready to leave. Bev walked us to the car. "Sara, you've been like a tonic. I got up this morning under a cloud and you chased it away. Promise you'll let me know how you make out at the Women's Center. I want to be able to cheer you on."

"I will," I said. "Thank you for a wonderful afternoon. Thank you a lot."

When I returned to Grady Gardens, my usual parking spot was taken so I had to park behind Verona Finch's unit. For a while I had suspected that the "business" my next-door neighbor had referred to the morning she complained about the exterminator sending cockroaches into her place was related to liquor, and now I was certain as I saw a man stagger out the kitchen door. Through the open door I glimpsed three men standing around the kitchen table, which held several liquor bottles. Verona Finch was running a bar, selling drinks in her kitchen! It could be worse, I thought, waiting until the door was closed and the man disappeared into the darkness before I hurried to my own unit with Adam, the roofer's knife secure in my hand. I was glad I had thought to leave a light on in the living room and the radio playing in the kitchen so it would look like I was home.

***

I didn't get to the Stalling Women's Center for better than a week after I saw Bev. The day after our Sunday visit Adam developed diarrhea. He was irritable and unhappy, and his lower gum was a swollen, angry red. Thinking that his problems were probably due to his teething, I waited a day before calling the clinic rather than taking him in. I didn't like taking Adam to the clinic, where I had to wait hours to see a doctor (once, for a routine visit, I waited five hours) in a room filled with coughing, sneezing, feverish children. The clinic was a place to catch an illness, not a place for a healthy infant. But when Adam was no better on Tuesday, I called and asked to speak to a doctor. "The doctors don't give advice over the phone," the receptionist said. "You have to bring the baby in."

"What if his problem is only teething?" I said.

"Then the doctor will tell you that."

So I took Adam to the Dearth Memorial Hospital pediatric clinic and waited two and a half hours surrounded by sick children and their unhappy mothers to be told by a pale young physician who had bloodshot eyes that Adam's problem was probably due to his teething. It seemed to me that the secretary showed more concern in verifying the information on Adam's Medicaid card so that the hospital would be paid than the doctor did for my son's discomfort.

Fortunately, Adam didn't catch any of the illnesses he was exposed to in the clinic. His first tooth came through on Thursday morning; his diarrhea stopped, and his sweet disposition returned. Relieved after three miserable days and nights, I called the Women's Center and made an appointment for Monday morning.

The Stalling Women's Center was in a white clapboard house in an old section of town near the university. Early for my appointment, I hurried up the cracked concrete walk, anxious to get Adam out of a chilly wind that was sending late-falling leaves skittering across my path. Although the sun was bright, it was colder than I had anticipated when I dressed the baby in a blue fleece jacket and pants.

The front door opened into a spacious reception area. Sun streamed in through a pair of windows, highlighting dark woodwork and moldings. I gave my name and the time of my appointment to the receptionist, a slender olive-skinned woman who was wearing tortoiseshell glasses too large for her face. "What an adorable baby," she said. "Make yourself comfortable while I check with Mrs. Mullen." She gestured toward a room behind a pair of partially open doors.

A coffee table covered with stacks of printed material that

described courses and activities planned by the Women's Center offered the only clue as to the room's use. Furnished with an overstuffed sofa and chairs, I felt as if I had stepped into someone's living room. I was taking off Adam's jacket and hat when a trim, gray-haired woman came up to me. "Sara Barefield?" she said, extending her hand. "I'm Frances Mullen, the director of the Reach Up program."

I rose, shifting Adam to my left arm so I could shake her hand. Her grasp was warm and dry. I could feel her evaluating me and was glad that I had worn a crisp white blouse and a simple navy wool skirt. "Please come to my office where we can talk privately," Ms. Mullen said.

Her office was a modest-sized room on the second floor. She went directly to a pair of green chairs facing a window through which there was a view of several large white pines. "I enjoy looking at the trees, especially at this time of year," she said. "Can I get you something, coffee or tea, before we start?"

"No, thank you, ma'am," I said, doubting that I could swallow. There was nothing intimidating about Frances Mullen, yet I couldn't shake my nervousness. My dream of going to college had grown into a desperate hope. I was convinced that my future and Adam's depended upon the outcome of this meeting.

"How did you hear about the Reach Up program?"

"I saw the article in the newspaper, the one about how you helped a woman named Yolanda Washington get a degree in nursing."

Frances Mullen smiled. "Yolanda is an inspiration. When she first came to us, she didn't have a high school diploma. Before she could go into nursing, she had to get her GED. It's been a long, hard road. It isn't easy when you're raising five children alone. How many children do you have?"

"Adam is my only child," I said, reaching into a front pouch of the diaper bag for a thick rubber pretzel-shaped toy to keep him busy.

"He's a beautiful baby," she said. "Please tell me a little about yourself and why you're here."

I took a deep breath. "I want to go to college like Yolanda Washington did. I've been on welfare since Adam was born."

"How did you support yourself before he was born?"

"I worked at Magnolia's and at a flower shop. Even with the two jobs, I couldn't have gotten by without WIC and food stamps."

"It's impossible to survive on a minimum wage without some subsidy. I wish the politicians who dole out the money for our funding were forced to live on a minimum wage for a year. They'd be a lot more generous." She smiled apologetically. "Sorry, sometimes I get carried away. Tell me what you did before you worked at Magnolia's."

"I was the school secretary at Creekside Elementary in Owings."

"How long did you hold that job?"

"Twenty years."

Her eyebrows rose. "Twenty years?"

"I moved to Stalling in March. I couldn't have held onto that job once I started showing."

"What about the baby's father?"

I didn't know how to respond. I wanted to be honest, to explain that Tully died without knowing I was pregnant, but I was certain that this woman had contact with the people at social services. Rather than say anything, I shrugged and made an empty gesture with my hands.

"Why did you come to Stalling? Wouldn't you have been better off remaining in Owings near your family and friends?"

"I don't have any family," I said, my voice flat and final.

"I assume that you have your high school diploma. Do you have any additional education, special skills like proficiency with computers or some background in accounting that you want to build on?"

"I want to be a teacher," I said.

"A teacher?" she said, clearly surprised. "I'm sorry, but I'm afraid I can't be of any help."

"Why?" I said, stunned. "You helped Yolanda Washington."

"To put it simply, it's a matter of money. We're funded primarily through the Carl Perkins Vocational Education Act and the Job Training Partnership Act. The JTPA wants a quick fix, women trained for jobs in six to twelve weeks, and although the Vocational Education Act doesn't specifically prohibit people from seeking four-year degrees, their programs are set up to get people through the system fast. Reach Up doesn't have the resources to help you become a teacher; we're stretching our money as far as it can go to help women get two-year degrees. The federal government isn't interested in women's cars breaking down or their child care problems. The government wants immediate results."

"But it took Yolanda Washington five years to get her degree," I said. "I'm not asking for more. I just want the same opportunity: five years so I can get certification as a teacher."

Ms. Mullen sighed. "It isn't that I'm unsympathetic to your desire to become a teacher. Teaching is a fine profession. But at Reach Up we have to aim for self-sufficiency if we want to keep our program going. We have to justify every person we accept. Yolanda Washington had nothing when she came to us—no high school diploma, no skills, nothing that would enable her to live decently on her own. You're miles ahead of most of the women we see—single parents and displaced homemakers lacking diplomas and job experience. You have sufficient skills to survive."

I had all I could do not to weep. How could I make this woman understand that the skills I had were limited, that my existence had always been a struggle, without appearing to be grasping? "Ma'am, after working twenty years as the school secretary, I was making $15,927 a year and had to watch every penny. I barely got by. If I could find another job like that, I'd be starting over for less money. There's no way I could pay for child care and support the two of us."

"We could help if you would aim a bit lower. Lee-Davis Community College has a one-year program that leads to a certificate in child care."

I immediately thought of Ardelle, who had worked in a child care center for five dollars an hour before getting a better-paying job at the laundromat. A woman working with Ardelle at the center had the child care certificate and was paid seven dollars an hour, which came to less than fifteen thousand a year. According to Ardelle, their tasks were the same; they were both glorified babysitters. I didn't want to be a babysitter. "I don't mean to sound unappreciative, but I really do want to be a teacher. It's been one of my dreams since I was in the fifth grade. I guess I shouldn't have come here. I'm sorry to have taken up your time."

I started to rise, unable to keep back tears much longer.

"Wait," she said, holding out her arm. "Even though our program can't help you, there may be a way for you to reach your goal. But it won't be easy."

I leaned forward. "How?"

Ms. Mullen smiled. "We'll get to that. First, I have to ask if you have a reliable car."

"The air conditioning broke, but the car is running all right, at least for now," I said. "I don't understand."

"Your two biggest problems, besides money, are going to be transportation and child care. Lee-Davis Community College is five miles from the center of town on a highway that isn't served by a bus route. A shuttle goes back and forth from town several times a day, but it's expensive, more than you'll be able to afford. Car problems have stalled more women than I care to think about. Where do you live?"

"Grady Gardens."

"The city." She shook her head. "Then child care is going to be a real mountain for you to climb. The city has no money in ESP—the Employment Services Program—for volunteers, which is what they call people like you who are going to school as a matter of choice. There is some ESP money in the county; however, that won't help you."

"But the city is in the county."

"That doesn't matter. The city and the county are different jurisdictions; their systems are completely separate."

She started writing on a pad that had been resting on her lap. "You can apply for a Pell Grant through the financial aid office at Lee-Davis that will give you twelve hundred dollars per semester. If you want to attend the summer session, you can get an additional five hundred dollar grant from the state. The five hundred probably won't be enough, so you'll have to use some of your Pell money should you decide to go in the summer.

"If you forget everything I've told you, I hope you remember this advice about the Pell money," she said, her eyes locking on mine. "The Pell money is tempting. Too many women spend whatever they have left after their tuition and books have been deducted. They get dental work done, they get clothes for their children. When you're on welfare, any extra money is a windfall, so they spend it and then they find they don't have enough to pay for the summer session or an emergency car repair. Hang on to whatever Pell money you have left as long as you can.

"You'll also be eligible for work-study, which pays four fifty an hour. You'll be told about it in the financial aid office. If you're thinking of starting school next semester, you should go there as soon as possible. I believe the deadline to apply for a Pell is sometime this month.

"What you want to accomplish is going to be very hard, but it's not impossible. I know of some women who have done it: one is a lawyer today, the other is an accountant. As I said before, child care is going to be a major hurdle. You might try the United Way. They have a waiting list; however, scholarships do become available. The Community Assessment Program also has some funds; it's run under the auspices of the Salvation Army."

Ms. Mullen wrote rapidly, then tore the paper off the pad and gave it to me. "You might be able to get additional leads from your caseworker. May I ask who your caseworker is?"

"Alexander Ryle."

"Good luck," she said.

Sometimes I wonder if I wouldn't have made a different decision if the doorbell hadn't rung within minutes after I got home. "I'm Anitra Taylor," said a woman about my age who had a round face and skin the color of nutmeg. She gave me her card. "Your unit is scheduled for inspection on Wednesday at one o'clock."

Anitra Taylor's name and the title *Community Coordinator, Grady Gardens* was printed on the card along with a telephone number. "Inspection?" I said. "What inspection?"

"A housekeeping inspection. All the units are supposed to be inspected four times a year, two housekeeping inspections and two preventative maintenance inspections."

"What do you do during this inspection?" I said, remembering how Lester and Monroe had covered my valuables when I moved to Lemon Street.

"We check every room. We look in the closets, cupboards, appliances to make sure the place is bein' kept clean. If we see things that need doin', we note them and come back to see that they're done."

"What gives you the right to come in here and go through my things?"

"This is public housing. You're livin' here at the taxpayers' expense. It's their property."

"This unit was never inspected! It was filthy when I moved in, crawling with roaches! With all the scrubbing I've done, I still keep the dishes and pots that I use in the refrigerator! So don't talk to me about any inspections! You just want to come in here and snoop and I'm not going to let you!"

The skin around Anitra Taylor's mouth tightened, but her expression remained cool. "Like I told you, this is public housing. The lease you signed gives us the right to inspect and that's what we're goin' to do. We got a new director and things is bein' done proper, not like before. We'll see you on Wednesday at one o'clock. If you're thinkin' about givin' us any trouble, you can also be thinkin' about movin' out. We got rules here and *everyone* got to follow them."

Trembling with anger, I shut the door. There was no doubt in my mind now: I was going to college so that I would never again have to experience the humiliations of poverty.

Before I went to bed that night, I took a slender box that was cracked and yellowed with age out of my top dresser drawer. Inside the box was a blue-and-silver pen that had been given to me by my fifth grade teacher, Mrs. Hartman. On the last day of school Mrs. Hartman had asked me to stay for a moment after the other children left. "I hope you will use this when you go to college, Sara Jean," she said, handing me a slender gift-wrapped box. "I have great expectations for you."

I had never used the pen. Finally, I would.

Although I fell asleep thinking of Mrs. Hartman, it was Mama who appeared in my dreams. *"Livin' in this place has made you as thick-headed as them cinder-block walls!"* Mama said, *puffing on a Marlboro. "You're outta your mind thinkin' that you can go to college! Outta your mind!"*

"I'm going," I said.

"Hah!" Mama chortled, as if it were a joke.

"I'm going, I'm going, I'm going," I repeated over and over until she vanished in smoke.

Chasing Mama out of my dreams was easier than the decision I had to make in the morning. I didn't know which I should do first, apply for a grant to go to college or make an appointment with Alexander Ryle. He had helped Yolanda Washington, but when I had told him that I wanted to go to college like she did, he had told me that I already had job skills. And he had hardly taken any time at all with the ESP pamphlet.

While I bathed and dressed Adam, I again recalled Frances Mullen's remark that I was miles ahead of most of the women in the Reach Up program. The remark was beginning to haunt me. Being miles ahead of women who had no skills didn't mean that I could make a living wage. I needed to earn at least ten dollars an hour so Adam and I could live decently, more if I had to pay for day care.

Based on the ads I'd seen in the newspaper when I moved to Stalling, I doubted I could earn enough as a secretary even if I learned how to take dictation and use a computer. But money wasn't the reason I wanted to go to college. A teacher had once given me the most precious of gifts: belief in myself. Until Mrs. Hartman, my teachers had made me feel the stigma of the Barefield name. They had made me feel unworthy. And I had accepted their judgment because I was a child and they were powerful figures whom I respected and feared; they were my teachers so they had to be right.

During the years I worked at Creekside Elementary, I had often overheard teachers in the faculty room pass on information about students, putting labels on them that stuck from one year to the next. Occasionally I knew things about the family histories and home lives of these children that the teachers didn't know, but my input wasn't welcome. There were many children I believed I could have helped.

I picked up Adam, inhaling his sweet, powdery scent. There isn't a better smell in the world than a baby fresh from his bath. "Yolanda Washington got her dream," I said, cuddling him. "There's no reason why I shouldn't try to get mine."

But I sounded braver than I felt. My pulse skipped when I made an appointment with someone in the financial office at Lee-Davis Community College for Wednesday afternoon at three thirty.

***

If I had any lingering doubts about my decision to apply for a grant to go to college, they were swept away by the inspection of my unit. The community coordinators were fifteen minutes late. Anitra Taylor was accompanied by a large woman named Gwendolyn Erby whose fingers ended in long, lacquered, decal-decorated fingernails that gave her hands the appearance of being rendered useless for anything more strenuous than signing her name and feeding herself. "It looks like you've settled in nice," she said.

I knew she was trying to be pleasant, but there is nothing pleasant about having your privacy invaded by strangers inspecting your home. "Where are you going to start?" I said. "My baby is sleeping upstairs."

Anitra Taylor was holding a clipboard and pen. "We'll begin here," she said.

Starting on the right, they walked methodically around the living room, looking at the door, the walls, the ceiling, the windows, the floor. They opened a small closet set in an alcove by the kitchen and went through the contents. "We have to check for anything flammable," Gwendolyn said.

Watching them poke through my things made me clench my teeth, although nothing was in the closet—several jackets, a raincoat, a broom, a dust pan, a mop and bucket—that I would normally consider personal. I had scrubbed every inch of this unit to make it fit to live in. These women with their prying, searching eyes were doing more than invading my privacy: they were making me feel violated. I had all I could do not to tell them to leave.

They went into the kitchen, again starting on the right. Gwendolyn opened the refrigerator; they both examined the stovetop and studied the inside of the oven, which I knew was spattered with grease from spareribs I had cooked for supper on Sunday. They opened the cupboards and looked under the sink. Anitra wrote on the clipboard. I wondered if they saw where the vinyl was coming up in the far corner and if they noticed the rust on some of the edges of the metal cupboard doors.

Upstairs, they inspected the bathroom and my bedroom, again beginning their circuit in each room on the right. I bristled when they opened the medicine cabinet; I could hardly bear to watch while they ruffled through the clothes in my closet. "My baby is sleeping," I warned as they were leaving my room. "The closet door in there squeaks, which could wake him."

The two women headed for Adam's room without an acknowledgment.

Gwendolyn opened the closet door. The hinge squealed and Adam woke with a cry. "Sorry," she said.

"Your inspection is over!" I said, rushing across the room to lift the startled, squalling baby out of the crib. "Get the hell out of here!"

His schedule broken, Adam didn't stop fussing until the motion of the car ride to Lee-Davis Community College put him to sleep.

A road off the highway that hugged the side of a mountain led to a sprawling, two-story building; there was a large visitors' parking lot in front. Carrying Adam, who was still sleeping in his car seat, I went in through the main entrance and asked a fellow dressed in jeans and a sweatshirt for directions to the financial aid office. "Go to the end of the hall and make a left," he said, gesturing with a tilt of his head.

As I walked down the corridor, I passed people of varying ages, students who looked impossibly young and others, graying and middle-aged or older, whom I assumed were on the staff. But when a black woman in her thirties came out of the financial aid office, I had to change my assumption. The woman was carrying books and had a form in her hand that looked like an application.

Not long after I gave my name at the reception desk, a tall, fair woman wearing a blue suit that flattered her delicate coloring came out of one of the inner offices. "Sara Barefield?" she said. "I'm Laurie Templeton. Please come in."

Laurie Templeton put me at ease so skillfully that soon I was talking about being on welfare and wanting to become a teacher without any hesitation. "I've been told that it would be easier if I aimed lower, but I don't want to," I said. "I really want to be a teacher."

"Then you owe it to yourself to try. It's your life," she said. "Once I was where you are, except I had three children, not one. I got my degree in business and accounting, and here I am."

My mouth fell open. "You were on welfare?"

"You got it! And there was no Reach Up program then to help out."

"Then how...?"

"My family helped, especially my mama. It would have been

much harder without her. But you find ways."

I thought of my own mama, taunting me in my dreams as she had taunted me when she was alive. Whatever I had achieved in life I had accomplished despite Mama. If Mama didn't want this, then it had to be right.

"You'll meet other women here; there are a number of them," Laurie said. "Now let's get to work. You're barely making the deadline for a Pell."

She gave me an application for federal student aid, and explained how to attach additional information that would reflect my current income. "I assume you'll want work-study," she said, giving me another application. "It pays four fifty an hour, and you can get up to twenty hours a week."

"I need the full twenty."

"You can make the request on the application, but it isn't guaranteed. Sometimes the hours depend on the job you're given," she said. "Have you registered for next semester yet?"

"No," I said. "I came here first to see if I could get the money. I was told that the Pell would cover all of my tuition and books."

"The Pell will give you twelve hundred dollars. It costs forty-five dollars a credit hour. If you take fifteen hours, that's six hundred seventy-five dollars. Books will run about another three hundred, and there's a five dollar student activity fee."

Adam woke and looked around sleepily. "He's adorable," Laurie said.

"Thanks," I said. "But he won't be adorable when he starts telling me that he's wet and hungry."

"I'm due for a break now. You're welcome to stay so you can change and feed him before you go pick up your application and a catalog."

"Thank you for everything," I said, thinking that I would like to have this woman for a friend.

Laurie smiled. "I'll look forward to seeing you next semester."

That night I worked on my applications. I made a list of things I had to do: arrange for my high school transcript to be sent to the college; pick one of the dates I was given to take an assessment test in English and math; call for an appointment with Alexander Ryle. For the first time in months I felt as if I were doing something positive.

***

On Friday morning I climbed the steep flight of stairs from the lower parking lot behind City Hall thinking that it was lucky I was able to get this appointment with Alexander Ryle so quickly. In one week I had accomplished what I had never thought possible: I had completed the first steps toward getting a college education. Now all I needed was help with day care.

As I followed Mr. Ryle through the maze of corridors to his office, I thought about the preparation I had done for this meeting, the figures I had gotten on the cost of day care, and the estimate of what I would earn if I went back to work as a secretary instead of going to college. The numbers were so clear that I was positive I could win his support.

"You want to be a teacher?" he said after I explained why I had made the appointment.

"Yes," I said, surprised at his tone, which was cutting, almost insulting. "I've always wanted to be a teacher. All I need is help with day care. I know I can do it."

He flipped through my file. "According to my notes, you were a school secretary."

"Yes."

"Then you can go back to being a secretary."

"I don't want to be a secretary. I want to go to college. I want the same opportunity Yolanda Washington had."

Ryle leaned back in his chair, which seemed higher than the last time I was here, as if there was a platform under it. "Yolanda Washington didn't have any skills when she started."

I took the ESP-JOBS pamphlet he had given me months ago out of my purse. "According to this pamphlet, people on ADC can get help with education."

"If you read the center section, you'll see that you don't fit into any of the targeted groups. It says *You may benefit most...* if you're a parent under 24 years old, if you haven't completed high school, if you have less than three months work experience, or you have received ADC for thirty-six of the last sixty months."

"But if I wait until I'm on welfare for thirty-six months, I'll just be wasting time. I want to start now, not three years from now. The faster I get my degree, the sooner I'll be off welfare."

"If you're that anxious to go to work, all you really might need is a six-week refresher course in secretarial skills."

"I can't support us on a secretary's salary," I said, unfolding the paper I had prepared. "If I could get a job for as much as I was earning before—which I doubt—I wouldn't have enough money left to buy food after I paid for rent, utilities, day care, and diapers. I made some calls yesterday. Day care centers charge one hundred twenty dollars a week for an infant. My rent and utilities would be at least five hundred fifty dollars. Diapers are another thirty-five dollars. Together, they add up to one thousand sixty-five dollars a month. My net paychecks from Creekside Elementary were one thousand sixty a month. That means I'd have nothing left, not a penny to buy food, clothing, gas for the car, and everything else we would need. I couldn't even afford a bar of soap."

I handed him the paper, sure that the clear figures would win him over. He glanced at it, nodding. "Well, it looks like you can't afford to go back to work, doesn't it?"

For a moment I was speechless. "Instead of trying to help me, you're telling me that I'm better off on welfare!"

"I never said that!" he retorted sharply.

"I've already completed my applications for a Pell grant and Lee-Davis Community College. If you would help me with day care, in five years I'll be earning enough to start paying back what I owe in taxes."

"You'll have to see the person in charge of day care," he said, rising to indicate that the meeting was over.

But after we went back through the labyrinth of corridors in silence, he left me in the hall near the reception area without telling me the name of the person I should contact. "If you've applied for work-study, make sure you go to the financial aid office to sign the social services notification form," he said before disappearing behind one of the nearby doors.

After coming this far, I wasn't going to let his dismissal defeat me. I went into the reception area and asked a young woman behind the counter whose face looked frazzled beneath her mop of blond hair if the person in charge of day care was available.

"Ms. Peverell is out sick."

"Is the person in charge of ESP available?" I said, determined to find someone to help me.

"Do you have an appointment?"

"I just saw Mr. Ryle."

The woman turned and looked uncertainly into the office area; no one was there. "What is your name?" she said, as if she weren't sure what she should do.

"Sara Barefield."

She made a call while I waited. "Mr. Maybee will be here in a few minutes."

Soon a man who had reddish-brown skin and a high forehead came into the reception area. He went directly to the counter. "Where is Sara Barefield's file?" he said.

"I don't know," the clerk said. "I guess Mr. Ryle has it."

"You're supposed to have files available for appointments," he said with annoyance.

Sure that he was Mr. Maybee, I approached him. "I'm Sara Barefield. I really appreciate your seeing me," I said, extending my hand.

His scowl changed into a broad smile that revealed a gold tooth. "Now that introduction showed initiative," he said, grasping my outstretched hand. "I'm Ernest Maybee. When we locate your file we can go to my office. It shouldn't take but a minute."

While I'd been waiting, I had had time to study the ESP pamphlet and its promises of education, day care, and transportation. What Mr. Ryle had told me was true: I didn't fit into any of the categories that would immediately enable me to qualify for the program. But it made absolutely no sense for me to wait nearly three years to go to college, not when I could start now, and when we were settled in his office that was what I told Mr. Maybee after I explained why I was there. I showed him the figures I had prepared for my appointment with Mr. Ryle. "I can't support us on a secretary's salary without getting help with day care anyway."

"You're what we call a 'volunteer,' someone who is self-initiated. Unfortunately, the ESP program is so strapped for money that we can only help targeted clients. Right now there is no money left in the pot for day care. For anyone. We have to wait for more funding."

"But you *could* help me after I've been on welfare for three years."

"I suppose," he said. "But you already have skills."

"But they are ordinary skills that will keep me close to poverty for the rest of my life. I'll earn far more as a teacher than as a secretary, so the government will get its money back and then some on the taxes I'll have to pay."

He sat back in his chair, studying me. "Is that why you want to go to college, for the money you'll make?"

His question stung. Afraid that I might offend him because he was black, I hadn't told him how much I wanted the same opportunity Yolanda Washington was given. "I've wanted to be a teacher since I was ten years old. I never had the opportunity. Looking at me now, it's probably hard for you to believe that a year ago I had a responsible job, a nice apartment, a decent life. I probably wouldn't have gotten as far as I did if it weren't for one teacher's encouragement. I know I can help children, that I can make a difference in their lives like that teacher did in mine.

"If I go to college now, I'll have my certificate to teach when I'm forty-six," I said earnestly. "If I wait three years, I'll be too old to start."

Mr. Maybee rested his chin on his hands, thinking. "You seem to have the desire and the determination to succeed. You deserve a chance," he said finally. "So listen up. I'm going to say this very carefully."

He paused while I leaned forward intently.

"I can't offer you any help at this time because you don't fall into one of the target groups. However, the ESP program can help people who are *already* in college. These people don't qualify for gas vouchers and other benefits, but they can come to us to get child care providing that we have the funds."

"I understand," I said gratefully.

"Meanwhile, you could try the United Way and CAP—the Community Assessment Program. You might get some help there."

"Thank you," I said. "Thank you."

Nothing could dampen my spirits for the remainder of the day, not even the notice I found in my mailbox when I got home stating that my oven had failed to pass inspection.

***

The United Way couldn't help me. "We do give out scholarships for day care, but most of the money we get is for the working poor," a soft-spoken fellow said. "I can put you on a waiting list."

"How long is the list?"

"It's close to a two-year wait."

"Please, I'd like to be on the list," I said, hoping I would fare better at CAP.

A pamphlet that was given to me stated that the Community Assessment Program was funded by local churches to help the less fortunate, which is another way of saying *the poor*, a label that immediately made me feel defensive. When I went on Tuesday, people were waiting in line to explain to two middle-aged women and an older man why they needed help. I heard pleas for money to pay utility bills, doctor bills, rent. It was a parade of misery, one heartbreaking story after another. When my turn came, I explained my situation as briefly as possible. Each word spoken to these strangers was painful. And their response—that they were sorry, they would like to help me but with their limited funds they couldn't—hurt even more. As I walked out of the Salvation Army building, it struck me that even the walls in this place, dull, scuffed beige, looked exhausted from all the sadness they'd witnessed.

After I got home and settled Adam for his nap, I went into my bedroom and wept. College was impossible now. There were no more possibilities. Oh, how I missed Tully. He was always able to show me possibilities where I saw none. But I doubted that even he could find a sliver of hope in this situation, and hope is what I had been living on: the hope that Yolanda Washington's path could be mine; the hope that I could give Adam a decent place to live instead of sidewalks claimed by alcoholics, drug dealers, and dice players.

The more I thought, the more I wept. I knew that if I didn't get out, I wouldn't be able to stop crying. I thought of Bev and recalled her mentioning that Tuesdays were usually quiet at the shop. I put a cold washcloth over my eyes so I would be presentable by the time Adam was up from his nap.

Bev was putting a centerpiece of gold-and-rust-colored chrysanthemums into the refrigerated case when we came into the shop. "What a wonderful surprise!" she said.

The telephone rang. While Bev took the call, I looked around. The refrigerated case was filled with Thanksgiving centerpieces. I had forgotten about the holiday, which was just two days away. "You're swamped," I said after Bev was off the phone. "I shouldn't have come."

"Everything is under control," Bev assured me. "I'm glad for the company. All these arrangements were starting to look alike!"

We went into the back so Bev could work while we visited. "I hoped I'd be going to college in January," I said after explaining all that had happened since we had last seen each other. "But without help with day care, it's impossible."

"There has to be a way." Bev paused, thinking. "Have you

considered hiring someone to take care of Adam instead of using a day care center? It might be less expensive."

"I can't afford to pay anyone."

"Aren't you going to be earning money with that work-study program you just told me about?"

When I had turned into the plaza, I had glanced guiltily at Magnolia's, thinking of Lolita; it had been months since we had spoken. The work-study money. Lolita. It was so obvious I should have seen it. If Lolita was willing, she would be perfect. "I think you might have solved the problem," I said excited about the possibility.

"That was quick," Bev said, laughing. "I have news, too. I've been out on two dates."

I immediately thought of Carl Shields. "That was quick."

"I guess I got lucky. Someone must have canceled an appointment because he was able to see me right away. He's invited me out to dinner twice, and I'll be seeing him again this weekend. He wants me to give him advice about his house. He's listed it for sale."

Bev's face was sparkling. "I'm glad for you," I said, thinking that she was too good for Carl Shields. He had listed his house for sale, which had to be the reason he had wanted it cleaned. I hoped he wasn't going to use Bev. She deserved better.

As I was leaving, Bev apologized for not inviting me for Thanksgiving dinner. "We're going to my brother's house," she said.

I recalled my last Thanksgiving spent at the Rutlands'. "Adam and I are going to have a fine time."

It was nearly five o'clock. Lolita always worked on Tuesday nights. I hadn't been back to Magnolia's since I had walked out when I was in labor. Some of my days there had been so difficult that even the best sales couldn't lure me in. But Lolita, my last hope, was worth enduring the sight of Linwood Cagle.

Mrs. Early spotted me and Adam as we came through the door. She hurried over to us with a welcoming smile. "I've been looking forward to seeing you for a *long* time," she said, letting me know in her smooth way that this visit was overdue. "What a beautiful baby."

Adam was as susceptible to Mrs. Early's persuasive charms as the customers. It wasn't long before she coaxed him out of my arms into hers, where he cooed happily until a light began flashing over a register. "Now why did that have to happen to spoil our good time?" Mrs. Early said, relinquishing the baby. "Y'all be sure to come back soon."

Finding Lolita straightening a rack of blouses was comforting. With a rush of feeling I realized how much I had missed this woman, who had risked her own job to defend me against Linwood Cagle. Lolita had made working at Magnolia's tolerable; she had made the long evenings pass quickly.

"Well, look who's here!" Lolita said, smiling broadly. "How you been doin', girl?"

"It's been rough, but we're all right."

"I can imagine," she said, her open arms enfolding us. Then she stepped back to gaze at Adam. "Ain't you somethin'! Lookit them eyes, so blue. Are you goin' to come to me?"

Adam went from my arms to Lolita's as though he did it every day.

"Are you still on Lemon Street? I never see your car when I go by."

"We moved to Grady Gardens in September."

"You *have* been havin' a rough time."

"But things can get better. I have a chance to go to college. I'd like to talk to you about it. Could we get together one day next week, maybe at your house?"

"How's Wednesday? That'll give me a chance to recover from the holiday. I'm havin' both families, and that damn Cagle wouldn't let me off tomorrow night," Lolita said. "Uh-uh, speakin' of the devil. There he is, headin' over here."

Linwood Cagle approached us, the expression on his face curious beneath his plastic eyeglasses. Though I would have loved Adam no matter what he looked like, I felt a sense of satisfaction when I saw a glint of disappointment in Cagle's eyes when he peered at my son.

"Are you ready to come back to work? We need cashiers weekends," he said, dispensing with even the barest greeting.

"I'll have to think about it."

Adam started to whimper. I took him from Lolita. "He's telling me that it's time for his supper," I said, eager to make my escape. "Lolita, have a great holiday. I'll call you next week."

***

I didn't want to go to Lolita's house empty-handed. On Tuesday morning I decided to make a pan of brownies, recalling Lolita's fondness for sweets. I had all of the ingredients except for the baking chocolate. Mail delivery at Grady Gardens was usually late on the first of the month, when everyone received their welfare checks and food stamps. Since all I needed to make the brownies was one item, I decided to go to Mayhew's Market, which was at the edge of Grady Gardens, rather than wait for my stamps and check before heading out to Lee Avenue.

Although the weather was ideal for walking, sunny and crisp with the promise of a warm afternoon, I drove to Mayhew's Market. I didn't want to walk past the men playing dice, past the drug dealers and the drunks nursing at their bottles in brown paper bags. No matter how often the police came and chased them off, the dealers and the drunks and the dice players returned to their spots and continued what they were doing as if they'd never been interrupted. They were as much a part of the landscape of Grady Gardens as the narrow strips of grass and the undernourished trees that bordered the sidewalks they claimed.

Mayhew's parking lot was on the side of the building. I pulled into a space near the street. There were about a half-dozen people in front of the store, all of them black, most of them males. Despite telling myself that Adam and I were perfectly safe in broad daylight, I held the baby with one arm and thrust my other arm deep into my jacket pocket, my hand gripping the roofer's knife.

A gaunt man whose skin was a deep brown came up to me as I

approached the store. He was wearing a torn jacket and jeans that were stiff with dirt. "I'll give y'all ten dollar's worth of food stamps for five bucks," he said. He held a book of stamps in his open palm, his eyes darting nervously from side to side.

He was standing directly in my path, and I could see that he had no intention of moving. I sensed the others watching. I also sensed that it would be better not to mention that selling stamps was illegal. "They're no good to me," I said. "No one will cash them without the identification card."

"Hah!" he snorted. "Are you kiddin'! They'll take stamps as fast as you can hand 'em over. Mayhew's don't give a shit about no ID card!"

"I didn't know that," I said. "I'm sorry I can't buy them. I don't have enough money on me."

Determinedly stepping around him, I walked into the store.

The prices in Mayhew's shocked me. Everything I looked at was priced from ten to thirty percent higher than the same items in the supermarkets on Lee Avenue. The price of the baking chocolate I wanted was two dollars and thirty-nine cents; on Lee Avenue the same box of chocolate sold for a dollar seventy-nine.

There were no customers checking out. I went to the only open register and put the chocolate at the end of the conveyor belt near the scanner. "You're probably the only cash customer I'll see today," said the cashier, a bleached blond whose hair was cut in jagged points around her face. She winked at me as if we were in on the same secret. "It's the first of the month. Soon all the freeloaders will be in here with their food stamps."

My jaw set, I pulled a book of food stamps out of my pocket. The cashier didn't ask for identification.

I hadn't baked brownies since Tully died and was pleased that they came out well. As I drove to Lolita's, I felt myself becoming anxious. My head was full of *what ifs*: What if Lolita wasn't willing to watch Adam? What if Lolita's husband objected? What if Lolita's house wasn't as clean as I had assumed it would be? What if the money I planned to offer—seventy-five dollars a week—wasn't enough? I had called the financial aid office and was told I would net approximately three dollars and eighty cents an hour for work-study after deductions were taken out. If I was given less than twenty hours, I would make up the difference out of my welfare check.

Lolita's house was on Decker Street. The homes were larger and better kept than those in the Fruit Belt. Lolita had once mentioned that she and her husband had bought the house at a bargain price because it needed so much work. "It was in terrible shape," she'd said. "But we took a chance because John can fix anythin'. Before he could even start workin' on the inside, he had to rebuild the porch and put on a new roof and new gutters."

When I pulled into the driveway, I smiled with relief. The slate blue clapboard house with its sparkling white trim and carefully clipped shrubs looked as neat and orderly as the racks Lolita had straightened at Magnolia's.

"Oh, brownies! You know sweets are my weakness," Lolita said, welcoming us. "I hope you didn't feel you had to bring somethin'."

"I wanted to," I said. "After all, I invited myself over."

"I'm glad you did. I'll put on a pot of coffee and we can have ourselves a good visit."

The house was immaculate. The windows glistened, the wood floors shone. I followed Lolita into the kitchen, where half the cupboard doors were missing. "John's strippin' the cupboards and repaintin' them white. Then he's goin' to put in new counter tops."

"I see he already installed a new floor."

"He replaced the floor after we moved in four years ago. I don't want to even think about the floor that was here."

I lifted Adam out of the car seat and put him on the floor. "He isn't as content sitting in his seat as he used to be. He's started to get up on his hands and knees like he's getting ready to crawl."

"I'll get a blanket. I don't like settin' babies on a cool floor until they're movin' about."

After Lolita returned, I told her about the Pell grant and my plan to become a teacher. "Would you be willing to watch Adam? I'd drop him off in the morning and pick him up before you have to leave for Magnolia's. I called social services and was told they pay sixty dollars a week for private day care. I can pay you seventy-five; that's what I hope to be earning with my work-study job."

We heard footsteps coming up the basement stairs. John Huggins walked into the kitchen holding an empty coffee mug. His skin was the color of mahogany; his features were strong, his demeanor as dignified as a bank president's despite the paint chips on his sweatshirt and jeans. "I thought I might find some fresh coffee," he said.

Lolita, who was eyeing the paint chips on his clothes as if daring them to drop on her gleaming floor, introduced him to me. "Sara wants to go to college. She's made me an offer to watch her baby," she said. "Seventy-five dollars a week."

"Seventy-five before or after deductions?"

"I hadn't thought about taxes and Social Security," I said apologetically. "I really can't afford to pay more."

"Social services is payin' sixty," Lolita said.

John looked at Lolita. "How do you feel about it?"

"You know how I enjoy babies," she said, bending to pick up Adam, who was biting on a doughnut-shaped rattle. "He's got a sweet disposition. And did you ever see eyes like his, so blue with that black ring around 'em?"

John smiled. "You sound like you've fallen for another fella."

"I guess maybe I have," Lolita said, laughing.

After John went back downstairs (with an admonition from Lolita to brush off the paint chips before he came up again), Lolita said, "He got called for a small construction job that'll start next week and last until Christmas. I want him to go into business for himself. John can do just about anythin'. I just know he'd be workin' steady once people see how skilled and careful he is. Maybe he'll take a chance now with the babysittin' money comin' in."

She paused. "Lookit your son. He's about ready to take off! Soon he won't be content to stay in the playpen."

Adam was on his hands and knees, rocking forward tentatively. For me the moment was bittersweet as I realized with a pang that Lolita might be the one to hear my son's first word and witness his first step.

***

Bev invited us for supper on the Sunday after Christmas. Her decorations were so beautifully done that walking into her house was like stepping into a Christmas card. The mantle over the fireplace had an arrangement of fresh evergreens, berries, and giant pine cones; the tree was decorated with all natural things—bunches of dried flowers, tiny painted wood bird houses, straw angels. Everywhere I looked there was something wonderful to see: a miniature nativity scene on a lamp table, a basket filled with round glass tree ornaments like richly-colored jewels, a small boxwood tree draped with delicate gold-twisted rope held by tiny gold bows. Bev's house made the decorations Mrs. Rutland expected me to exclaim over every year, her artificial Christmas tree and fat ceramic Santas, look sad in comparison.

There were presents under the tree for us, overalls and a shirt for Adam, and for me a beautiful blue-and-white flowerpot similar to one I had admired in the shop. I gave Bev a pair of knit garden gloves coated in rubber that she could use for planting and a sign on a stick that said **WEEDS**, which she could poke between her flowers. "Oh Sara, thank you," she said. "I've wanted these gloves; a friend told me about them. And this sign is a hoot! I can't wait to put it in my garden."

Bev made me feel good about what I gave her, even though it wasn't much.

While we ate a delicious dinner of ham and scalloped potatoes, I told Bev about the tests I had taken at the community college. "The English portion wasn't difficult, but I had a hard time with the math. I don't think I did very well."

"When will you get the results?"

"I have an appointment with an adviser tomorrow morning to plan my courses. Lolita will watch Adam. Thanks to you it all worked out."

"Sometimes when we're too close to a situation we can't see it as well. I just relearned that lesson."

I immediately thought of Carl Shields. "The dentist you were dating?"

Bev nodded. "I guess I wanted a relationship so badly that I made myself overlook things that I shouldn't have. He was so cheap, and I knew he was using me. I could go on, but there's really no point. In the end it was a good learning experience: I wasn't hurt because I was the one who ended it. I'll be more careful in the future."

"Then it was a successful trial run," I said, relieved that he hadn't hurt her. I hoped I would never be reminded of Carl Shields again.

We left at seven so I could put Adam to bed on schedule. I wanted us both to get a good night's sleep so we would be well-rested in the morning.

My appointment in the counseling office at Lee-Davis Community College was for nine o'clock, but it was nearly ten before an adviser, Linda Clark, called me into a cubicle. A small-boned, sharp-nosed woman of about fifty, she adjusted her wire granny glasses as she read my test scores. "You did exceptionally well on the English portion of your assessment test. You're in the ninetieth percentile, most unusual," she said, looking at me as if she expected an explanation.

"I read a lot," I said.

"You don't have an accent," she commented. Her Yankee a's sounded like ah's. "Where are you from?"

"Owings."

"Hmmm," she said, again looking at me expectantly.

This time I offered no explanation. The years of effort it had taken to erase the accent from my speech wasn't personal history I wanted to share.

"You passed the first part of the math section, but you scored less than fifty percent on Algebra II, so you'll have to take a developmental math course. You won't get college credit, but you'll get three hours of credit toward your Pell Grant."

It could have been worse; at least I had passed the first part. I had forgotten most of the math I had learned in high school. "Will it cost the same as my other courses?"

"Yes," she said. "But I'm going to be able to offer you something that will help balance it out."

Since I planned to transfer to a university, Ms. Clark advised me to take courses that would lead to an Associate in Arts degree, which would give me the qualifications for entrance into a degree program in education. After some discussion, my list of courses included College Composition, French, Introduction to Psychology, and History of Western Civilization in addition to developmental math. "There is one other course you are required to take," the adviser said. "It's a two-credit orientation. Because it's being funded by a grant, you won't have to pay for the two credits."

"Orientation?"

"All beginning full-time students are required to take orientation. Usually it's a one-credit course. But this is a special orientation for women like you. It will be run as a support group."

"What do you mean, *women like me?*"

"Women who have more pressures on them than the typical entering student, women who are considered at risk."

"You mean women on welfare?" I said, keeping my voice low so people in the reception area outside the cubicle couldn't hear.

"There is nothing to be defensive about. We want you to succeed. The Reach Up program has always had support groups for their participants."

"What do people do in these support groups?"

"They talk about their goals or their problems or about anything else that is on their minds."

"I don't think I'd be comfortable talking about those things with a bunch of strangers."

"Getting you to feel comfortable sharing your concerns is one of the goals of the group," Ms. Clark said brightly.

"I'd prefer to take the regular orientation course."

"I'm sorry, you don't have a choice," she said. "But you may want to drop one of the other courses. Going back to school isn't easy; there are adjustments to make. A lighter course load can make a big difference."

"I'll keep it as it is," I said.

"But it will be more difficult."

"I don't have the luxury of taking my time."

I glimpsed Ms. Clark writing in my file as I was leaving the counseling office, probably comments about my objection to the special orientation group and my unwillingness to take her advice and drop a course. It didn't upset me. It had taken me a lifetime to get here. I had to trust my instincts.

With one problem seeming to beget another, it took me over two exhausting hours to register for my courses. When I was finished, I was registered for seventeen hours, all but three of them for college credit; however, I would only have to pay for fifteen hours. The two credits for orientation wouldn't be charged against my account. "Will I be given a bill?" I asked the clerk who was helping me, a pleasant woman who had infinite patience.

"We'll deduct what you owe from your Pell when it's sent to the school," she said. "The bookstore will do the same. You charge what you need and it's taken out of the grant when it comes in."

I had left Adam with Lolita at eight thirty, thinking that I'd be back to get him well before noon, but between the wait in the advisement office and my troubles in Admissions and Records, it was nearly one o'clock when I returned to pick him up. Fortunately, I had given Lolita an extra bottle in case I was delayed.

Lolita came to the door feeding Adam. "We're havin' lunch," she said.

We went into the kitchen and she introduced me to her oldest daughter Janelle, then to Julia, and finally to her youngest son, six-year-old Jamal. "They're all named with J's, like their daddy. The oldest, John Junior, is playin' basketball at the playground. If he don't get home soon, he's goin' to miss his lunch."

"Then he'll just sneak stuff," said Janelle, who was twelve and looked like Lolita.

"No, he won't!" said Lolita.

"He do it every time," said Jamal, who had been looking at me. "Are you takin' the baby home now?"

"As soon as he's finished with his bottle."

"My mama say the baby got a soft spot on top of his head so not to touch."

"That's right."

He felt the top of his head. "I don't got no soft spot."

"That's because you're a big boy," I said. "Only babies have soft spots."

"All babies?"

"Yes, that's why we have to protect them."

"I won't let nobody touch Adam's spot."

"Thank you," I said, giving him a smile.

Later, Lolita refused to take the fifteen dollars I gave her. "Ten is more than enough," she said, returning a five.

"I hope it wasn't too hard watching Adam with your kids home on vacation."

"The girls loved havin' the baby so they could act like little mamas. Jamal was behavin' strange, but he'll be okay."

"He's used to being the youngest. He could be jealous."

"That must be it. I should have figured it out myself. Sara, you're goin' to be a good teacher!"

"I hope so," I said. "I really hope so."

1993

I took Adam in for his six-month checkup at the WIC clinic on the first Monday in January. "He weighs nineteen pounds!" the nurse exclaimed after placing him on the scale. "He's certainly thriving!"

I was told to return in six months, and was given vouchers for infant formula, juice, and cereal. As I was leaving, I reflected on how different WIC was from the Department of Social Services. The people at WIC didn't make me feel embarrassed or ashamed; they seemed sincerely concerned about my health and Adam's. And the vouchers I was given, which ensured that Adam wouldn't go hungry no matter what my circumstances, gave me a brief feeling of security.

That same week I took my car to be inspected, a chore I'd been dreading. Last year I had taken the car to Ready's Garage several weeks after Tully died, and Bob Ready had refused to charge me for the inspection. "Consider it on the house," he'd said when I had tried to pay him. I certainly didn't expect that to happen at the garage I went to on Lee Avenue, but I didn't expect a list of over nine hundred dollars in repairs, either. "I'll have to take my car somewhere else," I told the service manager, a harried-looking fellow who had a habit of clearing his throat every few minutes.

"Then we'll have to mark it Failed Inspection."

"There's nothing I can do. Nine hundred dollars is more than I can afford."

The service manager studied the list, then used a calculator. He cleared his throat. "Bare minimum, you need new brake pads and two new tires or no place in town will pass the car. With an oil and lube, plus the inspection, it'll come to two hundred eighty-six dollars."

I swallowed hard. For months I had been driving without insurance. I had gotten too far behind on the payments after Adam was born. But worn brake pads and tires had to be replaced, and driving with an expired inspection sticker on the windshield was advertising for trouble. Reluctantly, I took the Visa card out of my wallet. "I'll pay cash for the oil and lube and inspection. You can put the rest on my card."

The brake pads and tires came to two hundred fifty-three dollars. To keep the card active, I had deliberately charged a few things for Adam in November, and had paid the bill promptly with a twenty-seven-dollar money order. This new charge was approved immediately.

When I got home, I called Visa and was told that my minimum monthly payment would be fifteen dollars; nearly four dollars of the fifteen was interest. It would be the first money I set aside when I got my check every month. That little plastic card was my safety net, my only shield against disaster.

***

The spring semester at Lee-Davis Community College started on the second Monday in January. Too excited to sleep, I got out of bed before dawn. The day I had dreamed about and hoped for was finally here, and I couldn't wait to begin. But several hours later, at the moment I was to relinquish Adam into Lolita's waiting arms, I hesitated. Suddenly my feeling of anticipation was gone. With the exception of the two mornings Lolita had watched him, Adam and I hadn't been separated since he was born. I could hear the differences in his cries, I knew the things that pleased him. As ready as I was for school, I wasn't prepared to leave him.

Lolita gently took the baby. "He'll be fine, and so will you," she said with a reassuring smile. Then she turned toward the stairs. "But Jamal ain't goin' to be fine if he don't get down here to have his breakfast! Do you hear me, Jamal?"

I couldn't move. It was almost as if a spell had been cast on me. "Sara, you already had your breakfast. Now get movin' or you'll be late for your first day of college!"

The spell was broken. "See you later," I said, hugging them both before I hurried out the door.

At the college I followed a line of cars to the student parking lot. While I waited to get in, I looked at the Blue Ridge Mountains that stretched beyond the campus into the horizon, and I felt as if Tully were watching me, that he knew what I was doing and he approved.

I had deliberately arranged my schedule to leave blocks of time free for my work-study job. As a result, I went from class to class without a break all morning. My first class was English composition, my instructor a young woman who had long straight brown hair and slender, expressive hands that moved constantly while she talked. The instructor's name, E. Farrell, was written on the blackboard in block letters. "You will write in this class," she said. "You will write and write until you can express yourselves clearly, logically, and concisely. You will keep a journal in which you will write about your reactions to class discussions and assigned readings. You will also write essays."

I took notes while Ms. Farrell lectured about the form and structure of the essay, her hands emphasizing the points she made. "Your first assignment will be to write a five-hundred word essay about an incident that is important in your life," she said toward the end of the class. "It should be a recent incident based on your experience."

An unshaven fellow of about nineteen or twenty who was sitting next to me let out a low groan. "Aw shit, not an assignment on the first day," he said under his breath.

I ignored him. I was already thinking about what I was going to write.

My next class was French. All my life I had dreamed of going to Paris. Being taught by Madam Bourdon, whose French accent was charming, if sometimes difficult to understand, seemed almost as good. Before the class ended, we were already pronouncing our first words. "*Bonjour, mes amis,*" I repeated, trying to get my French accent right.

There was nothing charming about Arthur R. Farrish, the instructor in my Algebra II class. A large, lumpy man of about fifty, Dr. Farrish was wearing an electric-blue shirt, neon-yellow necktie, and brown-plaid pants. Although he looked like he had stepped out of a cartoon, what he had to say wasn't amusing. "Some of you may be falsely assuming that you won't have to work in this class because you won't be getting formal credit for it. Make no mistake: you will work and you will work hard. Expect to do three hours of homework for every hour you spend in class. There will be a quiz every other Friday. Only in rare instances are excuses accepted for missing a quiz. You will be graded on a standard curve; every missed quiz is counted as an automatic F. Your final grade will be either pass or fail."

He looked around the room, his eyes small gray pebbles behind his thick glasses. "If you are thinking that I am deliberately trying to terrify you, you are correct, and I am doing so for good reason: you cannot take higher level math courses, which some of you need to transfer into a four-year college, without successfully completing this course," he said with a satisfied smile. "Now that we understand each other, we can begin."

"I don't know about you, but I'm goin' to try to transfer out of this class," whispered a fat young woman sitting next to me whose hair was dyed the color of strained carrots.

I couldn't change my schedule; nor did I think it was necessary. For all his bluster, Dr. Farrish might be a good teacher.

Before I ate lunch I went to see Laurie Templeton in the financial aid office to ask about my work-study job. "I managed to get you eighteen hours. The way you set up your schedule really helped.

You'll be working here in financial aid," Laurie said. "Usually we have accounting majors, but an accounting background isn't necessary for the work you'll be doing. Mostly you'll be scheduling appointments, filing, and making photocopies."

"Do you have any idea of what my net pay will be after the deductions are taken out?"

Laurie smiled. "Somehow I knew you'd ask. Give or take some change, it'll be close to seventy dollars."

For the first time all morning I felt myself relax. There would be no problem paying Lolita seventy-five dollars for watching Adam.

"If your lunch is in that brown bag, you're welcome to eat here."

"Really?" I said. It was hard to believe, remembering how ugly Bert Sidley got if I so much as sipped a glass of water at my desk at Creekside Elementary.

"We're pretty casual. There's a machine at the end of the hall if you need something to drink."

I worked in the financial aid office all afternoon. Laurie showed me the appointment book and explained the filing system. "Mary Fitzgerald is the director of financial aid," Laurie said. "You'll meet her later; she's at a meeting. Mary doesn't like her appointments scheduled too close together. She generally gets the tougher problems, which can take longer."

Mary Fitzgerald came in at two o'clock. She was a matronly woman whose gray hair was combed into a severe bun; however, her smile was warm and her manner friendly, if a bit reserved. "Laurie had to hunt to get your work-study money," she said. "She seems to think a lot of you, Sara. I hope you don't disappoint her."

"I'll try not to," I said.

"I hope I haven't made you feel defensive. Laurie often goes out of her way for students. Even though I've cautioned her not to take it personally, she feels betrayed when they don't try. She puts a lot of herself into her job."

At that moment the fat young woman with the carrot-colored hair who sat next to me in the Algebra II class came into the office. "Here is a perfect example of what I was talking about," Mary said as the young woman approached us. "This is Amy Thomas, Sara."

Amy didn't so much as nod at me. "I went to admissions and records for my work-study job, and they told me I have only ten hours," Amy said. "I need more than that."

"Last semester you were given twenty hours, and you didn't show up for your job half the time. Other students could have used those hours and that money."

"My baby was sick," Amy said in a whine.

"Not all semester," Mary said. "Excuses won't work anymore, Amy. If you start skipping hours this semester, you won't be given work-study again."

Her moon face set in a pout, Amy marched out the door.

As I was getting ready to leave, Laurie gave me a schedule card. "This is for your orientation group."

"I'd rather be in a regular orientation class," I said.

"Oh, don't feel that way. Give the group a chance. Some of them are bound to be interesting. You never know what you'll learn that'll prove useful."

"Maybe," I said doubtfully.

It was five o'clock when I arrived at Lolita's. Adam was in a playpen in the living room, where Julia and Jamal were watching cartoons on television. Lolita shook her head and smiled. "Your son got a mind of his own. He wants to be near the kids. I had to move the playpen from the kitchen 'cause he raised such a fuss when they left him to watch TV. He sure let me know what he wanted!"

I stooped to pick him up. "Hey, Adam," I said, nuzzling him. "Did you miss your mama?"

Adam gave me a big grin, but then he wiggled around so he could see Julia, Jamal, and the television. "Well, I guess that tells me," I said, laughing.

Later, while I was bathing him, I said, "What a busy day we both had!"

To my delight, Adam began to babble. None of his sounds were intelligible, but to me they made perfect sense. "You did have a good day!" I said. "And so did I."

After I put him to bed, I sat at the kitchen table to do my homework. The books I bought had a crisp, new smell; for no reason other than pleasure I ran my finger down the straight spine of the algebra book before I opened it. Then I started to work. After I finished the algebra, I studied French vocabulary. I lost all sense of time. There was a feeling of accomplishment in each problem I completed, in each word I memorized. It was close to midnight when I finished writing my essay, which began...

All my life I dreamed of going to college. But this morning, when my dream was about to come true, I was prepared for everything except leaving my son.

***

My first class in psychology was even more interesting than I had anticipated it would be. The professor, Dr. Hugh Raymond, an intense man who strode back and forth across the room while he spoke, was alternately funny and serious as he told us what we could expect. "We're going to be examining human and animal behavior," he said. "We're going to talk about learning and memory, development and personality, emotion and stress. I'll be contributing to your stress by requiring the completion of a term paper at the end of the semester, as well as mid-term and final exams.

"But more about that later. In the course of our exploration, we'll gain a deeper understanding of ourselves and others, of why we behave the way we do."

The hour and a half I spent listening to Dr. Raymond passed so quickly that I left to go to my next class with no expectations. The History of Western Civilization was a required course, not one that I would have chosen, and I doubted that any instructor could be as fascinating as the one I had just heard. That was before I saw C. Alton Dillard.

"Now he's somethin' to look at!" said the brunette sitting next to me when he ambled up to the front of the classroom.

I had to agree. He was the handsomest man I had ever seen, about six feet tall, broad-shouldered, with chiseled features. His thick black hair tumbled over his collar. He was wearing a white button-down shirt open at the neck, a gray tweed sport jacket that had suede patches on the elbows, and jeans that were a perfect faded blue. He was so good-looking that it was difficult for me not to stare at him.

C. ALTON DILLARD he scrawled on the blackboard. Brushing chalk dust off his hands, he turned and scanned our faces, his dark brown eyes resting briefly on me and another woman who had creamy skin and wavy auburn hair. "This class is the History of Western Civilization," he said. "We'll be going back to some of our earliest recorded history, to *The Iliad* by Homer, to Sappho's poetry, to the *History of the Persian Wars*, to Exodus and Genesis and Matthew in the Bible. We'll cover the years up to 1500, ending the semester with Machiavelli's *The Prince*. I envy those of you who will be reading them for the first time."

I couldn't imagine him envying anyone. I noticed that he wasn't wearing a wedding band, although that didn't mean he wasn't married. Not that his marital status would make a difference. A man as educated and cultured as C. Alton Dillard wouldn't be interested in me. But I was looking forward to reading these great works, and having him as my guide was a pleasant bonus.

There was no time to eat after the class was over at twelve thirty; the orientation class was scheduled to begin at twelve forty-five. My stomach rumbling with hunger, I bought a soft drink at a vending machine. Since orientation wasn't an academic course, I hoped I would be allowed to have my lunch.

The desks in the classroom were arranged in a semicircle; there was a single desk at the opening, where a woman who had close-cropped brown hair was seated. I chose one of the unoccupied desks near the center of the circle. "My name is Adrienne Wakeman," said the woman at the separate desk. "Since our meeting time is during the lunch hour, any of you who haven't eaten are welcome to eat here. I hope lunch isn't holding up the others who are supposed to come."

While I ate my sandwich, I glanced at two white women whom I guessed were close to me in age, a white woman in her twenties, and a black woman who was leaning back in her chair with a cautious, rather skeptical expression on her face.

"We can't wait much longer for the others," said Adrienne at five minutes to one.

A few minutes later Amy Thomas came into the room; she moved sluggishly, as if she were unaware that she was nearly fifteen minutes late. Then the last member of the group arrived, a slender black girl who took the last empty desk, which was next to me. "Sorry if I'm late," she said. "I had to get some lunch."

"I understand," Adrienne said. "But we only have an hour, and one of the things I'm going to insist upon is that everyone makes an effort to be on time. Promptness is a sign of respect, and we're all going to respect each other here. As I said earlier, anyone who wishes to is welcome to eat during our meeting.

"In the time we have left, I'd like to talk briefly about the purpose of this orientation class. The class will be run like a support group. You are all single mothers who have returned to school to get degrees that will enable you to improve your lives and the lives of your children. Some of you have already been here for a semester; for others, this is your first semester. For everyone, this is a time of personal growth and struggle, a time in which you will have many common concerns and experiences that you can share.

"The success of this group depends upon everyone participating openly and honestly. We aren't here to judge. We're here to discuss what you want to accomplish, to focus on your own personal goals."

Adrienne paused to look around the room, her compelling brown eyes making eye contact with each of us. "I can't overstress the importance of not letting what is said in this group out of this room. What we share is confidential and must be kept confidential."

Again, she paused before continuing with a smile that revealed a set of dimples. "I've talked enough. Now it's your turn. Going around the circle, I'd like each of you to tell us your name and a little about yourself."

She directed her gaze at the white woman in her twenties wearing jeans and a stretched-out pink sweatshirt seated at the opening of the semicircle.

The woman folded her arms protectively in front of her. "My name is Rosellen Holmes," she said, her eyes focused on the floor. "This is my second semester here. I have four children. Last semester was rough. Me and the kids were all adjustin'—me to school, and the kids to where we're livin' and their new school. It's been gettin' better. There are more good days now than bad."

"Where do you live?" Adrienne asked.

Rosellen looked up. She had a heart-shaped face, a small pointed chin. "Falcon Trailer Court. It was the only place I could get after we moved out of Safe House—you know, the women's shelter. I try to keep to myself at Falcon. It ain't always easy with the kids."

Adrienne nodded. "What are you studying here?"

"I want to be a nurse."

"And you?" Adrienne said to Amy Thomas, who was seated next to Rosellen. "Can you tell us something about yourself?"

"My name's Amy Thomas. This is my second semester, too. I have a daughter eighteen months old. I want to be a teacher," she said, shifting her bulk importantly. "But right now I've got a problem. I was only given ten hours on my work-study job and I need more than that."

"You'll have to take that up with the financial aid office."

"I already did," Amy said, glancing at me. "They won't give me any more."

"Then you'll have to look elsewhere," Adrienne said.

"Didn't you tell us this is a support group? Aren't you supposed to help?"

"I'm here to facilitate, to help you help yourselves, not to solve your problems for you. Does anyone have any suggestions for Amy?"

No one responded.

"Then I guess we'll have to continue around the circle."

"But..." Amy started to protest.

"Perhaps you can bring it up again next week. We don't have a lot of time today, and there are others we need to hear from."

"I suppose that means me," said the woman sitting on the other side of Amy.

She was about forty, a striking woman who had perfectly applied make-up and streaked blond hair. Beneath her shaded blue lids, her clear blue eyes shone with a lively intelligence. "I'm Pat Sennett. The name Sennett might be familiar—Sennett Electric. That was our business. My husband and I built it up from scratch. I kept the books and did all the billin'. My husband died from cancer last year. He was sick a long time. We lost just about everything.

"After he died, I got a job keepin' the books for another electrician, but we—me and my daughters—couldn't live on what he was payin'. And he had the nerve to think of himself as a bonus, me bein' a widow and all. So I quit. But it was the same everywhere I went. Even with my experience, with no credentials I couldn't get much more than a dollar or two above minimum wage, and we couldn't live on that. It about killed me to go on welfare, it really ripped my pride, but it's the only way for me to get a degree so I can make a decent livin'."

"What are you studying?" Adrienne asked.

"Accounting," Pat said with a laugh. "In my classes last semester, we were workin' on some of the same stuff I did in my husband's business."

A wave of laughter rippled around the semicircle. Adrienne smiled, then turned to me.

Obliged to say something, I gave them my name, Adam's age, and told them I wanted to be a teacher. I didn't leave an opening for any questions. To my relief, Adrienne focused on the slender young black woman sitting next to me whose crossed leg had been swinging back and forth, back and forth, in an edgy rhythm. "I'm Tanya Wales," she said, leaning forward, her body taut as a spring. "This is my first semester. Like Pat, I want to be an accountant. I've always been good with numbers. For a while I worked in a bank, but they pay next to nothin' and there's no future unless you're in management. People like me don't get into management.

"My daughter's three years old. I got pregnant when I was eighteen. It was a big disappointment to my parents. I'm the oldest, and they expected me to go to college."

"Then they must be pleased that you're here."

Tanya nodded. "They're really supportive."

"You're lucky," said the woman sitting next to her. She looked to be in her early thirties; her hair was short and curly, her skin a tawny brown. She was wearing unusual earrings made of polished wood cut into circles and triangles that swung when she moved her head, brushing her long, elegant neck. "My family will never forgive me for goin' on welfare. No one in my family was ever on welfare, no one would ever take a dime."

"My family feels the same way," said Pat Sennett.

"So does mine," said Rosellen. "But I wasn't goin' to stay with my husband and get beat up anymore to save them their pride."

Her earrings swinging, the woman sitting next to Tanya nodded. "Sometimes pride is the glue that holds you together. It's a hard thing to give up. I've been strugglin' with mine for a long time."

"Can you tell us about yourself?" said Adrienne.

"My name is Kelsie Parks. Like I said, no one in my family was ever on welfare. I worked two jobs to support myself and my sons. But my older boy is fourteen now; the younger one's nine. They're at the age where they can get into trouble fast. Workin' two jobs, I had no way of knowin' who they was with or where they were at. When I discovered that my older boy was startin' to keep bad company, that was it. I wasn't goin' to sacrifice my sons to the street to stay off welfare. I should have come here long ago. This is my second semester."

"What are you studying?"

"I'm goin' to be a nurse," Kelsie said, her voice full and confident. "The pay's good and I'll never want for a job."

"I can't argue with that," Adrienne said, smiling as she looked at the last woman in the semicircle. "Please tell us about yourself."

Somewhere in her forties, she was the oldest student in the group, and time hadn't treated her kindly. The skin on her full face was patchy and rough; lines on her forehead gave her a permanent frown. She was clutching a notebook so tightly her knuckles were white. "I'm Wanda Birckhead. This is my first semester," she said, with a nervous quaver in her voice. "I'm here because my husband left me. He's livin' with a woman the same age as one of our sons—twenty-five. Lord knows what she sees in him other than a paycheck. He gets mean when he drinks, and he drinks a lot. I've got three sons. The oldest is married; the middle one's in jail. He was into drugs real bad. The youngest is in high school. I'm hopin' he don't go down that path." She shook her head, sighing. "I've had some hard, hard times."

"What are you studying?"

"I'm takin' a computer course and some business courses."

"What is your goal?" Adrienne asked.

"Goal?" Wanda said.

"What do you want?"

Wanda's face collapsed like melting ice cream. "I want to get off welfare," she wailed. "I want my husband back."

I glanced up at the clock on the wall and saw with relief that the hour was over. At that moment, all I wanted was to get out of this support group.

***

Adam had no trouble settling in at Lolita's. He went into her waiting arms happily in the morning (which hurt a little, I admit), and he enjoyed seeing Jamal and Julia later in the day. My going to school was as good for him as it was for me. I settled in easily to all of my classes except one: the support group. I just didn't want to be in there, although the second meeting seemed a little better than the first.

The session started promptly at twelve forty-five. "I'm glad everyone was able to get here on time," Adrienne said. "How did your week go? Did any of you have problems?"

Rosellen Holmes, seated at the same desk at the opening of the semicircle that she'd had the previous week, raised her hand. "I had a fight with a neighbor because of one of my kids. She accused him of takin' money from her purse, but he didn't do it. It was her own kid that took it. She demanded that I give her the money. Or else."

"What do you mean, *or else?*"

"She threatened that she'd come after me with a knife," Rosellen said, her tiny chin quivering, "so I fixed her good. I told her I was callin' 911 to report her threat and that if anythin' happened to me, they'd know it was her that done it.

"This fight has had me so upset. I did terrible on a test I took yesterday. I couldn't concentrate. I hate livin' at Falcon Trailer Court! It's next to impossible to keep my kids away from the other kids who live there. I've got to keep an eye on them every minute."

Tanya Wales nodded, her swinging leg moving in agreement. "I don't let my daughter play with the kids where we live. I keep her in or take her to the park."

"Where do you live?" Adrienne asked.

"Grady Gardens," Tanya said. "My name's been on the list for better housing for over two years, but I've never been called. Sometimes I wonder how those names move up, if you know what I mean."

Some of the others nodded as if they also suspected that the lists were rigged. They continued to talk about housing (I didn't say anything) until Adrienne said, "Have there been any other problems?"

Amy Thomas, wearing a pink sweatshirt that fought with her carrot hair, took a deep breath. "My aunt died," she said. "At the funeral—it was on Saturday—my cousin's girlfriend was wearin' my aunt's gold locket. I was supposed to have that locket! My aunt had told me that someday it would be mine because I always admired it. And that's what I told my cousin—that Aunt Lucy promised me the locket. He said, 'No way,' and we got into an argument.

"Now, instead of standin' up for me, everyone in the family is blamin' me for spoilin' the funeral when it's really my cousin's fault," Amy said with a whine.

"Why is it his fault?" Adrienne said.

"He gave his trashy girl friend Aunt Lucy's locket!"

For a moment everyone in the group seemed to be looking at the walls or the floor, anywhere but at Amy. I looked at the clock. Fifteen minutes left. What was the point of this support group? My time could be much better spent studying or working in the financial aid office.

Kelsie Parks broke the silence. She was wearing a black turtleneck sweater that accented her tawny skin. "I'm havin' a problem with my older boy. He's fourteen. This year he's at a new school. The kids who get free lunches are given orange lunch tickets. The kids who pay for their lunches get green tickets. He's been comin' home with bad headaches since school started. Finally he told me that he's been goin' without lunch because he's embarrassed to turn in an orange ticket."

"Can't he bring lunch?" Adrienne said.

"That's what I told him," Kelsie said. "I guess no one brings lunch. It ain't cool. But skippin' lunch is startin' to hurt his grades, and I can't afford to give him the money."

"My girls feel the same way about those orange tickets. They babysit to earn their lunch money," said Pat Sennett. "Maybe your son could get a job somewhere in the neighborhood."

"Jobs for boys are next to impossible to find in my neighborhood. He spent what little money he was able to earn last summer mowin' grass and weedin' yards on clothes and sneakers," Kelsie said, pushing up the sleeves of her sweater. "There's a lot of pressure when you're fourteen. Sometimes I get so mad at Michael Jordan and his damn sneakers! He's makin' millions pitchin' to kids who can least afford what he's sellin'. There should be some publicity on how many boys have gotten into trouble—stealin' or sellin' drugs—to get the money for Air Jordans. Probably thousands."

I wasn't thinking about sneakers; my mind was on lunch tickets. I leaned forward to catch Kelsie's attention. "I was a school secretary. We used the same color lunch tickets for everyone, but we marked the backs of the free lunch tickets with a special stamp. That way no one could tell who was getting a subsidized lunch unless they turned the ticket over. Maybe you could suggest the idea to the principal at your son's school. If you got a few mothers to join you, it might help. The principals I worked for were always impressed with numbers—the more parents who spoke up, the better they listened."

"Then I'll bring at least a dozen!" Kelsie said. "Believe me, they won't be hard to find."

***

I drove slowly, looking for a parking space. I didn't like coming home when it was dark. The men who bought drinks from Verona Finch (women drank there, too) parked in the spaces closest to my unit, so every evening I had to juggle the baby, the diaper bag, and my books in the darkness while I trudged to the mailbox and then struggled with the lock on my door. Unable to handle the roofer's knife with all that I was carrying, I felt like a walking target.

The only piece of mail in the box was a thick white envelope from social services, which I thrust into my coat pocket to read later. First I had to bathe and feed Adam, and then prepare my own supper. Since I had started school, my evening meals had dwindled to canned soup, a sandwich, and fruit. I couldn't spend valuable time cooking when I had barely an hour or two to play with Adam before I started doing my homework. He was crawling now, and curious about everything. He was growing too fast, precious moments that I had to enjoy because they were passing so quickly.

After I started undressing for bed, I remembered that the letter was still in my pocket. I shuddered with disgust when I turned on the hall light to go downstairs and saw scurrying cockroaches. No matter how hard I scrubbed or how many times the exterminator came, nothing short of burning it to the ground would rid the place of bugs.

Inside the envelope there was a form letter notifying me that a review of my welfare status was scheduled with Alexander Ryle on Friday, January twenty-ninth at eleven o'clock. There were also familiar papers in the envelope that I was to fill out and bring with me.

January twenty-ninth at eleven o'clock was impossible. At that time I would be taking my first Algebra II quiz. Dr. Farrish had announced the quiz that very morning, and had reminded the class what he had stated the first day: only in rare instances—so rare that he could think of just one—were excuses accepted for missing a quiz. I would have to call social services to change the time of the appointment.

But when I called the next day, Mr. Ryle told me that I was expected to keep the appointment or lose my benefits. "We don't reschedule appointments to accommodate the whims of clients," he said harshly.

There was no alternative but to speak to Dr. Farrish, a prospect I dreaded. I thought of the humiliations I had experienced during the past year—applying for food stamps and welfare, losing twice to Grover Daniels in court, pleading with Fletcher Hargrave to find me a place to live, making my poverty public and then enduring disapproving stares from people when I paid for my groceries with WIC checks and food stamps. Humiliation could be measured in degrees, in how deep a wound it made, in how wide a scar it left. Telling Dr. Farrish that I couldn't take his quiz because my welfare status was scheduled to be reviewed at that time was too painful to contemplate; I didn't know how I could do it. And it wasn't something I could delay. Dr. Farrish had office hours only once before the test was scheduled.

To my dismay, he shared an office with another teacher, a woman who was marking papers at her desk. He gestured for me to sit in a chair placed next to his desk. As usual, he was dressed like a character in a cartoon, in an apple green shirt and a purple-printed tie. "What brings you here, Ms. Barefield?" he said pleasantly, his gray eyes curious behind his thick glasses. I twisted in my chair so that my back was to the woman seated at the other desk. "The quiz on Friday," I said, reaching into my purse. I handed Dr. Farrish the letter from social services, unable to look at him. "I have a conflict."

Dr. Farrish scanned the letter. "I saw one of these several years ago," he said, returning it to me. "It belonged to a woman who came to me for the same reason that you have, and I asked her what proved to be a truly stupid question: I wanted to know why she didn't change the time of her appointment. To my astonishment, she wept. What she said still haunts me: *'Don't you think I tried to change the time of the appointment so I wouldn't have to endure the humiliation of letting you see this letter?'*"

He coughed to clear his throat. "Ms. Barefield, I would be happy to give you a make-up quiz at two thirty on Friday afternoon, if that is a convenient time. It will be here in this office."

My eyes brimmed with gratitude. "Thank you," I said. "Thank you a lot."

***

My appointment with Alexander Ryle was a brief replay of my initial intake interview. After he reviewed the new Base Document I had filled in, he said, "I see you are in the work-study program at Lee-Davis." He opened a desk drawer and pulled out a single-page yellow form. "Why haven't we received this from the financial aid office?"

"I don't know," I said, taking the form from him. It was an authorization for Lee-Davis Community College to release my financial aid information.

"How many hours a week are you working?"

"Eighteen."

"Then you're taking home about seventy dollars. That's a nice wad of money at the taxpayers' expense."

His insult made my face flame. "I'm using the money to pay someone to take care of my baby! I pay her seventy-five dollars a week."

"Really," he said, as though what I told him was doubtful. "To make sure our records are correct, I'm going to put a hold on your future checks and food stamps. It's too late to stop your February check and stamps; they went out this morning. But they are the last you'll get until we receive your financial aid information."

"I work in the financial aid office. I'll make sure the form is sent back to you right away."

"Yes, do that," he said.

"Why are you treating me like this?"

He looked at me coldly. "I don't know what you mean."

Despite my efforts, hot tears of anger formed in my eyes. "You're making it sound as if I deliberately didn't sign the form, that I'm trying to cheat somehow."

"I am here to make sure that *everyone* follows the rules," he said, rising to indicate that the interview was over.

In a hurry to get out of the building, I almost collided with a young woman holding a baby when I reached the glass doors that faced the parking lots. "Sorry," I said. Then I stared.

"Symone?" I said. There were circles under the girl's eyes, and there was a strained expression on her lovely face. The baby was a complete surprise. Symone was slender the last time I saw her.

Symone's smile was half-earnest, half-embarrassed. "How's Adam?"

"He's fine. He's crawling now and starting to get into everything. Is this your daughter?"

Symone lifted a corner of the pink blanket the baby was wrapped in. "Her name is Chandra, with a C, for my daddy. His name was Chester." She paused as a black Honda Celica pulled up opposite the door. "That's my ride."

I held open the door for her. "Say hello to your mama for me," I said, recalling how much Joletta had wanted Symone to go to college.

Although I had studied for the algebra exam I took several hours later, I had difficulty concentrating. Symone and the baby and Alexander Ryle's threat kept intruding into my thoughts. Several times I caught myself making careless mistakes. "I'm afraid I haven't done very well," I said when I was finished.

"I doubt that's the case," Dr. Farrish said. "But if it is, I'm sure you'll do better on the next one."

I hurried to the financial aid office. Laurie Templeton's door was open. "Are you free?" I said.

"My next appointment should be here in a couple minutes."

"I won't take long," I promised, closing the door.

Laurie's expression hardened as she listened to me tell what had happened in Alexander Ryle's office. "That bastard!" she said when I was done. I had never seen her so angry.

"I've signed the form," I said, placing it on the desk. "I know you're busy, but I'd be grateful if you'd send it back to social services as soon as you can."

"It will be done today before I leave," she said.

"Thanks. It's had me so upset I couldn't think straight for the make-up test I just took."

"Sara, I'm truly sorry this happened. I'd like to explain something to you, but I must have your word that what I say will never leave this room."

"You've got it."

"I imagine you've been wondering why I didn't have you sign the notification form sooner."

"Well...yes," I admitted.

"I know you're using your work-study money for child care, so I was hoping Ryle would let it pass. Depending on a student's need, some caseworkers will overlook the form; they'll 'forget' about it." Laurie framed "forget" with her fingers. "For years Alexander Ryle deliberately 'forgot' to obtain Yolanda Washington's financial aid form. I suspect the reason he isn't in your corner is because he wanted to be a teacher."

"What?"

"The story that went around is that he wanted to teach history in high school. He was told that he wouldn't be able to get a job because he's too short; the students wouldn't respect him. I heard that he was unemployed a long time before he became a caseworker.

"Once I turn your form in, the money you earn here will be counted as income and a deduction will be taken from your food stamps."

I could feel my shoulders droop. "How much of a deduction?"

"I'm not sure. They have a formula to figure it out."

"If I had a different caseworker..."

"It's too late to help you in this instance," Laurie said. "But if I were you I'd look for someone other than Ryle. You need a caseworker who's on your side."

"How can I find one?"

"Ask around. A good place to start would be the women in your support group."

All weekend I mulled over what Laurie had told me. I worried about how much would be taken out of my food stamps, and I thought about how unfair it was that some people were penalized for their work-study money while others weren't. Of one thing I was certain: I had to get a different caseworker.

When I went to the support group on Tuesday, I was careful not to mention anything about the incident concerning the financial aid form because of my promise to Laurie; once the women began talking, there was no telling where their discussion would lead. Instead, after Adrienne asked if anyone had any problems, I told them how Ryle refused to change the time of my appointment even though I had explained to him that I had a test that conflicted. "Last semester Ryle did that to me. At least you got to take a make-up test," said Amy Thomas resentfully. "I'm havin' a real problem. I've got a new boy friend. He hates it when babies cry, and my daughter always cries when he's around. It's like she knows and does it on purpose."

"How old is she?" Tanya asked.

"Eighteen months."

"How does he treat her?" asked Rosellen.

"He treats her fine," said Amy, her voice louder than necessary.

I listened with disappointment while the discussion veered off in an entirely different direction.

As we were leaving, Kelsie Parks came up to me quietly and said, "Do you live in the city or the county?"

"The city."

"Then you might want to ask to be switched from Ryle to Mattie Fuller. She's always done her best for me."

"Thank you," I said.

"I should be thankin' you. A group of us met with the principal of my son's school yesterday. He's goin' to see about changin' those lunch tickets."

"That's great!" I said, thinking that maybe the support group wasn't such a bad idea after all.

***

March first fell on a Monday. Anxious to open my mail, I didn't take off Adam's jacket and hat before I put him in the playpen. For weeks I had been worrying about the effect of the financial aid release that had been sent to social services. My welfare check was the same, but my food stamps had been cut by more than half, to one hundred five dollars.

I tried to ignore familiar stirrings of panic as I lifted Adam out of the playpen. Soon his jacket and hat would be too small. He needed new jerseys and overalls, a sweater for the spring. Even if I managed to find things for him at secondhand stores and garage sales, it still wouldn't solve my problem. I needed more than one hundred dollar's worth of food stamps a month to survive. It had to be a mistake.

After a sleepless night I called my food stamp worker, Daphne Slovene, in the morning. "The stamps were issued based on the money you earn in your work-study program," Daphne said.

"But I'm using every penny of the work-study money to pay for child care."

"What you're using the money for doesn't make a difference. The amount of stamps you receive is calculated by a strict formula. There are no exceptions."

I went to the financial aid office before my first class hoping that Laurie would know what to do, but all Laurie could suggest was that I call my new caseworker, Mattie Fuller. "She doesn't know me," I said. "I haven't had time to see her yet. When I'm not in classes, I'm working here."

"From what I've heard Mattie Fuller does what she can to help her people succeed," Laurie said. "It can't hurt you to call."

Mattie Fuller listened without comment while I briefly explained my problem. "Have you talked to Ernest Maybee? He's in charge of the ESP program that helps with child care. I don't know if his funding has come in yet," she said, the tone of her voice sympathetic. "I'd hate to see you give up."

So I called Ernest Maybee, wondering if he remembered me. "I have your name right here on the list," he said after I explained my predicament. "The program should be fully funded again by May first, sooner if the money comes early like I'm hoping. Hang in there, Sara. You'll get your child care. Don't give up."

But there were four and a half weeks in March, another four and a half in April, a total of nine weeks with two hundred ten dollars' worth of stamps. I sat in my classes going over and over the same figures, the numbers lining up as inflexibly as bars in a window. I had no idea of what Dr. Raymond was lecturing about in psychology; not a word uttered by handsome C. Alton Dillard registered in my brain. An entire morning of thinking yielded just one solution. It was, I believed, my only option if I were to stay in school.

I decided to skip the support group. They wouldn't have an answer. I was regretting that I had told anyone. After Dillard's class I went to work in the financial aid office, put in my usual time, and was able to leave school an hour earlier. Instead of going to pick up Adam, I drove to a supermarket on Lee Avenue where I cashed my welfare check and bought diapers. Before I left the supermarket parking lot, I put thirty dollars in one jacket pocket and the roofer's knife in the other. Then I locked my purse in the trunk of the car and drove to Mayhew's Market at the end of Grady Street. I pulled into the narrow parking lot and backed into a space so I would have a clear view of the front of the store.

I waited in the car for a while, watching the people who were coming and going, watching who was lingering outside. I also looked at the cars in the parking lot and those on the street to make sure I was the only one observing the activity in front of the store.

It was the busiest day of the month at Mayhew's Market. There wasn't a bank near Grady Gardens, so people who didn't have cars came to Mayhew's to cash their welfare checks and shop with their food stamps. Business was flourishing outside as well. Street dealers were selling crack and heroin, exchanging drugs for money with a sleight of hand that a professional magician would envy. Everywhere there were children, some going into Mayhew's, others waiting to be picked by one of the dealers to run an errand that meant easy money. Crack addicts were jockeying for position to be the first to offer their food stamps for sale as people approached the store. A late afternoon sun shone down on the activity, lighting it like a carnival.

I remembered how Tully used to say that sometimes a person has no choice but to take a deep breath and do what is necessary. I took a deep breath and got out of the car, my heart racing, my hands thrust deep in my pockets, thirty dollars in one hand, the roofer's knife in the other.

It didn't take me more than a minute to buy sixty dollars' worth of food stamps for the thirty dollars. The woman I bought them from was unquestionably an addict: her hair was matted in greasy clumps, her brown skin was rough as bark, her tattered clothes stank, a plug of spittle hung from the corner of her mouth. She was so anxious to get her hands on the money that her feet danced impatiently on the sidewalk.

I didn't allow myself to think about the woman, or that the stamps I had bought were meant for the woman's children. I didn't allow myself to consider the possibility that I could have been arrested for committing a crime, that I had risked Adam's welfare as well as my own. I didn't allow myself to think at all.

As I was driving away, I turned on the car radio for distraction. I had managed to keep the radio by sticking heavy black tag board over it to make the opening look empty. "Today is March second," a male announcer said. "I bet most people can't remember where they were or what they were doing a year ago on this date."

I gasped. I could never forget that day: a year ago on March second I went to the Department of Social Services for the first time. It seemed like a lifetime ago.

I slept no better that night than I had the night before. Mama appeared in my dreams after a long absence, Mama as she had looked near the end, her flesh eaten away by cancer. Smoke rose from a Marlboro in her hand.

"And you looked down on us," she repeated over and over. *"And you looked down on us."*

"I have to eat, Mama," I said in defense.

"And you looked down on us," was her unyielding reply.

* * *

With the exception of the first meeting, when she told the support group that her hard-drinking husband had left her for a woman the age of her oldest son, Wanda Birckhead had had little to say. Like me, week after week Wanda sat in the semicircle without participating. She would nod to herself when the women talked about their problems, as if they were confirming what she'd known all along: that the road of life was paved with misery. Whenever Adrienne asked her how she was doing, her reply was always the same, "As well as can be expected." So it came as a surprise when she announced in mid-March that she had decided to quit college.

The meeting had just begun. "Why?" Adrienne asked.

Wanda was wearing black polyester slacks and a lavender sweatshirt that had faded to a near gray. Her salt-and-pepper hair was frizzy at the ends from a cheap perm. "It's hard," she said, the frown lines on her forehead deepening. "I reckon I've been out of school too long."

"I can get help for you," Adrienne said. "Free tutoring."

"I appreciate it, but I've had about all I can take of welfare," Wanda said. "My youngest boy's birthday was last Thursday. He's been complainin' that all we eat is macaroni and hamburger. I knew he missed the steaks my husband used to bring home every week on payday, so I decided to make a nice birthday dinner even though it meant we'd be short at the end of the month. After school I went to Kroger and bought a steak, a couple nice bakin' potatoes, green beans, and a birthday cake. The cake was nothin' fancy, just one of them small cakes that has *Happy Birthday* on it. I got the chocolate 'cause that's what he likes. When I went to pay with my food stamps at the checkout, the lady behind me in line said, 'Now I've seen it all! Look at her payin' for steak and a birthday cake with food stamps! Those stamps are supposed to be for poor people!'"

Wanda wiped away a tear. "I could feel people lookin' at me. What could I say? That I'm poor? That it was my son's birthday and he's sick of macaroni and hamburger and this was the only present I could afford to give him?"

"What did you do?" Adrienne asked.

"Nothin.' My face was hot so I knew it was red. I picked up the bags and left.

"My son liked the steak, but I couldn't swallow a bite. It caught in my throat and just stuck there, it wouldn't go down. That ain't goin' to happen again. I got me a job so I can buy what I want with my own money and no one can say a word about it."

"Where?"

"At the Ramada Inn cleanin' motel rooms. I'll get five dollars an hour plus tips. That should give me plenty."

Kelsie Parks leaned forward, her unusual carved earrings swinging with the movement. "How much do you plan on makin' from the tips?"

The skin on Wanda's face broke out in bright patches. "The man who's hirin' me said I can get as much as five dollars from each room. If I work fast, I could get me an extra ten dollars an hour, maybe more."

"Not at the Ramada Inn, you can't," said Kelsie. "I know someone who just quit there. She was told the same as you, but the biggest tip she ever got was a couple of bucks. Most weeks she didn't get any tips at all; the other women didn't either. And they don't have enough people cleanin', so they gave her twice as many rooms to do as they told her they would when she was hired."

Wanda's face got redder. "Maybe she didn't get tips because she didn't do a good job."

"I'm sure Kelsie's friend did a fine job," Adrienne said quickly. "I've heard of the same thing happening, people being promised tips larger than they actually get. Wanda, I know your experience in Kroger's was upsetting, but I hope you won't let that one incident make you choose cleaning toilets over a chance to get an education that will help you get a really good job."

"I ain't partial to cleanin' toilets, but…" Wanda paused for a moment, chewing on her lower lip. "Social services is after my husband to pay support. He don't want to pay a dime, so he told me he's goin' to a lawyer to get a divorce if I don't get off welfare and support myself. I don't want a divorce."

"How long have you and your husband been separated?"

"About a year."

"Then perhaps the marriage is over," Adrienne said gently.

"Not for me," Wanda said, weeping.

"There's no way you can support yourself on five dollars an hour," Rosellen said.

"You'll be on food stamps for the rest of your life," Tanya said. Wanda wasn't convinced by their arguments and didn't respond until Pat Sennett spoke. "Why are you makin' it easy for him after he ran off on you? Shouldn't it be the other way around?"

"What do you mean?"

"He left you for another woman. It seems to me that he should be payin' for what he did," Pat said. "If you go to work, he'll have more in his pocket to spend on her. But if you stay in school and he's forced to contribute support, he might not have enough money to keep her interested. Then, no matter what happens, when you graduate you'll have an education that'll get you a better job than cleanin' toilets."

It didn't take Wanda long to decide. She took a tissue out of her purse and blew her nose. "I'm stayin' in school!"

***

Sometimes I felt that taking a seat next to Pat Sennett at the first meeting of the support group was a stroke of luck. We began meeting several times a week for a quick lunch before we went to our work-study jobs and soon became comfortable friends. Pat had lived the life I had once dreamed of with Tully—marriage and children, a successful business and a nice home. After I told her about Tully, she clasped my hand and said, "If I ever catch myself becoming bitter, I'll think about you and your Tully. At least Gary and I had those good years together. I wish you'd had that much."

Pat impressed me with her ability to grasp situations and get straight to the heart of them. "What you told Wanda yesterday will keep her in school," I said when we met the following day for lunch in the college cafeteria. "How did you think of it?"

She pushed her streaked blond hair away from her face and laughed. "It's simple accounting: Wanda's husband has only so much money to spend. If he has to support her, he'll have less for the younger woman he's trying to dazzle."

We both brought our lunches from home in brown paper bags. "I wish

I could see things in my own life as clearly as I saw Wanda's," Pat said, unwrapping a sandwich. "My accounting teacher is interested in me, but I'm not sure it's the kind of interest I want, if you know what I mean."

"Yes," I said. "I've been getting some attention from my instructor in the History of Western Civilization. It's been flattering. The man is gorgeous."

Pat put her sandwich down and looked at me with a smile that was half-serious, half-teasing. "I wouldn't have picked you to fall for a handsome face."

"I haven't fallen yet, but it's been lonely."

"Lord, has it ever!" Pat said. "But as lonely as I've been, somethin' is holdin' me back, a feelin' that his interest is just casual, that if it weren't me it would be someone else. I don't want to be a convenience for any man, somethin' that can be used and dumped like an empty soda bottle. I'm not goin' to be on welfare forever. When I come out of this I want to have at least some of my pride intact."

I thought of the devastating morning I had overheard Carl Shields talking about me as the cleaning woman. "You're smart to be cautious," I said.

"Probably the men who teach here think we're easy marks because we're older and alone."

Our conversation stayed with me all afternoon. Since the beginning of the semester when *The Iliad* was discussed in my Western Civilization class, C. Alton Dillard had made me aware of his interest. He had praised my remarks on the women's perspective of war, that their fears of the loss of their husbands and children hadn't changed from the early Greeks to the present. His praise gave me confidence, and I had led the class into a passionate discussion of Vietnam, of how young men were wrongfully sacrificed for a cause that wasn't theirs. "This country didn't give a damn about the men who fought in Vietnam, and nothing was done to help the ones who survived!" I'd said. Afterward I wasn't sure if the high I felt was because I had finally given public utterance to feelings I had held in for years, or if it came partially from Dillard's compelling brown eyes focusing on me as if there was no one else in the room. His gaze was intoxicating. It made me feel young and attractive. It made me forget welfare and food stamps and Grady Street. Hard as I tried, after that day I couldn't get C. Alton Dillard out of my thoughts; nor would he let me. He sought me out before or after class, always casually, luring me in like a fisherman sure of his bait.

Toward the end of the afternoon when there was a break in appointments, I went into Laurie's office. "What's on your mind?" Laurie said, flipping through a pile of papers on her desk.

I pulled up a chair. "C. Alton Dillard."

Laurie's expression sharpened. "Are you getting one of the famous Dillard *treatments*?"

"Treatments?"

"To Alton Dillard, sex is a sport. He's the hunter and you're the prey, even if you think you're chasing him. It's always his game, whether he allows himself to be caught or he snares you. He doesn't give a damn about anyone but himself. There are dozens of women who would like to attach a permanent sign on him that says, 'PROCEED AT YOUR OWN RISK.'"

It didn't take guessing to understand that Laurie was one of those women. I nodded, unsure of what to say.

"Maybe I can make up for the bad news with some news that's good. The Pell money is in. I know you'll be tempted to spend it, but try to hang on to as much as you can. You'll need it this summer."

We rose at the same time. "Oh, Laurie, how can I ever thank you?"

"You can become the best damn teacher in Virginia!"

***

When I went to pick up Adam at Lolita's on the Thursday before Easter, he was too busy pulling on the ears of a furry stuffed rabbit to pay attention to me. "Where did you get that wonderful bunny?" I said.

"It's from me and Janelle and Jamal and John Junior," Julia said proudly.

I put Adam down and hugged her. "Thank you for the bunny," I said. "And thank you for watching Adam and playing with him."

"Adam's fun. He's goin' to walk soon."

As if he'd been cued, Adam let go of the bunny, crawled to the coffee table, and pulled himself up. Julia put the bunny at the end of the table; we watched as Adam inched toward it, holding on to the table edge for support. "See!" Julia said.

Lolita came into the living room carrying a gift-wrapped box. "This is for Adam, too."

While Julia got permission to call for a friend, I carefully removed the Easter wrapping. Inside the box there was a matching jacket, hat, and overalls for Adam. "What a gorgeous shade of blue! It's adorable. This and the bunny...It's too much. How can I ever thank you?"

"All the children in this house get new clothes for Easter," Lolita said, as if it were a law. "When that outfit came into the store, I knew it was for Adam. Heavenly blue, the color of his eyes, a perfect match! When I saw it, I took it as a sign."

"A sign?"

"To quit!" Lolita said. "Last night was my last time at Magnolia's, and it feels good! Between John's new job with Wes Honeycutt and watchin' Adam, I don't have to walk into that store unless I need to buy somethin' there. Right now I can't think of anythin' I'd want bad enough to be willin' to look at Linwood Cagle again."

"I thought John was going into business for himself."

"He was until Wes Honeycutt heard about it and called him. Wes is a custom builder. He's gotten big these past few years, more on his plate than he can handle. John is goin' to be like a general manager. Wes wants him to oversee the projects. He'll work with Wes so there won't be a problem with some of the men takin' orders from him, if you know what I mean."

I nodded, thinking of men like my daddy and Ronnie Lee.

"It'll be year 'round. No more waitin' to be called in the dead of winter. Wes has more than enough work to keep busy."

Lolita smiled at me with a gleam in her eye. "Wes is tall and good-lookin.' He's about the right age for you, too. And he ain't married. He got divorced a while ago."

"Forget it!" I said. "I've got enough in my life."

"Not without a man, you don't," Lolita said, the expression on her face telling me that it was useless to argue.

There were no classes at the community college on Good Friday. In the morning I drove to Lee Avenue. As I approached the Westmark Plaza I thought of Bev and decided to stop and wish her a happy Easter. I had meant to call to tell her that school was going well, but there never seemed to be the time.

The shop was filled with flowers, with pots of lilies and azaleas, with tulips, daffodils, hyacinths, and hydrangeas. I must have been enjoying the beautiful colors and lovely scent too long because I didn't notice a pleasant-looking gray-haired woman who was putting an arrangement with others that I knew were ready for delivery. "Can I help you?" she said.

"I'm Sara Barefield. I've come to see Bev. I used to work here."

"She's in the back trying to finish some arrangements before they're picked up."

Bev must have heard us. "Sara, come on back," she called.

Her workroom was exploding with flowers. "Wow!" I said. "I've never seen it like this!"

"Isn't it wonderful!" Bev said with a wide smile. She put down her flower clippers and gave us a hug. "It's so good to see you! How is school?"

"Everything is going really well. And I can see that business here is blooming."

"Life has been good, and not just business. I've met someone," she said, glowing. "He came into the shop late on the Saturday before Valentine's Day. I was sure he was one of those last minute shoppers like my former husband, who didn't care what he bought as long as he had something in his hand to give. I was exhausted and had no flowers left, so I told him that I couldn't help him. Then he explained that his daughter had just had a baby. 'If my wife was alive, she'd know what to do, but she died last year,' he said.

"I filled a large white basket with plants, African violets, and ivy nestled in Spanish moss, and wound blue ribbon around the handle—the baby was a boy. He came back a week later to tell me how much his daughter liked it, and he asked me out to dinner. His name is Elliot Dennison; he owns a computer software company. I haven't enjoyed myself so much in years."

"He's very lucky," I said, truly happy for her.

The potted lilies were so lovely, I wanted to buy one for Lolita. At first Bev refused to charge me, but when I told her I couldn't just take it, she insisted that I pay no more than her cost. "It would ruin my Easter to make a profit on you," she said.

I left the shop wishing, as I had many times, that there was some way I could repay her for all her kindnesses.

Besides buying groceries, I also bought an Easter basket, green cellophane grass, and candy. While the checkout clerk scanned my order, I thought about how ridiculous it was that I could buy bags of candy with food stamps but not toilet paper, soap, and tampons.

I filled the basket while Adam was napping and took it to Lolita's late in the afternoon. Jamal answered the door. "This is from Adam for you and your brother and sisters," I said, handing him the basket.

"What do you say, Jamal?" came Lolita's voice behind him.

"Thank you!" he said so enthusiastically that I had to laugh.

Lolita was pleased with the lilies. "My favorite Easter flowers," she said, "and these are truly beautiful."

On Easter Sunday, I dressed Adam in his new outfit and took him to a park where the Stalling Chamber of Commerce was sponsoring an Easter egg hunt. It was a bright, balmy, cloudless day. Although he was too young to participate, Adam enjoyed seeing the children, the little girls in their ruffled, pastel dresses, and the boys in dress shirts and sport coats, miniatures of their fathers. A picture in blue, Adam watched the activity wide-eyed, jabbering happily.

Resting on the grass, I felt completely relaxed for the first time since Tully's death. The ever-present knots of tension in my neck and shoulders were gone. Ernest Maybee had called to tell me that the ESP program would pay for child care starting May first. Then I would be able to use the seventy dollars I earned in my work-study job to buy food and other necessities. Mr. Maybee had apologized for being unable to put me into the ESP program for gas vouchers, but that didn't upset me. Women who received the vouchers for ten dollar's worth of gasoline a week had to take them to every instructor to be signed as proof they were attending classes, a humiliation I was happy to forego. And I had one hundred seventy-five dollars left from the Pell grant after paying a long overdue telephone bill, which I could use for the summer session. I was already thinking about the courses I wanted to take.

The future looked as bright as the sunshine on this Easter Sunday. With Adam in my arms and college a reality, I felt as though I had been given a second chance at life.

***

As far as I was concerned, Amy Thomas meant nothing but trouble. Amy was unable to transfer out of Dr. Farrish's algebra class, and soon I felt as if I were paying the penalty. After the first few weeks, it seemed that there was always a reason why Amy had to "borrow" my homework: either her baby was sick or she was sick or a relative was sick or her alarm didn't go off or she forgot her book or she lost the assignment.

The first time Amy copied my homework I didn't mind, but when it started happening regularly, I began to resent it and came later to class, which didn't leave Amy sufficient time. "I know what you're doin'," Amy said nastily when she confronted me after a class. "We're in a support group together. That means we're supposed to help each other."

I was too astonished to reply. But I had plenty to say after Amy repeatedly looked at my paper during an algebra quiz in February. I knew Dr. Farrish had noticed; I saw him glance in our direction several times. Afraid that he might think I was deliberately helping Amy cheat, I confronted her afterward. "If you ever sit next to me in algebra again, I'll get up and move away from you. Is that clear?"

"I don't know what you're talkin' about," Amy said with a fleshy pout.

"Then I'll say it differently: stay away from me! You're not going to ruin my chance to get an education!"

Although I felt justified in what I had said, the wounded look on Amy's face upset me.

The women in the support group had also lost patience with Amy. It was her attitude that irritated them, her self-centeredness and her greed. Week after week she talked about her problems, resenting any intrusion, as though the group were meeting solely for her benefit. Once, when Amy was absent, Rosellen remarked at the end of the meeting that it was the best session ever because the barrel didn't have a bad apple. Everyone knew the missing bad apple was Amy.

Still, it came as a shock when Adrienne made her grave announcement at the start of a session in mid-April. "I was just notified that Amy and her boyfriend have been arrested by the Stalling police for the death of Amy's daughter. The little girl died this morning of a head injury. Doctors found extensive evidence of abuse on the child's body. It was on the noon news."

We sat in stunned silence, remembering that a month ago Amy told us that her twenty-month-old daughter had a broken arm. When Pat made the comment that it was unusual for a child under the age of two to break an arm because babies were relaxed when they fell, Amy became so upset by the implication that she had to be persuaded to stay.

Adrienne broke the silence. "What has happened is a tragedy. Some of us might have suspected that Amy had problems, but we didn't realize how deep they were. I think it would be helpful if we talk about discipline today, about how we were disciplined and how we discipline our children."

No one volunteered. "Rosellen, how were you disciplined as a child?" Adrienne said as the silence threatened to become uneasy.

Rosellen hunched her narrow shoulders. "My daddy used to whip me with a belt. I know he must've felt bad about it."

"How do you know?"

"He wouldn't have done it unless he thought I really deserved it. Sometimes I thought I saw tears in his eyes."

"Do you use a belt to discipline your children?"

"No!" Rosellen said. "No one should ever get beat with a belt! I don't beat my kids, but I do hit them. I'm tryin' to do better. I learned from my psychology class that when kids do destructive things, it could be because they want attention. Now when I see them doin' somethin' like pullin' stuff off shelves, I ask if they want my attention. The first time I was surprised to hear them say yes. I'm beginnin' to understand their behavior better. It takes time. The psychology course is good."

"So is Oprah," Kelsie said. "She has shows on how to discipline kids. I've learned a lot from her."

"How were you disciplined?" Adrienne asked.

Kelsie grimaced. "My daddy was an angry man. He was angry all his life, and he took it out on his family. I remember gettin' a whuppin' for nothin' at all. He was feelin' mean and I happened to be walkin' by. He whacked me so hard he sent me flyin' across the room. My head got split open when I hit the corner of a table."

"My daddy was angry, too," Wanda said. "It seemed like his hand would come at us from out of nowhere. I always tried to keep my distance from him so's I wouldn't get hurt."

In my psychology class, Dr. Raymond had said that children pattern their behavior after their parents, that abused children are likely to become abusive adults, an explanation that I couldn't make work for my mama. Mama's mother died when she was three years old, and Grandpa Loudermilk was a gentle drunk who didn't have it in him to harm anyone. Listening to the women, it came to me like a revelation: *Mama was angry*. Memories tumbled into my head: feeling the sting of Mama's hand across my face when there was no money to pay the rent, when the car broke down, when there was no food in the house. Whippings when Mama's tips were bad, when Mama lost a tooth. My daddy hit Ronnie Lee; I was Mama's punching bag.

I remembered Mama talking about how beautiful she'd been once, how she'd dreamed of becoming a model; Mama taking an instant dislike to anyone whom she sensed looked down on her; Mama fighting the world because she carried the name Barefield.

"Sara?" Adrienne said near the end of the session. "Is there anything you want to say? You've been so quiet. You look like you've been in another world."

"I have," I said, "and I'm never going back."

***

The familiar symptoms started on Sunday afternoon, and by that evening I was certain that I had a bladder infection. It couldn't have happened at a worse time; there was one week of school left before final exams. I had two term papers to finish and finals to study for. My previous infections had also occurred during times when I had been under pressure, but I didn't reflect on the effect of stress on my body as I might have with what I had learned in my psychology class. My one thought was to get medicine, fast.

"A doctor won't prescribe over the phone," the receptionist said when I called the OB/GYN clinic at Dearth Memorial early Monday morning. "You'll have to come in."

"But I've had this before," I said. "I know what's wrong."

"Then you can tell the doctor when you see him," the woman said curtly.

I went directly to the hospital after I dropped Adam off at Lolita's. The waiting area was already full when I registered in the clinic at eight fifty-five. A sign on the wall behind the reception desk asked for patience until the clinic relocated into the soon-to-be-finished new wing.

I settled into one of the pink upholstered chairs and studied, trying to ignore private patients who came and went in what seemed like minutes while I waited and waited and waited. I was already too late for my English class, and by ten thirty I knew that I'd miss my French and algebra classes as well. It was past eleven when my name was finally called.

To save time, I explained my problem to the nurse on the way to an examining room. The nurse disappeared after I gave her a urine sample.

The doctor who came into the examining room later was one I hadn't seen before. Short and pudgy, he had doughy skin that looked like it had never been exposed to the sun. "You have a bladder infection," he said. "You'll have to stay in the hospital until Friday."

Stay in the hospital. I stared at him, speechless. "I...uh...All I have is a bladder infection."

"That's right." He removed a paper from his clipboard. "You can take this down to admissions."

"I can't stay. I have no one to take care of my baby."

"You'll have to make arrangements," he said with annoyance.

I thought of Adam, of the term papers that were due, of my final exams. "I can't. It's impossible."

He thrust the paper at me. "You're here now, so obviously you can."

I wouldn't accept the paper. My mind was racing. Why was he insisting that I stay? After I had Adam I hurt so badly I could hardly walk, and they made me leave the hospital even though I didn't feel that I could manage on my own. Now, for an ordinary bladder infection, he wanted me to stay in the hospital for nearly a week. It didn't make sense. "What medication will you be giving me for this infection?" I asked.

"Macrodantin," he said impatiently.

"I've taken that medicine before. They're yellow and black

capsules. I don't need to stay in the hospital. I just need the pills, and to drink a lot of water."

I looked pointedly at his name tag, *Dr. Robert Poole*. "If you won't give me a prescription, Dr. Poole, I'll call the doctor I used to go to in Owings, Dr. Healy, and tell him about this. Maybe he can call a pharmacy for me."

Dr. Poole hesitated, his expression dark. "No doctor will prescribe for you over the phone."

"Dr. Healy was my doctor for over fifteen years. He didn't see me every time I had a bladder infection; he trusted me when I described my symptoms. He knew I wouldn't call unless there was a good reason. And he never thought it was necessary to put me in the hospital while I was on Macrodantin."

It was probably only a minute, but it seemed like forever before Dr. Poole responded. "I'm going to have to put a note in your file that you left against my medical advice," he said, his tone unmistakably nasty as he reached into his clinic coat pocket for a prescription pad.

I had the prescription filled at the hospital pharmacy, but my experience with Dr. Poole stayed with me after my symptoms began to ease. The more I thought about it, the angrier I became. I felt as though I'd been belittled and manipulated, that I'd been treated as if I were stupid. A bladder infection. That was all I had. It was ridiculous to be expected to stay in the hospital for five days for a simple bladder infection!

The next day the experience seemed even more outrageous, so impossible that I almost felt as if I'd dreamed it. When Adrienne opened the last meeting of the support group by asking if anyone had an issue to discuss before we began summarizing what we had accomplished this semester, I didn't hesitate: I told the women what had happened at the OB/GYN clinic with Dr. Poole.

"The same thing happened to me, but with a different doctor," said Rosellen. "I had a bladder infection, too, but I didn't know what medicine to take. When I told the doctor that I had four kids and no one to watch them, he said I could be out all day as long as I stayed in the hospital overnight."

"Is that what you did?" I said, astonished.

"I had no choice. If I wanted the medicine, I had to do like he said. My sister stayed at night with the kids while I slept in the hospital. They just wanted a body in the bed so they could collect the money for it."

Tanya's lean frame shot forward. "That hospital wants more than a body in the bed, at least from some folks! After I had my baby, I had some heavy bleedin'. When I went to the clinic, instead of lookin' for a simple cause, they told me I might have cancer in my uterus and they put me in the hospital. I was so scared. They had me in there for a week, runnin' every test they could think of. In the end it was nothin', just somethin' ordinary that happens sometimes after havin' a baby, and they had me believin' I was goin' to die."

"What hospital?" Adrienne asked.

"Dearth Memorial," Tanya said. "Same as Sara and Rosellen."

"They did that to me at Dearth Memorial, too," said Kelsie. "I get these headaches, migraines. I've had them for years. When I went in to get pain medicine for a really bad one, they told me the headache could be from a brain tumor. They ran tests on me for days, shot me full of enough x-rays to *give* me a tumor. They scared me to death when they knew all the time what it was."

"They think we're stupid because we're on welfare and Medicaid!" I said.

"Maybe," Pat said. "But I think it's really about basic accounting. Last week there was a report on the television news about an excess of hospital beds in Stalling. Hospitals are like hotels: they don't make money unless their beds are filled and their expensive machines are kept busy. If they had enough payin' private patients, they probably wouldn't bother with us. Even though we may not be their first choice, we're money in their pocket. Gettin' government money is better than gettin' no money at all."

"But tellin' people they might have cancer so they can use their machines and fill their beds," Kelsie said. "That's...That's..."

Kelsie couldn't find the word she wanted. No one could. Even Adrienne, who always seemed to know what to say, was speechless.

***

Pat and I celebrated the end of our final exams by going out to lunch at Burger King, where there was a special: two Whoppers for the price of one. It was my treat, a way of repaying Pat, who had offered to cut my hair. "Back in Owings, there's a restaurant called Franny's," I said after we started eating. "They had a Frannyburger platter, this wonderful burger with a mountain of the best fries I ever ate."

"Do you miss Owings a lot?"

"Who has time?"

"I know what you mean, especially after studyin' for finals. Most days I feel like I'm on a treadmill—school, homework, cookin', laundry. At least I get some help from the girls. It must be worse for you with a baby."

"When Adam is up he wants my attention, so I have to make every moment count when he's asleep. I've forgotten what it's like to have a few minutes to myself. Sometimes I forget I'm human."

"Then why are you goin' to summer school? You need a break."

"If I don't go, it will take me five years to get certified as a teacher. Going summers will reduce it by a year."

"I'm only goin' to take one course. I'd like to take more, but home is the right place for me this summer. Teenage girls can get into a lot of trouble, even good kids like mine. Gettin' my degree a little sooner isn't worth what it could cost if one of my girls takes up with bad company. With all the drugs and drinkin' goin' on, I feel like I have to be vigilant every minute. It was easier when my husband was alive. Now I've got the responsibility all by myself."

"Kelsie told me that she's staying home for the same reason."

"What did you think of the support group?" Pat asked. "In the beginning you hardly said a word."

"At first I resented having to go. I felt like I was being singled out because I was older and on welfare. But now I think the group was a good thing. It helps knowing that other people have the same problems and that they find ways of dealing with them. Even what happened in the hospital, that I wasn't the only one."

"I didn't mind goin' because I was curious. I also hoped to make some friends. Most of the friends I had when Gary was alive have disappeared. They're nice enough when I call them, but they don't call me and they're always *too busy* for us to get together," Pat said. "I don't know how much is due to my bein' a single woman, and how much is due to me bein' on welfare, not that it matters. The result is the same."

We had planned to go to my place afterward, but when we were getting ready to leave the restaurant, I started making excuses. "Is it that you don't want me to cut your hair or that you're worryin' over where you live?" Pat said.

She was too smart to fool. "It's Grady Street," I admitted.

"I'd probably be livin' there myself if my brother didn't have that little house for me to rent."

My apprehension was needless. "This isn't bad," Pat said, looking around after we arrived. "It would be nice if it weren't for the cinder-block walls. I wonder why they did them that way."

"To remind us that we're prisoners of poverty," I said.

The three-week break between spring semester and summer school was over too soon. It was the best time I'd had since Tully died; my days were filled with Adam. He took his first steps on Memorial Day weekend, toddling into my outstretched arms with an expression of open-mouthed delight on his face. He was talking, too. "Mama!" he said with his bright blue eyes fixed on me, "Mama, Mama, Mama."

Not even the A's I got in all my courses except one—a B in French—meant as much as hearing Adam say "Mama."

There was only one cloud in that otherwise sunny time. One afternoon when I went out to get the mail, I met Symone at the corner. Her baby was sleeping on her shoulder. "Symone, it's good to see you!" I said, thinking that she was even more beautiful than I had remembered. "Do you live here or are you visiting?"

"I moved in last week," she said, tilting her head toward the side street where Verona Finch lived.

"Are you all settled?"

"I'm tryin' to make the place look nice, but I guess it'll take a while," she said. "Look at how Adam's grown!"

"Too fast," I said, grabbing him as he started taking off down the sidewalk. "I hope you'll come by and visit. I live over there." I pointed with my free hand.

Now that he was walking, Adam wasn't content to stay in my arms very long, so I checked my mailbox and went back inside. I wasn't comfortable being out on the street, and not only because of the dice players and drug dealers. During this school break I had become aware of another activity going on: the unit across the street from mine, which had constant male traffic, seemed to have developed into a thriving house of prostitution.

I was surprised to see Symone at my door at ten the following morning. She was wearing a black knit top and white shorts that showed off her long, slender legs. "I'm about ready to take Adam to the park," I said. "Would you like to come?"

"Sure. I'll run and get a bottle and some diapers for Chandra. It won't be but a minute."

"You don't have to run. I'll be happy to wait. I'm parked near your unit."

"I thought that was your car," she said. "I remembered it from Lemon Street."

The park closest to Grady Gardens was already busy with young mothers watching their children in the wading pool. Adam seemed a little intimidated by the splashing and shrieking, so it wasn't difficult to keep him busy at a safe distance. "This sure is better than bein' cooped up at home," Symone said, relaxing on the blanket I had spread on the grass; Chandra was sleeping in her car seat.

"Sometimes days can be long when you're taking care of a baby."

"Are they ever!" Symone said. "'Specially when all of your friends are in school or workin'. What do you do all day?"

"I'm going to the community college. I started last January. Summer session begins next week."

"How can you manage to do that on welfare?"

"I have a Pell grant and I work."

"My friends are goin' to college in the fall. They all have jobs this summer."

"It must be lonely for you."

Tears welled in her eyes. "I didn't think it would turn out like this—havin' the baby, I mean. I knew about the others, but I thought I'd be different, I thought he would marry me. Mama didn't want me to move to Grady Gardens; she thinks I'll be stuck there for the rest of my life. She's after me to finish high school in the fall. There's goin' to be a program that'll help with child care and transportation, but…" She didn't finish.

"But what?" I prodded.

"I'll be older than the other kids," she said, her chin set.

"I'm the oldest one in a lot of my classes, but it doesn't bother me. In fact, I'm proud of it. Being there shows that I'm working on making myself a better future."

The sunlight shone honey-gold on Symone's flawless skin. I could see her pride, her disappointment, her deep unhappiness. "After you get your high school diploma, it'll be easier. There are people of all ages at the community college," I said. "Education is your ticket out of Grady Gardens."

She nodded, but I could see that she was far away. Afraid that I might have pushed too hard, I felt as though I'd failed.

***

On the first day of summer session, Janelle, Julia, and Jamal were waiting with Lolita on the porch steps when I came to drop Adam off. "How's my baby?" Lolita said, greeting him with outstretched arms, her face lit with the pleasure of seeing him again.

Adam was as happy to see them as they were to see him. And they all made such a fuss when they saw that he could walk that only Lolita noticed me starting to leave. "The children have been missin' Adam," she said to explain their behavior.

"I can see that," I said, smiling, thinking that no one had missed him more than Lolita.

The greeting I received when I returned to my work-study job in the financial aid office was as welcoming as Adam's had been at Lolita's. Both Laurie and the Director of Financial Aid, Mary Fitzgerald, told me how glad they were that I was back. "You did so well your first semester," Mary said. "Last week I had lunch with Ellen Farrell, your English professor. She told me that your final essay was one of the most outstanding she's ever had from a student."

Later Laurie stopped by my desk. "I know how hard it's been," she said. "Some days I'd just look at you and hold my breath. You sure haven't had it easy!"

"School wasn't so hard," I said. "It was surviving that had me worried!"

A substantial portion of that worry had been lifted. I don't think I could have made it through another month if Mr. Maybee hadn't gotten funds from the ESP program for Adam's child care. All I had to do to receive the money was sign an employability plan, which required me to go to school. Finally I could use my work-study money to buy food, and I would have enough to get clothes for Adam. During the three-week break I found a thrift store run by the Stalling Junior League that sold used clothing in good condition. Although I would have liked to buy Adam new clothes at the best department store in town, it was a hard fact that I couldn't even afford Magnolia's. At least I could keep Adam looking decent with clothes from the thrift store. I needed things as well; with the exception of maternity clothes, I hadn't bought anything for myself in almost two years. It would take a while to save for the necessities—bras, underpants, sneakers—before I could even think of buying a new pair of jeans. I could afford patience because I had what I needed to survive: shelter, food, and the opportunity to get a college education.

Laurie had gotten me a five-hundred-dollar grant that would cover the cost of the ten credit hours I was taking during the summer. With the remaining one hundred seventy-five dollars I had left from the Pell grant, I had just enough money to cover the cost of my books. I was getting a full summer of college for less than what the Pentagon paid for a single toilet seat.

By the last week in June, everything was going so well that on a blistering hot Monday morning when I heard a humming noise coming from the gas tank as I turned into the road that led to the college, I decided to ignore it. During the past year the car had made a number of strange sounds, rattles and squeaks that had amounted to nothing. But as I approached the student parking lot, the humming noise grew louder, and then the car died. Unable to restart it, I waved cars around the Buick until three fellows pushed it to the side of the road.

I half-walked, half-ran to the financial aid office. Laurie's door was closed, which meant that she was with a student if she was in. I knocked, then opened the door a crack. She was with a student. "May I see you a moment?" I said.

Laurie came out of the office. She shook her head sympathetically while I explained. "For my money, Long's Garage is the best in town. Mowbry Long is honest and his work is good. I'll look up the number for you."

I waited better than an hour in searing heat for a tow truck to arrive. The tow truck operator, a skinny unshaven fellow, wanted payment in advance before he would touch the car. I gave him my Visa card and told him to take the car directly to Long's Garage. "I'll call there and tell them to expect you," I said. When I called, the man who answered told me they were busy and wouldn't be able to get to my car until later in the day.

It was difficult to concentrate in my classes. I had no idea what was wrong with the car, but its stillness seemed ominous. What if I couldn't afford to get it repaired? Or worse, what if it couldn't be repaired? Without the car I couldn't go to school. Without the car I was stuck in Grady Gardens.

Laurie was leaving early for a doctor appointment and offered to drive me to the garage. Long's Auto Repair was off Lee Avenue about a mile from Magnolia's. Out of habit I walked into the garage through one of the open overhead doors instead of going to the front office. "Can I help you?" a mechanic asked.

"That Buick Century is mine," I said, pointing to the car, which was in the last bay.

"Y'all wait here while I get Mowbry."

Mowbry Long's gray coveralls were stained with grease and perspiration. A tall, big-boned man, he had sandy hair that was cropped close to his head. "You own the Buick?"

I nodded.

"You're lucky," he said, wiping grease off his hands with a rag he pulled from the back pocket of his coveralls. "It was only the fuel pump. When it was towed in, I would've bet on the engine. I've lost count of all the 1984 Buick Centurys and Oldsmobile Cutlass Cieras I've seen go bad. The problem in those 3.0 engines is in the bottom end, the crankshaft and bearings. They usually come in here after they get over sixty thousand miles on 'em; the rod comes loose and makes a hole in the block. It's happened with thousands of them vehicles, but people don't know that; they just know about their own. They have no idea of the scope of it. Yours has lasted longer than most I've seen. You've got over seventy thousand miles on that vehicle."

"Is there anything I can do?"

"If it was mine, I'd trade it in."

"I wish I could," I said.

The car wouldn't be ready until the next day at noon. Lolita borrowed a car seat for Adam from a neighbor and picked me up.

"You've done so much for me," I said as we approached Grady Gardens. "How can I ever thank you?"

Lolita sucked her teeth as we drove past drunks dozing on the grassy knoll at the entrance, their fingers curled around the necks of their wine bottles. "You can graduate so you and Adam can get outta this place!"

The last thing I needed that week was to lose income from my work-study job, but I had no alternative. I lost several hours on Wednesday so I could be home for the six-month housekeeping inspection of my unit. Anitra Taylor and a woman I hadn't seen before whose hair was woven in braids went from room to room, always starting on the right as they made their circuit, while I watched, barely containing my resentment at this violation of my privacy.

The following afternoon I had my six-month re-evaluation at social services with my new caseworker, Mattie Fuller. I brought a new Base Document I had filled in, and a residency statement that had been completed by the office at Grady Gardens. Mattie Fuller, a slender woman about my age, was wearing a print dress in browns and oranges that complimented the warm tones of her skin. "I've read through your file," she said after she went over the documents I'd brought. Her voice had a deep, soothing quality that made me relax. "How are things going? I imagine it's better now that you have child care."

"Much better," I said. "I couldn't have made it through another month."

"Then things are going well?"

After my experience with Alexander Ryle, I didn't know what to say. "School is fine," I replied.

"I realize this is our first meeting," Ms. Fuller said, looking at me with steady brown eyes. "You don't know me very well, so you'll have to trust me when I tell you that I'm here to help you succeed. If you're having a problem, run it by me. I can't guarantee you a solution, but you'll get a sympathetic ear and my best effort."

"My car broke down on Monday, and I had to have it towed. It needed a fuel pump."

"That's expensive."

"The tow and the fuel pump came to two hundred fifty-eight dollars. In January, it cost two hundred fifty-three dollars for brake pads and tires so the car would pass inspection."

"How did you pay for all this?"

"With my Visa card."

Ms. Fuller's eyebrows reached toward her scalp. *"With your Visa card?"*

I felt myself becoming defensive. "Two years ago I had good credit. I had a nice apartment and a decent job."

"I'm sorry," she said. "It's just that it was so surprising. Most people who come into this office haven't had a credit card in years; they've drowned in debt."

"That's what I'm afraid of—that I'm going to drown. I was paying fifteen dollars a month, most of it for interest. My new payment will probably be double. Somehow I'll have to manage it. The Visa card is all I've got to keep the car going. Without the car, I can't go to school. And if I can't get to school…" I couldn't finish.

"Do you have any money left from your Pell Grant?"

"Just enough to pay for my books this summer."

"Unfortunately, you don't qualify for full benefits from the ESP program, but that doesn't mean you should quit looking for help from other sources. Go to the financial aid office at the college and start investigating scholarships. Your first semester grades were outstanding."

"My work-study job is in the financial aid office."

"That's a real plus," Ms. Fuller said. "Don't give up if you can't find the help you need right away. You have to keep up your determination. You have to tell yourself every day that you're going to finish!"

"But if my car goes…"

"There's no point in worrying about it until it happens. Maybe it won't happen, and you'll have wasted all of that energy worrying for nothing. And if it does go, then you'll find another way like I did."

"You?"

"I paid a friend gas money to drive me. I wasn't going to live all my life on welfare, and neither are you! We'll meet each problem as it comes."

It was my turn to be surprised. "You were on welfare?"

"My husband left me with two infants when I was twenty-one. I had to go on welfare while I finished college. It was the most difficult experience in my life."

Ms. Fuller rose and extended her hand. "I want you to think of me as your partner. I'm here to help."

I stood there blinking like a fool. It was hard to believe what I was hearing.

Any doubts I had vanished the following afternoon when Ms. Fuller called me at the financial aid office. "I talked to Mr. Maybee, and he's found a hundred dollars you can use to pay for your books, which will free some of your book money to apply on your Visa bill."

"Thank you," I said, astonished. "I thought I didn't qualify."

"At certain times of the year there is a small amount of discretionary money. It usually goes quickly. You were lucky."

I agreed, but I thought my real luck was finding Mattie Fuller.

***

A week before the end of summer session in August, I asked Lolita for a favor when I picked up Adam on a sweltering Friday afternoon. "Could I drop Adam off an hour earlier next week? The final for the computer course I'm taking is on Thursday, and I haven't had enough practice time. I'll pay you extra."

"You can bring him earlier, but I don't want extra money."

"I won't feel right not paying."

"It's too hot to argue. No extra money, that's it!" Lolita said, spreading her hands, palms down, with finality.

"I'll feel as if I'm taking advantage," I said.

"It's not takin' advantage because I want to do it. Sara, you've got to learn how to accept from others when they want to give. You can't always be lettin' your pride get in the way. Acceptin' graciously can be as generous as givin'."

"You're right," I said, hugging her. "Thank you."

"Mama!" Adam said, clearly put out because my attention wasn't focused on him. He raised his arms. "Up, Mama!"

"Well, aren't you demanding," I said.

"He's quick to let you know what he wants," Lolita said with a chuckle.

"I've been noticing that, too. We'd better be careful or there will be no dealing with him."

"It's just a stage," Lolita assured me. "He'll be fine."

On Monday morning there was a black Jeep parked in the driveway when I arrived at Lolita's at six forty-five. Lolita's husband John and an exceptionally tall man were standing on the porch looking at a set of blueprints "Good mornin', Sara," John said as I approached them. "Go on in, Lolita's expectin' you."

"John," the man said, "aren't you going to introduce me?"

John smiled knowingly. "I thought you were in a hurry, Wes."

"I'm never in too much of a hurry to miss meeting a pretty lady."

"Sara, this is Wes Honeycutt."

Wes Honeycutt had to be at least six feet four or five. I looked up into cool green eyes under a shock of chestnut hair and the most dazzling smile I'd ever seen. No wonder Lolita was always mentioning him, I thought, conscious of how washed-out my shorts and blouse were. But my next thought—that he was so far above me socially that I didn't have to be concerned about my worn clothes and lack of make up—made me relax. "It's nice to meet you," I said, returning his smile.

Adam was trying to wriggle out of my arms. "Lo Lo," he said, leaning toward the screen door.

"He's looking for Lolita. I'd better get him settled."

Lolita was in the kitchen rolling out a piecrust. "Be with you in a minute," she said, skillfully lifting the crust and placing it over peaches in a glass pie plate. Her tone was distinctly frosty.

"Am I too early?" I said, watching her crimp the crusts together.

Lolita rinsed the flour off her hands before she took Adam. "I'd say you were right on time if you'd had enough sense to linger on the porch a few minutes. You still can if you're smart."

I understood. "I think it's smarter not to linger. I'll explain later."

"I'll be waitin' to hear *this*," Lolita said with exasperation.

Our difference over Wes Honeycutt stayed with me all day. As our friendship had deepened, I had come to appreciate Lolita's judgment, which always seemed on target. But as I mulled over our disagreement, I became even more convinced that my reaction to Wes Honeycutt was right: although he was compellingly attractive, any relationship with him would be an invitation to disappointment. The lesson I had learned with Carl Shields was far more painful than a toothache, and this is what I explained later to Lolita without mentioning the dentist's name. "After Adam was born, I had a brief relationship with a professional man. I foolishly believed that he thought enough of me to overlook where I lived and that I was on welfare. Then one day I accidently overheard him talking to his neighbor about me. It was one of the worst moments in my life. As I listened to him, I saw myself as he saw me: as trash. I won't let that happen again."

"You can't assume everyone's the same. Wes Honeycutt ain't that kind of man."

"He's human. He can't help but make judgments. Can you imagine him coming to Grady Street to see me? His Jeep would be stripped within five minutes after he parked it."

Lolita shook her head. "A man like Wes Honeycutt won't last. Someone's goin' to catch him."

"Maybe," I said. "But I can't be concerned about that. Right now I have to concentrate on doing well on my exams."

"I understand that. But when your exams are over, I want you to start thinkin' about the future, not just about teachin' but about your life after Adam grows up. Time goes fast. He'll be big before you know it and out on his own. You'll be mighty lonely if you give up your chances for happiness and end up alone."

Pat invited me to supper to celebrate the end of summer session. As I was driving to Pat's house late Friday afternoon, I was regretting that I had accepted the invitation. Exhausted from the strain of finals and the unyielding heat, all I wanted to do was sleep. But a cold beer and the warm welcome I received soon revived me.

The yellow-and-white cottage Pat lived in was three miles outside of Stalling on her brother's property. Although it had the same number of rooms as my unit in Grady Gardens, it was considerably smaller, the kitchen so narrow that only one person could be in there at a time. "I cook outside as much as I can," Pat said, taking hamburgers and corn off the grill. "It's easier than workin' in that kitchen."

I gazed past a wide expanse of lawn to the thick woods that rimmed the property. "It's beautiful here. I wish I had this to look at instead of Grady Street."

"It's a shame my girls can't hear you. They're babysittin'," Pat said. "They miss where they used to live—the big house, the neighborhood. This has been a real comedown for them. I try to point out that they're luckier than a lot of kids, but it's hard for them to accept when they think about what they used to have before their daddy got sick."

"I guess I'm lucky that Adam is too young to understand where he lives."

After we finished eating, Pat said, "My accounting teacher from last semester called the other night and asked me to meet him for a drink."

"Did you go?"

"Stupidly, I did," she said with an expression of self-disgust. "He showed up wearin' too much after-shave lotion, so I got the message right away. He didn't even have the sense to let me finish my drink before he hit on me. I told him that I was already involved with someone in case I have the bad luck to get him for another course. It killed me to say that when I really wanted to tell him to go to hell."

"You can tell him when you graduate."

"By then I won't care. I try to let go of my anger because it takes more out of me than the person I'm angry at. He's not worth my energy. I guess tellin' you is my therapy."

"Wait until you get my bill," I said.

Enjoying myself more than I had all summer, I didn't leave until it was dark. After spending time in a place that was peaceful and green, returning to Grady Street, to the long shadows of sleeping drunks, to the blare of boom boxes and the noise of overheated, overtired squabbling children out past their bedtimes, was an unwelcome dose of reality. The parking spaces near my unit were all taken, probably by Verona Finch's customers. Forced to park a block and a half from my front door, I took the roofer's knife out of my purse and slipped it into the pocket of my shorts, knowing as I did so that it might be impossible to use while carrying Adam, who was fast asleep.

I walked briskly, straining to see and hear anything that could be threatening, acutely conscious of Adam's vulnerability and my own. Thinking that I would be home much earlier, I hadn't left any lights on. As I hurried up the walk to the front door, I was vaguely aware that something wasn't right, but anxious to be inside, it wasn't until I turned on a lamp in the living room that I realized the air conditioning unit was missing from the window. I heard scuffling sounds and then creaking, and ran to the kitchen: the door was wide open and whoever had been there had escaped over the fence.

The television and the VCR were gone. My heart pounding, I opened the freezer and saw with relief that the cake I had hollowed out to hide my jewelry in was still intact. Nothing seemed to have been touched upstairs. I used a paper towel when I closed the kitchen door so I wouldn't disturb any fingerprints. Then I called the police. It was nine thirty-five.

I sat up until midnight waiting for the police to arrive. As the wait grew longer, I remembered what Joletta had told me when I first moved to Lemon Street: *The po-lice don't care what's stolen down here.* The two officers who finally came looked at the marks where the kitchen door had been pried open without much interest, and wrote what was stolen on a printed form. "When are you going to take fingerprints off the door?" I said.

"Ma'am," said the older policeman, who was carrying an extra fifty pounds in his belly, "I hate to tell you, but your stuff is long gone. It's already been sold on the street."

"But I heard them leaving at nine thirty," I said. "I heard them jump over the fence."

"You probably did," he said, nodding, "but that don't make a difference. The thieves that took your stuff got rid of it as fast as they could. They turned it over for cash and for drugs. If you've got insurance, you can make a claim."

If I could afford insurance, I wouldn't be living here, I thought bitterly.

For a moment I considered telling them about Verona Finch's bar business. If I had been able to park near my unit, I might have been home in time to stop the thieves. But fear kept me silent. Informing on Verona Finch would almost certainly mean trouble.

I missed the air conditioner more than the television. The heat was relentless, the humidity worse; the occasional breezes my windows managed to catch offered little relief. But the obligation of telling Bev that her property was stolen weighed more heavily on me than the humidity.

"I'm sorry, I wish I had the money to replace it," I said when I went to the flower shop on Monday. "Someday I'll get you another one."

"No, you won't!" Bev said. "You did me a favor by taking it. As a matter of fact, next weekend I'm going to start cleaning out the basement; then I'm going to work on the closets. I'm putting everything I don't want into a garage sale."

The twinkle in Bev's eyes was the clue that made me ask, "Is this more than a routine cleaning?"

"Yes," Bev said, beaming. "Elliot Dennison and I are getting married next spring."

"That's wonderful! I'm so happy for you."

"I believe in second chances," she said. Then she changed the subject. "It's a shame about your robbery. It must be rough living in Grady Gardens."

"The alternative would be a lot rougher. I'm grateful that you were able to get me what I have. My name is on the list for other housing, but there isn't much hope. People who were in my support group at school have been on the list for a couple of years."

"What list is that?"

"The Section 8 waiting list. I was allowed to sign up in January."

"*Allowed?*" Bev said with disbelief. "What do you mean *allowed?*"

"They have so many people waiting for housing that they only open the list once a year for thirty days."

"Really," she said, more to herself than to me.

As always, she wouldn't let me leave the shop without something in my hand, this time a variegated ivy that she insisted needed extra attention.

* * *

The robbery left me with a perpetual feeling of uneasiness. I was nervous when I went outside and more conscious of street activity that I could see from my windows, particularly from Adam's bedroom window. The worn path behind the units seemed to be in constant use, people walking to and from The Bottom. The drug market was the busiest place in the neighborhood. It was bustling, and one evening as I was getting Adam ready for bed I spotted a familiar figure walking down the slope to the level ground below. *Symone.* But where was Symone's baby?

Hoping that I might be wrong, I stood near the open window with Adam in my arms, my eyes fixed on the young woman. Now positive that it was Symone, I watched as she walked up to a teenage dealer, a tall, stringy boy who had a gold earring in his left ear. She held something in her palm that glinted as it caught the waning light; with her free hand she gestured strongly. From their body language I guessed that they were arguing. When the dealer started to walk away, Symone grabbed his arm and gave him what was in her hand. I couldn't see what she was given in return.

I rushed downstairs and put Adam in his stroller, hoping to reach Symone as she approached the sidewalk to make it look like an accidental meeting. But it was nearly dark, and as I hurried up the walk I realized that I hadn't thought about what I would say.

I didn't get there in time. "Symone," I called as she was about to cross the street.

Symone hesitated, teetering on the curb.

"I thought it was you," I said, noticing despite the darkness that her T-shirt needed washing. Symone had always kept herself immaculate. "How is Chandra?"

"Fine."

"She must have gotten big over the summer. I'd love to see her. Is your mama watching her now?"

"Uh…no…" Symone stepped off the curb. "Sorry, I got to be goin'."

She disappeared so quickly that the darkness seemed to swallow her.

Even though I told myself that I had been foolish to think that meeting Symone could accomplish anything, I went home feeling as I did that day in the park, that I had failed. Rationally I knew that I didn't have much influence over Symone, but I kept thinking about Joletta's kindnesses: Joletta driving me to the hospital when I was in labor, Joletta bringing me a meal and a gift for Adam when I came home. For days afterward my heart ached for both Joletta and Symone. My desire to get out of Grady Gardens became stronger than ever. I had to escape the evils of this place before they touched Adam.

Although the summer session had been harder than I had anticipated, with longer classes and more concentrated study, I was glad after the two-week break to be back at school. Finally I felt truly comfortable at the college, sure of myself and what I was doing. As I walked down the halls I met people I knew, students who had been in my classes and the women who were in the support group. I saw Kelsie and thanked her for recommending Mattie Fuller. "They're havin' lunch tickets all the same color again this year at my son's school," Kelsie said. "That sure was a good idea." Wanda was still in school, but Pat told me that Rosellen had dropped out. "Her ex-husband went to the trailer park and beat her up so bad she may not be able to come back. She's still in the hospital." I thought of Ardelle—the bruises, the black eye, the broken arm, the fractured jaw—and was thankful she and the girls had gotten away from Ronnie Lee. Maybe it wasn't too late for Darlene; maybe one day she would be herself again.

When the early September rush was over in the financial aid office, I talked to Laurie and Mary Fitzgerald about the possibility of getting a scholarship. "I got A's in all my summer courses," I said, handing Mary a copy of my transcript.

"Excellent, Sara," Mary said. "You could be a candidate for the Clairol Scholarship. It's one thousand dollars."

"It would count against her ADC and housing," Laurie said.

Mary shook her head. "Sorry, I'd forgotten. There is other money out there. We'll just have to do a little digging. We'll get back to you."

But a scholarship wasn't mentioned again until October when Mary asked me to come into her office. "Edith Newell will be here tomorrow afternoon at two o'clock to meet you," Mary said, looking pleased. "Wear a suit, something conservative."

"I don't own a suit," I said.

"Then wear a simple dress or a blouse and skirt. As long as it's conservative, it will be fine."

"Who is Edith Newell?"

"Your benefactor, I hope. Edith was a teacher who married very well. She and her husband didn't have any children. Three years ago they endowed a scholarship in the school of education at the university. The first few years they sat in on the interviews with the final candidates; it's my understanding that they had the deciding vote. Last year Edith's husband died. I don't know if she will be doing interviews this year or not, but I didn't think it would hurt to invite her to lunch and have her meet you."

"How should I act? What should I say?"

"Just be yourself, Sara, and you'll be fine."

That night I washed my hair and put clear polish on my nails. The only clothes I owned that seemed to fit Mary's specifications were a blue blouse and a blue challis skirt, an outfit I had bought in the fall before Tully died. I was down to my last pair of decent pantyhose and hoped, as I put them on in the morning, that I could make it through the interview without getting a run.

Mary returned to the office with Mrs. Newell shortly before two o'clock. Dressed in a plain brown suit, Edith Newell was a small, gray-haired woman who looked at the person she was speaking with in a pert, interested way that reminded me of a wren. "I understand you want to be a teacher," she said after we were settled in chairs in Mary's office. "Can you tell me what led you to this decision?"

I heard myself saying what I had said many times before, a recital that I feared might sound hollow after so many repetitions. I talked about my job at Creekside Elementary, about children I believed I could help as Mrs. Hartman had once helped me. "Mrs. Hartman sounds like a wonderful teacher," said Mrs. Newell.

"She made me feel that I could accomplish anything," I said.

"Certainly you can!" Then, smiling, Mrs. Newell paused thoughtfully. "Past applicants for the Newell Scholarship have been high school students. Since you are considerably older—not that there is anything wrong with being older, age isn't a handicap unless you allow it to be—I would appreciate it if you would tell me about yourself, about what motivated you to return to school."

An image of previous applicants, of fresh-faced, eager-eyed teenagers who didn't have the stain of welfare on them, the students for whom most scholarships were created, flashed into my mind.

There was no way that I could compete. All I could do was answer honestly. "My son," I said. "His name is Adam. He's almost sixteen months old. I want to be able to give him the security of a decent home. I want him to have opportunities that I didn't have when I was growing up."

"I understand you are a single parent. That must be difficult."

"My life would be more difficult if I didn't have Adam. It would be unimaginable. Adam's father died six months before he was born. I met Tully—that was his name—when I was seven years old. He was my whole world, the only boyfriend I ever had; not a day goes by that I don't miss him. So you see, Adam is a blessing."

"Yes, he is," Mrs. Newell agreed with a sigh.

Mary was beaming after the interview. "It couldn't have gone better," she said. "Sara, you should start working on your application to the university. I'd like you to get it in as soon as possible. Mrs. Newell mentioned at lunch that she'll be leaving in December to spend the winter in Florida."

"I'll call for an application today," I said.

That evening I was late picking up Adam. A large tractor-trailer had overturned on a sharp curve before the exit to go into town, scattering crates of squawking chickens all over the road. Some chickens that had escaped were dashing helter-skelter between the stopped vehicles, diving under cars or scooting off the highway into the woods, dodging the uniformed policemen who were trying to catch them. Watching the goings-on was more entertaining than most television shows. I laughed when a man in one of the stopped cars called out, "It looks like the chickens are winning!" If I hadn't been so concerned about the time, I wouldn't have minded waiting until the mess was cleared and the line of cars I was in was waved through.

Wes Honeycutt's black Jeep was parked in the driveway when I finally arrived at Lolita's. Recalling how attractive he was, my first thought was one of relief that I looked presentable. But as I walked toward the house, I told myself that getting any ideas about him was both risky and foolish.

Wearing jeans and a blue denim shirt, Wes was even taller and better-looking than I had remembered. I was aware of his green eyes on me while I explained why I was late, describing the policemen chasing the chickens. "I didn't know chickens were that fast," he said, laughing.

"I guess they're no different from other animals," John said. "Fright gave them speed."

Wes was leaving; he walked with Adam and me to the car. "Lolita says you want to be a teacher. It must be hard going back to school. I don't think I could do it."

"I'm enjoying it," I said, bending to put Adam in his car seat. "It's something I always wanted to do."

"Maybe you could tell me about it over supper, if you wouldn't object to going someplace casual where they don't mind jeans."

"I'm sorry, but I have to feed and bathe Adam and get him in bed to keep him on his schedule," I said, the words coming out of my mouth so fast that I didn't have time to think about what I was saying.

His eyes flickered with either surprise or disappointment, I wasn't sure. "Maybe another time," he said.

Any doubts I had about refusing his invitation vanished when I drove into Grady Gardens. The reality of my circumstances told me that I had done the right thing, but it wasn't much comfort. I couldn't help thinking how nice it would have been to be sitting in a restaurant with Wes Honeycutt instead of eating a sandwich alone in my small kitchen.

***

The application for the university came in the mail the last week in October. I used a typewriter in the financial aid office to fill in the forms and type my essay. Although some students might have found the topic of the essay, *Write about something that is important to you,* too broad, I had no trouble deciding: I wrote about Adam.

Working on the application was a pleasure until reality intruded. I couldn't afford to send the required twenty-five-dollar fee with the application and afford an additional seventeen-dollar-and-fifty-cent fee required by the College Scholarship Service to process my eligibility for financial aid. Attending summer session had been a financial disaster. The longer class hours meant that I couldn't work as many hours in the financial aid office. However, in July I didn't receive an adjustment in my food stamps to compensate for my lower income. Then in August, I didn't receive any food stamps at all. After days of calling, I finally reached my food stamp worker, Daphne Slovene. "Sorry," Ms. Slovene said. "I didn't get all my paperwork done before I went on vacation." Finally I did get the stamps, but too late to keep me from falling behind with my electric bill. In September and October every spare cent I had went toward buying clothes for Adam, who had outgrown everything and had nothing for the fall and winter. So when my November check came, the most I could afford was to purchase a twenty-five-dollar money order to send with my application to the university. The financial aid form would have to wait until January since I also wanted to apply to a small women's college near Roanoke that had scholarships for older students, for which I would have to squeeze a thirty-dollar application fee from my December welfare check. This plan meant managing with the barest of necessities, but it could be accomplished if I had no unforeseen expenses.

Believing that I had solved the problem of paying for the applications, I was surprised when Mary approached me the week after Thanksgiving. "I received a call from the university. Have you sent in your CSS form? They are aware of your financial situation, but they need the validation."

"The form is done, but I can't afford to send it in until January."

The following day Mary handed me an envelope. "I'd be happy if you'd accept this as an early Christmas present."

Inside the envelope there was a money order for seventeen dollars and fifty cents made out to the College Scholarship Service from

Sara Barefield. I could feel my face get hot with embarrassment. "I didn't mean…I hope you don't think…"

Mary put her arm around me. "I know you weren't asking. I know how proud you are. Please indulge me. Nothing would give me more pleasure than for you to use this."

I remembered what Lolita had told me, that accepting graciously could be as generous as giving. "Thank you, Mary. I don't think I've ever had a more thoughtful gift."

The expression of delighted relief on Mary's face told me that I had done the right thing. But it wasn't easy.

As it sometimes happens, my good news came all at once the third week in December. When I arrived to work in the financial aid office on Tuesday, Mary was waiting for me. "Sara, please come into my office a moment."

Laurie, who was already in the office, rose from her chair. "Is anything wrong?" I asked as Mary closed the door.

"I won the toss, so I get to tell you!" Laurie said excitedly. "You're going to get the Newell Scholarship! You're going to the university in the fall!"

"I got it?" Almost afraid that saying it aloud would make it untrue, my voice wasn't much more than a whisper.

"Yessss!" Laurie said, raising her arms in a cheer.

"Although it won't be official until the spring, after your grades for this semester are in and your financial assessment is complete, Mrs. Newell didn't see any point in waiting to let you know. She told me that of the scholarships she's given, this one pleases her the most," Mary said as joyfully as her dignity would allow. "With your scholarship plus the Pell, a tuition assistance grant from the state and work-study, all of your school expenses should be covered."

The university. Tears ran down my cheeks.

"Are you all right?" Mary asked with concern.

"I've never been happier in my life!" I said, laughing and weeping at the same time.

Later, as I drove to pick up Adam, I realized that this day

wouldn't have been possible without Lolita, who was the anchor that had kept our lives from drifting into nowhere. I laughed and cried again when I told her. "Oh, I've been prayin'," Lolita said, wiping away her own tears of joy. "I've been prayin'."

I cast my eyes upward. "It seems like you have a direct line."

"Not exactly," Lolita said, as if she weren't quite finished.

"I don't know what you mean, but I'm grateful. I'll never be able to thank you enough."

"Seein' you graduate and the two of you livin' in a decent place is all the thanks I want. And it'll happen, I know it will."

A letter from the Stalling Department of Housing notifying me that I was eligible for a Section 8 housing certificate was in my mailbox on Thursday. I was positive that it was a mistake. There were hundreds of people on the waiting list ahead of me.

But it wasn't a mistake. When I called the Department of Housing on Friday, I was told that I had to make an appointment to be interviewed. "Really?" I said, wondering how it was possible. Then I recalled Bev's interest in the Section 8 waiting list. This had to be Bev's doing; she must have talked to her brother. There was no other way I could have leaped to the top of the list.

I made the appointment but was unsure if I should keep it. As badly as I wanted to get out of Grady Gardens, moving would be a hassle and an expense that I couldn't afford.

For Lolita, the decision was easy. "Praise the Lord!" she said ecstatically, giving me a great hug.

"It isn't a done deal," I said, afraid that Lolita was overreacting. "I don't have much time to look for a place. School is more important. I have to keep up my grades for the scholarship. And I don't have the money to pay anyone to help me move."

"No problem," she said, waving my concerns away with her hand. "I have friends who know where to look for places. I'll find out from them. And as for movin', John and John Junior can help with that."

Adam toddled up to us carrying a toy truck. "See, even your son knows what to do. He's tellin' you with that truck to get out. Out, ain't that right, Adam?"

Adam knew that word and liked it. "Out," he echoed happily.

1998

It is impossible to describe how I felt on my first morning at the university. All of my life the first day of school had been special, but on that hot September morning it was the fulfillment of a dream. I had to keep telling myself that the sun beating down on me, the voices of the students greeting each other, the old brick buildings, the ancient trees and vast lawns were all real. And it was still hard to believe.

I must have stood on the side of one of the brick walks that connected the buildings for a while, because several students stopped to ask me if I needed directions. "No, thank you," I told them, showing the campus map in my hand. "I believe I can find my way."

Adjusting to the university wasn't as easy as I had expected it to be. The classes were not only much larger than they were at Lee-Davis, but they were more difficult; and unlike the community college, there weren't many older students. My classmates seemed to accept me easily, even though my life away from the campus was so different from theirs. While they thought of their weekends in terms of parties and playing, I thought of Adam and grocery shopping and laundry. Sometimes it was difficult not to envy them their carefree existence, but it was a wistful kind of envy. Never would I have considered trading the joys of my life with Adam for their parties.

There were times when I didn't think I'd make it to graduation day. My car died the first semester a week before midterms. "You're not so lucky this time," said Mowbry Long, who remembered me from the summer. "It's the engine."

"How much will it cost to fix?" I forced myself to ask.

"Over two thousand dollars, more than the vehicle's worth."

"I have no choice," I said after telling him about the scholarship and welfare. "I would be rejected for a car loan and I have to get to school."

Mowbry took off the cap he was wearing and rubbed his close-cropped sandy hair, thinking. "How would you pay for a new engine?"

"Visa."

"I've got an old Toyota out back. I had a judgment for the repairs and I just got title. You can have it for what I've got in it—four hundred eighty-five dollars. It ain't pretty and it's got close to two hundred thousand miles on it, but those cars don't quit. There's a lot of life left in that vehicle."

Visa accepted the charge for the Toyota, but I couldn't drive it until I came up with the money for the registration fee, personal property tax, and insurance. Mattie Fuller and Ernest Maybee rescued me with two hundred dollars from social services. "How can I ever thank you?" I said when I picked up the check.

"Graduate with your teaching degree!" was their reply.

Mrs. Newell gave me a check for five hundred dollars in December before she left for Florida. She invited me to her home for tea. I had never been invited to tea and had no idea what to expect, so I called Bev and told her about the invitation. "How am I supposed to act?"

The question made Bev laugh. "Relax and enjoy yourself," she said.

I was balancing the cup and saucer in my hand when Mrs. Newell gave me the check. "This is too much," I said, the surprise nearly causing me to spill the tea. "You've already given me the scholarship."

"Worrying about making payments on a vehicle that gets you to school could affect your studies, and I don't want that to happen," Mrs. Newell said. "When you're teaching you'll see students whose problems you can't help solve, and if you're as caring as I think you are, it will frustrate you. This car payment problem is easy for me to remedy. It's my pleasure."

"I feel like you're my guardian angel."

"Oh, my," she said with a chuckle. "I hope I was never that good!"

It wasn't difficult to figure out how Mrs. Newell knew about the Toyota. I had told Laurie my car story when we got together during Thanksgiving break, and Laurie must have told Mary Fitzgerald. Even though I was no longer attending the community college, Laurie and Mary were still looking out for me.

It seemed like everyone was looking out for me. Mattie Fuller told me about the new welfare law that was coming when I met with her for my six-month re-evaluation. "The welfare reform law is going to take effect July 1, 1995, and Plummet County is going to be among the first in which it will be enforced."

"How will that affect me?"

"I'm not sure," she said. "The new law requires able-bodied recipients to get a job within ninety days, and limits benefits to two years. I believe your attendance in school should count as a job."

Something in her voice made me nervous. "But you're not sure?"

Mattie gestured, her palms open and empty. "Governor Allen has been asked about recipients already in school, but he hasn't been willing to make a commitment. The law as it's written only exempts those up to age nineteen who are already enrolled in school full time," she said, her steady gaze meeting mine. "I think you should apply for student housing as soon as possible. If it becomes necessary to plead your case, it can't hurt to have your life totally centered at the university."

Adam and I moved into student housing on the day the new law took effect. Our apartment was located five minutes from the campus in a complex built for married students and students with children. It was a huge improvement over the HUD housing we had been living in when I moved out of Grady Gardens, where the neighbors spied on each other and where I was still subject to housekeeping inspections. My new neighbors were all graduate students, some of them with small children. Adam found playmates and I made friends.

My work-study job was considered employment, so I was able to stay in school. To my relief and Mattie's, I graduated with a Master of Education degree within the two-year time limit. I get breathless when I think about how close I came to not making it: if I had waited a year, or even six months to start school, I would have run out of benefits before I finished. Pat, who has a good job with a large insurance agency, is as grateful for her degree as I am for mine. "If we hadn't gone back to school when we did, we'd be stuck in low-paying jobs for the rest of our lives," she said.

In the fall after my move into student housing, I taught for the first time; it was in November, a lesson about Thanksgiving and the meaning of being thankful. After polishing the lesson plan for days, I stood in front of a second grade class both nervous and thrilled, feeling that I had prepared all of my life for this experience. And what an experience it was! In response to my question about the meaning of being thankful, an impish-looking boy who had a dark brown cowlick that stood straight up on his head raised his hand. "My mama says we should be thankful that Granddaddy comes for dinner only this once and at Christmas, because he takes his teeth out when he eats and he doesn't cover his mouth when he burps!"

The children laughed while I froze, conscious of the teacher evaluating me in the back of the room. But as I stood there I remembered how unpredictable children are, how I could always expect the unexpected from them, and I relaxed. "Why do you think he takes his teeth out when he eats?" I asked the boy when the laughter stopped.

"He says they hurt."

"Then what can we be thankful for?"

A curly-haired girl raised her hand. "We can be thankful that we have our own teeth! Last summer I didn't have my front ones and I couldn't eat corn on the cob."

I steered the discussion to other things to be thankful for and the lesson went well. Afterward the supervising teacher gave me a positive evaluation. "You handled Granddaddy's teeth like a pro," she said with a chuckle. "You're a natural."

I don't always feel like a natural. I just finished my first full year of teaching, of being on my own in a classroom, and every day was a challenge. I had several offers from fine suburban schools but chose instead to teach first grade at a school in a poorer section of town. Perhaps it was selfish of me, but I picked the first grade because I wanted to be the one to give children the gift of being able to read. It turned out to be a gift for me as well, a joy to see the light in their eyes at the moment they were able to read their first words. There is nothing I could do in life that would be more rewarding.

From the beginning I wanted to teach so I could give children what Mrs. Hartman gave me: I wanted them to feel good about themselves, that they could accomplish anything they set out to do. I never expected that they would give me more than I could possibly give them, but they have. There was a boy in my class who had been severely burned in a fire when he was an infant. The first time I saw Kendall I had all I could do not to gasp: his little face was as twisted and scarred as a mask in a horror movie; only a few tufts of fine hair grew from his scalp; all of his fingers had been burned off his left hand; on his right hand he had only his thumb and a portion of his index finger; his teeth were irregular, a result of the burns. I prayed that I would be capable of helping this child.

Although his appearance took some getting used to, his mind was bright and his personality was positive. Everyone in the class liked Kendall and accepted him as he was. Then something happened one day that I couldn't have handled if it hadn't been for the children. It was a few weeks before Christmas. I had stayed in the room to change a bulletin board during the art teacher's lesson. The teacher, a woman named Mrs. O'Connor who had once mentioned that she had been teaching for sixteen years, had told me that she planned to have the children make gifts for their parents, but I had no idea of what the gifts were to be. I was pushing a thumbtack through the corner of a child's paper when I heard her say, "We're going to make special pictures with our hand prints on them. We're going to do this by putting one hand at a time flat on the paper and tracing around each finger, starting just below our wrists and going up and around our thumbs like…"

Suddenly she stopped. I turned and saw Kendall's arm in the air, his thumb and stub of a finger. "I don't have a whole hand," he said. "What should I do?"

Mrs. O'Connor looked stricken, as if she were about to burst into tears. I felt like weeping, too. But then the child whose desk was in front of Kendall's, a girl who had shiny black hair and large dark eyes, turned in her seat and said, "Kendall, you can use my hands."

Then the boy sitting behind Kendall offered his hands. Another child offered, and then another, until all the children in the class were offering their hands. "Oh," Kendall said, his scarred face breaking into a great smile, "I have so many hands!"

I left the room quickly so the children wouldn't see my tears.

That night I was grateful, as I have been for many nights, to have someone with whom I could share what had happened. Wes Honeycutt and I were married a week after I graduated from college. Lolita, who was the happiest person at our wedding, says that I made Wes chase me until I caught him. As usual, she's probably right, but it wasn't an intentional plan on my part. After I started going to the university I had to drop Adam off at Lolita's earlier some mornings, and I kept meeting Wes there. Not too long ago he let it slip that he learned my schedule so he could *accidentally* see me. I did nothing to encourage him, which was all of the encouragement he needed. Apparently I was the first woman he'd met in years who hadn't shown a bit of interest in him. I'm guessing about women in the past;

however, I do know about women now. If I didn't feel as sure as I do of his love, I would be anxious all the time over the way females throw themselves at him. Sometimes I tease that he'll lose his admirers when he loses his hair, but I don't see that happening soon. Wes's chestnut hair is as thick as ever with just a few more gray strands than before.

Wes asked me out for nearly a year before I finally accepted. He tells people that he kept asking until he wore me down, but the truth isn't that easy. I was ashamed of being on welfare, embarrassed over where I was living, and my experience with Carl Shields had stuck fast. It was only after I moved into campus housing that I dared accept his invitation to go out to dinner. (Some of his other invitations had included the movies, picnics, a day at an amusement park, and ice skating; also rollerblading, which he confessed months later that he was afraid I might accept!)

Our dinner date was for a Saturday night. By Saturday afternoon I was so nervous I called Lolita. "Does Wes know that I'm on welfare?"

"I don't know. What difference does it make anyway? You should be thinkin' of yourself as a college student, as someone who's goin' to be a teacher, not as someone who's on welfare."

"But I am on welfare and that might make a difference to him."

"I doubt it. He's been wantin' to take you out for months. Don't you be lookin' to spoil it! Sara, you've got to stop lettin' the label welfare stick to you like a scab! It ain't goin' to be forever. Just relax and have a good time!"

Wes had made reservations at a restaurant a few miles outside of town that looked like a quaint country inn with its wide front porch and flower-lined walkway. He was compellingly handsome in a navy blazer, a light blue shirt open at the neck, and gray slacks, and I could feel the eyes of every woman in the dining room focusing on him when we walked to our table. After the waitress brought our drinks, he raised his glass. "Maybe this is what you need to relax."

"Is it that obvious?"

"I'm afraid so. I hope it isn't me, that I'm not the cause."

"Oh, no, it has nothing to do with you. It's about me, it's about my life. It's about…something you should know."

And then I told him. By the time we had finished eating Wes knew about welfare and Tully. He knew more about my life than I had ever told anyone at once because he listened with such quiet encouragement. When I told him about Tully's cars, he didn't look at me skeptically like Carl Shields did. "Tully must have left a sizeable estate," he said.

"Yes," I said, "but he didn't leave a will."

Then I told him about Mrs. Rutland and the funeral and my decision to leave Owings. "You have a lot of courage," he said.

"Not really," I said. "I just didn't see another option."

He leaned back, studying me with his sea-green eyes. "After all you've been through, would you make the choice you did if you'd known what you'd face?"

It took me a long time to answer. I thought about the things I didn't tell him, about Lemon Street and Grover Daniels, about Grady Gardens with its roaches and housekeeping inspections, about my humiliating interviews at the Department of Social Services. I remembered my despair when I had to tell Dr. Farrish the reason I couldn't take his Friday exam. But then I thought about how close I was to reaching my goal, and how fortunate I was that I had started school just months before the opportunity might have been closed to me forever. "People would probably change half the decisions they make in their lives if they knew in advance what the results would be. Right now I'm close to becoming a teacher, which is a dream I've had since I was a little girl. I can't say I've enjoyed some of the road I've traveled, but I'm grateful that I'll reach my destination."

"Fair enough," he said.

As we were leaving the restaurant, I realized that I knew hardly anything about him. "I can't believe I talked so much," I said apologetically.

He put his arm around me. "Sara, I can't recall having a more enjoyable evening."

Soon we were seeing each other every weekend. Wes made an extra effort to get to know Adam. "I don't know much about kids. I was an only child. My parents had me late in life. I was a real surprise!" he said with a grin. "And I kept surprising them, probably because it was so easy to do. They were so set in their ways."

From the beginning I enjoyed being with him. Wes is good company, funny and smart. He also has a serious side that he keeps to himself until he knows you well. What I like most about him is his honesty; Wes is a straightforward man.

After we had been dating a while, I asked him why his marriage had broken up. We were driving to my apartment after going to the movies. "It was a combination of things, I guess," he said. Despite the darkness, I could see his eyes growing distant, as if he were gazing into the past. "We got married right out of college. My degree was in architecture. I got a job and I hated it. The next job was even worse. I didn't like being inside all day. I wanted to be building, not just drawing. My head was exploding with ideas that I wasn't getting a chance to try. Finally I quit and went to work for a builder. The bottom line was that I wasn't earning much; our friends were all doing well. Money was a problem. So was conceiving. Susannah couldn't get pregnant. The harder we tried, the more uptight she got. When we finally learned the reason—that as the result of an infection she had early in our relationship, the secretions in her vagina were killing my sperm—it finished the marriage.

"The breakup was hard for me, even with nature telling us that our union was wrong. I hate failure. That's why I've been single all this time. I wasn't going to make a commitment until I was absolutely sure it was right."

He pulled the Jeep to the curb, turned off the ignition, and kissed me, a long slow kiss. "Marry me, Sara. It will be forever, I'm that sure."

I don't think any woman has ever had a more perfect proposal.

He had asked me to meet his parents a number of times, but I had always managed to find an excuse. After I accepted his proposal, I knew I couldn't hide behind excuses. I had to meet them.

His parents live in a large brick house just outside Richmond near the James River. As we were driving there I couldn't stop thinking about Mrs. Rutland, and it wasn't long before I was starting to feel physically ill. "Maybe we should do this another time," I said.

"Relax, Sara. My parents are looking forward to meeting you. They're nice people. You'll like them, and I *know* they'll like you."

Wes was right: they are nice people. Aileen Honeycutt greeted us with a warm smile. Although she's in her late seventies, she's still exceptionally attractive. She's tall—the same height I am—and she has snow-white hair and lovely, even features. Wes resembles her. His father, Cameron, is more reserved than Aileen. He has a sly sense of humor and infinite patience, especially with Adam.

The Honeycutts took to Adam right away. "I have something special in the kitchen that I think you'll like," she said to him, holding out her hand.

After a slight hesitation, Adam slipped his hand in hers and off they went. Seconds later we heard him squeal, "Chocolate chip cookies!" with such joy that we all laughed.

Aileen Honeycutt's chocolate chip cookies are so good that I could have squealed when I ate one for the first time. She has shared her recipe with me, which surprised Wes. "Those cookies are her secret weapon," he said. "You don't need greater proof that she likes you."

Before he retired, Wes's father was an engineer. He enjoys tinkering with old cars, rebuilding those he thinks he can save. Adam followed him out to their spare garage. After they were gone for a while, I went to check on them, concerned that he was bothering Cameron. I saw them with their heads together, Cameron explaining to Adam how he was rewiring a headlight. Adam was totally absorbed, watching and listening with such intense concentration that my breath caught in my throat. It's almost impossible to express how I felt at that moment. I couldn't have hoped to see anything more perfect.

Now when we visit, Cameron is waiting at the door for Adam, and they go to work in the garage after having chocolate chip cookies and milk. "I think my father was disappointed that I wasn't interested in fixing cars." Wes said. "Sharing his hobby with Adam has brought him great pleasure."

Wes and I were married in a small chapel on the university campus. I don't know who was happier, Lolita or Adam. "Oh, how I prayed for this day!" Lolita said afterward, her face lit with happiness.

I hugged her, my heart so brimming with gratitude that I couldn't manage a word.

Adam was far from speechless; he had been excited about the wedding for weeks. "Me and Mama are going to live with Wes!" he announced as we were leaving the chapel. "We're going to see him every day!"

My love for Wes isn't the same as the love I had for Tully. Tully was the love of my youth, of my dreams, the love I see every day in the face of our son. Wes is the man with whom I am spending the rest of my life. I have never been this happy and content. My heart is full.

Although Wes wanted me to take the name Honeycutt when we got married, I decided to keep the name Barefield. "I want Ardelle to be able to get in touch with me," I said after telling him about her and the children.

There was another reason besides Ardelle, one that I didn't tell him. After a lifetime I had finally learned to live with my name. I was no longer ashamed of being Sara Barefield.

Sometimes I think of my mama, how she held on to her anger like I clung to my pride, both of us defending ourselves against a world that didn't look upon us kindly. Mama isn't in my dreams anymore. I like to think that she wishes me well.

This past year Wes built a cedar-and-glass house for us on the side of a mountain that overlooks Stalling. Sometimes at night when I stand at one of the windows looking at the stars twinkling above and the lights of Stalling shining below, I feel that I am suspended at a perfect place between heaven and earth. I have been truly blessed.